esa —
Never be afraid to
take a chance!
♡ Helen
Boswell

LOSING ENOUGH

A Second Chances Novel

Book #1

Helen Boswell

Artemathene Books

To Janice P.
For encouraging me to take the risk.

Contents

Acknowledgments

My heartfelt thanks go to the following people that made it possible:

Janice Pia, for initiating this journey and taking it with me, and for always setting the bar high with your evil queen treatment. Stevan Knapp, for your brilliance and outstanding editor's humor. Elaine Braithwaite, Rosalyn Eves, Tasha Seegmiller, and Erin Shakespear, for your keen eyes, love, and support throughout the process. Kelly Schwertner, Ali Hymer, Carey Heywood, Mary Jo Tufte, Christina Pryor, Dani Morales, Keith Osmun, and Megan Paasch, for your wonderful insights and suggestions – your often humorous feedback made my day many times over. Mary Jo Tufte, Dr. Ryan Van Woerkem, Jared Wenn, for your unparalleled expertise and assistance with technical aspects. Aldo Pia, for your candor and for sharing with me your life experiences. Lynsey Taylor, for your utter genius in creation of the beautiful cover. My street team and manager Laura Helseth, for your enthusiasm and excitement as I venture into new territory. My blogger friends and readers, for your continued support and all of the hard work that you put in to support authors. My family, for your love most of all.

And my mom, for being my inspiration and who has shown me my entire life what it means to be strong.

1

Alex

Most of my friends go to the lake or beach during summer vacations. Not me. I spend my summers in Sin City with my parents. Have ever since I was twelve. Nine months out of the year, Dad's a certified public accountant. The other three, he's a professional gambler.

It's early June, and a blast of heat flies up my skirt as soon as I step out of the hotel and into the line for taxis. By the time I get into a cab, I feel like I'm coated in a sheen from my hairline down to my favorite strappy high-heeled sandals. The locals call it "dry heat," but that's what they tell visitors to make us feel inferior whenever we mention how hot it is. Even though I'm from the northeast, it's not a big deal. I've learned to adjust to summer life here, and I don't just mean the temperature.

I sweep my long red hair over my shoulder to get it from sticking to my neck and tell the driver, "QE2. It's on Paradise."

The driver nods and starts the meter, and I whip out my phone to check my texts. My flight got in a couple of hours ago, and my phone's been going nuts since I stepped off the plane. My friend Elle, who's a little insane in general, was crazy-thrilled when I called her up last week and told her I was coming out for the summer earlier than planned. I have a barrage of texts from her.

2 hours ago: *Text me as soon as u get off the plane*

1 hour ago: *U better come by the club as soon as your ass gets in. Did u land yet?*

45 minutes ago: *Dammit. Got slapped with double shift. Won't get off work til later but come by and we'll play*

There are more, but those are the important ones. Elle is twenty-two, has about that many tattoos, lives in black tank tops to show them off, and tends to have hordes of men drooling over her. When I met her at an over-under club a couple of years ago, she promptly spent the summer corrupting me in various ways. Besides my mom, she's my best Vegas friend. She's a waitress at the QE2, a club off the main part of the Strip, and I turned twenty-one last month, so this summer I'll actually be able to get in with my real ID instead of a fake one.

Thankfully, the driver isn't inundating me with small talk like some of them do, and I sit back and text Elle.

Had to check in and all that. Keep your panties on, bitch

5 seconds later: *Bitch, I don't wear any*

I laugh out loud and stare out the window as the cab makes its way down Las Vegas Boulevard. The sights settle over me like a second skin – casinos that look like they've been designed by someone on crack, garish lights and advertisements plastering everything, all of the crazy tourists wandering the Strip holding drinks bigger than their heads. I love this place. The energy, the insanity, how it's all disconnected from the rest of the world. I love all of it.

I tap my fingernails on my knee, frowning a little as I clear the e-mails from the afternoon off my phone. Mostly junk, but one of them is from the registrar's office at the University at Albany confirming the refund of my summer registration fees. That had been the original plan. I was going to take classes during first summer session so I didn't have as much to take in the fall. But then Dad called me after they first got out here at the end of May. Said that he was probably going to have to cut their stay short this year, so could I come out sooner? He sounded so uneasy, anxious, but he wouldn't tell me more than that. I tried to call Mom and ask her what was up, but she was just as vague.

I wound up waffling on it for a day because I'd already signed up for classes, but I ultimately went with my gut and decided to come out. Classes can wait. Summer vacation is officially here.

It's grittier and darker once you get off the Strip, but I like it because it's real. Elle's not waiting for me outside the club, but she wouldn't be if she's working.

The bouncer is one of the regulars that I recognize from the past two summers, a wiry guy whose body and face look as hard as steel. He scrutinizes my I.D. before staring me straight in the eye. I stare back, and he waves me through. I think that the really good bouncers play on fear, make that eye contact to see who backs down. It's the ones with guilty consciences who get busted for having the fake I.D.'s. This is the first time I've used my real one, and prior to that, I never got caught.

I automatically get a little high when I walk inside, like I always do. Not a chemically-induced high, but because QE2 is my favorite place in Vegas, full of dark places and music so loud it makes my heart feel like it's going to pound right out of my chest. I head straight for the bar, keeping an eye out for Elle along the way and squeezing through bodies until I make contact with the cool metal and glass surface.

I see a familiar face, and I wave to get the attention of a guy with deliberately shaggy brown hair.

"Hey, Tucker! You seen Elle?" I shout over the din. Tucker is the best bartender of all time because he always serves a heavy shot of sarcasm with all of his drinks. I can always count on him to engage me in a battle of smartass remarks.

"Alex. Hey! What, has it been a whole year already? Don't look so excited to see me." He flashes his teeth at me in a wolfish grin. "Yeah, she's working the floor. I suppose you're expecting a drink on the house?"

I grin back. "If you're offering, I won't argue. Manhattan?"

"Free Manhattan. I'd die of shock if you argued. Coming right up, babe." He slaps the bar with his hand, winks at me, and turns away.

I look away from the bar to see if I can catch a glimpse of Elle. The crowd looks fairly mixed tonight, but the rockers and goth types dominate the place as usual. The last guy I went on a date with would have made some dumb joke about how I blend in because I wear too much eye makeup. Only part of the reason I don't date much. Back home, I'm focused on working and school. Out here, dating doesn't make any sense. If this summer was going to be like any of the last few, it might come with a hook-up or two, but that's all.

Tucker's shout calling out my drink brings me back. As soon as my fingers close around the glass, an elbow smacks into my arm. Goddammit. My arm has more Manhattan on it than my glass has in it.

I whip around and shoot a death glare at the guy next to me. The bar is crowded, sure. But would it kill him to wait until there was actually room before plowing his way into a spot?

I'm face-to-face with a solid wall of dark blue, a t-shirt that's stretched over broad shoulders and a muscled chest that would probably give Elle an immediate hard on. My gaze lifts to a face with chiseled, strong features, full but firm lips, intensely blue eyes blazing in contrast to his tanned skin. That kind of eye color should not legally exist on a human being. I'm the one who's drenched in whiskey, but he's the one staring at me like he's pissed off at the world.

I snap in his direction, "Thanks for that. Now I'm soaked *and* out of a drink." I eye the stack of cocktail napkins next to him, but they're out of my reach. Not about to dive on him to get them.

Without saying a word, he takes a wad of napkins and unceremoniously shoves them at me. His fingers rake through his dark wavy hair, which is already messy like he's been pushing his hand through it all night. For some reason, everything about his appearance makes me think he rides a bike. I check him out again as I blot my arm dry. Striking. Especially with the slight stubble on his face, and with *those eyes*. Too bad he's kind of an ass.

"What, sweetheart? You want me to buy you a drink now? You'll have to sweet talk me more than that. Or I accept sexual favors, too." He says it half-heartedly, like he's reading it out of some stupid playbook of his.

Are you shitting me? Okay, make that a total ass. I cough out a laugh. "Yeah, right. No thanks."

He shrugs. "No skin off my back. People in this city drink too much anyway."

His voice is low and resonant, the timbre of it sending an involuntary jolt of electricity through me. The look he gives me and the way one corner of his mouth curves up is almost mocking. Not that I'm expecting any sort of chivalry on his part, but that had to be the worst apology. Ever.

I raise my eyebrows. "You might have noticed, but you're standing at the *bar*?"

"I'm not drinking, am I." He says it flatly, as a statement.

"No," I admit. "But you seemed pretty intent on shoving your way into a spot here, and there are less crowded places to go if you didn't want a drink."

He glances away, unfazed by my stellar display of logic. "Came here to talk to someone."

"Lucky girl. Or guy," I say with sarcasm.

Why am I even wasting my breath with this guy? I don't wait for a reply before shoving away from the bar. I briefly debate circling around and going to the other end to get another drink, but my nerves are crawling with irritation. And not just because my arm is sticky. I need to get away from anti-Prince Charming before I go into total bitch mode. I'm here to have fun, and normally things like that bounce off of me and don't leave any impression. But he got under my skin, and I don't like that.

I'm almost to the ladies' room when I finally see Elle.

"There you are!" she yells. She might be small, but she has a set of lungs on her. The volume of the music is no competition.

She throws her arms around me and hugs me a little insanely. I squeeze her back, feeling like a behemoth. Elle is like a little willow branch on caffeine, moving with grace that's always super sparked with energy.

I release her, grinning like crazy. So good to see her. We message each other a lot during the year, and now she looks me up and down in the way that good friends do. We're only a year apart and like-minded in a lot of ways. She figured out a couple of years ago that she wants to go into social work and has been working her butt off taking classes ever since. Same thing with me and nursing.

"You look fabulous. So you're single and free this summer?"

"As always. Do you even have to ask?" I retort.

"Oh, so if Wes has a friend, you're game?"

I shoot her a mock glare as she grins at me. Elle tends to date fast and furious, and Wes is her latest boyfriend. She goes through her men almost as fast as tissues, whereas I prefer to keep it light and not even let things get to that phase. While we differ on our attitudes, she at least gets that about me. I know she's teasing me about setting me up.

"Oh!" Her eyes widen like she just remembered something. "You know Alysa's Empyre is playing tomorrow night, right? I totally tried to get us tix, but they sold out like a minute after they went on sale. I was going to hit up the scalpers, but I'm kinda short on cash right now." There's a glimmer in her eye as she adds, "Unless… Is there any chance your daddy can get us in?"

Of course I know they're playing. Elle and I have been following the alternative indie rock band in Vegas for years. She introduced me to them a couple of years ago when they were starting out and playing in joints like QE2 to crowds of ten. They're one of the lucky ones that shot up to rock-stardom and fame, and it's crazy to think that they're one of the most popular indie bands in the country now.

But the venue is The House of Blues, and I'm pretty sure that Dad can only get comped tickets for events at our hotel.

"I can ask, but I kinda doubt it." Though it's not really anything I can do about, I still feel bad. Elle is a serious fan of the band. "Sorry, dude. We can try the scalpers tomorrow night. I'll pay for you."

She shakes her head. "Nah, I couldn't have you do that. 'S okay. I guess we'll just have to settle for telling people 'we knew them when,' buy their shit on iTunes to support them, stuff like that, right?"

"Right. But hey, I *will* ask my dad, okay?"

"Okay." She threads her arm through mine but freezes. "Why are you so sticky?" she shouts. "Did you take a bath in whiskey?"

I shoot a look over my shoulder, but anti-Prince Charming is gone. "Pretty much. Had a little mishap with some jerk and lost my drink."

"I have just the solution." A few strands of Elle's long spiky hair fall over her eyes, and she pushes them back before tugging me toward the dance floor. "C'mon. I have to do a couple of things, but I'll set you up with a challenge first."

"Already?"

My laughter tumbles out of me, the edginess I carried from my encounter with the guy at the bar effectively wiped clean. Elle is always good like that. Thinking about ways to get us both into trouble. I don't remember who started the glorious summer tradition of "the challenge." It might have been me, it might have been Elle. Either way, it was inspired by one too many drinks one night. Now we play it in some form or another whenever we go out. It's like the bar-version of double dog dare.

We walk to the edge of the dance floor. There are a lot of bodies out there, and the deejay is playing some slow, heavy, sexy remix that's bringing everyone close and grinding together. It's been almost six months since I moved against anyone like that, and I feel a slow heat spread through me as I watch the couples in front of us.

The gears in Elle's evil brain are cranking as her eyes sweep through the crowd. I know she's trying to pick out someone to challenge me with, and my adrenaline surges in anticipation. Elle's challenges are usually pretty fun. That's the entire point.

"Him," she decides, elbowing me in the ribs. I follow her line of sight and see them standing at the edge of the dance floor. Two guys checking out the crowd like Elle and I are checking out the crowd. One with longish dark hair, bronzed skin, and some extensive ink on his arms. The other one is broad-shouldered with good-boy surfer looks, sunned skin and blond hair falling over his eyes.

"Your challenge, if you choose to accept it," she says. "Dance for two songs with him and then make him buy you a drink."

"Which guy?" I ask.

She shrugs one shoulder. "Your choice. Both if you want. Oh, and I like the ink on that one guy. See if you can find out where he got it done, if he got it done local that is."

"Ooh, is that all?" I narrow my eyes at my potential targets. "You sure you don't want anything else? His phone number or anything?"

"Only if you want it," she says cheerily. "Hey, it solves your problem about losing your drink. By the time you're done with him, I should be finished with my stuff and we can actually hang out."

She has a point. She probably feels bad that she couldn't get off work earlier on my first night in town. It doesn't matter to me either way if I'm alone or not, but Elle is fairly prone to guilt complexes.

Plus, neither guy is hard on the eyes. And I do love to dance. The throb of the bass continues to draw me in and tantalize me, and Elle is still standing by waiting for my answer.

My sights hone in on the guy with the ink.

"Challenge accepted."

2

CONNOR

I'm not in the fucking mood to be here right now. But Elle called me right as I was getting off work and told me to swing by the club. Should have known that the Friday night crowd would make it impossible to find her. I don't feel like talking to anyone but her, and I already had to get into a near-conversation with some redhead who got her panties in a twist over her drink spilling at the bar.

The bartender, Tucker, always makes it clear that he doesn't like me. Elle says he's being protective of her, but I'm her cousin for chrissakes. He's just a bartender at some club where she happens to work, so I don't even pretend to get that. I order a Guinness from him and ask if he's seen her.

"Haven't for a while, Con. Maybe she took an early break. Or maybe she knew you were coming and clocked out early."

The way he calls me "Con" rakes against my nerves, but I shrug it off. I didn't expect him to give me a straight answer, knew he'd feed me some bullshit line.

My gaze flicks over people as I walk through the bottom floor of the bar in search of Elle. Overall, the crowd looks pretty harmless. Lots of goths and emo types. A few tourists that stick out like beacons. Still don't see Elle, but she could be out on the floor, working the upstairs, or maybe Tucker was actually telling the truth and she's on break. I grab my phone and call her, but it goes straight to voicemail.

Out of anyone in my family, Elle's the only one I have any connections to. She grew up in Albuquerque in the same crap neighborhood as me. Our mothers are sisters, only hers stuck around and mine left when my brother and I were kids. Elle's three years younger than me, and I was always secretly jealous that her family wasn't nearly as dysfunctional as mine. They were as poor as we were, but she'd at least had a mom and dad that gave a shit about her until she was seventeen. As soon as she graduated high school, she moved to Vegas to try to make it as a singer. By then, I'd already finished my SEAL training and was on active duty.

Elle and I were the same in that respect. We both jumped on the first chances we had to get out of that hellhole where we grew up. My twin brother Cruz hadn't. He got mixed up with a bad group back home, claimed his stake in the world of criminals.

There. I catch a glimpse of her by the dance floor, but when I get closer, it's some other chick with short dark hair that only vaguely looks like Elle. Even if she is out in that mess somewhere, she's only five foot two, and the bodies in front of me are so densely packed that there's no way I'd find her.

I'm turning away when I get a glimpse of the redhead from the bar again. She's tall and stands out in the crowd, and I don't know why, but I stand and watch her. Watch as she sways to the music with her eyes closed, her lips parted, her arms lifting over her head. I can't tell if she's dancing with the blond guy in front of her or if he's trying to move in on her. He's wearing a white t-shirt and jeans, and she's in a black dress. If they are here together, my guess is that they didn't come here that way.

He closes the distance between them, his hands landing on her hips, and she doesn't miss a beat as she pushes his hands off her and turns away. But he comes at her again from behind and grabs her waist, pulling her close so he can grind into her like an animal.

I've seen it a million times at these clubs. But for some reason, it reminds me of Cruz…

and Laura, a voice grits out in my head

…and my anger ignites to see it, to see this guy push the boundaries with this girl. The redhead makes this sort of shimmy move to get away from him, though, and I feel some of the edge wear off. I'm glad she can take care of herself, but still, it pisses me off.

It pisses me off even more that I even give a shit enough to watch. I try and tell myself that I'm doing what I always do, watching and waiting. Looking for signs of trouble.

The redhead suddenly leans close to him and says something in his ear, and he nods and takes her hand before leading her to the bar. Just goes to show that I was imagining the whole situation. She wasn't being harassed on the dance floor, which begs the question – what the fuck is my problem?

I walk away too, to check the back room to see if Elle's waiting on any of the tables there. I get ten steps through the mess of a crowd before a woman slams into me. She staggers back, a shot held high to save it from spilling.

"Watch it, frat boy!"

I'm as far from a frat boy as she is. She's blonde, has a pretty face, and is wearing expensive jewelry. Quality stuff all around and just my type, but I'm in too shitty of a mood to do anything about it.

I cock an eyebrow and say half-heartedly, "Fuck me, and all is forgiven."

Her eyes grow almost comically wide right before she shoves her way through the crowd to get away from me. I hear her yell over her shoulder, "Dickhead!"

I laugh then, some of the tension finally easing off of my shoulders. I feel a hand on my arm at the same time.

"Hey, dickhead. Is that your new fab way of hitting on women?"

I turn around and grin when I see Elle. She slides her empty serving tray under her arm and shakes her head in disgust, but I can see the gleam in her dark eyes that reveals that she's glad to see me. No one would guess we were cousins aside from the fact that we both have dark brown hair. But Elle spikes hers, and with her large tribal ear piercings, heavy eye makeup, full tattoo sleeves, and destroyed black tank top and pants, she looks like she walked straight off the stage from an emo band.

Her expression changes to one that's more serious, and she steps forward and slides her arm around me. "Sorry to drag you away from work."

I wave it away. I have an hour before I have to get to the airport to pick up a client. Pimping myself out to high rollers as a private security guard was never on my list of dream jobs, but opportunity struck when I moved to Vegas two years ago. While it isn't something that I can see myself doing for the long haul, for now, I'm too good at what I do to want to stop.

When you grow up shit-poor with a dad who was high on meth half the time, it's hard to want to let go of anything that's even remotely good.

I grab Elle around the neck in a hug. I haven't seen her in almost a month because I've been working my ass off, as always.

"It's okay. I have a short break now," I say. "What's up?"

She glances to the back of the bar where I was heading anyway, toward the booths and tables shrouded in darkness and a semblance of privacy. "Let's go back here for a minute," she says, leading me to the shadows.

The booths are oriented like they're in a theater for a Vegas show, curved and facing outward with a small table fixed in front. I gesture toward one of the free ones, and she moves to slide in first. She gives me a smile before she sits, but it's a nervous one. Shit. If this turns out to be about Cruz, I might bust something.

The last time I'd seen Elle, she'd invited me out to lunch and then proceeded to tell me her unwanted opinion that I should seriously think about reconciling with my brother. My anger fills me now like a slow burn to think about it. Elle knows what kind of person Cruz was and what he did before I left for the military. She *knows*. And she knows how unforgivable it is.

She draws in a breath. "Cruz is here. He's in Vegas, and he wants to meet with you."

My hands clench into fists on the table, all of my resentment from the past boiling to the surface at the mention of my brother's name.

I can feel Elle's eyes probing me as though they're desperate for a response, but I don't know what to react to first. I rake my fingers through my hair, my thoughts jumbling together in an angry mess. Cruz. Here. I haven't heard from him or my drug-addict father for seven years. Not since Cruz did what he did to Laura… I cut off my own thoughts before they become too murderous.

"He's here," I repeat flatly, dangerously. "You invited him?"

Elle's posture is tense, and I see my own anger reflected in her eyes. "No, I did *not*. He decided to come all by himself. And the last time I saw you, I was trying to warn you about this possibility, but if you recall, you threw a hissy fit and stormed off."

More like I'd gotten up from the table at the restaurant and walked away before I exploded. I think about walking away again, right now, but if Cruz is actually here, I need to know details. Like if he's here to see me or Elle. If he's going to be parked outside my house when I get home tonight. And even if Elle hadn't initiated this visit, I also need to know how much she said to him, what she told him about me and my life.

My life is private, and I need to keep it that way.

"You talked to him already?"

"Just on the phone. Right before work tonight."

Fuck.

Her expression softens, and she lays her hand on my arm. I stare down at her fingernails that are black and decorated with little skulls as she goes on. "Hun, I know you don't ever want to think about that hellhole we grew up in…"

She has it all wrong. The place hadn't been the problem – it was the people who'd made it hell, and now one of them is here. I look away from her, into the darkness.

"… but Cruz told me he's been making changes. Good changes."

I look at her incredulously. Sometimes her level of blind faith in people could be staggering. I don't understand it. "People can't change that much. People can't come back from evil in seven years, let alone a lifetime," I growl.

She raises one of her pierced eyebrows. "I understand that you're still angry with him, but Connor, this is your twin brother. This is your blood, like I'm your blood." She attempts a smile, but it's weak. "And I'd like to think that you wouldn't ever tell me to fuck off and die."

Yeah, I get it. That was essentially what I'd told Cruz before I left town. Because he deserved it.

"Don't," I say coldly. "Don't compare yourself to him."

Elle purses her lips. "The least you could do is talk to him."

I glower at her, my fury threatening to cloud my head. Elle had raged with me when I told her what happened between me and Cruz. She tried to help me work down from that so I could walk away from it, but some things you can't forget. She's the only one in the world who gets me, who understands where I come from. Or at least I thought she understood, but now I'm starting to wonder.

"No," I snap. "And if you tell him where to find me, you can fuck off, too."

She works her jaw, her eyes flashing angrily. "You don't have to be such an asshole."

I shrug and meet her glare with one of my own. "Maybe not, but at least I'm not a meddlesome bitch. I have nothing to say to him."

"Coward." She abruptly stands up, still glaring down at me.

I stand up, too. "You don't understand," I grind out. But in actuality, I know that she *does* understand, which is exactly the reason why I'm on the verge of raging.

She lifts her head high. Fighting me, challenging me. Elle is my cousin, and I love her like a sister, but she doesn't have the right to tell me what to do. If Cruz is here and she wants to see him, fine. That's her business. But she'll have to do it alone.

She looks at her watch and curses. "I need to get back to work but I have a break in fifteen minutes. We are not done. Do *not* go anywhere."

I don't say anything back, and I watch her weave through the crowd with her tray, anger and resentment burning through me. I raise my beer bottle, but it's empty. And fuck it all because I need a drink, but I have to get to the airport soon.

I grit my teeth and head to the bar for another one.

3

Alex

I'm way drunker than I should be.

My heart thuds in synch with the heavy thumping bass of the music, my head spinning and putting me off-balance. Maybe the drinks tonight are just stronger than what I'm used to. Maybe it's the effect of being kissed for the first time in forever.

An Adelita's Way remix is playing, and the hot blond boy and I are sitting in one of the booths in the back room of the bar. Everything is more muted back here – the room is dimly lit in purple hues, and the shady corners are full of silhouettes.

Usually the music isn't as loud back here either. But it keeps thumping into my head like I'm drowning in it.

He has his arm around me and his other hand on my knee. My head tilts back, and he kisses me, his tongue going at it in a rhythm that's a little too regular. Like a metronome.

In, out. Tick, tock. No clue how long I've been here.

I open my eyes, going cross-eyed because of how close his face is to mine. He pulls back and gives me a slow smile as he trails his fingers along the back of my neck. Across my shoulder. Back again to fondle the nape of my neck, his fingers threading through my hair. I close my eyes, feeling myself float into a haze. Elle. Elle told me to go for him or his friend. And his friend had been with some other girl. So this is okay. Even if Elle hadn't told me to go for him, this would still be okay.

Except I don't feel like myself. My limbs feel disconnected, and my head is all floaty like it's not attached to my body at all. What's happening to me?

"Here. I ordered you another drink."

Thank God. It's like a million degrees in here. I'm dying and I need that drink. I lean away from the pretty surfer boy and take another sip of my third – or is it the fourth? – Manhattan. He's been paying for all of my drinks, which means I won the challenge.

Elle's challenge. Where is Elle, anyway?

"What's your name?" I hear him ask over the music. I realize I don't know his either but don't really care.

I have to think for a second.

"Alex Lin."

He looks at me dubiously, and I sip at my drink. "Yeah, I know. Sounds like an Asian guy, right?"

So I prefer being called Alex instead of Alexis. And I don't look as Chinese as my surname. My dad's only half-Chinese, and I have my mom's overall build – five-foot-ten and big-boobed. What my mom calls "well-proportioned" but what the boys in high school used to call "Amazon." Surfer boy's eyes trail down the front of my dress. He seems to like the boobs.

"Where are you staying, Alex?"

Too many questions. I pull my hair back as his gaze roves from my chest downward. I think hard, my head throbbing from the effort, but I can't remember the name of my hotel. I can't remember, and it bothers me more than the fact that I don't know the name of this guy who had his tongue almost down my throat.

"I'm staying with my mom and dad," is all I come up with. My words run together, but it still feels like it takes me forever to get them out.

He barks a laugh, and it sounds uncomfortable. "Here on vacation with the 'rents, huh? For how long?"

I don't want to answer his question because I don't want him to know. I don't want him to know me. I almost wish he would kiss me again, not because he's that good at it, but because then he won't be able to ask me any more personal questions.

I shift to get closer to him, and he grabs my face and kisses me again. His tongue plunges into my mouth, almost making me gag. His fingers shove their way up my skirt and touch me through my panties, but I can hardly feel it. It's like my brain is dissociated from my body, and I shiver.

He starts rubbing me too roughly, and I can feel *that* but not in a good way. I flinch, and he pulls away from me as my vision swims to get him into focus.

He treats me with that lazy smile again. "You wanna go somewhere?"

Do I? The question repeats itself in my brain like a distant echo. I tear my glance away from him and look around the room. For a second, I can't remember where we are.

He moves his hand down my thigh so his palm rests on my knee, and I briefly close my eyes. I feel dizzy.

"I need to find my friend. She might be worried about me," I mumble. The room wavers in my view again, and I blink until it stops.

"Relax. Your friend knows you're with me. She knows you're okay."

I try to muddle through how that's even possible, but surfer boy's face gets closer to mine again, and the room starts to spin. I let my head fall back, my eyelids fluttering shut as his lips graze against me. His breath tickles my ear, and I giggle in spite of myself.

"Stop it, Chase." My own voice sounds like it comes from far away. I hear just the music for a while and then a short humorless laugh.

"Chase, huh? Is that your boyfriend? I won't tell him if you don't."

I don't answer. Chase was my last real boyfriend, but that was so long ago. Almost three years ago. I don't even know why I thought about him.

Surfer boy kisses me again, harder, hungrier, tasting like beer mixed with smoke. Song after song plays as I sit with his tongue in my mouth and my fist knotted in his hair. His hand tugs at my panties, fumbling inside. I feel numb. I feel nothing. This isn't right.

"C'mon. Let's go."

His voice sounds like it comes at me through a long tunnel, but when I drag my eyes open again, he's right there. He takes my hand and tugs at me to come out of the booth, and my feet and legs automatically follow. My head is really spinning now, the floor tilting under my feet as the bass-line of some remix pounds into my head.

I hope we're not dancing. I don't feel like doing anything except for going home to my apartment and crashing.

Wait. I'm on vacation. I can't go home.

He trails around the perimeter of the room until the walls transform into heavy, dark curtains. My feet continue to follow him as he slips through a gap in one of them. I blink, trying to get my eyes to adjust to the lighting. We're in a hallway that branches in two different directions. There are doors on either side of us. What look like offices or storerooms. I stand back and watch as he tries the doors, but they're locked.

We're all alone, and I know what he wants. I'm not a rookie. I've hooked up with guys before, and on another night I might have wanted something like this. Maybe. But I can't do this the way I'm feeling right now.

"I want to go back out front," I say, my head seriously pounding. He advances on me, and my heart freaks out like a bird's trapped inside my chest and trying to get free.

He presses me up against the wall. He smirks.

"I don't bite. We were having a good time before. Just chill and keep having a good time, yeah?"

I shake my head *no*, but he forces his mouth onto mine, his hands everywhere, yanking down the shoulders of my dress and roughly grabbing at my breasts. He's a couple of inches taller than me, and his whole body presses against me, the bulge in his jeans hard. His body heat sears into me, the only thing I can feel. His hands grope under my dress and pull my panties down. The sound of my pulse hammering in my ears is the only thing I can hear.

The blood rushing through my body.

Time rushing. Everything rushing.

Except for me. I can't move. Even though I know I don't want to be here.

"Wait," I think I say, but he straightens again and presses his mouth against mine, and the word never hits the air.

I feel him shift away as he fumbles with his belt buckle and undoes the fly of his jeans. He grabs my arms and shoves me back against the wall.

"You want it as bad as I do?" he grunts. I can feel his erection grind against me, and my stomach turns.

No. No, I don't. Let me go.

But I'm pinned and can't move, and my throat is so dry I can't speak. I squeeze my eyes shut, hold my breath, my heart beating way too fast. I open my mouth to call for help, but nothing comes out.

"Alex? Holy shit… Hey asshole, get the fuck off of her!"

My eyes fly open, and I see Tucker advancing on us from the curtain opening with fury in his expression. I'm suddenly not pinned to the wall anymore, and I stumble forward. Nausea rips through me, turns me inside out. Tucker rushes forward and grabs my arm, and surfer boy backs away.

"Dude, it's not what it looks like."

"Really." Tucker peers down at me, his eyes fixing on where one of my boobs is practically spilling out of my dress. He lets go of my arm and advances on surfer boy, all anger and testosterone. "Looks pretty fucking clear to me."

My equilibrium is off, but I manage to pull down on the hem of my dress. Cross my arms over my chest. See my panties on the floor and say to hell with them.

Somehow I make my legs move. Somehow I walk out of there, my heart still going at a million beats a minute as I pass through the curtain. I shuffle through the room to the main part of the bar, and I see Elle there with her tray.

A wave of nausea rides through me again, and I wobble on my feet. But I keep pushing my legs and stagger toward her, my whole body shaking. She's frowning and talking to some guy, but she looks up abruptly, a mixture of surprise and relief on her face when she sees me. And then horror.

"Alex!" She drops her tray, her tiny but strong hands clasping my arms as I stumble. "What's wrong? Girl, what happened?"

"Elle," I moan. It's the only thing I can say. I feel like I'm trying to speak through water, my shakes getting worse. I sag against her, the tears springing to my eyes.

"Connor!" Elle grabs me tight and yells past me. "Help me get her outside!"

The guy she'd been talking to doesn't move, his expression looking annoyed. Elle starts shouting at him again, and he yanks on my arm and pulls me away from her right as I taste the bile in my throat. I grab my stomach and double over, throwing up everything I had to drink.

I hardly have time to register that I know him from somewhere. The bar – messy, dark wavy hair, illegally gorgeous blue eyes, anti-Prince Charming himself.

4

CONNOR

I should have taken off when Elle left the table, and now I'm stuck in her mess. Literally a fucking mess. Elle wants me to meet with Cruz, says she'll come with us like we need to be chaperoned. We stand by the bar and keep arguing back and forth about it. If it was anyone else but Elle, I'd walk away.

Her whacked-out friend stumbles over in the middle of everything, and Elle screams at me to help her. Right before the redhead pukes out her guts.

The redhead. The same one as at the bar, the one I'd seen on the dance floor. I'm holding her arm over my shoulder to support her and cursing Elle out in my head.

"Lemme go."

I ignore Red's slurred protest as I wind her arm over my shoulders and hoist her up, careful not to get any of that shit she'd just thrown up on my clothes. But it looks like it all made it onto the floor. Not envious of the employees here for having to clean up that one.

A guy named Will is working the front door tonight, and he steps over when he sees me hauling the redhead to the door. As far as the staff go at this club, he's one of the few decent ones. Elle tails me with a cup of water she grabbed at the bar, yelling at me to be careful. For hell's sake. She's damned lucky I'm doing this at all. And if the redhead pukes again... I shake my head and dump her onto one of the benches outside. Elle flies past me to catch her before she slumps over.

"Jeez, Connor. Have a little care," Elle snaps.

She sits down next to her friend and murmurs something as she brings the water up to her lips. I give Elle a stony look before glancing at my watch.

"Need me to call a cab for her?" Will looks like he's keeping his distance from her too, his expression impassive.

Elle shakes her head as he reaches for his phone. "No! I want to make sure that she actually gets back to her hotel room. I'm off in forty-five minutes..." She looks up at Will and pleads, "Can she hang out here with you while I wrap up?"

"Won't be able to babysit her, Elle. I got my job to do, too." Will looks at her, his forehead creasing with doubt.

The redhead's head lolls back as she mumbles, "I'll take a cab. I'll be okay."

I nod. Perfect. I have just over a half hour to get to the airport, and I start toward the parking lot, more than satisfied with the resolution. "See ya, Elle. Will."

"Connor! Wait." Elle's voice is bordering on authoritative, and I bristle. She whispers something else in her friend's ear, then calls out to me, "She's staying on the Strip. It's not far – you can take her."

"Sorry, cuz." I turn but keep backing away, lifting my arms by my sides. "You and Will aren't the only ones who have to get back to work."

She jumps up and stalks over to me with a furious expression on her face. "I can't dump her into a cab," she hisses. "And I doubt a driver would even take her like this."

"Not my problem." I don't want the redhead in my car either. Being late for clients with anxiety disorders – I'm convinced they all have them to some extent – is bad for business.

Elle's face flushes, and she says through her teeth, "If you do this for me, I'll owe you."

Elle's tenacious, and something about her equal unwillingness to stop harping on me about her friend gives me pause. Owe me? Elle knows I don't hold things over people's heads like that. This girl means that much to her? I give Red a second look. She's sitting with her elbows braced on her knees, and she slowly raises her head, her eyes meeting mine before she drops her forehead back down into her hands.

There's something in her gaze that stirs up a long-ago memory. Not a good memory.

I walk over to her and kneel down, grabbing her chin and forcing her to look up. Some of her hair is plastered to her forehead with sweat, her eyes averted. "Look at me," I say firmly.

"What the hell are you doing?" Elle is next to me in a flash, but I push her away as her black nails grab at my arm.

"Look at me," I repeat, ignoring Elle.

Red's gaze slowly rises to meet mine, and I stare at them. Her pupils are blown, a small ring of cocoa brown showing around the edges. Shit.

I stand up, all of my instincts shouting at me to walk the fuck away.

"She's high."

Elle's whole body tenses up, and she starts in on me again. "Whatever. So she had a little too much to drink. Like you've never –"

26

I turn on her, my patience finally at its limit. "No. Look at her eyes. She's either tripping out on E, coke, something..."

Red attempts to sit up tall, her shivering worse as she glares at me. "I don't do that stuff."

"...or someone dropped some shit into her drink," I finish.

Elle stares at me with wide eyes before diving down into a crouch next to Red. "Hun, what happened with you and that guy after the challenge?" Her expression hardens as the redhead mumbles something back. Elle lifts her head to look at me, her expression full of agony. "Omigod. This wasn't her fault. You *have* to take her to her hotel. C'mon, Connor. Please. Make up for the past."

"My purse," Red suddenly moans. "I think I left it in the back room."

"I'll look for it. Stay here with her," Elle shoots in my direction with a pointed look before she runs back into the bar.

I don't answer because I'm fuming, my hands fists by my sides. Make up for the past? Low blow, *cousin*.

My better judgment is still telling me to walk away. Walk away right now. But Elle's words make me think about things I don't want to think about, the same things as when I saw Red on the dance floor with that guy who kept advancing on her.

Cruz and Laura. All over again.

Overshadowing my anger is guilt, and it claws at my conscience. I stare at the girl on the bench and think about the seconds ticking, the fact that I have to be at the airport. I fight the urge to punch something. Because I know I can't leave Red sitting here drugged up like this. It's like Elle guessed what I'd see, knew I wouldn't be able to walk away, and I hate her a little for that.

Elle runs back out a minute or two later with Red's purse. She stands and faces me, worry lining her eyes.

"Fine," I snap. "I'll take her to the hotel."

A flicker of relief crosses her face. "Good. I'll call you tomorrow, okay? We'll do lunch and come up with a game plan."

"Don't push it," I growl.

Elle grumbles something about how you can't choose family, her cue for me to respond with another cynical comment like I always do when we argue back and forth, but I don't jump in this time. I don't answer her, don't say goodbye, just haul Red off the bench and drag her to my car.

I pause to look down at her before disengaging the Audi's alarm system.

"Listen, Red. Show any signs that you're about to puke again, and I'm kicking you out of the car, got it?"

She wobbles on her feet but lifts her chin and looks me in the eye.

"My name's Alex," she mutters. "And don't worry, Prince Charming. I won't puke in your precious car."

I frown as I drive back to the Strip. For some reason, *this* had to happen tonight, right after I got the news about Cruz. Fuck my luck.

Alex leans her head back on the headrest, her eyes closed. She looks young, though she's obviously at least twenty-one to have been in the bar, unless she used a fake I.D. to get in. I noticed it before when I was watching her, but she has a pretty face — it's pale right now, but with high cheekbones and perfectly curved lips, dark eyelashes, dark red hair.

I'd bet the fact that she puked actually helped get most of the shit out of her system, which means she'll probably be okay.

If only Laura had been so lucky.

I briefly close my eyes after braking at a stoplight. This isn't déjà vu; it's more like some sick form of karma spearing me in the guts and refusing to release me from the past. Alex is a stranger, but what happened to her tonight, the thought of what could have happened to her, brings back pain. Pain that I don't want to remember.

Too late.

Alex's head tips back as I accelerate on the green light, and I give her a sharp glance. I don't want her to pass out, should talk to her to keep her awake.

"Hey." I reach over and jostle her shoulder. "You okay? Do you remember your name?"

She turns her head to face me. I think I see some emotion register in her eyes — anger, or fear. Something strong, but it's gone in an instant.

"Don't shake me," she mumbles. "Yeah, I remember my name. You remember yours?"

Funny. "It's Connor. Connor Vincent."

She snorts. "Parents couldn't decide on one first name, huh?"

I raise my eyebrows. Still has an attitude even though she's messed up. "Vincent's my last name, wiseass. Didn't really have a choice in that, did I?"

I quash the fleeting thought in my head, the fact that I did have a choice, that I could have picked any last name when I moved out here. Vincent is Elle's middle name — a family name passed down to her from her mom — and I chose it for mine because it gave me a connection to her.

Alex doesn't respond, just rubs her eyes, and I wager with one hundred percent certainty that she's going to have one hell of a headache tomorrow. I pull up to one of the service entrances, watching her with growing impatience as she fumbles with her seatbelt before finally reaching over and undoing it for her.

"Got your hotel key? You know your room number?"

Her eyes flick down to my hand, and I realize I'm still holding onto the seatbelt. I release it and pull away.

"I'm not an idiot," she grumbles. Her eyes are still bloodshot but maybe a hair better than they were.

"I never said you were. Though you gotta admit, you were stupid enough to take multiple drinks from a stranger even after you were probably already feeling like hell."

She makes a strangled sound that might be a laugh. "You sure have a way with words."

"So do you know your room number or not?"

"Yeah, but I'm not gonna tell it to you," she shoots back. "No offense."

"None taken." I look past her and spot a staff member I know fairly well, a guy named Jordan who works as concierge. He's outside smoking a cancer stick, and I lower Alex's window and shout over to him.

"Hey, Jordan, can you help me out?"

He flicks ash from the end of his cigarette and saunters over. "Sure thing, Connor." His eyes fix on Alex, his eyebrows immediately knitting together in a frown. "Oh. Hey, man. I don't know…"

I grit my teeth and grab my wallet, rethinking the whole "owing" thing between Elle and me. I reach over Alex, holding out a fifty like bait to Jordan, and he automatically extends his hand to take it, like I knew he would. Throw in money, and you can always find someone to do you a favor in this city. You just have to know how much to throw.

"Make sure she gets to her room safely," I bark out.

He pockets the bill smoothly. "Of course. You have my word."

I nod, knowing at the very least that he'll be able to use the service elevator and be discreet about it. He opens Alex's door and steps back to let her out, but I catch her wrist before she can move.

"Hey. You know you're lucky, right? If you hadn't puked out most of that shit, or if that guy you were with laced your drink with something like GHB, we would not be here right now. I'd be dropping your ass off at the E.R."

She looks at me, her pupils still slightly dilated but almost normal again. Her gaze is warm, and it burns into me.

"I get it. See ya around, Connor Vincent."

I stare at those lush lips as they form the words, as they say the name that's not really mine.

Yeah, I remember my name. You remember yours?

I have exactly nineteen minutes to get to the airport now, and she's nothing more than an inconvenience, something standing in the way of where I need to be. There's no way I'll be able to walk her upstairs and still be at the airport on time.

Then why the fuck do I want to?

I watch Alex follow Jordan, not realizing I'm still staring until they get to the service door. Jordan opens the door to let her through, and he places his hand on her back to guide her. Right before they go in, I see his hand drop down to her ass.

My hands clench around the steering wheel, my knuckles white. I have to go. I wasted precious time babbling, and now I'm staring after Alex like an idiot dropping off a date. What's gotten into me? I throw the car into drive and take off, fighting the urge to look in the rearview mirror even though I know they went inside.

Trying not to think about Jordan copping a feel. Trying not to think about Cruz and Laura. Failing miserably. The ghosts from my past are haunting me too strongly right now for me to ignore.

I run my hand over my face. "You're going out of your mind, Connor," I mutter. And now I'm talking to myself.

I briefly consider calling my business partner to cover me but immediately nix that thought. The client I'm supposed to pick up at the airport tonight isn't just anyone. It's Maya Coplin. Maya was my very first client. She got me the start in this business, and she's the reason I have the good rep that I do. She'd pitch a fit if anyone else but me picked her up from the airport. I *cannot* be late for Maya.

I check the flight information on my phone in case there's a change in status. Meant to check back at the bar but didn't have the chance.

Flight from San Antonio (SAT) to Las Vegas (LAS) delayed. Est arrival 30 minutes.

A fraction of my stress dissipates off my shoulders as I blow out a breath, and I silently thank whatever forces in the universe are intervening tonight. Luck doesn't always make a habit of being on my side, but when it is, I try not to take it for granted.

I circle around and drive a little too fast until I get back to the service entrance – luckily there are no cars coming. None of this makes sense, nothing that I'm feeling or doing right now. Not the urge to call Neil to sub for me or the need to make sure Alex gets to her room. But I'm operating only partially on logic right now.

I grab my keys from the ignition and run to the service entrance, beating myself up for being out-of-my-head insane.

When I catch up to them, Jordan doesn't give me my fifty back, but he does give me access to the right service elevator.

"She said she was in the Platinum Tower." He shrugs and gives me a questioning look that I ignore.

I manage a brief smile, though it feels like my jaw is going to crack. I also want to punch him for touching Alex before. "Thanks, man."

"Sure thing, Connor. See ya around."

Alex walks into the elevator without saying a word, seeming not to register or care about the change in guard. She crouches down on the floor and buries her head in her arms, and I give her a shrewd look. She was coherent in the car, enough to be a smartass. Probably just dealing with the effects of the drugs wearing off. The best thing for her right now is to go to her room and sleep it off.

I say to the top of her head, "You're going to have to at least tell me the floor you're on. Unless you want to sleep in the elevator."

She slowly raises her head to look at me.

"Oh, it's you," she mumbles. She puts her hands on her knees and gets up to a standing position, staring at the elevator buttons for an interminable amount of time before stabbing one of them. "Can't stay away from me, huh?"

"Apparently not," I say drily. "I had to make sure you got to your room."

If she says anything in response, I miss it. I'm staring at the lit-up button on the elevator display.

We're heading up to one of the VIP floors.

I check her out again but with more scrutiny than I'd done on the drive over. She's playing with the ends of her hair with fingernails that are even but not particularly well-manicured. Black dress is a good cut but doesn't look expensive. No jewelry to speak of except for a leather wrap bracelet set with cheap crystals. Sandals are scuffed and not new.

I'm guessing not a high roller, though some of them can definitely be quirky, and others dress down on purpose so they don't draw attention, especially when going out. But I've never seen one go out to someplace as seedy as QE2. And her personality… I'm still on edge, but I can appreciate the attitude she put out tonight, even in face of all of the shit she went through.

She's probably the daughter or niece of the VIP guest. A slimmer chance that she's the girlfriend. And now my curiosity is piqued as to who that VIP might be.

The elevator stops and the doors open, but Alex doesn't move to leave. Her keycard is already in hand, but her forehead is furrowed, a few messy strands of long hair falling over her face as she digs around in her purse.

"All you need is your key right now," I point out. "Go to your room and sleep it off."

Her gaze lifts and locks onto my face, and I read anger in her expression. "I was trying to tip you, Mr. Impatient Bossypants. But someone took all of my cash. Probably that douche canoe I was with," she grumbles.

I laugh, the sound surprising myself and from the looks of her glare, pissing her off. I explain. "The name-calling. And you don't have to tip me." The elevator doors start to close, and I stick out my hand to stop them as I look at her more seriously. "How much cash did you lose?"

She sighs. "About two hundred." She steps out of the elevator and starts to walk away. "I know it's not a lot," she tosses over her shoulder. "Not in a city where everyone gambles."

"Two hundred is a lot," I disagree. "And not everyone gambles."

She hesitates, and I watch as she turns to face me. I see an emotion flash in her brown eyes. Anger at her situation. Something that makes me think that this girl has fire in her.

Her words pour out of her in a rush. "Not that I care what you think of me, but I don't do this. Get all drunk and hook up with some random guy whose name I don't even know. If I want to hook up with someone, I do it because I really want to, you know?"

"Don't beat yourself up about it," I say brusquely. "Tonight wasn't your fault."

"Yeah…I guess. See ya." She walks away just as the elevator doors close.

I don't know why she bothered saying all of that to me. I don't know why I'm not immediately pressing the button to get back down to the first floor. I don't know why I'd gotten out of my car in the first place.

But I do know that I didn't do any of this for Elle. Or for her friend.

I did it for Laura.

5

Alex

I wake up with my heart in my throat and an army of evil minions going at my head with jackhammers. I bolt up to a sitting position – ugh… way too fast – before flopping back into the fluffy bedding.

What happened to me last night? Something. Something bad, but I can't remember what. My emotions are slippery, and I press my cheek into my pillow and try to figure out why I feel so out of control.

The scent of crisp linens permeates my fog, and I realize I'm lying in a field of pillows that aren't mine and that I'm not in my own bed. I sit up again in a panic, swiping my hair out of my eyes and feeling relieved when I see that I'm in my hotel room. No army, no jackhammers, just my pounding head and mounting horror as I realize how much of last night was a blur, much of it a total blank.

Crap. I do remember getting a ride back to my hotel room, riding in the elevator… And I have a faint recollection of making out with some guy at the bar last night. But I can't remember how far we went. Like, at all.

I slide my hands down my body. Still wearing the same dress I'd gone out in last night. Still wearing my bra, which is godawful uncomfortable. But my underwear.

My underwear. Is. Missing.

Oh my God. Really? Why can't I remember *that*?

I press the heels of my hands to my forehead and moan as my ears start to buzz. I'm not a total lightweight. I've been hungover plenty of times. But not like *this*.

My phone rings loudly from somewhere in my bed, and I grope for it under the sheets. The display says it's Elle. It also says it's just past nine in the morning, which is way too early to be calling.

"Hey," I croak, rubbing my eyes. The drapes in my room are still shut, my room in mostly darkness. Thankfully. My head feels like it might split into a billion pieces.

"Oh, thank heavens you're alive, woman!" Elle shouts. I wince and hold the phone away from my ear as she goes on. "I mean, okay, so I did hear from my cousin last night, but I was worried you died in your sleep when you didn't answer any of my calls this morning!"

Cousin? I have no clue who she means. Yet another thing on the list of what I don't remember about last night. I grimace as I rub my forehead. I don't like things being taken out of my control like this.

"Sorry. I'm okay," I say, though that's still up for debate. "Sort of okay. Still in bed… What's that about your cousin?"

She makes a choking noise. "Omigod. Okay. How much do you remember about last night?"

She's speaking carefully, like she thinks I might freak out if I do remember what happened. Not good. But her cousin? The sea of people Elle's introduced me to over the past two summers is infinite. Lots of musicians, people she works with, random acquaintances. I think I do remember meeting one of her cousins once, a woman with glossy dark hair that seemed ditzy. But I don't remember if she was there last night.

Elle is talking a mile a minute, so it winds up being much easier to puzzle this out in silence than to try to think of a response.

She goes on. "… so Tucker beat down that guy for dropping that shit in your drink…"

I sit straight up, ignoring the protesting throb in my temples. "Wait, what? *What*?"

My horror compounds as the memories began to trickle back. Elle giving me a challenge. Going up to those two guys and getting surfer boy to dance with me. And then what? The blood rushes to my face, burns my cheeks with anger as I realize why I can't remember anything. Why my underwear is missing…

"Hold up, Elle," I interrupt. "What did Tucker say? What was I doing when he found me?"

She quietly swears to herself before sighing. "Oh, hun. You sure you wanna hear this? Okay. He said you were in the back hallway by the stockrooms. That you were flopping over like a rag doll with that guy all over you with his jeans undone."

I blow out a furious breath. I was drugged. I got freaking roofied. I don't know whether I want to scream or to storm out of here and hunt down that chickenshit who did this to me so I can tear him a new one. But I'm angry and terrified at the same time. And grateful, so grateful that I walked away from that. I press my hand over my eyes and try to get control of my breathing. I owe Tucker, big time.

"I'm so sorry. The challenge… I had no idea." Elle says, her voice suddenly quiet. "Hun, you okay?"

"No, I'm not okay." My head pounds as I struggle to sit up in bed. "I'm mad about being so stupid, and I'm still kinda wrecked." In the midst of all of the emotions churning inside me, I feel a bit satisfied that it had been Tucker to find me. Favorite bartender to the rescue. "Did Tucker mess him up pretty bad then?"

"Enough to teach him a lesson," Elle sighs. "But Trey walked in on them and broke it up before it could go too far."

Trey is the owner of the bar. "Okay, well…" Elle sounds really upset, like she's blaming herself for this. I clear my throat. "Hey. You had no idea that he was a creep and was going to do that. Maybe we should always use the buddy system from now on. For future challenges, you know?"

She barks out a laugh. "Girl, you're insane. That you're even thinking about future challenges." Her voice registers relief. "I'm glad you're okay."

"Yeah, me too."

Elle's starting to say something else, but I hear a soft knock, and I groan. "Hey. I think my mom's at the door. But I'll call you later."

She huffs into the phone, maybe out of relief. "Yeah, cool. Go, go have fun with your mom and call me later. Heart you, dude."

I'm not sure about the having fun part, but I climb out of bed, my head threatening to explode. I wobble over to the door, almost tripping over my sandals in the middle of the floor. I need to get my act together. And I need coffee. Plus ibuprofen. Not to mention a do-over on my first night of summer vacation.

I'm a big believer in signs from the universe, and if last night isn't a huge flashing neon sign, I don't know what is. Part of the reason I'm here is because I want to see what's going on with my parents, not to party the whole time and get wasted. Granted, my current state is not totally my fault. But still, the universe is obviously reminding me of why I'm here.

I open the door, and Dad's eyes widen at me in undisguised shock. I probably mirror his expression with mine – I hadn't gotten to see him last night because he was on the clock when I first got to the hotel. When he's in Vegas, he works the floor like it's his job because for the time that he's here, it is. Dad may be a professional gambler, but he isn't one of those high rollers that flies in by chartered plane and has a winter home in the Caymans. He works hard all year to pay for this trip. He comes here not to impress strangers but as an escape from everyday life.

He's wearing his lucky blue button-down shirt with a simple blazer jacket and basic Dockers, and I notice right away that his hair, once dark brown, is peppered with more grey than last time I saw him. That was what, right before spring break?

"Morning, Dad." I try on a smile, glad that it doesn't feel too unnatural.

"Alexis." He doesn't smile back. "I'm glad you made it in last night."

I'm not sure if Dad means last night after going out or my flight last night. I realize how I must look dressed like I just came back from a club. And my makeup and hair must be totally destroyed. Not exactly what a father wants to see in his one and only daughter in the morning. I hope my cheeks aren't flaming red.

"Was your flight okay?" he adds, and I feel absurdly relieved.

"Yep. Only one short layover. Thanks for making the reservations and all that."

He finally smiles, and the awkwardness between us seems to clear. "Of course. I wanted to catch you this morning before I go back to work. I have something for you."

His eyes show an excited shine in them, and he beckons for me to follow him into the living room part of the suite. He sits on the couch, and I perch next to him.

Dad reaches into his inner jacket pocket, and I open my mouth to object – I don't expect spending money from him anymore. But he holds up his hand before I can say a word.

"It's for the whole trip. Don't argue. It's my winnings from last night. I want you to have it."

"Dad…"

"You're twenty-one now, Alexis."

He places the bills in my hand and practically jumps up off the couch before I can say anything. That's typical Dad. When he decides on something for anyone in the family, there's no further discussion on the topic. Especially when it comes to money.

I watch him walk over to the door to the master bedroom on the other side of the suite, seeing a spring in his step that always means he's doing well at the tables. I wait until he disappears into his room before checking out how much is in the stack.

It *is* a stack, and it's almost ten grand.

Holy crap.

There's some myth out there that casinos pump pure oxygen into the air to give players more energy. The myth itself is complete bullshit, but right now, I kind of wish it was true because I'm feeling light-headed. Ten grand is about nine and a half grand more than he's ever given me for spending cash, and he hasn't given me spending cash since I was seventeen. I know it's probably chump change compared to how much some players drop at the tables, but… Ten. Freaking. Grand. He'd said it was because I'm twenty-one, like that was all of the explanation that I needed. But what does that mean exactly? Is he expecting me to go out and gamble with this?

My first impulse is to immediately call Elle and tell her we need to ramp up the plans for the summer. The possibilities are endless in a city like this. But my more reasonable voice points out that this is not totally in character for Dad.

I'll stick the cash into my room's vault until I figure out what's going on.

"Oh, and Alexis?" Dad pokes his head out of his room. "I passed your mother on her way downstairs, and she wanted me to see if you were up for a swim. She tried knocking before she left, but you were still asleep. If you're still tired…"

Mom and I both love to swim, and when I was younger, our summer days would start off with us getting up early and doing laps in the hotel pool. We'd go until we were famished and then treat ourselves to a giant room service brunch. But she and I haven't done that in a couple of years, probably not since I was nineteen.

They don't call this city "The Capital of Second Chances" for nothing. The universe is speaking, loud and clear. My parents need me today.

"Thanks, Dad," I say. "I'm not tired. I'll head down in sixty seconds."

Saturday morning, and the lap pool is mostly empty except for a guy doing some hardcore freestyle in one of the far lanes and two elderly women chatting as they do a slow frog-style stroke in the middle. Mom is lying in one of the lounge chairs reading a Vogue, huge sunglasses on and her strawberry blonde hair swept up in a perfect twist. I saw her briefly last night right after I got to the hotel and as she was getting ready for bed.

"Hey, Mom," I say to her hair.

She looks up, a smile on her face as she sets the magazine down and reaches for me with outstretched arms. I sit down and hug her, and a faint mist of Chanel engulfs me.

"Alexis! So glad you came down, baby girl. Did you have a nice time with Elle last night?"

"It was fine," I lie. Only Mom gets away with calling me baby girl. I squeeze her but let go when I feel her wince. "You okay?"

"I'm fine. A little sore from my swim yesterday, I guess. I'll stretch out better today."

I throw my towel and bag onto the chair next to her, and we both start our stretches. Whatever that jerkwad put into my drink last night feels like it's still clinging to my bones. But I vaguely remember someone telling me that I was lucky, that it could have been a lot, lot worse if I hadn't puked my guts out. I bend my leg back and grab my foot, gently tugging to stretch my quads, and I know this must be true.

Mom's body is all grace as she reaches up to the sky and arches her back. If Dad has some more gray peppering his hair these days, Mom is the opposite. Her hair shines in the high morning sun, her eyes sparkling as she looks over at me and smiles. She turns forty-nine this year, but everyone says she looks like she could be my older sister. I'm good with that.

Her hazel eyes sweep over me and miss nothing. "You've put on a little weight."

"Thanks a lot." I roll my eyes. I could be as skinny as a twig and she'd probably say the same thing. Ever since I could remember, she's been on a strict diet to counteract the influences of her own mother. My maternal grandmother is originally from England and is famous in the family for her hearty food.

"Well, you look great," I add, which is totally true.

"Why, thank you." She smiles serenely, looking pleased. "This is lovely, isn't it?" she sighs.

"Yes," I agree wholeheartedly. Especially since my ibuprofen is starting to kick in.

"So what did you girls do last night?" She bends over and touches her toes, and I wonder if she's going to go through an entire sun salutation routine.

"Went out to the club where Elle works. Dancing and stuff, you know?"

She nods and looks at me as if she wants more details, but I clam up. I would rather make up stuff than tell her what really happened last night.

"And Elle is well?" she prompts. "Does she still sing?"

"She's great. And I think she still sings. Sometimes?" I say, though I honestly don't know if Elle does very much anymore now that she's working full-time and also going to school.

"Did you know that I used to sing at a club?" She straightens again, and I stare at her with wide eyes. There's an almost wistful expression on her face. "It was a long time ago."

"Really?" I've seen Elle sing before at the club, and I try to picture a younger version of Mom doing the same thing. She's never mentioned it before. "Does Dad know?"

Her face falls, her brow puckering. "Yes. But, well… Maybe don't mention that I told you."

"Okay…" I say, but I wonder why not.

"If you know of any shows that Elle's doing, or of any good concerts this summer, let me know. That would be fun. Ready?"

My arm is resting against my head, my other one pulling back on my elbow for a stretch, and I lower both of them. It takes me a second to register that Mom just switched topics.

But if she doesn't want to talk about it, I'm not about to push her.

"Sure." I pull my t-shirt over my head, and unbutton and kick off my shorts. "Let's go."

We get into the pool at the same time, and I go into my bubble. It's what Mom taught me when I was little and first learning to swim. I was afraid of putting my head under the water, but she told me that if I learned to hold my breath and go all the way under, I'd be protected by a special bubble. That it would quiet the noise of the world and fill me with a special strength.

I remember the first time I tried it. How the shouts and echoes of the other people in the pool became muffled and the noise of the world filtered away until it didn't matter anymore. And then I kicked my legs and moved my arms, and I glided through the water with what felt like no resistance.

I cleave through the water now, the warmth from the heated pool feeling so, so good on my skin. I become stronger, my strokes more powerful, and I push myself until my lungs burn. I grab a breath of air from the surface and submerge again, pulling myself through the water farther and farther until all of the bad stuff from last night dissolves and I'm left clean again.

My mom told me about the bubble when I was five, and I still always envision it that way when I'm in the water. Because it feels good sometimes to muffle all of the noise. Because we all need something now and then to rejuvenate us and make us feel stronger than what we really are.

6

CONNOR

I'm normally much better at doing this. Turning off my feelings, being exactly what I need to be and to hell with everything else.

Now is not one of those times.

I drift halfway in and out of sleep, the smell of smoke from the bar filling my senses, and the thought of the redhead from QE2 forces its way into my head.

Red. Alex. I got a series of annoying texts from Elle shortly after I dropped her off and was on my way to the airport. Had Alex made it back to the hotel? Had she made it back to her room? Had I seen to it first-hand? Was I absolutely sure she was okay? My responses were yes, yes, yes and then stop fucking texting me. Even though everything worked out in the end, I hate the fact that I even thought about calling Neil to cover me. Alex hadn't been an emergency, she'd been a moment of weakness.

A moment of weakness who's staying on the VIP's floor.

It means nothing. The high rollers come and go as fast as their money, and I'll probably never run into her again, not even if I work 24-7. I don't know why I'm dedicating any of my brain cells to thinking about it. Especially given the real bomb that dropped last night about Cruz being in Vegas.

I open half an eye to the sun blazing through a crack in the blinds. I see the head of platinum blonde hair on the pillow next to me a second later. Shit.

The apartment belongs to Bethany, a hot little blackjack dealer that I hooked up with a few months ago. We aren't dating, but we use each other when it's convenient. Bethany texted me right after I dropped off Maya Coplin at her hotel. She said she'd just gotten off her work shift and would make it worth my while if I stopped by. I made sure it was worth her while, three times.

It works. She's a known entity, gorgeous, and a great lay that comes with no strings attached. But I sure as hell hadn't wanted to fall asleep here.

The warmth of her skin intermingles with mine as she rolls over and spoons me, and I stir as one of her arms slides around my shoulder. Her fingers trail lightly from my neck to my chest to my stomach, but I catch her wrist before she can go any lower.

"Well, look at you. You're awake after all," she purrs into my ear.

"Barely," I mutter.

She tosses her hair back and sits up, her hair sexy-messy and falling in her face. She parts her lips, licking them as she gazes down at me.

I know that look, and I cock an eyebrow. "You can't be ready to go at it again."

"I'm game if you are."

She rises up to a kneeling position, and I drink up the lithe curves of her body – perfectly naked except for the tiny triangle of fabric that masquerades as underwear. I keep watching her as she stretches, closes her eyes, pushes her hands through her hair and moves her hips more seductively than some of the best strippers in town. Bethany spends hours at the gym to keep that body in top form, and I know she's intentionally giving me a show and loving the fact that I'm watching every move. Her palms run slowly over her breasts, and the sheet that's still twisted around the lower half of me starts to rise like a tent.

Her lips curl in a sly smile as she notices. But then her gaze flicks over to her alarm clock and her smile vanishes. "Oh, shit. Actually I have to meet someone in a bit." She pauses before adding, "You want to stay? I shouldn't be gone for too long."

The invitation is enough to totally kill my mood. Bethany and I had fun until the early morning hours, sure. But the more time we spend together, the more awkward it gets.

"I have to get to work."

She shrugs and climbs off the bed, her eyes sweeping over me a little greedily. "See you sometime soon?"

"Sure." My tone is noncommittal as I get out of bed and grab my jeans from the floor. She narrows her eyes at me as I take out a dollar bill from my wallet and walk over to her.

"Thanks for last night," I say with a smirk as I tuck it into her thong.

"You're a pig, Connor," she shoots back, but she winks and takes the dollar. She flounces over to the master bathroom, and I laugh. It's a joke that we have going. Sometimes I'll leave the dollar by the nightstand before I take off, other times she'll leave me a dollar on the pillow for when I get over here.

I hear her start up the shower, and my mood feels a shade darker as I snatch up the clothes I'd worn last night.

I get dressed, stepping my way through the piles of Bethany's clothing littering the carpet. The coffeepot is programmed and already going when I get out to the kitchen, and I'm grabbing a mug from the cupboard when my phone rings.

Elle again. Of course.

"That does it. I'm changing my number," I mutter into the phone without preface.

"Chill the hell out," she snaps. "Although you might not be able to when you hear this." I hear her intake and release of breath. "I just saw Cruz."

My grip tightens on the phone, my jaw clenches. Thanks to the whole puking incident, I hadn't gotten the information about Cruz I needed from Elle last night, and now her tone makes it sound like I'm out of time. Elle's words are drawn-out and heavy, her tone grave, and while it speaks volumes, I need cold facts, not her feelings on the subject. The back of my neck pricks uncomfortably, as if Cruz is in the room with me right now, watching. He'd always been observant, watching and sizing people up. He's like me in that way, but only in that way.

"Where is he now?"

"Don't know. My guess is he's staying with friends or at a cheap hotel —"

"I gotta say, Elle," I interrupt. "For a second, I was sure you were going to say he was staying with you."

She huffs. "Look, hun, I'm not masterminding any of this. And I'm actually on your side, in case you forgot. I'm just the messenger here."

I make a mental note of this. "Right. And how is it that he even found you?"

"Cruz found me exactly like you found me," she says with exaggerated patience. "By asking my overly-trusting parents for my address. Believe me, I didn't ask for this." She hesitates. "He wanted to know where he could find you today, but I didn't tell him anything."

Maya is on the docket for the day, and I can picture her reaction if she ever sees him – so much like me in his appearance, but so not like me in all of the important ways. The last thing I need is for my twin brother to track me down and show up out of the blue when I'm with a client.

"What did he say? Why is he here now after all this time? Elle, don't you think that if he actually gave a shit about you, he would have made the effort a little earlier?"

She falls silent, and I know my comment hurt her. I don't totally blame Elle for all of this, though I do suspect she encouraged him to come more than she'll ever admit. Cruz is a wild element, volatile, and unpredictable. He's impulsive, where I try not to be. We both went through the same shit growing up, but I finished high school and then literally pushed myself to my limits as a SEAL. Cruz dropped out of school when he was fifteen, landed himself in juvie for disorderly conduct and again for aggravated assault by the time he was seventeen. Guilty of a multitude of other crimes but no jail time, at least not yet.

He and I might be blood, but we're as different as night and day.

Bethany walks into the kitchen, her hair damp and her eyes settling on me with interest when she sees I'm still in her apartment and drinking out of one of her coffee mugs.

"Hey, I'll call you back in a minute," I mutter to Elle before ending the call. Bethany's pouring coffee into a travel mug, but I can tell by the interested look on her face that she's eavesdropping.

"Hot date?" Bethany asks breezily. She snaps the lid on her mug and raises it to her lips, one eyebrow lifted in a delicate arch.

"No." I leave it at that, hoping she will too, but I feel her blue gaze bore into the side of my head.

"You know it's cool if you do, right?" She hesitates. "Hey, Connor. Can I tell you something?"

Hell, I should have taken off when I had the chance and suffered until I could get to a Starbucks. I hate morning-after-sex conversations, and this one is rapidly becoming unbearable. My gaze finally meets hers, and she unfortunately takes that as encouragement to go on.

"I started seeing someone. We've actually been dating for a couple of weeks." Her cheeks flush pink. "You and me, babe – what we have is pretty amazing, but… I'm sorry. I guess I should have told you last night, huh?"

The way she's looking at me is like she's trying to soften the blow. But that's the thing – there isn't one. I'm not surprised one bit that Bethany's screwing someone else. There are thousands of reasons why we aren't more than we are, and I don't want to think about any of them.

And now Bethany's looking at me with a mixture of regret and hope in her eyes, like she wants me to say that everything is cool and that I'll still come by. But I know in this moment that I won't. We'd had our fun, but I have no desire to be the "other guy." Not for anyone.

I move the distance between us and touch her chin. She tilts her head up, and I lean down and kiss her coolly on the forehead.

"Good luck with everything."

"Oh. Yeah. You too." She draws back from me, the flush that was in her cheeks now gone, and forces a smile. "I had a good time. We could have been something maybe."

I doubt that. I feel her eyes on me as I leave, but I don't look back.

51

I stand outside the door to one of the VIP suites, running through my mental file of her.

Maya Coplin. Thirty-seven years old, Texas native, inherited most of her money from her grandfather. Loves her jewelry and likes to dress like a fifties Hollywood starlet. Her poker face is a mixture of sultry and flirtatious looks, but she's as cool and calculated as any of the boys, and she has bigger balls than most of them.

The first time we met was in a different casino, and I was trying my luck at poker out on the main floor. I noticed her right away – anyone with a working set of eyes would notice Maya. I also noticed the worthless piece of shit across the table from me checking her out as she walked out of the high roller room. He cashed out right away and followed her off the floor. I tailed both of them to one of the elevators and grabbed him right after he pushed her into the doors and snatched her purse.

Maya had asked me for my name, and I'd given it to her. She approached me the next morning after she ran a check on me. The Navy SEAL background had clinched it for her, and she came up with an offer that was too good to turn down. I had nothing else lined up at the time and had been trying to figure out what to do next. At the very least, I figured I'd help her out while she was in town. I had no idea how well connected she was.

I owe a lot to her – all of my initial clients were referrals that she sent my way, and now Neil and I both have a respectable list of exclusive clientele that keep us busy.

For the next fourteen days, I'll provide more than security for Maya. I'll also be her companion, conspirator, and protection against bad juju (so she claims).

I dial up the appropriate level of charm before I knock on her door. I'm wearing a dark blue t-shirt, dark jeans, and a casual jacket to conceal the Sig Sauer I keep on my belt. She prefers me dressing like her boy toy instead of a hired thug – her words. She's particular about a lot of things.

I hear the click of high heels, a pause as she checks that it's me before flinging the door open. She doesn't disappoint – she never does. It's just past noon, but she's decked out in an evening dress, pink silk with a plunging neckline, her hair shining in soft blonde waves that flow over one shoulder.

Last time I worked for her was back in the middle of April. She was lucky on that trip, gambling big and winning big, and when I picked her up at McCarran last night, she acted relaxed and happy.

I smile at her. "Hi, beautiful. It's been too long."

Her eyelashes flutter over baby blues. "Fourteen hours is too long to be away from you, you tall, gorgeous, drink of water." Her voice is sultry and smoother than honey.

It's how we always greet each other, the cheesier the better. I laugh, and she gives me a perfect pink smile, but the expression in her eyes stays cool. The clock is ticking, and I need to get her down to the casino floor so she can play.

I offer my arm. "Ready?"

"Of course I am." A sparkle flashes in her eyes. "What a silly question, darling."

I can almost feel the excitement flow through her as she slips her hand through my arm. High rollers are all junkies in a way, addicts looking for their next rush that comes from taking the risk. Even though I'm out on the floor almost every single day with them, I work hard to distance myself from all of that. The kinds of highs and lows that serious players go through are equivalent to the shit that I had to watch my father go through with drugs, what Cruz was starting to get into when he was a teenager. Gambling's the same, just a different drug.

Thinking about Cruz makes a dark place in my gut roil with hatred and contempt. I shove the feeling back down, where it can't do me any harm.

"Connor," Maya drawls. "I have missed you. Are you sure you can't offer 24-hour security for your oldest client?"

I cock an eyebrow, and she winks. Maya knows I keep everything professional with my clients, no exceptions.

"If I didn't prefer older women, I might take you up on that, Mrs. Coplin," I tease. "But you can't be a day older than twenty-one."

We come to a stop in front of the row of elevator doors, and she fans herself for show. "Goodness. What would the late Mr. Coplin think if he could hear the things you say to me?"

I never met the late Mr. Coplin, and only know from what Maya said that he'd been older than her and that he's dead. Don't know more than that and don't want to. I don't like to know what my clients' home lives are like, whether they're happy in other aspects of their lives. As long as they're happy with me, I'm good.

She lifts her chin as she tucks her evening bag under her arm. "I thought we'd go visit Max today."

I raise my eyebrows. Maxwell's Room is the high-limit poker room, and it has a ten thousand dollar buy-in, minimum. Maya usually doesn't hit Maxwell's at the start of her stay. Plus, that's where she cleaned up last time, and she's always been superstitious about playing the same place twice in a row.

"You sure?" I know she won't be offended by me asking.

She shrugs delicately, as if the decision is nothing. But I know otherwise, that she worked out a strategy in her head. "I have a good feeling about this, darling."

"Then you got this," I say easily.

"With you by my side, always."

It's all banter. Nothing is guaranteed in this city, and we both know it.

But I feel off today. As we walk through the casino floor, every time I see my reflection, it's as if Cruz is glaring back at me like a fucking ghost.

Maxwell's is excessive, from the guards posted at the entrance to the stakes involved. It's busy today, and I take up position to the right of Maya as she takes out a marker for her buy-in. A few minutes later and the dealer pushes her a stack of chips worth a small fortune. It used to be harder than it is now, watching players like Maya take a marker for thousands of dollars from the house like it's nothing, to watch her count out the money to cover her losses. Just another thing I learned to distance myself from.

Two hours later, Maya pushes her chips over to get changed over to larger denominations, passing the dealer a hundred dollar chip for a tip and telling me to collect the rest. She was up almost eighty thousand at one point, but with her chips colored up, there's not even enough to rack. I'm used to her being quiet after she loses, but I notice more strain around her eyes than usual when I stand to face her in the elevator. She needs the downtime in her room before going back out there.

I know that Maya's perfect exterior is how she shows the world that she's on top. But the financial and emotional stress for the high stakes player can be off the charts, and I noticed over the past few visits that she stays away for longer after a heavy loss. Given how hard Maya played over the past two years, I wouldn't be surprised if she stopped making Vegas trips soon. It's inevitable, and it goes against my better judgment to care. Still, I hope she doesn't crash too hard when it's all over.

She lets go of my arm as we approach her suite. Inside, she glides over to the couch, and I follow with her chips, setting them down on the coffee table.

"You don't want to have a drink with me before I have to go back downstairs, do you?" she asks, her eyes intent on me. Her words drag out a bit, her drawl more pronounced than usual.

I hesitate because it's out of character for her to ask. I never drink when I'm on the job, not even with Maya.

"Not while I'm working," I remind her. "But I'll pour one for you before I leave."

She puts her feet up and rests her elbow on the high arm of the couch, her hair spreading out in golden waves around her shoulders. "Pity," she sighs. "All right then. A gin and tonic. A good stiff one."

Maya's eyes are still fixed on me when I return with her drink.

"See you in an hour, gorgeous," I say lightly.

I wait for her usual comeback, but she just sips her drink and nods. I wonder what's up, but Maya is a big girl and formidable in her own right.

Whatever's eating her, I'm sure she can handle it.

7

Alex

Mom's in the living room, Dad's working the floor, and I'm taking full advantage of the giant bathtub in my bathroom. I sink down so my chin is engulfed by bubbles, willing myself into a state of total relaxation.

But my brain doesn't cooperate. I can hear Mom singing, and I listen to her sweet soprano voice lament about love and broken promises. I remember she used to sing in the community choir back home, but she gave it up when I was little. I can't stop thinking about what she confided in me when we were at the pool this morning, and I wonder what else she's had to give up.

I know she gets stressed out during the rest of the year when she has to deal with reality. Back home, Dad is a total workaholic. He says he does it all for her, but the fact is that he's gone a lot because of it. Mom gets restless and anxious over it, and then they fight. Vegas is their place to come to make things good again, which is why hearing that Dad might have to cut the trip short makes me worry.

I need to take Mom out to see a show, like she asked.

I dunk myself completely in the tub, hair and all to more fully wash out the chlorine from the pool. Elle is at her social work internship this afternoon, but prior to me jumping into the tub, she and I were texting each other about what to do about the Alysa's Empyre concert tonight. She's stressing out about it and wants to try our luck with the scalpers.

The lead singer of Alysa's Empyre is super-talented, her voice and energy both inspiring. It's the entire reason that Elle loves the band so much, and if there's any concert worth going to this summer, this one's it. But even if we could manage to get three tickets from scalpers, they'd be for tix on the floor. Mom wouldn't be able to handle that, and there's no way I'd let her deal with the all of the b.s. that comes with being shoved around by the general admission crowd.

Elle had been the one to ask if there was a chance my dad could get us in, and I'd told her I'd ask. Never hurts to ask, right?

I finish shampooing and rinsing my hair, pop the drain, and drag myself out of the water, wrapping my body in one of the big soft hotel robes and my hair in a fluffy towel. The suite is quiet again by the time I'm out, and Mom's door is closed, which means she probably went to lie down for a quick nap before dinner.

I sneak over to the desk in the suite and perch on the edge of the chair on rolling wheels. It's Dad's desk, or at least it is for the time he's here. My hand runs over the smooth polished mahogany surface. I know his iPad is sitting in the top drawer, and all I have to do is unlock it to see his schedule for the day. He plans down his days to the minute, the same as when he's at home working as an accountant.

I pull open the drawer, my finger hesitating less than an inch above the screen. When Dad's on the floor, he's in another world. He doesn't want us around him. I have vivid memories of Mom telling me this time and time again when I was a kid. She'd almost look scared when she said it. We were not to approach my father when he was working, not under any circumstances.

Yeah, well, I'm going to take my chances this time. I want to surprise Mom with this.

I unlock the iPad and go into his scheduling app to find his list for today. He doesn't always play in the casino where we're staying. Right now it looks like he's at the high roller room in the casino across the street, and it looks like he checked in an hour and a half ago. I don't know everything about Dad's method, but I do know one thing. For every two hours that he plays, he walks away for a half hour, minimum. Even if he's winning. And that means he'll be coming out soon.

I run in bare feet to my room and throw on my favorite t-shirt (the one with skulls) and favorite rockstar grunge skirt (the one with the grommets). I take a few minutes to apply light makeup, and I run a pick through my hair. It'll dry pretty much instantly the second I step outside, anyway.

I start to put on my favorite sandals but considering the distance I'll have to walk, throw on a pair of sneakers at the last second. Nobody's going to care.

Casinos are super annoying if you ever want to leave in a hurry because they're designed so you have to walk forever to get to the exits. I suppose they do that on purpose, figuring they can entice you with an additional mile of poker machines before you can find your way out. I jog that mile, ignore the machines, and hold my breath as the hundred plus degree air slaps me in the face when I push the doors open to the outside.

Not in the clear yet. Las Vegas Boulevard is like an obstacle course right now, packed with slow-moving tourists fanning themselves with fliers. Every ten feet, I'm accosted by someone who jumps out at me with one of those same fliers, trying to get me to try out some prime rib or check out a new comedian or "ladies only" show. Yeah, no thanks. I glance at my watch and grind my teeth together. This almost feels like the universe throwing small roadblocks in my way, but I refuse to acknowledge them this time.

I breathe easier when I make it across the street and inside the casino. Until I realize that I have no idea where the high roller room is. It's not like there's a sign pointing the way, but I should be able to figure it out.

The casino has a tropical theme, and I walk through a simulated rainforest and around the perimeter of the main gaming floor, the lights and sounds from the slot machines bouncing off me as background noise. I glance at the time, and my heart skips a beat. By my estimate, Dad's due to be out of the high roller room soon, and the size of this place is insane. I veer directions and stop by the nearest cashier to ask where the high roller room is.

The woman looks about ninety, her skin brown and wrinkly like a walnut. She shrugs. "Those who are suited to go there do not need to ask where it is."

Huh. I wonder if she has a slip from a fortune cookie back there that says this very thing. I bare my teeth in a smile. "Well, I'm trying to find my father, who *is* suited to go there. If you can't tell me, I can always ask your supervisor."

Her lips press into a thin line as I continue to stare her down. Finally, she points behind me and to my right. "Past the blackjack tables. Corridor behind the fountain."

"Thanks. You've been so helpful." I smooth back a strand of hair from my face and walk away, shaking my head. Some people should not be allowed to interact with the general public. Seriously.

I walk past the blackjack tables and spot the fountain. I also see some guy in an expensive-looking suit walking with some dude in tow. I've observed the high roller crowd enough to know that there are two types. Type one always walks alone. Type two always has someone as an escort, usually some thug-like dude who I assume is an overpaid bodyguard or sometimes a drop-dead gorgeous woman that looks more like a good luck charm. My dad happens to be the type that always walks alone.

The type two heads down the short hallway off the main gaming floor, and I follow.

Bingo.

There's a thick, muscular guy complete with an earpiece and black suit posted outside a set of heavy-looking doors made of opaque glass. His jacket is loose, and as I walk past him, I see the butt of a pistol sticking out of a belt holster. Cold eyes graze over me as I go by, dismissing me as insignificant. But as he is armed security, I sincerely doubt he'll tolerate me hanging out by the doors to wait for my dad, so I keep walking until I get to the end of the hallway. It's a dead end, occupied by a lit sign advertising some of the shows at the casino, and there are restrooms off to the side. It's almost time for my dad to be out anyway, so I linger near the ladies' room door and whip out my phone. The sound of a voice stops me before I can dial.

"Good afternoon, Reggie."

"Afternoon, ma'am."

I glance up at the sound of the Texan drawl and see another type two. She's beautiful, blonde, perfect. But that's as much as I notice about her. Because the guy with her, her escort who doesn't look like a thug or a good luck charm, is looking over at me.

And he has the most intense blue eyes I've ever seen.

This morning I struggled to recreate events between pounding down Manhattans and puking my guts out. But I remember *him*. The guy who spilled my drink on me at the bar last night. The same guy who wound up driving me to my hotel. Anti-Prince Charming. Connor something-or-other.

He's wearing a black t-shirt, jeans, a dark blazer jacket. His gaze locks with mine right before the guard opens the door, and I see something in his expression that's more than simple recognition. Like he's looking at me but seeing more than me.

Like he's not happy about what he sees.

He doesn't say a word, but the unspoken judgment in his eyes surprises me. I tense up, even though I have no reason to feel defensive, and glower back at him.

His jaw tightens, and he breaks off the eye contact. The beautiful blonde walks into the high roller room, and I watch as he follows. The door shuts behind them, and I'm alone in the corridor with the guard.

My hand clenches into a fist, my fingernails digging into my palm as I turn away. What was his deal?

"Alex?"

I'm still in the same place – by the ladies' room and slightly annoyed – when the sound of Dad's confused voice brings me down off the ledge and fills me with a different sort of edge. Damn. I almost lost focus as to why I'm here. All thanks to tall, dark, and jerkface.

Dad hurries toward me with concern written on his expression. His questions come out rapid-fire, his voice low.

"Alex, is something wrong? Why are you here? Is it your mother?"

Yikes. I hadn't banked on him panicking when he saw me, though maybe I should have. How else would he react to his kid showing up at his "work" if I've never done this before?

"No, no." I add quickly, "I was hoping that you might be able to help me arrange a surprise night out for Mom."

"Oh!" He exhales out of relief, a genuine smile breaking out on his face. "What did you have in mind?"

"There's a band playing that I think she would really like. And my friend Elle also, if that's possible."

I catch a flicker of something on his face – sadness maybe? – before he nods, and it makes me curious as to the reason behind it. "When is it?"

"It's tonight at The House of Blues. But it's sold out." It sounds insane as I hear myself say it. I fold my lips inward, waiting for his reaction.

He nods again, and I can almost see his mind switch over from dad to businessman. "I can make this happen. Come with me."

Dad extends his arm out to me, and I slide my hand into the crook of his elbow. We walk through the tropical-themed gaming floor together, and he drops little facts as we go. How much it was said to cost to make the simulated rainforest. How they'd originally put plants in there that they later found to be poisonous (and had removed). Rumors about the next casino and what theme it'll have. And it's like a magical switch turns on that wipes away any of my worries. He's always so centered, focused, a calming influence that balances out my own fire. And as he reaches over and affectionately pats my hand that's nestled in his arm, I'm glad that I came to find him. That he doesn't always have to walk alone.

Important-looking casino personnel in expensive suits keep giving him courteous nods as we pass. It's cool. My dad is a VIP, and it's like being at a concert with backstage passes. We stop at the VIP lounge, and I hang back as Dad speaks to the suit behind the counter.

I automatically wander toward the bar, but after what happened last night, I could probably stand to be sober for an entire year. I pour myself a glass of orange juice on the rocks instead, glancing through the lounge and vaguely wondering if I'll see anyone I know. But the Strip is like a city in and of itself, and the chances of running into someone you know are slim to none.

Except that I just did. That guy from the bar. Connor.

No clue why he got to me like that when we were outside the high roller room, but I'm still feeling slightly prickly about the whole thing. I look at my reflection in the gilded mirror above the bar, trying to see what Connor saw in me that made him look so…I don't even know. Disgusted? It's not like my boobs are popping out of my shirt or my ass hanging out of my skirt. My hair maybe looks a little wild but has a natural wave to it today. My makeup is light but fresh. I look *good*. Not like that angry pukey mess that Connor met last night.

There's no need to second guess myself. I push back a strand of hair behind my ear, summoning up all of my good energy as soon as I have the thought.

"Done," my dad suddenly says from next to me. "The tickets will be waiting for you at the box office tonight under your mother's name. One for your friend Elle, too."

I release an audible gasp. "Dad! Thank you! How did you do that?" Elle will probably scream and then die when I call to tell her the news. "What about you? Will you come with us, too?"

He chuckles but shakes his head. "Oh, no. I wouldn't dream of it."

I beam back at him, feeling absurdly and sublimely happy. "The casino really got us tickets? For free?"

He pats me gently on the back and glances at his watch. "Nothing's for free, Alex. I'll go work it off." His eyes rest on my face, a thoughtful expression on his, and a brief smile touches the corners of his mouth. "Would you like to come with me for a bit?"

"Really? Like your good luck charm?" I backtrack quickly, thinking about the type two high rollers. "I mean, I'll hang out in the background and watch, so I don't disturb you. Unless you want me to do more… like, um… what do you want me to do?"

Dad barks out a laugh. "Just come and sit with me. And don't tell your mother," he adds with a wink.

We go back to the high roller room, back to the guard and the heavy doors made of opaque glass. And when we step across the threshold, it feels like we cross into a different dimension. The room is bathed in soft lighting that gives the atmosphere a hazy, dreamy feel, the air cooler and lightly fragranced with something that reminds me of rain and springtime. The walls are made of the same opaque glass as the door, but they are layered with floor-to-ceiling metal partitions that gleam under the lights. The carpet feels as lush as a forest floor under the soles of my sneakers. We walk past a table that holds a towering arrangement of branches holding pink orchids.

I've eavesdropped on my parents enough to have heard all sorts of stories about the high limit room, the room where high rollers came to play. Someone losing the deed to a house in a single game of poker. Crazy stuff that I never imagined would really apply to my dad in any way shape or form.

But we're here now, and it's so surreal to see Dad step up to a baccarat table and the dealer smile at him like he's greeting an old friend.

"Welcome back, Mr. Lin." The dealer is an older man who looks Chinese. After the more formal greeting, they start to speak in Mandarin. I can understand bits and pieces when other people speak it and can insult people in Chinese, and that's about it. But when my dad rests his hand on my back, I sit up straight. I recognize a few words and hear my name in the mix. He introduces me to the dealer as his *baobèi*, a term for someone who's precious to you.

"It is a great honor to meet you, Ms. Lin. I have known your father for many years. A great man." The dealer bows to me, and I smile and bow back.

"I've known him for many years, too, and I agree. A great man."

Dad laughs a happy laugh and puts his arm around my shoulder. He gestures for me to sit, and I perch on one of the leather seats at the baccarat table. My eyes bug out as Dad hands something to the dealer and gets a huge pile of chips in return. This is my *dad*, who scrimps and saves all year long. Who started a college savings account for me when I was born so I wouldn't be slammed with student loans.

The other players at the table are all men, and before the game starts, my dad introduces me to everyone else. He knows all of them by name, which surprises me a little.

Dad nudges me as the game starts, the cards and chips moving quickly – from the dealer to the players and back again. I smile to watch my dad fist-bumping the other players whenever someone wins.

I've never seen him like this. I've never seen him smile so easily, never seen him cut loose like this and roar with laughter. When he's at home, he always seems to have a shadow of a frown on his face. But not here. That shadow is gone without a trace.

I look up at one point and see Connor standing across the room from us by the poker tables. His arms are crossed, and he's off to the side of the beautiful woman with the Texan drawl. And he's watching me. More like his eyes are lasered in on me. My glance skates over his chest, arms, and boldly down to his jeans before landing squarely on his face again. His answering look is unsmiling, so intense that I feel the color rise to my cheeks.

I turn away and let myself get swept back up in the excitement of the game, but I can sense that Connor's still watching me. Not in the same way as he was doing in the hallway, either. I don't think I just imagined the interest in his expression, but it's not the kind of interest I'm used to getting. Not lustful, not exactly. It's more like he's curious about me. Confused, even.

I try not to look back over at him. It's hard not to.

8

CONNOR

Maya is doing a hell of a lot better now, as if this afternoon was a rehearsal and tonight is her public performance. She's sitting at the high-limit poker tables, the only woman amidst all of the boys, and she emasculates them, hand after hand. I know I should probably be happy for her, be glad that she's doing well and in a better mood than yesterday. But instead I stand behind her with my arms crossed, feeling stiff and restless at the same time, and far from fucking happy.

Unlike *her*. Unlike Alex, who is on the other side of the room and in complete contrast to me.

My eyes keep drifting over to the baccarat table. It's a totally different scene over there, where the game is interrupted by frequent and raucous laughter. Even though Alex isn't gambling, it's like she's one of them, bumping shoulders with the guy next to her and cheering every time someone wins.

Alex's head turns a little, and her gaze catches mine before she looks away.

I should look away too, but I can't. When I'd first seen Alex outside the high stakes room, I thought it was my eyes playing fucking tricks on me. God knows I've been on edge ever since finding out Cruz was in town. And when I saw her, it was like a reminder of the ghosts from my past. Like some figment of my imagination that wanted to drill into my head the thought of what I'd done last night in helping her out of the club, in taking care of her and personally making sure she got to her hotel room

in making up for the past.

Alex looks a lot better today. Not just in comparison to the doped-up mess that she was last night, either. She's obviously at least twenty-one, to have been at the club and now in the high stakes room, but I again have the thought that she looks young. It has nothing to do with her body – she has a sensuality about her that speaks to the opposite. It's more of her energy and her vitality, the way she grins like a kid at the guy she's with. And that does makes me wonder how she's out here laughing away like nothing happened to her last night. I totally don't get that.

The guy. He's a lot older than her, definitely old enough to be her father. But he looks Chinese, or at least a good part-Chinese. And she doesn't. Her red hair, for one thing. But maybe? Her cheekbones are high and sharply defined like his. Her eyes…

Don't know why I'm even trying to figure it out. It doesn't matter. I'm just irritated at myself for being distracted. The player to the left of Maya is drunk and starting to get too chatty with her, and I need to keep an eye on him.

The couple times this afternoon I've had the chance to call Elle, she hasn't answered. The times she's tried to call me back, I haven't been able to answer. Worst fucking game of phone tag I've ever played. I already feel like my nerves are exposed, as if Cruz is going to walk around the corner at any moment with his cocky swagger and attitude of entitlement. I'm wound up tighter that I need to be, than I should be, given that I'm supposed to be providing security for a client right now.

I look over right as Alex claps her hands together.

"Good one, Dad!"

Dad. The guy with her *is* her father, which mostly surprises me because of how different they look. But there's a part of me that isn't surprised, that thinks it makes sense because of the way she is with him. She turns to him, her whole face aglow, and I feel something inside my chest tighten.

He nudges her with his elbow, and her expression grows serious before she points to a spot on the table. He's letting her place a bet for him.

I watch as her father pushes forward a stack of chips and as the dealer sweeps his hand over the felt. He passes cards out of the shoe to the players before flipping two over for himself, and I hear Alex give a happy squeal. She throws her arms around her father's neck, and he hugs her and rocks her back and forth a little.

This is right out of one of those fucking feel-good movies that Elle's tried to drag me to see in the theaters. Life isn't feel-good, not like that. And even as I'm seeing real people act out one of those moments in real time, I have a hard time believing it.

Out of anyone I know, Elle probably has one of the best relationships with her parents that I've ever seen. Her parents fed her, clothed her, and her father didn't beat the shit out of her like mine did, which in my book makes him father-of-the-fucking-year. But her parents were never outwardly affectionate, not like *this*. And as soon as she turned seventeen, they told her she had to support herself, like they'd been counting down the days until they could claim that they put in their time and were done. I know Elle goes back to see them for Christmas sometimes, but I also know she does it more out of the same sense of duty.

At the end of the next hand, Maya turns around to face me. It's the first time she's spoken to me since we got to the table.

"Watch my chips for me while I go to the ladies' room, won't you, darling?"

"Of course, sweetheart." I smile at her, eyeing the guy to the left of her as I take her spot.

He's definitely wasted. And an idiot for drinking so much with such high stakes on the table. He swings his head around to look at me, the stink of whiskey coating him, and I turn my head away in disgust.

"Hey. Your old lady sure knows how to play a mean game." He has a heavy accent, sounds like he's from Long Island or Brooklyn.

"She's not my wife," I mutter, staring at the glass in front of him.

"Sorry, sorry." He holds out his hands as though trying to appease me. "Girlfriend then." His voice gets lower, like he's trying to conspire with me on this one. "Or whatever that fine piece of ass is to you. I'm curious, always wondered about the lady players. Does she only put out on the nights she wins?"

My elbows are braced against the table, but I shift now so I'm full-on facing him. "I'm her security," I growl. "And I think you need to demonstrate some fucking respect to your fellow players. You know what I mean?"

I spout it off without thinking. I do *not* talk to anyone except for my clients when I'm on the job. I'm a fixture, part of the scenery, not part of the game. And I just broke the rules by engaging one of the actual players. For all I know, I threatened the CEO of some fortune five hundred company who'll demand my head as retribution for my mouth. Luckily, the guy backs down and shuts up, but I still feel like I'm sitting on a bed of nails.

I raise my eyes from Maya's towers of chips, my gaze drawn across the room for the hundredth time in the last hour. Alex and her dad are leaving the baccarat table, his hand on her back in a possessive gesture. Or maybe it's a fatherly one, but I wouldn't know.

And then she looks straight at me, her smile like a ray of fucking sunshine. My throat constricts, like she put me into a stranglehold.

I've been hanging onto Cruz more or less all day, and she can turn everything off just like that? It's obvious she remembers me. So how the fuck can she let go and smile at me, the guy who watched her vomit all over the place and lectured her about being stupid?

She's not playing by the rules, either.

Near the start of hour three, Maya turns around and looks at me through her lashes. "I think I'm getting hungry, darling. What about you?"

Drunk guy left a long time ago, but the person who took his place is annoying her even more because he's chatting her up in between hands. As far as I can tell, the guy is stone cold sober, and he's tried at least five different ways to find out the name of the casino where Maya's staying. He's dark-skinned, his voice smooth, and I estimate that he's older than Maya by about twenty years. The guy's Italian suit probably costs as much as my car.

Maya came up with this plan and a set of code phrases our very first year together. This one more or less means, "I've played enough. Now get me the fuck away from this asshole."

"Yeah, I'm starving," I say. "Let's go." I extend my hand, and she takes it while the guy in the suit stares at me thoughtfully. He can think whatever the hell he wants, that I'm her hired help or her plaything. The latter is the kind of the look Maya wants me to go for anyway, and I think it's exactly because of assholes like the guy in the suit.

"So. Would you like to join me for dinner then?" Maya says it quietly as she slides her hand through the crook of my arm. I stare down at her in surprise as we walk away from the table, and she lifts a shoulder in a delicate shrug. "What? That gorgeous body of yours does need occasional sustenance, doesn't it?"

We leave the room, and I start scanning the crowd as always. "Mrs. Coplin. You're not asking me out on a date, are you?"

"No. But I did well tonight, and I feel like celebrating." Her tone is heartfelt, and when I glance down at her again, she's looking back at me in earnest.

I hesitate, and she adds, "I don't want to eat alone, Connor. It's what I always do."

Maya always has her meals delivered to her suite, and dining with her in her room definitely falls under my no-socializing-with-clients clause. One of my hard-and-fast rules that I put in place for our mutual protection. But when we get to the elevator, I feel her sigh against me, and I reconsider. This is Maya, and if it's a simple dinner that she wants, I can do that.

"It would be my pleasure, Mrs. Coplin."

She squeezes my arm. "Oh good. And don't worry, darling. The late Mr. Coplin approves of you. He told me so."

I don't try to figure out if she's playing or serious with that one. My clients are all highly unusual, in one way or another, which is totally their prerogative. And I have no problem with the late Mr. Coplin approving of me as a casual dinner date, but no more than that.

We get back to her suite, and she waves for me to sit while she goes to the phone. I remain standing, not totally good about being in her room despite the fact that I should be – after two years of pick-ups and drop-offs, I should feel more at ease with it, not like my skin is crawling.

I feel even more out of place as she picks up the phone and asks the front desk to patch her through to a restaurant at a different casino. I recognize the name – one of those fancy steakhouses where the chefs cut your meat for you right at the table and act like they have college degrees in anatomy. If I remember correctly the price of the things on that menu, she could order me bread and water and I'll be happy.

She hangs up the phone and perches on the edge of the couch.

"If you're going to stand there and hover, the least you could do is pour me a glass of wine," she drawls.

I nod once and walk over to the bar where a bottle of Merlot is sitting next to two glasses. Two glasses.

Maya's rooms are always set up exactly to her liking because she demands that everything is arranged for her and only her. Always one pillow on her bed, one set of towels. One glass at the bar. There's only ever one glass set out at the bar, and while it's entirely possible that some casino staff member placed two there today by mistake, I somehow doubt that it's the case.

I stare at the second glass and realize that Maya planned this, that even before she did well at poker today, she planned on sharing this wine with someone. With me. I brace my palms against the counter of the bar for a second, breathing in once and out again. I'm tempted to walk out that door, but don't want to risk upsetting her. I can't do that to Maya.

I pour just one, leaving the other one untouched. Maya doesn't look surprised when I hand her the wine, and I relax a little. I'm being paranoid, unnecessarily suspicious of everything. It's because I've been waiting for Cruz to show up all day, but that doesn't mean I have to project my demons onto Maya.

"Thank you, kind sir." She makes a graceful gesture to the rest of the couch. "You don't have to stand over me, you know. Consider yourself off-duty. But paid for your time, of course," she adds quickly. She kicks off her shoes and curls her feet under her.

I'm not paid hourly like that, but I know what she means. Maya just ordered me a hundred-dollar cut of steak, and I feel strangely uncomfortable about it. Clients have paid for far more expensive dinners for me before, and I've had no qualms.

"Tonight's on the house, Maya."

It's a gesture on my part, but I realize how big of a gesture it is as soon as the words are out of my mouth. I don't mess around with money. Work is work.

I'm totally not myself tonight, and I don't like it. It's because of Cruz, because my goddamn phone has gone off on me at least four times in the last hour. It's also because of Alex. I keep hearing the sound of her laugh, and it makes no fucking sense why I'm even thinking about her.

Maya's eyes are wide, like she's seeing me for the first time. "Connor Vincent. I've known you for two whole years, and that is the first time you've ever called me by my first name."

I frown. Had I? Shit. I'm off my work game if I did that, and it irritates me to no end. I open my mouth to apologize, but she sits up straight and interrupts me before I can.

"Don't fret over it. It's fine. I actually prefer it. The Mrs. Coplin title comes with the widow label and everything that goes along with it."

She says it matter-of-factly and with maybe a tinge of bitterness, and I think about the wine glasses. The one set of towels. The hem of her dress rides up her thigh a little, and she adjusts it in a gesture that's demure for her. She catches me looking at her and smiles at me almost sadly, and it hits me that I'm seeing the real Maya beneath the act, the real deal, right now. Out on the floor, she's a tigress, but really she's just a woman trying to escape a lot of hurt. Like all of us.

I finally sit down next to her. "You don't need to accept those labels. You're smart, resourceful, young, and gorgeous, and while being a widow might technically be true, that doesn't define you." I mean every word.

Her face registers surprise, the expression in her eyes clearing, softening. She leans forward. "And what defines you, Connor? I'm curious."

I freeze. It was a mistake for me to come here. I don't let people get close to me like that.

The bell to the suite rings right then. Thank God. I get up and walk swiftly to the door to answer it and find out that Maya didn't only order us steaks – she ordered the service too. The awkward moment between us is over, and we both move to the dining table to spend the next forty minutes or so being entertained by one of the chefs from the steakhouse. The vulnerable Maya is gone, her mask solidly back in place.

I don't acknowledge her question about what defines me.

I don't know the answer.

I get behind the wheel of my car, glaring at my own reflection in the rear-view mirror. Today can go and fuck itself.

I can blame Elle for not answering the phone the times I've tried to call. Maya for taking me off guard tonight by trying to get through my defenses. Cruz for deciding to come to *my* city. But Elle has her own life, Maya's lonely, and I'm just one of the two million people that live in this city. Cruz and all of the other people who pass through here have as much a claim on it as I do.

I try Elle again as I'm starting up the engine.

"Hey," she barks. "Finally."

I'm not in the mood for Elle's usual crap, but oddly enough, the tightness in my shoulders relaxes as soon as I hear her sharp voice.

"I just got off work. You at the bar?"

"Nope, *I* get to see Alysa's Empyre tonight," she announces proudly. "VIP seating, baby."

Alysa's Empyre. Some indie rock band that Elle likes. She dragged me out to see them with her a couple of winters back before they got all big and went commercial. I like their music all right, but that's not what gets my attention.

"Who's the VIP?"

She hesitates before saying, "Me. Obviously." Her tone is guarded, and I know, I *know* she's going with Alex.

Doesn't matter. If Elle's going to a concert, that's two hours more, minimum, that I'll have to wait to talk to her. I feel a heaviness settle through me and swallow my pride. "Do you have a second to talk? This Cruz shit is making me crazy, Elle."

"Hey." Her voice softens. "I know it's gotta be killing you, having to think about everything all over again." She stops, and the silence spreads out into seconds, maybe minutes. I close my eyes and hang onto it until she speaks. "I'm so sorry. Look, I'll come over to your place right after the concert and we'll figure out what to do. But I'm just on my way out right now to meet my friend. She has the tickets, and oh hell, Connor. I feel so selfish for doing this to you, but I really want to go to this show."

"It's fine," I grit out. "Come over after the concert."

"Promise. And Connor?" she adds. "I'm glad you're finally letting me help you out. No offense, but you were acting like an ungrateful twat before."

She ends the call, and I stare out of the windshield, the edginess creeping along my nerves until my skin pricks.

Ever since I made the decision to take control of my life, it's been important to me that I've kept it. Kept control of situations at work. In everything. Right now, I need to get control of this situation, to put this Cruz thing to rest.

All I need is ten minutes of Elle's time, max. Alysa's Empyre is playing at The House of Blues. I can be there in less time than that.

9

Alex

Elle seriously needs to chill. My hand that's applying lip gloss jerks as my phone goes off again, and I roll my eyes. Ever since I called Elle up and told her we had VIP seating for the show, she's been freaking out. I know that Alysa Trane is her idol, but still. I don't know if I can deal with her all night if she doesn't calm the hell down.

I ignore the latest call and dab on a little more lip gloss. Elle can wait. It'll be good for her.

"How do I look?" Mom's voice sounds from the bathroom door of my suite.

Mom is wearing a gold shimmery top that looks utterly fab with her hair, black leather pants, and three-inch black heels. Her hair is up in a soft-looking classic French braid.

"Wow," I say with genuine admiration. "You look hot, Mom. Twenty-something boys, beware."

She laughs, the sound producing a happy echo in my bathroom. "Oh dear. I'm not one of those so-called cougars, am I?"

"Definitely not! Not unless you're going out and prowling the clubs for boys when Dad's busy. And if you are, I don't want to know about it."

"Who's prowling the clubs? Is this you, Grace?" Dad suddenly appears in the doorway. I didn't hear him come in, and from the sound of Mom's gasp, she's as surprised as I am.

"James," she scolds. "Are you eavesdropping on us girls?" Her voice has a slightly sharp edge to it when she adds, "Better me prowling for boys than Alexis."

I almost choke. "Um, yeah. You don't have to worry about me doing that."

"Good," Dad says, but he's facing my Mom with a closed expression, not even a trace of a smile left on his face. "I was only joking, Grace."

"And I wasn't?" Mom's brow draws together in a frown, and she comes to the mirror to stand by me like she needs an ally.

Never a good idea to take sides in parental squabbles, no matter how minor. I press my lips together to keep from saying anything, though my gut instinct is to side with Dad on this one. You know, since he's the one treating us to this night out in the first place. But I do my best to ignore it. They're always trying to get little jabs in at each other. They've always been like this.

Actually, that's not totally true. They used to be a lot worse. Their marriage was way more full of ups and downs when I was younger, and I remember the panic and devastation I felt when they almost got divorced. I was eleven, and Dad moved out into an apartment for about a month while Mom wandered around the house like a zombie and left me to fend for myself for most meals and to make sure I got to school every day (I didn't always). They eventually worked it out – somehow – and Dad moved back in.

Things got a little better when we started coming out to Vegas every summer, but they still get into little spats like this all of the time. I'm pretty convinced by how they act with each other that they can't ever totally escape the past. I don't think anyone can.

I hear Dad's retreat and the sound of Mom's shoes clicking on the marble floor as she steps away, and I know she's examining me. I brace myself for the commentary. I'm wearing a simple black off-the shoulder t-shirt that I like because it makes the red of my hair pop and a skirt that's probably too short.

"Would you like me to fix your hair before we go? It will take just a minute," she says.

Oh, *that*. My hair is swept up in an updo that I did myself. It probably won't last the night. "Sure. Thanks."

I sit down on the little stool in front of the mirror, and she stands behind me and goes to work. Her fingers are like magic, and I close my eyes as they weave through my hair.

Against my better judgment, I say, "You could have been a little nicer to Dad a second ago. He was just trying to have fun."

Her fingers stop moving for a second, but I don't wish I could retract the words. Even though I usually try not to take sides, I mean what I say. It might be the memory of having so much fun with Dad this afternoon and wishful thinking that she and my dad could be like that too. While they sometimes show outward affection to each other, I can't remember the last time I saw them laugh together.

Her hands start flying through my hair again, gently pulling on this piece, tucking in that piece.

"I looked up some of Alysa's Empyre's songs this afternoon when you were out…" She pauses as if giving me the chance to tell her where I was, but I don't. "I love the voice of the lead singer. She has so much emotion, and I adore the lyrics."

My shoulders relax, and I don't realize how tense I just was until they do. Her statement is a little funny to me because a lot of Alysa Trane's lyrics are pretty explicit. But I also recognize that Mom going out of her way to listen to the band ahead of time is her way of trying to connect with me.

"Yeah, she does," I say. I reach up and back over my shoulder to her, and she squeezes my hand after pinning one last strand into place.

"All done."

Mom had swept back most of my hair into a deliberately messy but secure updo with a few stray tendrils touching my cheek. I look transformed, not like my usual self. Older, more sophisticated. Pretty damned hot, if I do say so myself.

"Thanks, Mom." I stand and give her a hug as my phone goes off again from the counter. I peek over at it this time and smirk.

"Elle's downstairs. We should get going."

She hugs me back, but then leans away from me. Her eyes are misty, and I stare back at her in surprise.

"Alexis, you know that the way your father and I bicker all of the time, it's normal. That's just how some couples communicate. We really do love each other."

She's still dwelling on my comment, and I feel a little bit bad that I made her go on the defensive like that. I suppose I know that they do love each other, and I guess the bickering might be normal for some people. But I don't care about what other couples do. All I know is that neither of my parents communicate with *me* that way.

I also know that when it comes to me and whoever I wind up with someday – in the far, far, indiscernible future – it won't be that way with us.

We're just in the limo, but Elle is so hyped up that she might as well sign up to be the opening act. She takes a seat across from me and my mom, dressed up by her standards in a long tattered black skirt, prized Alysa's Empyre tank top, combat boots, and an armful of random black bracelets.

"Dude. I love you. I want one of these cars someday, like for general use." She beams at me then turns to my mom. "I mean, I love all of you. Alex, could I come up and visit you in your digs soon and personally tacklehug your dad?"

I laugh and shake my head. "Right, because that would not make him feel uncomfortable at all."

"Grace, I can't tell you how utterly gorgeous you look tonight. Especially in that top." Elle nods, her spiky hair bobbing up and down. "Oh my God, but I don't mean that in a creepy stalker way like I'm staring at your boobs or anything. This is going to be one epic night, you know? Did you know that Alysa Trane is my ultimate inspiration? Her voice is so smooth but also totally edgy, which is what I would love to pull off with my own voice. Oh! Not that I can even compare…"

I grin at her ramblings. Elle is very funny to listen to when she's excited. Or I wonder if Elle's nerves are going haywire because my mom is here with us, though Mom is being a good sport, nodding and smiling gently at her. She confided in me once that she thought Elle was "spunky."

"Yes, Alexis has told me that you are quite the singer yourself," she says. "How often do you perform?"

Mom sits forward, her hands clasped around her knee, and I see a brightness in her expression. I wonder if she'll bring up the little-known fact that she used to sing in clubs.

Elle shrugs, shooting me a quick, narrow-eyed look that screams, *oh no, you didn't.* "Not much these days. It's hard to fit it in with a job and now I'm doing an internship and taking classes at UNLV."

"I'm glad you're going to the university, but don't give up on what you love," Mom says, her tone firmer, and I immediately recognize her "mothering" voice. While she rarely uses it with me anymore, she sometimes still drags it out for my friends. Not mortifying at all. "You have a gift, and it's for a reason."

"Yeah? You think so? I guess so." Elle shrugs one shoulder again, but I can tell that she's eating up the encouragement. Elle hardly talks about her family, just that she grew up in Albuquerque and that she goes home every Christmas. But that's it. I get the distinct impression that her parents aren't super supportive of her musical talents.

"Yeah, Elle," I chime in helpfully. "You never know who's going to be in the crowd watching. Some big music producer could stop by when you're doing your thing."

Elle coughs a laugh. "Right. On the nights they used to let me sing at the QE2, I knew exactly who was in the crowd. The staff and a couple of local alcos who had nowhere else to go."

"You never know," Mom repeats. She tugs on a strand of her hair as she looks out the window at the Strip, and I wonder what happened to make her give up singing.

The limo comes to a stop in front of the casino, and Elle makes a noise that sounds like a mouse getting caught in a trap. The driver opens the door for us a few seconds later, all smiles as we pile out of the car and onto the sidewalk. Alysa's Empyre fans are swarming all around us, and an excited current charges through me.

"Compliments of the hotel, Mrs. Lin. Enjoy the show."

I look over at the driver, and he's handing a laminated card on a lanyard to my mom.

"What's that?" I peek over her shoulder as she takes it. "No freaking way! An all-access pass?"

Elle emits another high-pitched shriek before clapping a hand over her mouth. She looks around like she's afraid of making a scene, which is funny, because she's so obviously freaking out.

"Here. I guess you get to rub shoulders with rock stars tonight," Mom says, handing it to Elle with a twinkle in her eye.

"Oh," she gasps. "I couldn't. No, you or Alex should take it."

"No," Mom and I say simultaneously. I grin at Elle. "Alysa Trane is your idol. You should go and see if you can meet her in person."

"I *love* you guys." Elle waves her hands in front of her like a set of hummingbird wings. "I swear, I'm not crying."

"We love you, too." I poke her in the ribs, and she loops the pass around her neck and sniffs. She'll be in crazy company when she goes backstage, though I'm sure she'll love it. Originally being from Vegas means that every sort of fan comes out of the woodwork whenever the band plays here.

We walk into the casino linked arm in arm. The buzz of energy filling the entryway is almost palpable as we join the hordes of Alysa's Empyre fans racing through the front door. Some of them are wearing fan gear like Elle. Others made themselves into lookalikes of the lead singer Alysa Trane, with bleach-blonde pixie haircuts and black knee-high platform boots. We make a wide circle around the perimeter of the gaming area to get to the venue, Elle making commentary on all of the Alysa clones along the way. But I notice she keeps glancing at her phone. Don't know if she's expecting a call or if someone's texting her, but if she is getting texts, she's not actually taking the time to read them.

I duck my head down to her level and whisper, "Dude, everything okay?"

"Yeah." She wets her lips like she suddenly realized they were dry, even though they aren't. "Some minor cousin drama. Sorry."

No clue why she's apologizing. And I still have no memory of this cousin she supposedly introduced to me at the club.

"Oh." I keep my voice low so Mom won't hear. "The same cousin I met last night? Is it bad of me that I don't remember this person?"

Elle's eyes widen. "How much of last night did you forget?"

I frown down at her. "Not everything. And shush," I whisper, although Mom doesn't look like she's eavesdropping. The background noise of the casino is loud, the noise from the people flocking to the entrance of the venue even louder. "Why? Did I do something totally stupid to embarrass myself in front of her?"

I don't dare say the rest of what's running through my head. That nothing could possibly be worse than getting roofied.

She coughs, but it sounds more like she's trying not to laugh. "No, no worries..." But then she trails off, her expression flooding with worry. "Holy shit. Look at the line. It's longer than the one for Thunder from Down Under on cougar night."

I snap my head up and follow her line of sight. "Whatever," I laugh, hoping Mom didn't hear that last part and think I told Elle about the cougar joke. "The line's not that bad."

Unlike her, I'm not surprised to see the massive crowd waiting to get into the House of Blues. It snakes around the rows of velvet ropes that lead to security before stringing out almost as far as the sign pointing to the buffet. Full of hardcore fans like me and Elle.

"We don't have to wait in that line," Mom says from the other side of me. "We get to go over to *that* one." She points with her pinky finger to a cordoned-off area that only has two people standing in it. VIPs only.

We don't have much of a wait at the box office, and Elle and I hang back as Mom gets our tickets. After giving the person behind the counter her name and showing her ID, she turns to us and hands me the envelope.

"Four tickets?" I look up from the envelope and at Mom in confusion. Dad could have come with us after all. If he'd wanted to.

"Oh, the man said there are two tables reserved for us. Two chairs per table," she explains. "Right on the end of the balcony. Your father got us some of the best seats in the house."

Elle's expression brightens, but then her eyes narrow as she focuses on something through the crowd. Her face darkens like a storm cloud. "Shit," she mumbles. "My cousin."

I crane my head around to see who she's looking at, and Elle steps away from us and waves her tiny hand in the air.

"Connor!"

I feel like I'm encased in cement as my brain wrestles with that name. Connor? The same *Connor* is Elle's cousin? The guy who was staring at me in the high roller room. Oh, man. I must have missed the introduction last night somewhere between all of the laced drinks and vomit.

"Hey. Glad I found you in this mess…"

The sound of that resonant voice sends a warm shiver through me, and I slowly turn to look at the man with dark hair and intensely blue eyes. This is becoming ridiculous, the numbers of times that we keep running into each other. But this time, he doesn't even look at me before he takes Elle's arm and walks away with her in tow, completely oblivious to the fact that she's with other people.

"I'll be right back, Mom," I say quickly. "I need to make sure Elle gets her ticket."

She nods in understanding, and I give chase. I weave my way through the poker machines, scanning the crowd. Crap. I can't see them anywhere. Connor had been moving so fast in his hurry to get away, or to get Elle away. Seriously, who does that? But it's a good thing he dwarfs Elle by about a foot because I finally spot his head of tousled hair over the crowd. I duck through a row of slot machines to intercept them, almost bumping into a middle-aged woman who's getting up from the machine on the end.

"Sorry!" I toss over my shoulder, and I keep running.

Elle looks like she's digging in her heels to slow Connor down. It doesn't look like it's doing her much good.

"Elle! Your ticket!"

She whips her head around and sees me. A determined look settles on her face as she shoves Connor in the side, and he lets go of her as she wrestles herself the rest of the way free. She stumbles forward, gratitude in her expression, and I stand like a statue as she throws herself at me.

And Connor… He stops and turns at the sound of my voice, his gaze connecting with mine. Recognition flashes in those electric blue eyes as they linger on my face, and I feel a warmth slowly radiate out from my core to the surface of my skin. I might be imagining it, but for some reason, he doesn't look as surprised to see me as I am to see him.

"Oh, thank God," Elle says. She snatches her ticket out of my hand and steps back, clutching it to her breast with all of the appropriate drama. "Okay, so yeah. You go ahead without me, and I'll catch up with you and your mom inside." She rolls her eyes back at where Connor's standing and mutters, "The cousin drama I mentioned."

The source of drama is still staring at me, like he did earlier today. My God, those eyes of his. The rest of him is standing stiffly, shoulders rigid and arms tense, but there's something almost fluid about his eyes. Like they're shifting through a whole mess of emotions and unable to settle on one.

What the heck are you doing, staring at the guy? Elle has her ticket. Walk away.

"Everything all right, Alexis? Elle?" My mom appears at my side. She doesn't disguise her pointed look at Connor, and I half-cringe and half-laugh inwardly as I realize that Mama Bear mode has gone into effect.

"Everything's cool," Elle says quickly. "This is my cousin. We were trying to connect all day, and I guess he remembered I'd be at the concert." She gives him the stink eye before continuing with introductions. "Grace, this is Connor. Connor, you obviously remember my friend Alex, and this is her mother."

"Lovely to meet you, Connor." Mom approaches him with an outstretched hand, all grace like her name. He finally turns that scorching gaze away from me.

"Same here, ma'am. Sorry to pull Elle away, but I needed a minute to catch up with her." He steps forward and takes my mother's hand, a smile and dimples appearing out of nowhere. Actual dimples. Calling my mom "ma'am." What is this guy's deal? He's like a real-life Jekyll and Hyde, only a lot more…hot. He's minus the jacket now, and my gaze takes in how good his body looks in that t-shirt and those jeans. My own body responds with a flush that I'm sure makes its way into my cheeks.

Mom continues to stand there, her hand clasped in his like he's already won her over. "We do happen to have another ticket for the show and a table where you and Elle are welcome to catch up. Would you like to join us?"

Wait. What? She did not just invite Connor to come with us to the concert, did she? This was supposed to be a night for my mom, for Elle, a time for us all to bond.

He'll probably say no.

But…I kind of wish he'd say yes.

His eyes flick over to me before he answers, and he gives me that cocky-as-hell half-smile again before addressing my mom.

"I'd like that. Thank you."

10

CONNOR

Elle's behaving like a half-brained fangirl, complete with annoyingly high-pitched squeals. It's a far cry from her usual badassery, and I'm irritated. Not only with her, but also with myself for turning up the charm with Alex's mother and getting myself invited to a concert with thousands of people. I did it without really thinking, mostly because I needed to talk to Elle.

But maybe it had a little bit to do with Alex.

She looks really good tonight. Sexy in that shirt and with her hair all done up like that. She brushes back a stray strand as we walk through the doors, and I catch myself staring at the long line of her neck. I tell myself that it doesn't mean anything that I'm noticing. I'm used to noticing people.

I bring up the rear as some burly dude dressed like a secret service agent escorts us into the elevator. I stand next to him while the ladies stay on one side, following them as the doors open and they parade out into the balcony.

There are two circular tables adjacent to one another that say "Reserved" on them, and Alex pauses to drop her bag on one of the chairs. She glances up and sees me looking at her, and her eyes roll before she turns away. I smile in spite of myself. Looks like I'm not the only one not thrilled about me being here.

The balcony area is side-stage and exclusive, and it takes me all of two seconds to sweep through it. I'm relieved at least that it's so secluded. The two tables they scored are the closest ones to the stage and arguably some of the best seats in the entire joint. Alex and her mother stand at the railing and look down at the crowd, and Elle starts to follow. But I'm not here to socialize, and I need to talk to her before she gets swept even further into the whole concert deal.

I look around, and everyone's excited to be here but me. It's like I'm the only sober person in a crowd full of drunks, only they're all drunk on good vibes and I got left holding onto all of the crap. What the hell had I been thinking, that this would actually be a good idea?

Before she can get away, I catch Elle's hand and pull her back to one of the tables. My nerves feel raw, edges exposed and ready to fire off at any moment.

Her eyes narrow for a second, but she sinks into a chair, and I take the one opposite her.

"So. Cruz."

"Yes…"

Elle trails off and bites her lip, and I wait and wonder. Wonder what she saw when she looked at him for the first time in so long. The three of us grew up together, and Elle was just thirteen when Cruz started making all sorts of bad choices. I used to think that if I hadn't met Laura when I did, I might have been in danger of going down a similar path. That in that way, she saved me…

…*even though I couldn't save her.*

I close my eyes for a second.

Elle clears her throat, and I bring myself back to the present and concentrate on her voice. "He came by this morning. We went out to brunch."

"And I wasn't invited? My feelings are hurt." Maybe I should be surprised at the fact that she's already buddies with Cruz, but I'm not. "So don't tell me you just sat across from each other and had brunch. He wanted to meet with you to find out about me, right? The same way we're doing this right now." I gesture between us. "So what did you tell him?"

"Hey," she says sharply. "He also wanted to see how *I* was doing. Did you ever think of that as a possibility?"

Pain floods her expression, but she quickly tucks it away where I can't see it anymore. Elle was friends with Cruz, too. She was maybe even closer to him than she was to me when we were growing up. Out of the two of us, he was always the more outgoing one. But she saw less and less of him as he became more involved with the people that he eventually embraced as family. I know it hurt Elle when he changed.

"Yeah. Sorry, Elle. I'm a dick."

"I know that." She gives me a half-smile but it vanishes. "He wasn't like he was when we were back there," she says in earnest. "He's been going to rehab, and he's not using anymore."

I raise my eyebrows. "And what, I'm suddenly part of his twelve-step program?"

Elle reaches over like she's going to touch my hand but thinks better of it at the last second. "Maybe. Would that be so bad?"

I don't bother responding to that. "So he's clean. Or so he says. What about the street gang? The protection rackets? Is he done with all that too?"

She chews on her thumbnail instead of answering, which is enough of an answer for me.

"Yeah, that's what I thought," I say. "Elle, you can't possibly believe that he came here to make amends with me."

She sits up straighter, stops fidgeting. "Actually, that's exactly why I think he wants to meet with you. That's what he told me, and why wouldn't I believe it?" she demands, defensiveness creeping into her tone. "Just because you think he's a certain way? You can't always stick people into these discrete little categories all of the time, Connor. People are complex, and they're interesting. And they change."

That again. That unwavering faith in people that Elle has. I disagree with her, and now I'm annoyed that she feels the need to lecture me.

"Listen," she says. "He's different, I'm telling you. He kept asking me if you were happy, what you were doing these days, if you settled down and got married." She smirks at this, like it's outside of the realm of possible things. I ignore the jab.

"And you told him what?"

"Nothing. Only that you're doing well." She leans forward, her eyes pleading. "I really think you should meet with him. He's going to stay for a while —"

"Exactly how long is a while?" I interrupt. This city has no room for the type of scum Cruz used to run with. Unless he's running from them.

It feels like every muscle in my body tenses as a scream erupts from the crowd below. The band is coming out now, and my first impulse is to get up and leave. Leave Elle along with her naïve optimism and her rich VIP friend.

As if she heard my thoughts, Alex dashes over to the table.

"Hey! You can't sit here all night," she says to Elle. "They're coming out, right now!"

"What? Omigod! No opening band?" Elle scoots out of her chair and rushes over to the railing.

Alex stays standing by the table, grinning after her. I catch the faint scent of her perfume, sweet and vibrant but with an edge. It suits her. Pretty and fresh but also with an attitude.

I watch from my seat as she rummages in her bag and pulls out a bottle of ibuprofen. She pops the top before she notices me watching.

"Headache?" I ask.

Her gaze zeroes in on mine, holds it steady and sure. It surprises me a little. I bet she doesn't take shit from people too often. If at all.

"My mother has one. But thank you for your concern." Her tone isn't snarky, though it could have been.

I glance over at her mother, who's standing with Elle at the railing and smiling gently at something she's saying, despite the headache. There's a resemblance to Maya there, but it's slight. Blonde hair, though Grace's is more of a strawberry blonde. Same air of refinement, which is maybe accentuated by a faint British accent. But even though Maya showed me some of her vulnerable side today, she's always all show and glitter when she's out in public. Alex's mom seems more real.

Alex taps two pills out into her palm and goes on. "She gets them a lot. I always make sure I have stuff for her just in case."

No idea why she's chatting me up, telling me personal things like this, but maybe she's being nice to me because I'm Elle's cousin. Her fingers close around the pills, and her eyes settle on my face, an openness in her expression that I'm not used to. For some reason, I feel obligated to say something back.

"I'm sorry to hear she's not feeling well. Will she be okay?"

"Sure. This stuff is pretty potent."

She smiles at me, and it's not the same sunny smile that she gave me when she was walking out of the high roller room. That one had been incidental, because she'd been having fun with her father and I happened to be in the path of that happiness. This one is for me.

That smile of hers stirs up something in me, and I'm not totally sure what it is. I glance over at her mother, whose arm is resting around Elle's shoulders as they look down at the stage. Elle's twirling the cord of a concert pass around her fingers. I saw it before in the elevator and when I was talking to her – an all-access pass – and notice that she's the only one out of the three that has one.

They gave Elle the only all-access pass?

Alex is looking past me now, her hand waving in the air as she tries to get the attention of a server who's taking drink orders in the middle of the balcony, but the server doesn't see her and starts to head in the other direction.

I stand up. "Water?"

She stares at me. "What?"

"Your mother. Would she like some water to take those?"

"Yeah, that would be great." She nods. "Thanks."

"You want anything?" I shoot over my shoulder as I start toward the server. I remember the drink I spilled on her at QE2 last night and add, "A Manhattan?"

I don't normally go out of my way for people that I don't know, but as I go get water from the server, it somehow feels right this time."No thanks," she says. "I don't think I'll be able to stomach one of those for a while. And I don't let guys buy me drinks anymore. I don't want to be *stupid*."

Ha. She's got me there.

I watch Elle from across the table as she belts out the lyrics to every song in the set. And she's doing it in a voice that should be heard by more than just me. Elle's got real talent, and I hope she realizes it, hope she knows that she should be out there singing to everyone, not only the employees at that dive of a bar where she works. She deserves more than that.

The guilt punches through my brief reflective moment. I feel bad that I haven't asked her how all of that's going lately. I know she has all of her friends and the people she works with, but we grew up together, and I'm her family. I frown, thinking about the fact that I haven't been very close to her lately. Busy lives or not, no wonder she glommed onto Cruz right away.

Call it reflection, call it resolve or realization, but it's in this moment that I decide. I'll meet Cruz. If he's here for a few days (assuming that's what Elle means by "a while"), he'll either pester her about me until she gives in and tells him everything she knows. Or she'll start to resent me for pushing him off, if she doesn't already. The bottom line is I have to figure out exactly what I'm going to say and do when I see him. Killing him is out of the question, though it almost makes me crack a smile to think about it.

Yeah, I'll listen to what he has to say. But that's it. I'll give him my time, which is a hell of a lot more than he deserves, but I'll do it for Elle.

I don't know why I come up with this decision right now, but maybe it's because I'm feeling chill for the first time in what feels like weeks. It could also have something to do with the fact that I'm having a beer, listening to decent music, and surrounded by people with positive energy.

Alex is part of that. She's sitting across from her mom and on her second Jack and Coke. She's not singing, but she has that glow again like when she was with her father in the high roller room earlier today. I'm watching the show, which is a pretty epic production with lasers, lights, and graphics. But I'm still aware of Alex.

I freeze with my hand on my beer as she leans over to our table. Her lips part, and I stare at them.

"Let's dance, Elle. Mom."

She grabs both of their hands, and the three of them laugh and move away from the tables. With them standing off to the side of the railing, I can still watch the show, but my eyes drift over to them more often than not. Alex dances like Elle sings, like it comes naturally to her and with emotion. Like the music is washing through her and making her move.

Elle shimmies over and grabs my hand. "C'mon, Connor. Dance with us!"

I stay seated. "Fuck no, crazy girl."

"Don't be such a bore. Come dance!"

The song is deep and slow, heavy on the bass and full of Alysa Trane's low, sultry voice. I watch as Alex's hips sway in the same sexy rhythm, feel my heart rate speed up. I stand without thinking, and Elle grins like a wicked witch before leading me over to the railing.

Alex watches my approach, and I catch a flicker of surprise cross her face, but it disappears as she turns to Elle. The two of them get kind of touchy feely as they dance together, and I'm torn between thinking that it's hot and mentally kicking myself because Elle's my cousin, for fuck's sake.

The band starts playing a faster song, and I hold out my hand to Alex's mom. She smiles and takes it, and I dance with her, switching off my dark thoughts associated with Cruz and Laura. The hatred. The guilt. Try to let it all go for now.

Elle catches my eye and smiles as I spin Grace around. I know this was her intention all along, to get me to chill the fuck out, and I roll my eyes at her. But I have to admit that it's all good right now. Maybe even better than when I go out, because I'm just having fun, for once not planning my next move.

The first song transitions to another fast one, and I keep dancing with Grace. She seems a little breathless by the end and excuses herself to go to the ladies' room.

"Thank you for the dance, Connor," she says, fanning a hand in front of her face. "I haven't danced like that in a long time."

I'm holding her other hand, and I give her a semi-formal bow. "The pleasure was all mine."

She takes her hand back and pats me on the arm before retrieving her purse from the table, and I'm left alone with Alex and Elle. The next song is a lot slower, and I freeze as Alex walks right up to me.

"Hey," she says. "Thanks for dancing with my mom. She looked like she was having a lot of fun."

She's standing close enough to me that I can smell her perfume. Close enough that if I took a half-step forward, we'd be touching.

"You're welcome," I say lightly. "But you don't need to thank me for that." Elle is standing by the railing singing again, and I raise an eyebrow at Alex. "Want to dance?"

She hesitates, and I almost say never mind, but then she shrugs.

"Sure."

She takes that half-step toward me, and my senses fill with her as she slides her hands up to my shoulders, as we move together like we've done this before. And maybe it's easy because this is just what I do when I go out and this is what she does when she goes out. But I think it's also because it's her. One of her long legs brushes against mine, and I stare down at her face. My skin heats up because of her nearness, her touch, and I lose track of anything else when I bring my hands to rest on her hips. She smells so fucking good. Her lips are slightly parted, and she looks so sexy that I wonder if she tastes just as good.

I lean down, and she freezes, her grip tightening on my shoulders. I pause with my lips just inches from hers, the anticipation hanging heavily between us. Her breath becomes mine as I descend, her eyes closing as my want turns into full-blown need.

But then Elle shrieks from right next to us, contributing to the high-pitched screams from the crowd as the laser show goes into overtime. Alex's eyes fly open as the moment between us is torn away, and she runs her hands from my shoulders down my chest but draws back, her cheeks flushed. She gives me a smile, and there's a little feistiness to it and a shine in her eyes to match. And Elle – fuck, I'd about forgotten she was even here – is gawking at us like her eyeballs are going to fall out of her head.

"Connor." She shakes her head at me. "Whatever you're thinking about doing, you need to keep it in your pants, okay? This is my *friend*."

Alex laughs, the tension of the moment dissolving. "It's not a big deal. We were just dancing."

She seems like she's being careful not to look at me as I say it, and she turns and links arms with Elle as the next song starts. Yeah, not a big deal except that my body's jacked up now because it still wants that kiss. I go back to the table, take a swig of my overpriced beer, and watch them dance from a distance.

I don't normally pay attention to women unless I'm trying to figure out if they're worth getting into bed. When I look at Alex, it's a little like that, not gonna lie. But it's not only that – I'm trying to figure her out.

Not that this makes any sense either. I don't usually sit and try to figure out people, not like this. I keep telling myself it's because I'm sort of hanging out with people in a totally casual setting for once. That the part of my brain that's so used to assessing people is working overtime.

Grace comes back from the restroom, and instead of sitting where she was, she takes the seat across from me. I feel a momentary jolt of panic when I realize that I'll have to make small talk, but then it hits me. She's a VIP, which means that technically she's a prospective client. I'm used to making small talk with people like her. I *should* make light conversation with her – it's as easy as flipping a switch with me, and I go into business-mode.

I might be thinking of Grace as a prospective client, but there's an astuteness in the way she's looking at me right now. Like she's also sizing me up but in a different way.

"Enjoying the band, Connor?"

"Yes, ma'am. They're a good band. Thanks again for the ticket." I pause before adding, "Are you feeling better?"

My question throws her off, and I see it like a small break in her poise before it settles back over her again. "Oh. Alexis told you I wasn't feeling well?"

I realize my mistake, that Alex might have not wanted me to tell her mother. A small pit forms in my gut at that realization. I'm not entirely comfortable with that, at being taken into confidence.

"I think she was just worried about you," I say truthfully. Grace nods, glancing off to the side at her daughter while I tell myself to keep my damned mouth shut.

"I'm fine," she finally says. "Swam a little too hard this morning. We take full advantage of the lap pool during the summer."

I nod understandingly. "Don't blame you. I spent a lot of my summers in the water."

"Oh, did you used to lifeguard?" Her eyes graze over me as if trying to see if I fit the type. "I think Alexis always wanted to do that for a summer job, but we always came out here in the summers, so she never could."

"No, ma'am. Navy SEAL."

Green eyes settle on me with definite interest.

I hear Alex's laugh from my left as she and Elle drop back into their chairs at the other table, and it hits me. I know what that look is now. It's not one I've been on the receiving end of since I lived back in Albuquerque. Laura's mom used to look at me the same way, like she was going through a running checklist to see if I was boyfriend material for her daughter.

Hell no. That's the last thing I want.

"Is that still something you do?"

"Not anymore." I give her a crooked smile. "I moved on."

She leans forward, as if ready to trade secrets. "And what do you do now?"

Walk away from this one, Connor. Write it off.

I shrug. "I provide personal security for high rollers."

"Oh!" She looks surprised, and there's a change in her demeanor, like she's interested for other reasons. "How did you get into that line of work?"

I guess it's a normal thing to ask. Purely conversational. What do you do? How did you start out? Only I've never had anyone ask me before. The vast majority of my current clients have been referrals, Maya being the exception to that. If she were here, I know exactly how she'd answer that question.

"It was all luck."

Grace is silent for a moment as she considers this. She's probably waiting for me to elaborate. I don't.

"Well," she finally says. "Considering the city you're in, I suppose that's appropriate. It's a good thing to have luck on your side."

11

Alex

"No, you didn't." I stare at Mom, not sure I know how to take this.

She has to be kidding. She did not actually invite Connor to come swim laps with us. I remember seeing Mom talk to him during the concert last night, and she had danced with him for those songs. But I didn't think she'd be so... susceptible to him? Though I have to admit that I've caught myself a couple of times thinking about that moment. The one when I was sure he was about to kiss me. When I was sure that I wanted it, too.

Okay, I've thought about that almost-kiss a *lot*.

Mom shrugs, completely unaffected by my reaction. She primps herself using the mirrored wall of the elevator.

Not because of him, though. This is not some cougar thing, right? Ugh. I kick myself for even thinking it.

"No need to make such a big deal about it. All I did was mention that you and I swim laps every morning, and that he was welcome to join us. It was a natural course of conversation. He's a nice boy, Alexis."

Complete and total mortification achieved. I suddenly feel like I'm back in junior high, when I towered over all of the boys in my class and wished I could shrink myself down into nothingness. *A nice boy*? If Connor is a "boy," I'm that same girl that I was in eighth grade.

I take a breath and release it as the elevator doors open. She's right. This is not a big deal. Chances are that he won't show up anyway, and if he does, so what? It's a free country, and if he shows, he shows.

Still, when Mom and I get out to the deck, I feel almost ridiculously relieved. The only other people in the lap pool are the same elderly women that were here yesterday morning. They gossip happily as they do the breaststroke, and I close my eyes and tilt my head up to the sun. I start in on my stretches, going for more of a yoga-type stretch than what I did yesterday. Reach to the sun first, then touch my toes, shift my weight and pick up with an extended side angle stretch…

"He's a little old for you anyway," Mom says from next to me. I guess she might have reconsidered the "boy" part of her description of Connor. "Did you know he was in the military?"

"No, I don't know anything about him aside from him being Elle's cousin, and that's good enough for me." My tone is firm as I switch sides. "I'm here to spend time with you and Dad. And Elle, you know?"

"Oh, I know." She sounds surprised, but I can hear past that, see through the act. "That's exactly what I was trying to say."

"Uh huh." A side of my mouth tilts up in a smirk. "Ready?"

"Almost," she says. "My leg feels a bit tight today. Let me work it out a little more."

I give her a concerned look, but she's just stretching out her hamstring. The pain relievers did the trick last night, and she's seemed fine so far this morning.

"Did you ever get to see Dad last night?" He was gone when we'd gotten back to the room last night and was already gone by the time I got my butt out of bed.

"Yes, for a bit." She sighs. "He's been working too much this summer."

"Why don't you tell him that then?" I gather my hair back as I watch her reaction. Sometimes she acts afraid of my dad, like she's terrified of how he'll take things. But he's so cool about everything whenever I approach him, so I don't get that.

"Oh no. I couldn't," she says quickly.

It's what I predicted she'd say. I cross my arms over my chest, not wanting to let this go this time. "Is everything okay, Mom? Why are you guys having to cut the trip short and everything?"

"Everything is fine, Alexis. Your father has less to play with this summer is all."

I think of the ten grand that Dad gave me, and I know this can't be the whole story. Or the story at all. But Mom stares at me with a plea in her eyes, and it makes me back down, at least for now.

She takes off her coverup and folds it before setting it neatly by her towel. I kick out of my shorts, pull my shirt over my head, and toss them both onto the chair next to hers. I'm wearing my new bathing suit today, a simple black halter-style bikini, and I swing my arms a little to keep them loose as I walk to the edge of the pool.

A shriek sounds over from somewhere in one of the other pools, and I cringe. My ears are still ringing from the concert last night, and maybe also from Elle screaming in my ear the whole ride back to the hotel. Not that it wasn't completely warranted. She got to go backstage after the show and see Alysa Trane for an entire thirty seconds. And Alysa *signed* her tank top, which means Elle is going to be in a state of complete giddiness for the rest of the summer.

I used to think she found her passion in life when she decided to go into social work. She was so excited when she first told me about her plans to go to UNLV, and that was about the same time that I decided I wanted to go into nursing. But after last night, I can see that Elle's true passion is singing. Though it would have been cool to have gone backstage, I'm glad it was Elle.

Mom dives into the water, and I follow her lead in the lane next to her. I wait for it, smiling inside as my bubble gives me silence. And strength.

Mom is out of the water and sunning herself on one of the chaise lounges, but I'm still going. We're supposed to meet Dad for Sunday brunch in an hour or so, which means going to the all-you-can-eat buffet. If I can work off those calories before we get there, I'll be happy.

I sprint for fifteen laps before surfacing at the end of the pool. Mom isn't on the chaise lounge anymore. Connor is.

His broad shoulders are slightly hunched over, his elbows braced on his knees, his hands loosely clasped in front of him. And those startling blue eyes are resting on me like they've been watching me for a while.

I kick up, propping myself on the edge of the pool with my arms as I catch my breath. "Hi. What did you do with my mom?"

He cocks his head at me. God, his gaze is so, so focused in on me like they were in the high roller room, like laser beams. I wonder if he's always so intense. I let go of the pool's edge and sink back into the water, my toes touching the bottom.

"Nothing." He stands, not breaking eye contact with me. "She told me she was going to go back to her suite to shower. Asked me to keep you company and remind you that brunch is…" He glances at his watch. "…in fifty minutes."

"I know when brunch is," I say simply. "But thanks. And as for keeping me company, I'll be swimming for about twenty more minutes and then going inside, so don't feel obligated to babysit."

I'm not trying to be rude, just straight with him. I don't need any company when I'm out here. I push away from the wall, my head still out of water so I can hear him in case he responds.

I stare at him as he throws his watch on his towel, right before he pulls his shirt over his head and drops it. I try not to gawk, but he has a great body, all tanned with well-defined muscles. I'd felt some of those muscles when we danced last night. He walks forward, swimming trunks slung low on his hips, and crouches down by the side of the pool. My head is right at the level of his crotch, and I fight to drag my gaze back up to his face.

My mouth is suddenly dry. No harm in looking, right? He was just watching me swim for however long without me knowing. I can make out a pretty big scar on his left shoulder, and I wonder what it's from.

"You don't seem like the type who requires babysitting," he says in a low voice. His jaw is shaded with a little bit of stubble today, like he slept in this morning and didn't have time to shave. I stare at his lips and finally manage to swallow.

"You're observant," I say back.

"Yeah, I have to be," he says, standing up again.

Oh geez. I have to crane my neck up uncomfortably in order to not stare at his swimming trunks again. Is he flirting with me? I suppose he might be, but he's so *serious*, and honestly, I don't want to figure it out, either way. I drift backward in the water in a float, the sun high enough now to blind me for a second and force me to close my eyes. I open them in time to see Connor diving into the lane next to me.

Better. I flip over and dive into the water to start in on my laps again. Connor's a powerful swimmer, and he goes fast and strong with even strokes. There's no way I can catch up, but this isn't a race, either. Still, I push myself hard until I reach the end of the lane, tucking myself into a somersault and kicking against the opposite wall before hitting the second half of the lap. I can see him ahead of me, and I pull myself through the water with stronger and stronger strokes. I'm not feeling that usual piece of calm energy that I do when I'm in here. Energy, yes. But none of the calm.

It's stupid and illogical for me to be all wound up inside because there's some guy swimming in the lane next to me. A guy who almost kissed me last night and who happens to have a body that I could stare at all day. A guy who is also sort of enigmatic... But no, that's stupid. He's only enigmatic because I know nothing about him, right? Except I do know that he was with an absolutely gorgeous woman in the high roller room for part of the afternoon yesterday. And that he'd been standing over her like he *was* her babysitter. It's enough to be another factor of intrigue.

Oh, hell. Speaking of other factors...what would Elle think if she knew I was ogling her cousin's hot body?

Twenty laps later, and I close in at the end. I can see half of Connor through the water, standing and waiting for me at the end of the pool, and my lungs burn like hell as I take the rest of the lap without resurfacing for air. My hand grabs the edge of the pool first, and I pop up right after and touch my feet to the bottom.

I'm breathing hard from the last lap, and Connor looks like he's just getting warmed up. He's tall, maybe six foot two, and my eyes come up to his chin. I stare at the slight stubble leading up to his mouth. It doesn't help my breathing any.

I push my hands through my hair to squeeze out some of the water, and his gaze trails over my face and down, down to the front of my swimsuit as I lower my arms. It's a lingering look, and I know I'm not imagining the heat behind it.

"You're a good swimmer," he says. It's a statement of fact, but I pick up a hint of something else in his tone. Not quite like admiration. Maybe more like approval.

"So are you."

He smiles slightly, and it's a shadow of that cocky grin. "It's almost time for your brunch."

I quirk an eyebrow at him. "What? Didn't my mom invite you to that, too?"

"No. Even if she did, I have to go to work right now."

Now that I've stopped moving after so many laps, I feel a slight chill from standing still in the water. Throwing a quick sideways glance at him, I hoist myself out of the pool. I wish I could say that I sprung out with grace, but yeah, that would be a huge stretch.

Connor's the one to float back away from me this time, his eyes moving up to my face. I can read something like lust in his eyes, and I have a pretty good feeling his eyes were planted firmly on my ass prior to that.

"Thought you had to get to work." I don't ask him what he does even though I'm curious. I wrap myself up in my towel and grab my shirt and shorts as I kick my feet into my flip flops.

"I do, but I'm doing one more lap first," he says. All traces of that previous smile are gone, and he's suddenly extremely serious again. "You'll be here tomorrow?"

I freeze in place with my clothes in my hands, telling myself that it's just because I'm cold. "Yes. Better chance than not."

"See you then. Better chance than not." He holds the eye contact with me for a few seconds longer, and then does this really cool flip to get his body under the surface of the water. He's off, and I force myself to breathe again as I watch him slice through the water like a machine.

I know that they like you to rinse off by the pool, but all I can think about is how serious Connor comes off. How his stare is like fire and ice at the same time. How he smiled at me. And how I wish he would kiss me.

My feet slap back over to the casino entrance in a hurry. There's no way I can take the intensity of that man's stare for one more second.

12

CONNOR

Ten in the morning, and I'm finally on my way to get Maya. Yesterday was a complete wash. Aside from my brief swim at the pool with Alex, I was idle most of the day. When I went to pick Maya up in the afternoon, she bagged out on her game, which she never does. Elle is evidently doing some internship for college credit this summer, and she's working on some paper. No texts or other word from her about Cruz. I'm not used to having leisure time, in any form, and I'd gone for a long run early this morning to take the edge off.

I knock on the door, and Maya opens it a good minute later, talking on her cell phone and dressed in silk pajamas. I try to hide my surprise. I'm right on time to pick her up, and I've never seen her look so *not* ready to go before.

"Hold on a second, will you, David?" She places her hand over the phone and whispers to me, "Connor, could we reschedule for an hour from now? I need to take some calls."

Her eyes even look puffy. This isn't the usual Maya, but it's not my business to say anything. It's not a problem to reschedule, and I nod as she's already closing the door and speaking to this David guy.

I frown as I head back down the hall. I hope Maya will be ready when I come back for her, that she doesn't bag out on this set of games like she did yesterday. It's not my style, but I'm worried for her. There's a certain formula that determines how often and even how much high rollers are supposed to play to get all of the royal treatment in return. I know Maya's connected to some powerful people in this city, but I doubt any casino would let her hang out and get all of the comps without having to work for it, no matter how influential she is.

I check my watch, even though I know it's a few minutes after ten. An hour is hardly enough time to let me leave the Strip and come back again. I could use the time to make some calls of my own, though.

Elle starts in without prelude as soon as my call goes through. "No thank you's are needed. I only ask you to acknowledge that I did this because I love you."

The tension automatically creeps into my shoulders. What the fuck did she do now? "Enough with the drama. What's going on?"

"You told me you wanted to see Cruz, so I talked to him for you. He said he'd be at the QE2 tonight at eight if you want to meet him."

My teeth grind together. Figures. It's just like Cruz to make it so he's calling the shots. He shows up in my city. He decides on the meeting place and time. Luckily my schedule is mostly free tonight.

"Fine," I snap.

A pause, then, "You know what? I take it back. A thank you would be nice."

"I need to meet with him alone, Elle."

"And I'll leave you two alone, I swear," she says quickly. "Monday nights are always pretty dead. I'll be helping with inventory and stuff like that in the back." She hesitates again before adding, "He treated me to the nicest dinner last night, Connor. He said he's looking forward to seeing you again, and I want you to believe that."

Right. Extortion money can buy lots of nice dinners. And I bet he is looking forward to it. I have a few guesses as to what Cruz wants with me, but I'll leave judgment for when I actually see him.

"So I'll see you then? And you promise to be on your best behavior?"

It's condescending as hell, and I have zero patience for this coddling shit. "I'll be there. I gotta go, okay?"

I end the call, my hand curling around my phone in a fist. I'd already made up my mind to meet him, and now I just have to get it done and over with. And then I can move on from this. Again.

The elevator opens, and I step inside, feeling the old resentment and anger rise up. I need a recharge of positive energy, and I hope I can get my shit together before I have to go back and pick up Maya.

I think I know exactly where to get that recharge.

I stop by my car to drop off my jacket and Sig and walk across the street to the casino where Alex is staying. She might be done swimming by now, but I'm hoping I can catch her.

I try not to think about why I'm going out of my way to do this, but I can't help it. Despite our rocky start, Alex is cool, pure and simple. The way I've seen her take things as they come. Alex is positive, and that's what I need right now.

And let's face it. I liked seeing her all dressed up the other night, and I liked it even more watching her at the pool when she was wearing almost nothing at all. Alex looked fucking hot in that black bikini, and I'd be kidding myself if I told myself that's not part of it.

If I'm going to meet Cruz tonight, I *need* this one little indulgence before having to endure that.

I was hoping for the path of least resistance, but I recognize the woman checking keycards at the pool. She's named DaNae or maybe it's Denean. I can't remember, but we hooked up a while back. A few months ago? A year? I remember she was working with some of the hospitality team back then. I don't feel like making conversation with her and hope she doesn't remember me.

I flash my staff pass to get into the pool. It's one I got from someone who works security at the hotel. I shouldn't even have it, but it sometimes comes in handy.

"Omigod. Connor."

Shit. So much for path of least resistance. She leans onto the counter, brushing a strand of long blonde hair away from her cleavage while I check her out. Fake boobs. Fake smile. Had I really gone for her before?

She looks at me through her eyelashes. "Haven't seen you in forever. Here for a swim?"

"That's the plan."

"Fu-un." She says it in an annoying sing-song voice and turns around to grab me a towel, even though I don't need it because I don't actually plan on swimming. When she hands it to me, she eyes me like I'm on the menu for lunch. "I'm on break in fifteen. Mind if I come and join you?"

"Maybe another time." Or not. I'm definitely off my game today. And I don't care.

Her face falls but then she gives me a hospitality-worthy smile. "Oh. You're here to meet someone, huh?"

"Yeah. I am." I look around, already feeling distracted. And damn, but I'm looking forward to the rest of that distraction.

I walk out onto the deck, my sights zeroed in on the lap pool. I can already see Alex in the distance, and my internal temperature cranks up a notch. She's wearing a purple bikini today and looks like she just got out of the pool. Her body is still dripping wet, all tall curves, and she's standing by one of the chairs with her phone in hand. Part of me wants to slow my pace to enjoy the view, but I pick it up instead in case she's taking off.

She suddenly looks up from her phone and sees me coming. Her hair is loose, and she raises a hand to push a strand back behind her ear.

"Hey." She doesn't look surprised to see me.

"Hey. What did you do with your mom?"

It's a joke on my part, but she frowns and hits something on her phone before sticking it into her bag.

"She got up to come swimming but went back to bed. Said she had another headache." She shrugs, but I can see the worry in her expression. "I was just texting to check on her."

"Sorry to hear that," I say, and I realize I mean it.

She tilts her head to the side a little, her eyes examining me and missing nothing. She picked up on the fact yesterday that I'm observant, and I think she's the same.

"I didn't think you were coming today," she says.

I rake my hand through my hair. "Yeah, I'm sorry…" Second time in thirty seconds I'd said sorry and meant it. Not something I usually have an easy time doing. "I actually had work, but things got pushed back for an hour."

"So you came to find me? Cool."

I stare at her, and she stares back, a smile playing on her lips. It's like she's slowly breaking down my walls with her words, her smile, her openness, and I don't know what to say.

She starts to walk back to the pool, and I watch her move, the way she places one foot almost directly in front of the other, the sensual sway to her hips, her very sexy ass…

She throws a glance at me over her shoulder. "You swimming, or what?"

I shake my head. "I didn't bring swim trunks."

She shoots a smile in my direction. "Swim in your underwear then. Who's gonna care?"

Probably everyone. But the grin breaks out on my face anyway. How does she manage to do that?

"What if I'm not wearing any?"

She laughs out loud and turns so she's walking backward away from me. "Then they might care."

I smirk, looking around. Besides the lifeguard, there's us plus two other people doing laps and a few people sunning-slash-sleeping on one of the lounge chairs. Alex is standing by the edge of the pool, a hand on her hip, and it's like her stance and entire attitude is challenging me. I don't miss the brief flick of her gaze down my body, like she's trying to figure out if I'm really walking around commando. For some reason, that does it for me.

Fuck it. I pull my shirt over my head and throw it on the nearest chair. Aware of her eyes on me the entire time, I strip down to my underwear and walk to the pool.

I've been with plenty of women over the past two years. Maybe too many. And I think that's why I expect Alex to react to me like the rest of them do. Or maybe I'm being a cocky bastard to think that she'll check me out as I'm walking toward her in nothing but my boxer briefs and the start of an erection.

But she looks me in the eye, giving me one of her sweet smiles before she turns away. "I'll race ya."

She dives into the pool and I follow, getting into the water as fast as I can. Not sure how the hell I'm going to swim with a hard-on, but I don't really have a choice.

But hitting the water calms me down, soothes my nerves. When Cruz and I were eight or nine, we started escaping the house in the summers by going to the community pool. It was pretty ghetto, hundreds of kids there every day, dirty as hell, but it was still somewhere for us to go, and it's when I first became like a fish in the water. I obviously added more things to my physical training regimen as I got older and decided to go for the SEALs, but swimming has always acted like a stress reliever for me.

I'm still pissed off about the way Elle went about things today, how she called to inform me about the plans made on my behalf. But I can almost feel my anger melt away with each stroke through the water.

Alex had a huge head start, but I can see her standing at the end of the lane instead of coming back. I break through the surface next to her, and she's suddenly giving me that look again, the one that strips down my defenses. Just like how she stripped down the rest of me to get me into the pool, and the thought of it makes me smile.

She bobs down in the water, tipping her head back to wet her hair. "What's so funny?"

"I thought you didn't need company when you swam."

"I don't need company. But I don't mind that you're here."

Damn, I like how she's so straightforward, how she speaks her mind like that. She raises her arms over her head to smooth some of her hair away from her face, and I feel this kind of raw need rise in my gut. The water feels warm, small currents eddying around us like they're urging me to get closer to her. I resist the temptation to close the distance between us, to tuck that stray strand of hair behind her ear.

"So are you staying at this casino too, then? Because you need a key card to get in here." Her question is direct, her gaze equally so.

"I'm not staying here," I admit. "But I have a security pass that I can use to get in here, even after hours if I want. For work."

"Yeah?" She tilts her head. "So what's work?"

I drift away from her in the water. "Another full lap, and I'll tell you."

I hear her laugh at that, but I'm already taking off down the lane. I'm surprised that she doesn't know what I do for a living, that her mother hadn't told her. But maybe I was wrong about Grace trying to set me up with her daughter. Fine with me. I hate having expectations laid out on me like that. I always hated that about Laura's mother, that she *hadn't* approved of me. But that was seven, eight years ago. None of that matters anymore.

I get to the wall first and wait for Alex to surface. She makes it and pushes her hair back, blinking water away from her eyes as she waits for my answer.

I give it to her. "Private security for high rollers. Didn't your mother tell you?"

"You're kidding." She looks at me with this incredulous expression, and I feel myself grow defensive. So now I'm going to have to explain myself because she doesn't believe me. But then she laughs, and that hard edge in me softens.

"My mom didn't mention it. But okay, so that makes sense now," she tacks on thoughtfully. "Is that what you were doing in the high roller room? Security for that woman you were with?"

"Yeah." I don't feel comfortable saying anything about Maya, *can't* say anything else because my clients are in my confidence. But there's that whole observant thing about Alex again.

"So what, did my mom hire you to protect me?" She sounds suspicious now, like she wouldn't put it past her mom to do something like that.

"No. I only protect assets and the people carrying them." I'm glad about it, too. Neil has horror stories about VIP's twenty-something daughters trying to get into his pants when I first brought him in as a partner. He and I came up with a contractual clause about our level of interaction with spouses and children of clients. We do not interact one-on-one with them, period. "Do you honestly think your mother would hire someone like me to protect you?" I challenge.

"Actually, no." Her smile widens. "Definitely not someone like you."

"You and your mother seem pretty tight. You and your father, too." The statement comes out as a simple observation, but it hits me hard as soon as I hear myself say it. It's not anything I can relate to.

She doesn't answer right away. Maybe I expected her to say yeah, they are. But then her eyes lock with mine, and I detect something stirring deeper in there.

"I guess we are close. Me being close to my mom and close to my dad. Not with each other as much." Her hand trails through the ends of her hair, twisting a few wet strands around her fingers. "You ever notice how a lot of people wind up married even though they're not good for each other?"

I look past her. I guess I know but I don't, not really. My parents hadn't stayed married, and I have no idea if they were good for each other or not. All indications pointed to no, but I never knew the whole story of why my mother left us.

When Alex catches my gaze again, she's looking at me curiously.

"Your parents. Are they not together anymore?"

"No. My father's a drug addict. My mother walked out on him when my brother and I were eight."

I don't know exactly why I answer, but there's something about her straightforwardness that's contagious. I also don't know how I expect her to react. Maybe with shock or sympathy. Not with the completely serious nod that she winds up giving me, like she's seen it all before.

"That sucks. Sorry, dude."

I shrug, and I have the strangest urge to smile. She's talking to me like I noticed she talks to Elle, which is kind of funny. Or maybe that's how she is with everyone.

"It's cool. You asked, I told you."

She nods again, and I can't tear my eyes from her mouth. She has a pretty mouth, perfectly curved and slightly pouty. I can only imagine what that mouth is capable of doing. Fuck. I knew Alex would help to distract me, but at this rate, I'm never going to be able to get out of this pool, not unless the water becomes a hell of a lot colder.

"What you said about marriage. You speaking hypothetically or from your own experience?" I ask, suddenly wary. She's not wearing a ring, not that this necessarily means anything. Divorced is fine, but if she's attached, I'm walking away.

"What?" Her eyebrows draw together in confusion for about two seconds, and then she bursts out into laughter. "Omigod," she chokes out. "*I'm* not married. You think I'm married?"

I shrug, still smiling at her. "Or given the nature of your comment, divorced. Why not?"

She sinks down in the water, her hair floating out around her shoulders. "Uh, because I just turned twenty-one? And because I'm going to school, working, and don't have time for that sort of thing?"

"Oh, right," I say with the same level of sarcasm. "Because I would have known that."

She laughs again and starts to float away. I catch myself wishing she'd come closer, not move away.

"Okay, after the next lap it's your turn," she says.

I stare at her, not comprehending. "My turn to do what?"

"Your turn to ask me something about me. Something personal."

I cock an eyebrow. "I thought I just asked you if you were married."

"Nah. That was part of the same question. Ask me something different."

She kicks off the bottom and floats on her back, her eyes closed. Her navel is pierced with a small jeweled barbell that flashes in the high morning sun. It's sexy as hell, and that slow-burning fire stirs in me again. We're separated by the floating dividers between our lanes, and I suddenly wish they weren't there.

I take the lap a lot slower this time, follow Alex's lead as she does the backstroke to the other end of the pool. No clue what my question is going to be when I get to the wall, but it surprises me that I'm even trying to think of one. I actually do want to know more about her. And the anticipation of asking her something personal is making my nerves fire up like they're super-charged.

This isn't how I operate. Conversations with women are always just a means to an end. It's only ever about the sex, a one-time mutual physical gratification, an in-and-out operation. Nothing beyond that.

At least that's how it's been since I moved to Vegas. I don't let myself think about how I was back in Albuquerque.

When I get to the end of the lane, Alex is waiting. She's breathing a little hard because of the exertion, and I try not to stare as she adjusts the straps to her bikini.

"Okay. A new question." I throw it out there. "How long have you known Elle?"

Those cocoa brown eyes of hers appraise me, probe me, as if searching for meaning behind the question, but I don't give her anything else to go on. I want to hear her answer without any prompts on my part.

"I met her a couple of summers ago. We hung out all last summer when I was out here."

I nod. I don't ask why I haven't met her before this summer. I was out of the picture for most of last year. Out of Elle's life when I shouldn't have been.

"And you gave her the only all-access pass last night?"

Confusion flashes across her expression, but she doesn't shrug off the question. "Yeah. Because she really admires Alysa Trane, you know?"

"I know," I say. *Tell her thank you. How different she is from the VIP brats that you've met. How you really want to fucking kiss her right now.*

I put my hand on the divider between us. "I have one more question."

She quirks an eyebrow. "Shoot."

I lift up the divider and slide underneath. She stands still, but not in a tense way or anything. More like she's just waiting for my move. My gaze locks with hers, and the water around us makes those eddies again, this time like the currents are magnifying the attraction between us.

I move forward until I'm only inches away from her and she has to tilt up her head to look at my face. Her lips part, her cheeks reddening. It's stupid, but I feel a sort of twisted sense of pride that I made the cool girl blush.

"I'm gonna kiss you, okay?"

"That's not even a legitimate question," she breathes.

"I know," I say.

She drifts over to me, her leg brushing against mine, and the way she's looking at me is like an open invitation. I move my hand through the water and find her, run my hand across her hip. Damn, her skin is so soft, her curves so sexy. I keep my touch light but really want to grab her and pull her over to me.

"So?" She challenges. "You going to kiss me or not?"

My mouth tilts up in a sideways smile. She's fiery, and I like that. That's why I originally came here looking for her, and this... *this* is just extra but now that the moment's here, I want it. Hell, I think I need it. I thread my fingers through her hair, press my lips to hers and drink her up with a soft kiss. She moans against me, and that kills the soft for me. I take the kiss deeper, and fuck, how she responds, matching every stroke of my tongue with hers, her taste deliciously sweet, her fingers knotting hard in my hair before raking over my shoulders and down my back.

I want to get closer to her. Want it so fucking bad, but there's too much water stirring between us. I slip my hands around her waist, and she pushes her body up against mine. We're skin on skin, slick and hard against wet and soft. It's like every touch of hers leaves a charge behind that electrifies and pulses through me. I'm rock hard, and my hand slides down to grab that gorgeous ass of hers as I grind against her.

A small sound of need escapes her throat, and I groan. I seriously consider carrying her out of the pool and finding an open room so we can continue this in private. Her room. Laundry room. Somewhere. Anywhere but here.

She breaks off the kiss, tilts her head back as I lean down to suck on the very sexy curve where her neck meets her shoulder. "My God," she moans.

I smile against her skin. "Not yet I'm not."

Her hand slips between us, presses against my chest and pushes me away, but she's smiling back. "You're so arrogant."

"You're so fucking sexy," I growl.

She drifts away from me in the pool, and it takes everything I have not to pull her back over to me again. It's killing me to work myself down from that kiss, from the feel of her skin on mine. But I need to at least rinse off and put my clothes back on – minus the boxer briefs – and go back to work.

I reach out to her and touch her hair, attempting to slow my breathing so I sound human again. "This was fun, but I gotta go."

"It's okay." Her cheeks are flushed, her voice husky. "I think you got your kiss."

I glance behind me, seeing more people out on the deck now. "You want to get me my towel, too? I don't think I can get out of here without it."

She laughs, and it's full of that positive energy that I so desperately needed when I sought her out here today. I tuck away that sound in my memory, knowing I'm going to need it again later.

Alex glides over to the edge of the pool and gets out, the water trickling off her as she walks away. I push my hand through my hair and watch her. I hope Maya's phone calls are going to be enough to distract her from noticing how out of my head I am.

Fuck, that kiss totally messed me up. But that was hot.

13

Alex

Holy crap. My legs are all noodly, my entire body thrumming. I can still taste Connor, a mixture of mint and yummy manliness. No idea how I manage to walk over to the chairs to snag our towels, but I do.

I bring his back to him and hold it out as he climbs out of the pool. The whole time, I make a pretense of drying my hair, but I'm really not-so-secretly gawking at him, enjoying the view as he wraps the towel around his waist. His gaze lands squarely on my face like a shower of cool blue sparks, his cocky grin in place as he catches me looking.

God, there is something about him that fires up my curiosity, makes me want to know what's really brewing beneath the surface. There's definitely some arrogance there, but I don't think he's one of those guys who's *defined* by that. He opened himself up to me before, enough to tell me that way personal stuff about his family. So, he's arrogant, yeah. But at the same time, there's this kind of vulnerability to him.

He did come all this way to my hotel during a work break to find me.

Something about that makes me want to reach out and run my hand over the slight stubble on his jaw. I lift my hand but graze it against the scar on his arm instead. It's longer than I initially thought, and I can see now that it goes from the front of his arm and curves back around to his shoulder. The line is jagged, the skin stretched and shining in contrast to the rest of his skin. I wonder if it has to do with that military background my mom mentioned.

"What's the story behind the scar?"

That spark I saw before in his eyes abruptly dies, and something darker replaces it. "No story."

His face is tight as he turns away, and he strides to the chair to grab the rest of his clothes without another look in my direction. Like he's suddenly closed from further discussion.

I go to my chair and kick my flip flops on as he starts to walk away. Okay, obviously his scar has to have a story, and it's cool if he doesn't want to share it. But to flip a switch like that? Now I'm feeling a little bristly. I mean, what is his deal? He initiated that kiss, that sexy as hell kiss. And in the blink of an eye, he backs off from me like that and turns into an iceman? The high I was riding mere seconds ago is totally gone, and that's *not* cool.

I'm not an attention whore or one of those needy girls. Forming summer attachments with guys doesn't make sense in my world. I'm usually the one to run away from them.

But he's not like those pretty boys I'm used to hooking up with. He's interesting. And I think I like him.

I frown as I gather up my things. These thoughts need to be nipped in the bud, right now. Connor's almost to the pool house, and I briefly close my eyes and take a breath. Oh, crap.

"Hey!" I shout.

He stops walking and turns around, his face still stiff. I stalk over to him – well, as best as I can in my flip flops.

I come to a stop by the side of the pool house, only a step or two in front of him. He stares down at me, his expression giving way to surprise. But his eyes are still clouded with anger. Or pain. Something.

"What's up?" Definitely guarded.

"I never thanked you," I blurt out.

His mouth twitches slightly, like he's trying not to smile. "For what?"

Oh, God. He probably thinks I'm talking about the kiss, and I'm not. Though now that I'm inches away from him, I am very aware of his body and the warmth of his skin. My own body responds with an ache. A need to close the distance between us and touch him again…

Girl, you need to focus.

"You know. For taking care of me the other night. Making sure I got to my room all right." I pause before adding, "Not too many guys would have gone out of their way like that. And others might have taken advantage of the fact that I was messed up."

He nods once. "No problem."

It's a no-frills answer to my rambling, but the way he looks at me holds more emotion than his words. His eyes search my face as if we're back in the elevator and he's trying to make sure I'm okay.

I nod back. "Just wanted you to know. And sorry to keep you. Maybe I'll see you at the pool again sometime."

It's all I wanted to say. Nothing urgent but nevertheless important because I don't know if I'll see him again to tell him. I turn to go, glad that I got the words out.

"Alex."

His voice is low, sexy. He catches my hand.

I spin around to face him, and he slides his arm around my waist and pulls me forward. Tugs on me so I'm pressed close against his chest and hard against his towel.

"You're not leaving Vegas soon, are you?"

His skin feels sun-warmed, his eyes like endless blue pools. I swallow hard. "No. I'll be here through the month. At least through the month. I'm not su…"

My legs turn back into jello as his mouth covers mine, and whatever walls he had up before, I can't feel in this kiss. It's warm and wanting, and it fires me up again like we never got out of the pool. I wind my arm around his neck, knot my hand in his hair. His grip on my back tightens, and he groans deep in his throat as I boldly move my hips against him. My other hand runs across the muscles of his chest, moves lower over his abs, not caring about the fact that we're down by the pool with other people around the corner. I wonder what he'd do if I got rid of that towel.

As soon as I have the thought, he ends the kiss. My vision is blurry, my heart rate about to go through the roof.

"Good," he says. I swear to God I can hear his heart beating as fast as mine. He lets go of me and steps back toward the entrance of the pool house, his eyes intent on mine.

"I'll see you again. I'll make sure of it."

My voice is lost somewhere, and I nod at him mutely. Even if it is some prefabricated line he gives women, he has me believing it.

He walks away, and this time, I let him.

"So?" Mom is curled up on the couch with a book, and she puts it down and smiles as I walk out of my room. "How was your swim?"

I'd entered the suite through my own room about twenty minutes ago and cooled myself down in the shower for about fifteen. Mom's eyes scour me right now like she's looking for hickeys. Luckily, there aren't any. I checked.

"Really, Mom? That's not really what you want to ask me, is it?"

Her eyes widen. "What? I'm just wondering if you had a nice swim. And yes, I admit that I might be hoping that you had company after I abandoned you."

"You didn't abandon me. I had a nice swim. And I did have company for a while."

She beams at me. "And when are you seeing him again?"

"We're not *seeing* each other. But I have no idea," I say lightly.

He'll make sure that I do.

It's my turn to scrutinize her. She looks pretty, with her hair hanging loose around her shoulders, which she rarely does. And her expression is relaxed, serene even. "Hey, but how are you? Feeling up to going out for lunch?"

"Much better. But I already had room service bring me a late breakfast." She picks up her book and pages through to get back to her spot. "Your father's in the VIP lounge and said he'd take you to lunch if you'd like."

"Yeah, sure." I give her one more hard look to be sure that she's okay, but it seems like her painkillers are doing the trick.

"I'm glad you and Connor had a nice pool date," she says into her book.

"Oh my God. Mom." I fight the temptation to roll my eyes.

I get the hell out of there before she can say anything else, but I have to laugh to myself as I walk down to the elevator. Between the stunts that both Elle and my mom have pulled so far, this summer is already turning out to be a lot more interesting than usual. I hope I can make it out of this city in one piece.

I go downstairs to the VIP lounge and pull open the heavy door, the scent of luxury wafting out in a perfumed cloud. The lounge is pure opulence, excessive in decor complete with velvet upholstery that melts over thick carpet. Dad is sitting and reading a newspaper in one of the overstuffed chairs. I don't think he's actually reading it though, because he jumps up almost as soon as I set foot in the room.

"So," he starts as we walk out together. It's how Mom had greeted me when I came out of my room, and I almost stop in my tracks. If he somehow knows about my non-date with Connor and is about to ask me about it, I might die.

"What did you think about baccarat the other day?"

Oh, that's all. I relax as we head to a high-end Chinese restaurant.

"I kept confusing the rules with blackjack rules at first," I admit. "But I figured it out after that."

He gestures for me to go in before him, and the host at the door greets my dad with a shallow bow.

"*Lín xiānshēng. Nǐ hǎo.*"

Dad gives him a nod, and the host leads us to a circular table and pulls out a chair for each of us before handing us our menus.

"Enjoy your lunch. The server will be with you shortly." The host bows at each of us and quickly retreats, leaving us to decide. Dad gives the menu a cursory glance before putting it down.

"The trick to playing baccarat is that there's no true skill involved," he says. "It's a guessing game. More of a social game than anything. The rules don't matter."

"I don't understand…" I trail off, honestly confused. "The rules don't matter? How can you win if you don't know the rules?"

"The strategy doesn't come from the rules," he says patiently. "You saw how it's played. A child could do it. All you have to do is guess whether you or the banker is going to have the best hand. Ultimately, the house has the advantage, but you can come out ahead if you know when to walk away."

I don't quite get it. "Sounds like you're describing how to cut your losses instead of actually winning."

He smiles at me, pausing his lesson as the server sets a pot of tea down in front of us.

"Some hands you win, some you lose. But winning only comes from knowing how much you can stand to lose."

I wonder if that's a translation of some old Chinese proverb. I feel like I'm sitting in one of my classes where the professor keeps trying to explain something over and over again and I don't get it.

"Okay, so… you're saying you win when you've decided you've lost enough?"

He nods and leans forward, like we're conspirators in a game. "In the long run, yes. Still have that money I gave you?"

I sip at my tea. "I do."

"After lunch then." He reaches out and pats my hand. "We'll try your luck at the tables, and I'll show you what I mean."

Whoa. What? My head swirls for a second as I try to put meaning to his words. "Are you serious? You want me to actually play?"

He nods. "Not on the same level as me obviously, but yes. Believe it or not, there are good lessons that can be learned from this." He looks a little sheepish. My *dad,* who always has a handle on things, looks sheepish. "But you need to promise to keep it our little secret."

Keeping this a secret from my mom is a no-brainer. She'd freak if ever she found out. I hold up my pinky like I used to do with him when I was a little girl.

"Pinky promise." I grin at him, and he grabs my little finger with his.

"We'll go across the street again, same place as yesterday," he says with a satisfied nod.

Across the street again. A current of excitement sparks through me, and I press my lips together as I realize why. It's only partly because I'm going out with Dad for my first actual gambling session. It's because I know Connor's also working right now, out there doing his thing. Maybe in that same high roller room.

Dammit. I'm *hoping* he'll be there.

14

CONNOR

"I'm out." Maya throws her cards down with thirty plus grand on the table, her declaration almost a snarl.

She's going down in flames, and there's damn little I can do about it. Making bad calls. Being snappish with the other players at the table. Nothing that would warrant the casino personnel asking her to leave, but she's not her usual gracious self. Something's definitely throwing her off today, and I'm guessing it's that phone call from earlier. I wonder if I should use one of our code phrases to get her out of the high roller room, but those are for her to use. Not my decision to make.

She turns in her chair, placing her hand on my sleeve. "Go get me a pack of Virginia Slims, won't you?" Her tone is brusque, lines of tension around her eyes evidence of strain.

I frown. True sign that something's eating at her. Maya doesn't smoke, or at least I've never seen her light one up before. But again, not my place to say anything. We all have our own shit that we do to take the edge off, and if this is what she needs, I'm happy to do it.

There's a convenience store in the lobby, and I leave Maya's side and walk through the gaming floor, my thoughts somehow drifting to Alex. On kissing her outside the pool house. On how I wanted to take her inside with me to the showers. The time with her at the pool wound up being a little more than I intended, more than a mere distraction. I don't tell people about me, ever. When she asked about the scar, I had to walk away, but it was only because a small part of me was tempted to answer her.

I'm surprised at myself for having told her as much as I did. My past is not exactly a badge that I wear proudly. Elle's the only one out here who knows anything about my parents.

Speaking of which, I can only imagine the shit Elle's going to give me if she finds out about my little swim with her friend. Though honestly, Alex doesn't strike me as the type of woman who gives up the dirt on the guys she messes around with. I remember what she said that night in the elevator, that she doesn't hook up with random guys, that it's only when she really wants to.

Damn. I'm looking forward to seeing her again. Too much. The anticipation of it gives me a little high, and I'm not totally comfortable with that. I can't remember the last time I felt that.

Sure I can. But it fucking hurts to remember.

I slam down that thought, make myself come back to earth. I'm on the job with Maya, and she's already off her game. I need to get my head on straight and keep it there until I clock out. And then go home to chill the fuck out before I have to meet with Cruz.

The convenience store is busy with tourists, and I get in line behind a Spanish-speaking couple. They're talking in low voices, but I hear the woman tell the guy that she wants a hundred dollars more to play blackjack.

"*No tenemos más dinero,*" he mutters back.

She argues with him until they get to the front of the line, and they walk away still arguing. Precisely why I don't gamble. I don't claim to be a saint, but I see enough of what it does to people to ever want to get into it.

The cashier looks like he's in his late teens. He has earbuds on and looks bored out of his mind. I grab my wallet from my back pocket.

"Pack of Virginia Slims."

He doesn't move. "Cigarettes suck," he says in a flat tone.

Interesting sales technique. He might as well tell people how addictive gambling is while he's at it. "Thanks for the unnecessary commentary. I still need a pack."

"Fine. You sure you don't at least want a more manly brand?" He drops the deadpan look and raises an eyebrow caustically.

Everyone has to be a fucking comedian these days. Though I can't totally blame him for trying to make his job more entertaining, even if it's at the expense of customers.

"They're not for me." I take out a ten and slap it on the counter. "Just give me the goddamn cigarettes."

"Yeah, yeah, okay." He shrugs. "I get it. Show your girlfriend you care. Give her lung cancer."

I shake my head as I take the pack and leave the store. The guy's attitude reminds me a little of Cruz in his forwardness, the way he takes jabs at people at every possible opportunity.

Cruz. I need to prepare myself for our meeting tonight, except that I can't because I only have vague guesses as to what he wants with me. My stomach is already tied up in an automatic knot at the thought of him, the old rage I keep hidden inside threatening to surface.

Dammit. I can't react like this when I see him tonight. He'll see it like a fucking billboard, use it to his advantage. Cruz has always been good at that, finding and exploiting people's weaknesses, and I can only imagine what he's like now. I won't give him the chance to do that to me, though. I'll let him know in no uncertain terms that he and I were done seven years ago, that he can't show up like this and expect me to welcome him with open arms.

Yeah, I need to be straight with him. Like Alex is with people. I don't know how she does it, opens up so easily and speaks her mind.

And now I'm back full circle to what I was thinking about when I left the high roller room. That woman has definitely worked her way under my skin. I wish I could get her under me, period.

I'm in a significantly better mood when I get back inside.

Maya's on her second cigarette and doing marginally better at her game when Alex walks into the room.

She's in my sights right away, and she looks good. Wearing one of her maddeningly short skirts again. A shirt that comes down in front in a deep V before hugging her breasts. I have this crazy urge to walk over, but I keep myself in check. I'm not about to leave Maya's side. Plus, Alex is with her father. Can't even imagine what I'd say if I had to introduce myself.

Hi, my name is Connor, and I'd really like to fuck your daughter.
Ha. Maybe not.

Alex scans the room for about two seconds before her eyes lock squarely with mine. It's like she was specifically looking for me, and this feeling of need spikes in me as she continues to stare. At the same time, the thought that she could have deliberately come here to find me is scarier than hell.

I watch as she places her hand on her dad's arm and whispers something into his ear, her eyes fixed on me. Shit. She's walking over to me. Now. While I'm working.

I see Maya's water glass is almost empty and quickly lean down to grab it. Thankfully, she doesn't look up or otherwise register the interruption. Interfering with a client's game is like a cardinal sin in this business. Without a word, I walk to the sideboard holding the drinks and appetizers, some of which probably cost more per plate than my entire weekly grocery bill. Alex approaches me as I'm filling up the glass.

"Hey." She gives me that purely happy smile.

"What's up?" I glance over at Maya, but she's still deep in the same game. "I'm working now," I say in a low voice. "I can't really talk when I'm working."

"Oh, sorry." Her cheeks become rosy, like her perfectly luscious mouth. "But it would be weird if we totally ignored each other, right?"

"You're right." I give Maya one more glance then turn my full attention to Alex. Honestly, I'm glad that she calls me on my shit. "How do you do that?"

"Do what?" She looks up at me curiously.

"Talk to people so easily."

"I don't know. I open my mouth and words come out. It's not hard. Should it be?"

I laugh out loud, the sound surprising me. Alex rolls her eyes at me but her face lights up with this kind of joy. I'm struck by it, by how pretty she is, and I reach out and finally tuck that strand of hair very gently behind her ear. She freezes, her eyes wide as my fingers trail down and touch her chin.

She takes a step back, her eyes shifting over to her father. "I gotta go. See ya soon, Connor."

She gives me a small smile, but it's brief and looks almost nervous before she averts her eyes and walks away.

What, all of a sudden I make her anxious? Or had her father caught me touching her and given a look of disapproval? I don't want to read into it, so I don't. I go back to my post and watch as she sits down with her father at the baccarat table. Looks like the usual exchange of nods and introductions, and then Alex reaches into her purse and takes out a stack of bills.

Oh, hell no.

The dealer passes her a sizable pile of chips. At least five grand. Maybe ten. This is not the same woman who was upset over losing two hundred dollars. My first instinct is to go over, to tell her to stick her money in her purse and walk away, but as soon as I think it, I force my feelings back down. My reaction makes no sense. She's an adult. It's her choice to be here. Still, if I ever saw Elle do that, I'd feel the same way. Not that Elle would have close to that amount of money to drop on the tables.

I look back over right as Alex picks up a small stack of chips, hesitates, and sets them down on the top of the pile again. Her father nods as if giving her the go-ahead, and she picks up a bigger stack and places them on the felt. And now she's frowning down as the banker deals the cards from the shoe. I watch her play a few hands, noting that the whole table is alive with conversation, laughter even. All except for Alex, who sits like an unsmiling statue.

"Connor."

I look down and see that Maya's staring up at me. Fuck. How long was I ogling Alex from across the room?

"What's up, sweetheart?" I try to relax and give her a smile, but my heart's not in it.

"I'm done. Rack up for me." Her stiff tone and posture as she pushes the chair back reveal that she's *not* happy with me right now. I do as she says, scouring my brain for something to say to make up for slacking on the job. Nothing comes to mind, and it's just as well because Maya's already walking away.

I allow myself one brief glance in Alex's direction on my way out. Her eyebrows are drawn together in a frown, her arms propped on the edge of the table as she leans forward with her all of her attention focused on the action. My jaw is tight as I force myself to look away. This isn't the place for her, but it's also not my place to say.

Maya steps out in the hallway first, and I follow. There's an angry light in her eyes when she turns to face me, and I know she's about to chew me out. I totally deserve it for falling short on the job.

"Do you know them?"

I raise my eyebrows. "Who?" I keep my tone light, but as soon as I hear the question, I know that Maya saw. I know that she pinpointed exactly why I was distracted in there.

She takes out another cigarette and lights it, drawing in a long breath and exhaling before answering. "That pretty girl with the red hair." Her voice has a sharp edge to it. "Do you actually know her, or were you just fantasizing about getting your dick wet with a VIP?"

That gets my full attention. Maya does not usually talk like this. There's only one time that I can remember, and it was when she first approached me and offered me a job. Thanks to the background check, she already had the information about me she needed, but she'd been almost as blunt.

Like back then, my gut tells me I need to answer her truthfully. "Both," I admit. "I know her, yes."

Her eyes glimmer, and I realize that the spark that I saw in them earlier might not have been anger. More like interest. "And what about her father? Do you know him?"

"Haven't met him." I don't know where she's going with this, but I feel my back go up. I've worked for Maya for two years, but beyond what she knows from the investigation about my past, she doesn't really *know* me. Or ever ask me questions like this.

"All right." She takes another long draw of her cigarette and walks down the hall.

I catch up to her in three strides, glad that she seems satisfied. But curious now as to what the hell that was all about. I offer her my arm like I usually do, and she slips her hand through. And for a moment, everything feels almost back to normal.

"To your room?"

"Yes, I need to freshen up for din…"

We reach the end of the corridor, and Maya stops walking, her hand suddenly tight on my arm. I follow her frozen gaze and look off to the side.

He's leaning against a wall, his arms crossed over his chest and a vigilant expression on his face. Watchful. Waiting. Like a predator that's recently killed but interested in scoping out possibilities for his next meal. His eyes travel up and down Maya with an unacceptable level of boldness, and seeing it makes rage roil deep inside.

His attention shifts to me as he picks up on it, and he pushes up from the wall in a deliberately lazy move. He saunters forward, a shit-eating grin on his face.

"Brother. You are one difficult fucker to find."

15

CONNOR

Son of a bitch.

I can feel Maya's eyes flick between me and Cruz, blazing with curiosity and a little bit of fear. I need to get her out of here and away from *him*. But I don't want to be the first to break eye contact. I know he's intentionally fucking with me by showing up here, and the amusement I can read in his expression tells me he thinks he already won this round.

He has a harder set to his face than he used to, leaner and angular lines to his features that look carved out by years of drug use. His hair is longer than mine, slicked back and adding to the starkness of his appearance. It's not totally like looking in the mirror, but it's no mystery Maya was shocked when she saw him. He might have fooled Elle into thinking he's cleaned up, but I take one look at his eyes and can see that he's keyed up.

His attention isn't on Maya anymore, which is a good thing because every muscle in me is loaded and ready to strike. If he touches her or so much as takes another look at her like he was doing when we came around the corner… My hand twitches by my side, and Cruz's gaze immediately hones in on the slight movement. No doubt he's carrying, too.

Chill the fuck out. Roll with this.

"We're not doing this here. You were supposed to meet me tonight." My throat feels constricted, like my words have to drag through gravel to get out.

"I had a slight change in plans." He says it off-handedly, as though speaking to me after so long is nothing significant. His mouth twists in a smirk. "So you gonna ditch the bitch, or am I gonna have to take care of her, too?"

He doesn't say Laura's name, but he doesn't have to. It's like the seven years since I left Albuquerque never happened, and the fury within me erupts. I take a step forward, my free hand clenched in a fist. Maya lets go of my arm, releasing me to charge forward.

But then Cruz slowly crosses his arms across his chest, and I catch sight of the tattoo. It's a tribal design, in the shape of a scorpion that curls around his forearm, and I stop in my tracks.

The tension in the air is so thick I could chew on it. Cruz barks a laugh, and Maya… The tigress in her has her claws out, and she stares at him like she wishes she could set him on fire.

Without taking my eyes off him, I say to her, "I need to take you to your room. Now."

Maya doesn't respond verbally, but she pulls on my arm. If she shoots me a look at all, I miss it. Cruz and I are still locked in a stare-down, and he gives me a curt nod as we pass, his gaze as cold as ice.

"I'll be waiting right here for you, *little brother*."

Not going to bother replying to that, but his comment makes my blood boil. Born nineteen minutes earlier and that somehow gives him lifetime rights to talk down to me. That's gotta change. Right after I make sure Maya's safely in her room.

The edge of my anger blurs into concern as we head to the elevators for Maya's tower. She reaches out and squeezes my hand, and fuck, but it's not a gesture a client would give. Maya's genuinely concerned, worried *about me,* and I stare down at her, something in my chest constricting. It's bad news that Cruz hunted me down now of all times, that he saw me and Maya together. If he knows we walked out of a high roller room, then he knows she has money. Might as well paint a bright red target on her forehead.

I struggle for something to say to her. But I got nothing.

No clue how Cruz tracked me down, how he was able to find me here. He wouldn't have been able to find me by my current name.

A pit suddenly forms in my gut as I think I know. Elle.

If Elle betrayed my confidence, if she told him what I do for work, Cruz would have known to stake out the high roller rooms. But even then, what are the odds… Unless he paid off guards to watch for me and alert him when they spotted me. I wouldn't doubt it. Cruz always had this way of making things happen so he gets his way. Except when it comes to me. He didn't get his way when I left. Prior to that, he'd had grandiose visions of Cruz and Connor Marino, brothers in crime, like some original fucking miniseries for HBO.

Connor Marino. He ceased to exist as soon as I got to Vegas and changed my last name to Vincent. I'd kept my given name all through the SEALs because it was less complicated, but as soon as I got out here, I wanted a clean break. I didn't want anything linking me to my father or brother anymore.

Just goes to show that you can run all you want, but where you come from eventually catches up to you.

Maya stabs out her cigarette in one of the ashtrays by the elevator doors before swooping into the nearest one. I follow and punch the buttons for a random number of floors above and below Maya's floor, in case Cruz follows us and tracks the elevator to see where it stops.

She watches me do it, her forehead creased in a frown. "How much trouble are you in, Connor?"

"Don't know," I mutter, and it's not a lie. I rake my hand through my hair, my thoughts too scrambled to explain. "My brother and I aren't…on good terms."

She makes a sound that's not quite a laugh. "Yes. I figured out that much."

A group of teenaged girls with wet hair and towels dash into the elevator as the doors are closing. They hit the button for one of the lower floors, giggling over how many of the other buttons are lit up. I know they think it's a prank, and I wish to hell it was. Still holding hands, Maya and I ride in silence while the girls go on and on about some hottie that talked to them at the pool. One of them glances back at me furtively before giving me a shy smile, and I look away, my stomach dropping like a stone.

The pool. What if Cruz was tracking me all day? Spying on me and Alex? I have the craziest desire to call Elle to get Alex's number, to give her a heads up about… fuck, I don't even know. That my psycho twin brother is in town and she should run if she sees anyone who looks like a tweaked-out version of me?

Gotta keep my head on straight. I keep Maya's hand in mine, our fingers tightly interlaced as I walk her to her suite. It's a gesture that's usually too intimate between me and clients, but right now I need it, need the reassurance that I can keep Maya safe at least in this moment. I feel hyperaware of my surroundings, the back of my neck prickling every time I see a peephole that's blacked out instead of letting light through. Shit. I'm being overly paranoid now, and if I don't get it under control, Cruz *will* win.

Maya unlocks her door but hesitates, still frowning as she peers up at me. "I obviously don't know the whole story between you and your brother. But if there's anything I can do to help –"

I shake my head before she can finish. "No. You can't get involved in this. He's way too fucking dangerous."

Her eyes widen in alarm, and part of me wishes I could take the words back, but I feel like she has a right to know. I release her hand, taking a breath to steel myself for the rest. "Mrs. Coplin, I think it would be best if my partner took over your protection during the rest of your stay."

Her mouth forms a round "O," her hand flying up to cover it. And damn if I don't think I see moisture spring into those baby blue eyes before I glance away like a coward.

"His name is Neil Dufort," I say to the door. "Of course you can do the background check on him if you'd like. He served with me in the same platoon. I trust him with my life, or I wouldn't be asking you to do the same."

"No, honey. I only work with you."

I stiffen at hearing the endearment, and she goes on in a softer tone. "I'll bag out on my evening session. I can make up the time later. Honey, I don't want you to feel like you're in this alone."

That "honey" thing. She's not saying it like we do when we banter back and forth. I shouldn't matter to her. I *can't* matter to her. Her tone has a tinge of desperation to it, and I have to stop this.

I channel a tiny bit of Cruz and look her in the eye with calculated coldness. "I can't ask you to do that. I'll call Neil and have him fill in for me until further notice."

She blinks. "Connor, I don't understand. Did I miss something downstairs? Your brother only said he wanted to talk to you, and you told me that you didn't know what was going on. Why don't you see how things go with him first and then decide?"

I switch tactics, lift her hand to my lips and kiss it as her eyes continue to plead with me for understanding. "Maya, my brother is a threat that I can't take out by conventional means." I grit my teeth for a second, wishing to hell that it would be that easy. "The choice is ultimately yours, but I would feel better if we went this route. Just for a day or two."

She looks down at her hand after I release it, and tigress Maya is finally all the way subdued. "All right. For a day or two. And your partner... Neil? I'll work with him under the condition that he checks in with you every day."

"Deal."

"What does he look like, so I know it's him when he shows up?"

I nod, thinking the same thing. "Black guy around my age, a few inches shorter than me, brown eyes, cleft chin, muscular. Dresses pretty casual."

Maya nods back and strokes her hair a little absently, like her head's already somewhere else. I wait until the door clicks behind her and the bolt engages before I walk away.

Neil Dufort and I were SEALs together, and he's a totally solid guy. He's originally from Colorado Springs but after his deployment was up, came out here to help his ailing mom. She passed away last year, and he's been working on getting his engineering degree, doing the security thing part-time. The only reason he partnered up with me is because I asked him if he would. He has a different working style than I do, simple and with very little small talk. Given how short Maya has seemed the past day or so, maybe that'll be a good thing.

I go to my contacts list and hit his number. He and I don't call each other unless it's an emergency. Even though we're business partners, we have our own client lists and work mostly autonomously these days.

"What do you need?" he says right away.

"I need you to take Maya Coplin for me. At least for a day but potentially longer." I give him the lowdown of her schedule in brief. "Can you do it?"

His silence fills the line. He knows exactly who Maya is, and he also knows that the fact that I'm turning her over to him isn't good. But Neil is a strictly need-to-know guy, and he doesn't ask me what's going on.

"I can do it."

"Thanks, man. I owe you one." I take another minute to fill him in on her details. Hotel name, room number, the agreement that he check in with me every day. I have a feeling Maya will either try to work her charms on Neil or give him hell. Either way, he can find out about her eccentricities himself. "And Neil?" My hand clenches into a fist before releasing. "My brother is in town. Tell me if you see him. We're twins, so you'll know it if you do."

There's another small hesitation. "Sure, Connor. I'll check in with you in the morning."

I end the call, feeling like the burden is only slightly off my chest. Neil's a formidable and dangerous guy — not that I'm not, but he's more of the thug type than the boy toys that Maya prefers. She'll be in good hands with him, especially if I'm not around to draw Cruz near.

Maya's statement about waiting and seeing what Cruz wanted was perfectly logical. Except it wasn't accurate — I told her I didn't know how much trouble I was in, not that I didn't know what's going on. And Cruz said much more than that without verbalizing it. He deliberately displayed his tattoo on his arm to me, like a beacon and horrific reminder of who he is.

Message received, loud and clear. He's here representing the gang.

Cruz is standing in the same place, leaning against the wall but now with half a glass of whiskey in his hand. He doesn't look at me or acknowledge my presence until I get within earshot.

"God, I love this fucking city. I need this kind of sweet action back at home." He nods appreciatively as a cocktail waitress walks by.

I bite back what I really want to say, that I'll get him all of the cocktail waitresses he wants if he gets the hell out of my city.

"What do you want?" I demand.

Cruz turns his full attention to me, his gaze hard, impenetrable. "You haven't changed a bit, little brother. You still have shit for patience."

"Interesting you'd say that." I keep my voice steady, low. "You're the one who couldn't wait a few short hours to meet as planned. Might as well get down to business."

He raises an eyebrow before tipping back more whiskey. "You wanna do this here then? Or somewhere where we can actually talk?"

Talking to him like this feels too familiar, like we picked up right where we left off seven years ago. I don't like it.

I start walking toward the sports bar, which isn't too crowded this time of the day, Cruz matching me step by step. We're a world away from the streets of Albuquerque. But something about us being together now stirs up the same feelings as back then. Cruz exudes that same insane level of confidence, like he's invincible and can take out anyone that gets in his way. I'm sure that attitude is what got him picked up in the first place by the street gang, one of dozens in the city. He'd talked up the lifestyle to me, tried to convince me to join him.

If that's why Cruz is here now, if he wants me to join, I can tell him to go to hell. I was never affiliated with them, aside from having Cruz as my brother. But I can totally envision Cruz getting himself into a mess back home and trying to pull some shit move. Trying to use his Navy SEAL brother as collateral or something.

We get to the sports bar area, and I gesture to a free table against the wall. Cruz nods his assent and takes the lead again, beckoning to a waitress as we sit down. She walks over briskly, her eyes shifting back and forth between me and Cruz. I know her from having been here with clients before, a brunette named Heather who's working her way through law school at UNLV. She's good at her job, doesn't take shit from customers, and I'm honestly sorry she's going to have to deal with my brother.

"Hey, Connor. Didn't know you had a twin." She balances her tray on her hip, giving me a wink. "What can I bring you two?"

Cruz leans back in his chair and grins. "My brother probably wants a Guinness. And I want you on your hands and knees after you get off work. Unless Connor's already fucked you, then bring me someone else."

Heather's eyebrows shoot straight up, and she flicks me a look that reads, *Are you shitting me?*

"You can go up to the bar and get your own drink," she snaps at Cruz. "Connor, what do you want? And no offense, but your brother's an asshole."

I stare back at her. Oh…hell. The look is meant for my brother, but it stirs up a recent memory. That's pretty much exactly the look that Alex gave me the very first time I'd met her. At the bar when I hit her with a line not any better than Cruz's.

It's a miracle that she even talks to me. And let me kiss her. My brother's an asshole, but I haven't been any better than him in that department.

"Make that a Sin City Amber for me." I give her a grim smile. "And yeah. Tell me about it."

Cruz looks amused as she leaves, and when he turns to me, his entire demeanor changes. He sits up straight, a greedy shine in his eye. My guard is already up, but I heft on another layer.

Stay cool.

He bares his teeth in a smile. "Elle tells me that you've been doing well for yourself here."

I bristle at how he says it, like he and Elle are tight and I'm the one that's been out of the picture for almost a decade. "You have her fooled into thinking that you're a good guy now, but she'll catch on to you if you stick around. She's not stupid."

His eyes narrow. "She believes what she wants to. We all do. She believes that *you're* good, doesn't she?"

I know how Cruz is, know how he good he is at manipulating people. But what he says hits me hard anyway. Because Elle does believe it, that I'm a good guy, and I'm not sure I totally deserve that. Some things you can't leave behind, no matter how hard you try.

I try to hide my reaction from him, but he's watching me like a hawk, and I know from the smirk on his face that he sees it. But Heather walks over right then with my beer, her body language deliberately shutting Cruz out.

"Here you go, hun. I put it on your tab."

"Thanks, sweetheart."

Cruz's eyes zoom in on her ass as she walks away, and I notice it more this time. I force down the bile in my throat as he turns to me, his eyes gleaming. "Goddamn. That's some prime pussy right there, yeah?"

"Wouldn't know," I grit out. "But I can tell you that she's more than that."

He barks out a laugh. "Yeah, well, she looks like a cocktail waitress to me. Same fucking thing." He smiles, but it doesn't reach his eyes. "You know what? I'm really happy for you. It's obvious you found yourself a good little niche out here."

I lean forward, my patience at its limit. "C'mon. You don't give a damn about me or Elle, or anyone unless you want something. So tell me what it is. You were the one who hunted me down today. Why? Afraid of Elle being around to witness your bullshit?"

He drums his fingers on the table, his smile gone. "She has good intentions, but I don't want her involved in this, no. Elle served her purpose in telling me how to find you."

I can see it, how he thinks he's wearing a badge of honor because he's sparing Elle from this madness. Never mind the fact that she *wants* to give Cruz a second chance, that she actually has some hope from him. As far as I'm concerned, I don't want him around anyone I care about. He's totally unpredictable, a loose cannon that can fly off the handle at any moment. But I know it's going to hit Elle hard if he breaks off contact from her after this visit.

"You and I were done seven years ago." I stare at him in contempt. "Don't tell me you're here to ask for my forgiveness."

He narrows his eyes. "I'm gonna be straight with you. Things have been kinda crazy at home. Dad's been really sick lately. In fact, he's dying. Lung cancer, in case you give a shit…"

Cruz's home, not mine. And no, I don't give a shit about our father. Not even if he's dying.

"…and business has been okay lately. I've been doing all right. But not as good as you're doing. And it got me thinking. You and Elle being out here living the good life and me all by myself."

I suddenly know where he's going with this. No. Hell no. His "business" isn't even equivalent to what I do, not equivalent to what any sane person would do. If he says what

I think he's going to say, that he wants to be out here, that wants me to hand over even a fraction of what I've worked so hard for, I'm gonna lose my shit.

"Leave Elle out of this," I growl. "This is between you and me."

"I told you. Elle's out. She doesn't owe me like you do, anyway."

Owe him. After what he did to Laura, I owe *him*? I'm tempted to take him out, to put an end to this right now. If it weren't for Elle, I just might.

"What are you talking about?" I snap.

"Right after Dad went after you with the bottle. When things got a little better after that." He leans forward, his eyes still narrowed and glinting like a slice of malice. "You didn't forget about all that shit we went through before you ran away to the Navy, did you?"

He glances at my left arm, and I hesitate. Of course I remember.

We were fifteen. Don't know why I bothered, but I was picking up beer bottles that our father had littered throughout the living room. I didn't realize one was almost full and spilled almost all of it on the carpet, not that it should have even mattered, because our carpet was pretty much trashed with spills and burn marks. But our father walked in and saw me trying to clean up the mess, and he happened to be high out of his mind. Smashed one of the bottles and came after me. I tried to fight back, but the broken glass sliced open my arm before I could.

I'll never get the image of Cruz out of my head from that day. Came rushing out of our bedroom with a baseball bat and yelling at the top of his lungs. Cracked our father across the shoulders and didn't let up on him when he crashed down to the floor. Cruz went ballistic, kicking him over and over again, his face twisted with murderous rage.

Things did get better after that. Our father never laid a hand on either of us again, and I focused on getting the hell out of there. I'd decided by that time that I'd try to get into the military and started spending my afternoons after school at the YMCA. My uncle – Elle's dad – knew a guy who volunteered there who was Navy SEAL, and he became my mentor, helped me prepare for the physical screening test and get my contract when I was eighteen.

"Why do you think Dad left us alone after that?" Cruz's voice is low, steady and in control. "You think he suddenly woke up one day and felt bad about everything? Or do you think maybe we got protection from someone else?"

Protection. It's like all of the air left my lungs, and I can't get another breath. I fight for it, struggle to understand.

"You...you got that gang of yours to protect us?" I stare at him in horror as he sits back in his seat with a smug look on his face. "Why? We were both pretty much out of the house by then. We survived that long. We would have made it without *gang protection*. You didn't have to do that."

His expression contorts, flips from smug to furious in two seconds flat. His hands clench into fists, his body almost shaking with rage.

"But I did. And now I'm here to collect," he snarls. "Elle told me what you do. I want a piece of your action here, brother. Hook me up with those rich assholes you work for."

"No." I keep my voice even, firm. "That would never work, not with your background."

He shrugs, like he already knows this. "I'm not talking 'bout working for you. These fuckers are so rich you could easily skim off their winnings without them knowing. Pay me a percentage of their winnings – I'll let you decide what you can get away with – and in exchange I'll offer extra protection." He grins, looking all the more like a wolf. "From me."

I feel like I'm burning up inside. I don't want to listen to any more of this bullshit, but now that he has the opportunity, he won't shut up.

"Or give me an in to this city. You have a lot of local contacts here. Bellhops, concierges, dealers, cocktail waitresses. All you gotta do is make the introductions, set up my street cred for me here, and I'll take care of the rest. Expand out on what I'm already doing back home." He taps his temple with a fingertip. "See, I thought it out ahead of time so I could provide you with all sorts of options."

I shove back my chair and stand up. He stays seated, looking calmly up at me, and part of me feels sorry for him. I'm sorry he felt like he's had to make the choices that he did. I'm sorry he feels like the only way he can ask for help is by using Elle and threatening me. If anything, maybe I can appeal to the criminal logic that sure as hell has to be up in his brain somewhere.

"You're crazy if you think you can come to Vegas and do what you've been doing back in Albuquerque. Vegas territory is all staked out by people way more powerful than you. They'll bury you within a week if you try to pull your bush-league shit here, get that?"

He looks taken aback, but just for a second before he recovers. "Aw, that's sweet, little brother. You still care."

I glare at him. "Go back home. Start over. Clean up your life."

He glances down at his tattoo. "Can't do that. I got special permission for this little vacation, to catch up with family. I'm here through the month, so you have plenty of time to decide on your answer. We need to get over this bad blood between us, Connor. Look…" His voice changes, becomes smoother. "I know you'll never forgive me for Laura. I've accepted that. But I hope you'll be willing to move on."

Motherfucker.

He has no right to say her name. The guilt over Laura, self-loathing for myself, hatred for Cruz, everything I've harbored inside me mixes like chemicals in a volatile reaction. I've kept it all inside me for years, and it suddenly detonates. I jump across the table and grab him, and I have just enough time to register his grin before I throw a hard punch to his jaw. He staggers and falls back into his chair, and I really want to go after him again, to bust open his face for that comment.

Fuck this. I'm breathing hard, every muscle in my body tight because he riled me up, and he's sitting there shaking from silent laughter as he rubs his chin. He can go to hell.

"The answer's no," I snap. "And that's not ever gonna change." I start to walk away, but he calls out my name.

"Connor." His voice is sharp, and despite my better judgment, I stop and listen.

He stands up too, walks over to me, and leans forward so the stench of whiskey fills the space between us. His face turns hard, all traces of humor gone.

"If you say no, I *will* go to Elle. She has contacts in this city, too. And I might be wrong, but she actually still likes me." He adds firmly. "I'll give you til the end of the month to think about it."

The end of the month — just over three weeks away. I won't need that long to tell him *no* again, but throwing Elle into the mix like that makes me hesitate. I think he's bluffing, though I do have to wonder what the hell he's going to be doing here for that entire time. It's been years, but I still know my brother, and there's no fucking way he'll just be sightseeing or lying by the pool.

At the very least, I'll convince Elle what a bastard he is. I start to walk away.

"Connor, who is she?" he calls from behind me. "*¿Quién es la puta?* What's she to you?"

Who's the whore? I stop in my tracks, an angry tic in my jaw as he adds, "She's one sexy piece of ass. Though I gotta say. I thought you always went for the blondes, not the redheads."

My hands clench, my blood rushes, and when I turn around, he's wearing that shit-eating grin, the same one he had when I first spotted him in the hallway. Before I played into everything he wanted.

I almost go after him again for making the comment about Alex. But if he already has the advantage in this game, I can at least demand one thing in exchange.

My hand lands on the butt of my Sig, and I know he sees it. "Okay," I spit out. "I'll give you an answer at the end of the month. But on one condition. You promise to stay the hell out of my life until then. And leave the people in it alone."

He holds up his hands in mock defeat. "Sure thing, brother. I promise I won't interfere. But I'm gonna be vacationing here on a regular basis soon, and that's a fact you're gonna have to live with."

I walk away without another word, the implications of all of this tearing at me and leaving a gaping hole in my gut. He can't, he *can't* be in the same city as Elle and me.

16

Alex

I'm on a crazy ride, and there better be a way off soon. Lose almost all of my chips in the first half hour. Get some back more in the next half hour. Dad keeps patting my back and telling me that I'm doing great, but throwing away almost five grand in an hour makes me feel like puking all over again.

When I was thirteen, Dad gave me a quarter and let me play it in a slot machine. Totally illegal. But I wound up getting ten quarters back, I was excited, and I went to spend it on something dumb. The end. *This* is nothing like that. This is too much more of a roller coaster with no seat belts. I must be wired more like Mom because I have no clue how Dad can possibly enjoy it.

It's the end of a hand, and I slump back in the high-backed seat and look around for Connor. But he and the woman he works for aren't in the room anymore, and I sag even further in my seat as I feel let down.

My eyebrows knit together in a frown as I catch myself feeling this way. Stupid of me to feel disappointed that he didn't say goodbye before he took off. Oh, man. Elle's going to give me such crap for this if she ever finds out. Tease me for having kind of a thing for her *cousin*. You'd think I'd never gotten with a guy before. And I haven't even gotten with Connor.

Though judging from the way he kisses, I think I'd probably like it.

My phone vibrates in my bag, and I peek inside. Don't recognize the number, but it's from the 702 area code. Probably Elle calling from the club, which is very likely the universe's way of getting back at me for thinking terribly impure thoughts about her cousin.

"Be right back, Dad," I whisper.

He gives me a distracted nod, and I move away from the table like I've noticed some of the other players doing to take calls. I hit answer as I'm walking past the towering pink orchids.

"Hey," I say.

There's a short pause, and a male voice says, "Alex?"

Oops. *Not* Elle. "Who's this?" I ask cautiously. No one else in Vegas knows my number besides Elle.

"It's Connor. I made Elle give me your number. I need to talk to you…"

I blanch. It's official. The universe is definitely messing with me. Something's off about his voice, and it takes me a second to even recognize it as being Connor. He sounds way on edge, and it makes my own anxiety levels rise.

"Yeah, sure." I perch on the edge of a velvet-upholstered couch. "What's up?"

"Not on the phone. Can we meet in person? Somewhere private?"

Whoa. I think his voice just cracked. I don't know the guy, not really, but I'm suddenly worried about him. I lean forward and glance over at my dad. He's still playing, not looking around for me or anything, and I'm going to go out on a limb and say my first high limit gambling lesson can end early.

Connor's silent on the other end, and I rack my brain for somewhere to go. I'm *not* about to invite him to my room, but all of the VIP floors have these little lounges that are usually pretty dead.

"Sure. You want to meet me in the lounge on my floor? I can be there in about fifteen."

He exhales. "Great. See you then."

He ends the call before I can ask him if he remembers which floor I'm on. I tap my fingers on my knee, thinking. Maybe I should call Elle to see if she knows what's going on, but I'm pretty sure she's at work right now. I give it a shot anyway, but it goes straight to her voicemail. It's just as well – I'd have to explain too much. Plus, given that I told Connor fifteen minutes, I have to get a move on.

I go up to Dad and tap his shoulder, and he jerks in surprise. Like he maybe forgot for a minute that I was gone. "Oh, Alex." He blinks at me. "Is everything all right?"

"Yeah, I'm fine. But I need to meet a friend right now." I feel a huge sense of relief as I hear myself say it. So glad that I'm done. "You want the rest of my chips?"

"No, no. Take them to the cashier cage. Yours for next time. Did you have fun?"

I smile at him. This is a big deal for my dad, I know. Kind of like the first time he took me fishing (still not my favorite thing).

"It was great. Thanks."

"Good job today." He reaches out and pats my arm before turning around, and I bite my lip. I think about asking if he means that this is going to be a daily thing, but I save it for later. Cashier cage. Right.

I walk my chips over to the cage and hand them over to a rail-thin man. He doesn't make eye contact with me as I ask for hundreds. He's probably trained to do the whole discreet thing, and I kind of marvel at how quickly his bony fingers separate out my chips into different denominations. I glance down at my phone and see I only have twelve minutes left.

"Ma'am?"

I look up, and stack of bills is sitting on the counter for me. It's a lot smaller than when I walked in but still a hell of a lot more than I'm used to carrying around.

"Cool. Thanks!" I stuff the money in my purse and flash him a smile, and he looks at me in mild surprise and gives me a tentative smile back. Maybe I should have used a similar tactic with the grumpy cashier out in the main floor the other day instead of responding to her with bitchiness. Some people just need a little bit of sunniness and they respond in kind.

Speaking of needing some sunniness, I need to hustle and see what the hell is eating at Connor. He'd sounded wrecked, honestly. I'd been so intent on trying to think of a place to meet when he mentioned it had to be private, but instead, I should have demanded to know why the urgency. I pick up the pace and hurry through the rainforest and across the street, trying to kill all of my speculations, but my uncooperative imagination keeps cranking out possible scenarios. Maybe he got tired because he came over to talk to me in the high roller room. Or he's undercover for the Nevada Gaming Commission and is secretly trying to get dirt on my dad. Or he has a wife or girlfriend and wants to come clean with me after kissing me twice.

Oh, shut it, Alex.

He's waiting for me in the lounge when I get there. I'm not exactly surprised because I'm a good five minutes late, but I'm surprised at *him*. He's pacing around restlessly like a caged animal, his eyes wild as they zero in on me. His gaze travels over me from head to toe like he thinks I might be missing a limb.

My own eyes are drawn to his waist, where I can see just the handle or butt (whatever it's called) of his gun sticking out of his jacket. Okay, had something big happened in the high roller room that I missed? Now that I'm actually here, there's no point in speculating. The lounge is set up with a few café-style tables and reading chairs, and more importantly, there's no one else here. I point to the nearest table.

"Hi. You want to sit?"

"Yeah." He does that big exhale thing again, like he was holding his breath while he was waiting. We sit across from each other, and he pushes his hand through his hair.

My turn to wait as his eyes drop down. "I don't know where to start," he says, and he sounds completely miserable.

His fingers drum nervously on the table. One second I'm staring at them and the next I'm reaching out and putting my hand over his. He surprises me by flipping his hand over and grasping mine.

"Start at the beginning?" I suggest. His hand feels nice, warm and strong and a little rough.

He coughs a humorless laugh, no trace of a smile on his lips. Those very sensual lips. I collect myself, focusing back on him.

"We'll be here for hours if I start at the beginning," he says.

"Okay. Give me the bullet points then."

He nods, his forehead creasing as he concentrates.

"I have a twin brother named Cruz. Haven't seen or spoken to him in seven years. He's bad news, loses control easily, relies on violence instead of reason. He's part of a street gang back where we grew up." He takes a breath and frowns down at our linked hands. "He's in Vegas now. He tracked me down, wants to edge in on my action. Wants to make contacts and expand his operations here. Threatened to involve Elle if I said no."

Shit just got real. This is heavy stuff. Okay, granted, when I first saw Connor in the lounge, it *might* have crossed my mind that he was all upset because he shot someone, which would be equally heavy. But that was a fleeting thought, more inspired because of the way he was acting so off and because I'd seen his gun.

The way he's talking, this sounds like it might be just as bad.

"Oh, Connor…" I close my hand more tightly around his, trying to get a handle on this at the same time. "So, okay. I'm sorry if I'm slow, but he wants to edge in on what you do with security? Incorporate it into the gang stuff somehow?" The words are so foreign that they feel strange coming from out of my mouth.

He nods once, still looking miserable. Man, I wish I had a magic wand to make all of this go away for him. But I still don't get why he's telling me these things, why it was so crucial that he got my number from Elle and meet me. That edge that's in Connor's voice slowly creeps over to me.

"You just met with him?" It makes sense, given how night-and-day he is now compared to when I'd talked to him in the other casino.

"Yeah." His voice is raspy. "He caught me and my client coming out of the high roller room. Probably paid off a guard to call him when he saw me."

The high roller room. I shiver, thinking about how I'm mostly glad I missed that whole thing. But also what a sight that would have been, to see Connor and his twin brother facing off.

"How bad of a guy is he?" I ask.

He finally lifts his gaze and meets mine, the expression in his eyes dull. "Bad."

I swallow. "Has he ever killed anyone?"

"Sure."

Sure? My mouth opens, but what I was about to ask doesn't come out. *What about you, Connor? Have you ever killed anyone?*

"Why are you telling me all of this?" I whisper.

"He or someone who works for him saw you and me together, Alex." His jaw tightens. "Either at the high roller room or at the pool. He made a point of bringing it up."

My hand jerks away from his like he burned me. I didn't think it could get any worse, but I gape at him as a series of mini-heat bombs go off in my chest.

"What? What do you mean he made a point?" I manage to keep my voice low and steady, even though I really feel like yelling. What is Connor even saying? That his evil twin thinks I'm a potential "contact," whatever the hell that even means? He'd better answer me instead of sitting there like a grim-looking lounge fixture.

"What. Was. The. Point?" I repeat.

He shrugs. "Scare tactic."

That's it? That's all he's got? Well, as far as scare tactics go, it seems to be working. I close my eyes and make myself take a few slow breaths. Inhale. Exhale. The smartest thing for me to do would be to walk away right now. Or run.

My eyes fly open. Elle. This Cruz guy is her cousin, too.

"What about Elle?" I demand. "Does she know about any of this? I'm assuming she knows how dangerous he is?"

"Don't know if she realizes how dangerous he is. He was good to her when we were kids, and she remembers that."

I search Connor's face, and he looks as conflicted as his voice sounds. Like he's afraid to put an end to this guy Cruz's madness because he's afraid of how Elle will take it. But that's not acceptable. At the very least, he needs to make Elle understand. If she doesn't realize it, and *I can* within ten minutes of listening to him, he didn't try nearly hard enough.

"What do you mean you don't know? Why don't you know?" I snap. "Did you even *try* telling her?"

My irritation finally seems to hit home with him, and he looks at me angrily. About time. At last something we can use.

"Of course I tried," he growls. "But she's at work and won't answer anything but texts."

I'd tried to call her too and it had gone straight to voicemail. "You should have tried harder," I say in a cutting tone.

"Right, because leaving her a message or text with all of this would be the way to go," he says sardonically. "Or storming over there and making her freak out during her shift. At least I was able to get your number from her." He rises, his chair almost tipping back in his haste to get up. "Don't know why I fucking bothered."

His eyes are full of fury as he glowers down at me, but I'm not afraid. I stand and plant my palms down at the table and glare back at him.

"You bothered because you like me. And it's a damned good thing you did because now I'm going to drag your sorry ass to the bar so you can talk to Elle like you fucking well should."

Oh boy. His overuse of profanity is rubbing off on me. I'm breathing hard, and he stares back at me in shock. And then he coughs that almost-laugh again.

"Fine." He might even be smiling a tiny bit. "You win. Drag my sorry ass to the bar."

I surprise him again by reaching out and taking his hand. He becomes very still for a second but then I can almost feel some of that tension in him dissipate as his fingers close around mine.

Looks like this one responds well to a mixture of sunniness and bitchiness.

"Fine," I say back. "You drive."

17

CONNOR

Laura was my first girlfriend, the only "real" one I've ever had. Platinum blonde hair that smelled like apples, beautiful creamy skin, a great smile that lit up my whole world. She moved to Albuquerque in tenth grade, and amazingly, she liked me. In retrospect, maybe it was because I was the guy she shouldn't have been with, the boy from the wrong side of the tracks. We promptly lost our virginity to each other at a party one weekend, and that's mostly what we did after that. Hung out on weekends when she could manage to sneak out of the house. Had sex a lot.

I knew she was intrigued by him from the moment she met him. Even back then, Cruz was the one who could lay on the charm so thick but in a way the girls didn't know what hit them. By then, he was already running with the gang and was coming to school less and less, but he still showed up at the parties. Sometimes I'd catch him staring at me and Laura, and I didn't think anything of it.

Cruz was my *brother*, and I thought that there was no way he'd betray me.

It was graduation weekend, and Laura and I had been together for two years. I'd been seeing her less frequently by then because I was so busy with my physical training. Cruz had already moved out of the house, and he convinced me to move in with him. He was able to afford a two-bedroom apartment with money from his "job." I didn't exactly know what he was doing out there, only that he was pulling in enough money to pay for most of our expenses. The place was pretty much a hole, but it was ours.

I ran up the steps of our building that night, late for a date with Laura because my mentor kept me at the gym longer than I planned. I heard Cruz and some chick getting it on when I walked into the apartment. That was another difference between us – Cruz never brought the same one back to his room twice. He mocked me because I'd been exclusively dating Laura, gave me shit about how stupid I was being free for the first time of my life and tying myself down.

Our bedrooms in the apartment were across the hall from one another, and I headed into mine right as Cruz came out of his, bare-assed and holding a bottle of whiskey in one hand and an empty glass in the other. I knew he was high as soon as I saw his eyes.

Anger I didn't know I had shot to the surface to see him like that. I knew Cruz drank, but to see him get high exactly like our father sparked my contempt for him. We'd agreed to never use, that we wouldn't travel down that same path that had led to our misery when we were growing up.

"What the hell are you doing?" I barked.

His eyes grew wide, his palms showing out in a defensive gesture. "Whoa, bro. No need to get all up in my face. Just having a little party."

Bullshit. I glared at him, my hands balling up into fists by my sides. "No drugs. We made a pact," I said through my teeth.

He swallowed hard, and I could almost taste his fear. But he shook it off in the next second.

"Aw, lighten up. I didn't take that much – gave most of it to my date," he boasted, but then his smile faded and he looked away.

I glanced down at the glass in his hand and saw the pink lipstick marks on it when I heard a moan from his room. I frowned. Cruz's whole attitude was off. And there was something about that moan, the color of that lipstick…

I stared at him as the sick realization hit me.

I pushed past him and into his room. And found Laura, naked and barely conscious. He'd gotten her drunk, drugged her, had sex with her.

I froze. I should have taken her to the hospital right then and there, but I fucking froze because I was afraid of being arrested if I brought her to the hospital like she was. Or at the very least I was afraid that I'd be brought in for questioning. I left the apartment, called 911 from the gas station on the corner.

Laura wound up making it, but she almost didn't. She almost died.

I hold onto Alex's hand like she's mine, and I don't want to let her go.

Elle does a double-take when Alex and I walk into the bar together. I realize what it must look like with us holding hands like this, but I don't care.

She storms over, a grin on her face. "Whoa! What's going on, you two?" She stops in her tracks and glances at her watch, her smile disappearing as she looks at me. "You're not due here for another three hours. Just came here to hang out, or what?"

Alex gives me a sideways look, and I walk up and put my arm around Elle's shoulders. "No, I came here to talk to you about Cruz."

Elle's eyes shift from between me to Alex in confusion.

"I told him to come," she says with a shrug. Alex's expression is open, encouraging. "You need to hear this."

"O...kay."

Elle looks around to see if anyone needs service, but including us, there might be a total of five people here. She dumps her tray at the bar, and the three of us head to the back room. It's quickly becoming our regular place for slamming each other with Cruz-related news.

We crowd into one of the curved booths, Elle and Alex on either side of me. Alex slides her hand into mine again, and I lace my fingers with hers.

It feels better somehow, having her here with me.

"Cruz found me earlier today. He was staking out the high roller room." I glance down at Alex. "The room where Alex and I both were."

Elle's face turns as white as a sheet, but I keep going before she can say anything. I tell her everything Cruz said to me, aware that Alex is also hanging on every word. Elle sits like a stone until I'm done.

"Oh, shit." She turns away, but not quickly enough to hide her tears. Her silence is my answer, the answer to the question Alex asked me about whether Elle knew what kind of person he is. I don't doubt that he fed her all of the bullshit lines that he could come up with, and I don't doubt that she desperately wanted to believe him.

Like the bastard said, we believe what we want to.

I slide my free arm around her and hug her hard to my chest. She half sobs-half gulps, and I rest my chin on top of her head. "It's gonna be okay, Elle."

She pushes away from me. "How? How the hell is it going to be okay? He's not going to take no for an answer. He could ruin your business that you worked so hard to build up." She swipes at the tears that are flowing freely down her cheeks now. "This is my fault. I shouldn't have ever taken his calls."

"Not taking his calls wouldn't have stopped him from coming here and finding Connor." Alex says it in a quiet but firm voice. "You know that, right?"

"Yeah… I guess." She sighs and looks at me through wet lashes. "I'm so sorry, hun."

I pull her to me again, and she sags against my side. Now that I came here and told her, I don't know what to say to make things better for her. Alex squeezes my hand, like she can feel the pain ripping through me.

"We have until the end of the month to figure out how to get him to go away," Alex says.

I stare down at our linked hands, currents of warmth going up my arm as her thumb strokes my palm. She included herself in that statement, and I can't let her do that. I can't let either of them involve themselves in this.

"*I* have until the end of the month to figure it out," I correct. "This is my problem, not either of yours."

"If you really and seriously think that, you can go screw yourself, Connor," Elle says loudly, glaring at me. "Alex and I. We're smart, we have connections in this city too, and we'll come up with something to help you."

"Hell no," I growl. "You two don't understand what you're saying."

Alex nods, and there's fire in her eyes. "I think we both do, and I second all of Elle's words. You're stuck with us."

Elle crosses her arms, her jaw set to match her stubborn stance. The prospect of either of them approaching Cruz about this is enough to make me sick, crazy, or both. But if I tell them to stay out of it, that'll pretty much guarantee they'll act on whatever brilliant idea they come up with. Without me.

"Fine," I concede, but I hope my expression reveals how unhappy I am about it. "You can help think of ideas, but you have to promise not to *do* anything aside from that."

They exchange silent glances, Elle looking dubious and Alex looking more confident.

"Promise," Elle finally says.

"I promise," Alex adds.

We leave Elle after agreeing to get together later in the week, and I drive Alex back to her hotel with the music cranked up in an attempt to drown out the thoughts crashing in my head. It's bordering on ridiculous. I've been trained to kill when necessary, but I can't do that in this case because it's *him*. I'm trained in intelligence, but somehow Cruz is the one who's given himself the upper hand by using Elle and even Alex as collateral. I glance over at Alex and know I did the right thing by warning her.

"What the most important thing to Cruz?" she suddenly says.

I turn down the volume and consider this. She's been pretty quiet since we left the club, like she's been thinking as hard as I've been. I don't know the answer to her question, but it's an interesting one. Still, I wish she'd let it go.

She's sitting with her sunglasses on, her head turned to look outside. It's just before six in the evening and the brightness of the sun is a little surreal. It feels like it should be midnight, this day has been so long. I hear Alex's stomach rumble as if in agreement.

"You wanna grab something to eat?"

She turns her head and looks at me. The fire that was in her eyes, in her entire attitude since I first broke the news, is dimmer now, and a tired smile flickers on her face. "Yeah, weirdly enough, I could eat."

"Nothing that weird about it." I vaguely think about Maya's comment about needing occasional sustenance and remind myself that Neil will be checking in with me in the morning to report how that's going. Hopefully he's still in one piece.

Alex nods absently and starts tapping out a text. "Dad made dinner reservations at some French restaurant, but I'll tell them to go ahead without me."

I brake at a stoplight behind a huge line of cars to get on the Boulevard, and shoot her a look. "You sure? I can drop you off at your hotel."

"Nah. Honestly, I could go for a burger." She points to the In-N-Out Burger sign that's towering over I-15.

"Okay." I shrug. "We can do that. If you don't mind slumming."

I look over my shoulder and edge over into the lane that'll take us off the Strip. We creep forward with maddening slowness – it's typical of this time of day, but it makes my nerves feel even more shot than they already were.

Alex's fingers pause, and she sets her phone down on her lap as she whips around to face me. "Excuse me," she says in a sharp voice. "Exactly why am I slumming? Because of the burger or because of you?"

"Take your pick," I say wryly. "You're here on vacation with your family. You should be going to concerts and the spa and lying around the pool. Throwing away all of your cash at the tables with daddy. Not here with me trying to involve yourself in my gangster brother problem."

That spark is back in her eyes again, and it's out of anger. "Holy shit. You can be *such* an asshole sometimes."

"Another reason to stay away from me," I point out.

"You think that I'm just some spoiled rich kid? That I'm with you right now because your brother's in a gang and I want a little action with some hot and sexy 'bad boy'? Fuck you." She mutters, "You're not even that much of a bad boy."

I laugh out loud, hard. And it's like a floodgate opens that temporarily washes away everything. Anxiety over having Elle and Alex involved in this. Concern over Maya and how she's dealing with the change. Anger over Cruz having any sort of power over me.

"No?" I calm myself down and cock an eyebrow at her. "But you think I'm hot and sexy?"

Alex's face is still flushed from anger and annoyance, but she presses her lips together like she's trying not to laugh. "Like I'd ever tell you that. Hey. Drive-through, okay?"

I nod as I pull into the parking lot of In-N-Out, my mood crashing again. The burger joint is always busy because all of the people passing through on I-15 and locals getting off work shifts on the Strip. Don't know why I should care that she doesn't want to go in and eat with me, but I do.

This isn't like me. But given the wringer Cruz has put me through today, it's no wonder.

"What do you want?" I ask Alex as we start going through the line.

"A double-double, hold the onions, large fries, and a large chocolate shake." Her eyes widen innocently when I look at her. "What? I haven't had anything since brunch. A girl's gotta eat."

I shake my head and smile. She digs out her wallet from her purse as I edge the Audi up to the speaker to order, and I put my hand over hers to stop her.

"Let the asshole buy you dinner, sweetheart."

"Power," I say.

Alex and I sneak our dinners into the movie theater in her hotel. Some comic book superhero movie is playing, and we sit in the back row and start passing the bags of food around. I don't care about the movie – I'm mostly glad it's not some feel-good romantic comedy.

"Power?" She looks up from her fries and squints up at the screen.

I poke her arm. "Not up there. You asked me what the most important thing to Cruz is."

As far as personalities go, Cruz and I are evidence that having the same DNA doesn't mean much. Even when we were little, Cruz was always exerting dominance over other kids whereas I was more concerned about fitting in. He didn't try to exercise control over me, not at first anyway – growing up, he'd been protective of me more than anything else.

Cruz never told me what he was up to when he left the house, and I thought he was doing something like I was. He made his own choices, but I still wonder if things could have been different for him if I hadn't been so entrenched in my own thing. I'd noticed when he stopped coming to school, of course, but he insisted he was fine, that he'd gotten a job so he could get the hell out of the house. The aggravated assault charge came after he was involved in the gang, and thinking back on it, he should have spent more time in juvie than he had.

Power. Violence. My brother in a nutshell.

All of the signs were there. Maybe if I'd pressed the matter…

"Power hungry, huh?" Alex says, breaking through my reverie. "I guess I'm not surprised."

She doesn't say anything else about it, concentrating on eating and watching the movie instead. Sharing her fries and chocolate shake with me like we're on a date. We don't hold hands again, but she leans against my arm when we're done with the food. The movie winds up being a double feature, and I don't even mind – for the first time in years, I'm not on a schedule.

It's good, watching superheroes bust up stuff and save the world, and listening to Alex's detailed commentary about the characters and plot.

"How do you know so much about this stuff?" I ask at the start of the second movie.

She shrugs. "Graphic novels? I sort of got hooked on them when I was in high school."

"Yeah?" I glance at her, and maybe I can see this about her. "What else are you into? What do you like to do when you're back home?"

She's silent, and at first I think she's not going to answer my question. But then she lifts her chocolate shake and gestures to the screen. "I like to do stuff like this. What we're doing right now."

"Oh. Going out on dates, you mean." I can imagine the guys from New York wanting to be all over her, and I nod because it makes sense. What doesn't make sense is the flicker of jealousy that hits me.

I dismiss it, though. Alex and I are just hanging out, and it's nice. Though I'm very aware of how good it feels to have her pressed up against my arm. Much too aware of how her bare knee is just inches away from touching my leg.

She flicks a glance in my direction. "No, I meant I like to watch movies with friends. I don't really go out on dates very often." She hesitates. "Or lately, really ever."

"Me either," I say simply.

She doesn't ask me why not, and I don't ask her, either. We all have our reasons for what we do, and I get the distinct impression that she doesn't want to talk about hers.

We both fall silent as an explosion rumbles through the theater speakers, and I watch as a city becomes engulfed in flames. But I quickly lose interest in what little of the storyline there is, my attention shifting more to Alex. My interest in her far outweighs anything that the big screen could offer.

When the movie's over, I ride up the elevator with Alex and walk her to her room. Second time in the same day that I'm making sure that a woman I actually care about makes it back to her room okay.

Women I care about. It's a foreign thought to me, but it's true. Of course Maya, because of our long working history and because she opened up doors for me that wouldn't have been otherwise possible. And Alex. Because she has that spark and an attitude but also compassion. Because she's the cool girl who's not afraid to call me on my shit. And because I like her.

"Thank you," I say. "For dragging my ass to the bar."

"You're welcome. Thanks for dinner and going to the movies with me." She hesitates, her eyes searching my face like she wants to say something else.

I beat her to the punch. "This is going to sound all wrong, but I don't want to leave you alone tonight." It's not a pick up line. And it's impulsive of me, but I mean it. I'd feel better if I could be in the same room with her for at least some of the night.

Her lips part, and I watch as she draws in a deep breath. "My parents are two rooms down if I need them." Her voice is husky, and I want to *ask* her if I can come in this time. Instead, I nod and turn to leave.

"Connor," she whispers. "Wait."

I turn around, and she's holding the door wide open for me.

"Don't go."

18

Alex

I don't invite guys into my hotel room. I don't.

But I just did. Not because I felt like I wanted to be protected. Because I wanted to, and now Connor's stepping inside as I hold the door open. My pulse is hammering so hard that there's no way he can't hear that. He walks past me and into the room, and I shut the door behind us.

My room is pretty standard-sized with its own bathroom, and the majority of it taken up by my queen-sized bed. It's just as well because all I ever really do in here is sleep, but I suddenly wish the room was bigger so that the bed wouldn't have to be the focal point.

I sling my purse onto the dresser, and he walks the length of the room until he gets to the two armchairs by the window. He takes a seat in one and runs his hand through his hair, his eyes on me as I kick off my shoes.

The way he's sitting there doing that unsmiling intense thing that he does when I've seen him working – it's a little unnerving, like he's watching over me. If he's going to go all security guard on me, maybe we'd be better off talking. Not about Cruz, though. I've been working too hard trying to get him to relax for the past few hours to start that up again.

"Despite all this," I say, gesturing around me, "I'm not a rich kid. Or spoiled."

Connor's expression doesn't change, like he's absorbing my words and taking what I say very seriously.

"I can tell you're not spoiled. I honestly don't care how much money you have."

"Okay…" His answer surprises me, but I'm not completely sure why. "But for what it's worth, I want to tell you," I say. "My dad's a CPA, and he does fine, but he socks away every single dime so he can do this each summer. I guess I've always thought it was his way of treating us to something nice when he's so busy the rest of the year. And my mom makes and sells custom-made jewelry on Etsy so she can buy new dresses and other stuff for the trip." I squeeze my eyes shut for a second. "Incidentally, if you ever tell her I told you that, you die."

He laughs, and it's the same one he let loose with in the car, like he's finally, finally, letting go. His laugh is resonant like his voice, and it's so sexy. I smile back at him, glad that my plan of burgers and movies helped him chill out a bit. I mean, really. If you're gifted with dimples like that, you might as well use them.

"I promise I won't tell her I know her secret." He cocks his head. "So what do *you* do? You said you were taking classes and working. Doing what?"

I perch on the edge of my bed and shrug. "Pre-nursing classes right now, and I'll be applying for programs this year. And I work part-time in a hotel restaurant so I can pay for my living expenses. Volunteer in the hospital when I have time."

I brace myself for some pervy comment about how he wouldn't mind me being his nurse, but he must be going for the strong silent type because he says nothing.

He's definitely not the same cocky jerkface that he was when he dumped my drink on me. Maybe because that kind of stuff is usually what people present on the surface, and Connor and I have gotten to know each other better since then. But even at the bar, he went out of his way to help me out.

It's not even midnight yet, but it feels so much later than that. I scoot back on my bed and sink into my veritable forest of pillows. Kissing Connor at the pool seems like it happened days ago instead of just this morning, and I close my eyes for a minute.

"You mind if I take this off?" I hear him say.

My eyes snap open. "Take *what* off?"

He lifts an eyebrow, pushing back the side of his jacket so I can see his gun. "My jacket and piece. Unless you want me to do more than that."

Ah, there we go. Pervy. But not really, because his comment doesn't come off as feeling creepy to me. More like he's teasing me for my overreaction. Like a friend would tease a friend.

"Haha. Sure, knock yourself out. Only your jacket and piece, I mean," I say pointedly. I lie back into my pillows again, and I'm suddenly very aware of the fact that he's checking me out as I stretch out. I'm all about equal opportunity, and I openly admire his body as he shrugs off his jacket. He's wearing a blue button-down shirt that looks custom-tailored to fit and absolutely amazing on him, but I almost renege and tell him he can take that off too.

"You ever have to use that?" I ask as he sets the gun on the table.

"I've had to pull it a few times."

I look him in the eye. "You ever have to kill anyone?"

He falls silent, and I feel the blood drain from my face.

"I'm Navy SEAL, sweetheart," he says quietly.

"Oh," I say. For once when dealing with him, I don't have a quick comeback. I hadn't known about the SEAL part, just what my mom had said about him being in the military.

"Why did you quit?"

"You never really quit the SEALs."

It's an evasive answer, not really an answer at all. He goes silent again, a slight frown furrowing his brow. Okay, so given the whole Cruz thing, maybe talking about his past, which (eek) may involve killing people isn't the greatest idea right now.

I close my eyes again. The entire rest of the suite is quiet, and except for the occasional noise from the corridor, it feels good to have temporarily shut out the craziness of everything outside my door. And I'm glad that Connor's here, because no matter how fearless I presented myself to him earlier, I think I would have been jumpy if I had to be here alone.

I meant what I told him, that I'd try to help him figure out a way to get rid of his brother. True, everything I know about street gangs could fit on a dust particle, but I'm good at working through problems and staying levelheaded while I do it. From what little I know about Cruz, I think staying levelheaded might be necessary.

"You going to sleep now?"

He says it quietly, and when I open my eyes, he's watching me. Probably has been the entire time.

"No," I say, but thinking about it makes me yawn anyway. "Going over things in my head. Sorry I'm such boring company."

"You're not." He'd unbuttoned his sleeves and rolled them up while I was busy being so boring. I watch as he flexes his arms in a stretch, enjoying the sight of the rest of him while I'm at it.

I don't usually go for guys like this. Not ones that are carrying around so many scars, figuratively and literally. But then again, I'm usually just looking for a good time. There's so much more to Connor than his sex appeal. Though I have to admit that it's definitely part of the draw.

I smile at him. "You can come sit next to me if you want. My bed is way more comfortable than that chair."

I hope I'm not blushing. So many ways Connor could take that statement, but the fact is that I invited him into my bed. I don't regret saying it, though. He's all the way over there, and I'm way over here, and I feel like we should be closer than that.

That gorgeous blue gaze of his sears through me. But he hesitates, like he wants to be sure my invitation was serious. There's plenty of room next to me, but I shift over even more so I'm facing him with my legs curled under me.

He takes my cue, gets out of the chair, and slowly walks over to the bed. He has a natural swagger to his walk, and the way his hips move is so hot that it makes me flush. I hold my breath until he stops, until he stands and looks down at me like he doesn't know what to do. My God. This beautiful man who's trained to kill looks completely unsure of his next move.

I hold out my hand to him, and he crawls into bed, reminding me of a prowling animal. He sits down so he's facing me, his fingers closing around my hand. A delicious shiver courses up my arm as he lifts my hand to his lips and kisses it. I turn my wrist so I can rub the slight stubble on his jaw.

He closes his eyes and exhales slowly. "I walked away from the SEALs because it was more of a means to an end than anything else."

My hand stills as I listen, and he presses it to his face as he goes on. "To prove to myself that I could do it. Originally it was my way of escaping the shitty situation at home. I worked so hard for it that I think I actually believed it was what I wanted, but once I was in the thick of things, I couldn't see myself making a career out of it." He opens his eyes and gives me a wry smile. "Not that I can see myself doing what I'm doing now for a career, either."

"Sounds to me like you just haven't found the right thing yet," I say. "Better to keep your options open than lock yourself into something. It's not like you're not doing well for yourself. I mean, look at you. Expensive car, nice clothes… fancy dinners at In-N-Out."

"Stop." He shakes his head at me, dimples in full effect. I love it when I can make him smile like that.

"Who knows?" I add. "Maybe I won't like being a nurse once I actually get to be one. I went through three different majors before I decided."

"No. You seem like you follow through with things."

I'm about to respond to that, but he lets go of my hand and trails his fingertips down my jawline, and whatever I was about to say flies right out of my head. I hold my breath as he traces a line along my collarbone, my skin tingling at his touch. His gaze locks with mine as they hesitate at the neckline of my shirt.

"I'm sure you do, too," I murmur. "Follow through with things."

He doesn't release me from his gaze as his fingertips follow the V of my shirt and travel over the swell of my breasts. I stare up at his face, little excited currents radiating through my belly as his hand hovers. On the verge of touching me. Leaning forward, his face so, so close. Deliberately keeping me in suspense.

Kiss me.

I close my eyes as he touches his lips to mine. Gently. That same surprising softness that he started with when he first kissed me in the pool. Gentle and slow, like he's tasting me for the very first time. Like he's not sure where I am with this and he's asking. I wrap my arm around his neck and kiss him harder to show him.

But he draws back a little, continuing to tease me with that slow and lazy kiss. His tongue flicks lightly against mine, his fingers make feather-light circles over one of my breasts, his knee brushes against my leg, and oh my God, every molecule of me aches for more. We're still sitting next to each other, and one of my pillows is wedged between us. Too much physical space separating us. Too many lingering worries in my brain. I want all of it gone except for him. I just want him.

I grab the pillow and chuck it to the side, slide my hand beneath his shirt, press my palm against his abs. His body tenses and then relaxes against my touch, and I move up slowly and revel in the feel of him, in the heat of him. Like he's on fire inside to match the beautiful burn that's starting to unfurl from my core. I spread my fingers out, feel him inhale and then slowly release his breath.

That shirt of his is too tight and has got to go. Really, and right now. I find his collar without breaking away from the kiss, my fingers flying down the front of his shirt undoing the buttons. He's all about gentle right now, and I'm not. I spread my hands out across his shoulders and push his shirt off the entire way. Break off the kiss and wrangle his t-shirt up and over his head. Incite a groan from him as I move to straddle him.

He runs his hands up my thighs, his eyes fiery and hungry and full of emotion. I'm wearing a skirt and very conscious of his touch, even more aware of the hot length of him through his jeans.

"Alex." His voice is rough. "I don't want to use you."

I stare at him, my heartbeat going wild as I try to make sense of what he said. Not that he doesn't want me but that he doesn't want to use me. Like having sex with someone equates to using them? Or is there more meaning behind that? I don't know, but the way he says it, the way he's looking at me in earnest makes me want to melt right into him.

I reach up and touch his forehead, push a stray curl back. I breathe, "Then don't use me."

The expression in his eyes shifts. Still desire, still hot, but like another flame burns on top of that.

He smiles a little bit before he leans into me. His mouth finds the sensitive part where my neck curves into my shoulder, and I whimper as he kisses me, as he applies more pressure and sucks. That softness from before is gone. Strong arms wind around me, and he lifts me up and then lays me down on my back. He braces himself up over me, his eyes searching mine for the longest time.

"Stay still," he whispers. "Don't move."

It takes everything I have to not throw myself at him. But I give him the tiniest nod, and he shifts his body down on me while I try to be still.

I'm trusting you.

My eyes flutter shut as he pushes my shirt up and kisses my navel. His tongue swirls around my piercing, his teeth nipping at it before his lips lay a slow path of kisses upward. He's holding the rest of his body away from me, and it forces me to focus on the singular sensation of his mouth on my skin. He pulls my shirt over my head, and I arch my back and help him. He pushes my bra down and out of the way, engulfs me in the warm and wet of his mouth, draws the moan right out of me.

I don't listen to orders. Run my nails over his shoulders, going crazy as his hand strokes my thigh with a commanding touch. Knot a hand in his hair when he gets to my panties. Hold my breath as he so, so slowly slides them down.

Please. Yes.

I gasp as he takes my nipple between his teeth. Releases me and lowers his mouth onto my other one so it doesn't feel left out. Caresses my inner thigh as I spread my legs apart for him. His fingers explore me, dipping into my wetness before centering on the spot that aches for him the very most, and my God, he knows exactly what he's doing. He's already pushing me toward the edge of bliss.

I don't want to go over without you.

He lifts his head like he heard me. I close my eyes as he rubs me in slow circles, as he makes me want more. Makes me want all of him.

"Alexis." His voice is low, raspy, and so amazingly sexy. It's the first time he's said my real name, and it feels good to hear it. I want him to say it again. All he wants.

I feel him shift his body up so his head is level with mine.

"Look at me."

I obey, and my heart stills for a moment. The expression in his eyes is hungry, but it's so much more than that. It's open, tender, full of emotion for me that I'm not sure I deserve. He covers my mouth with his again, his tongue sliding in at the same time that his fingers slip into me.

Oh. Oh my God.

He kisses me deeply, moves his fingers in the same rhythm, and I grab the sheets in a fist before letting go. Try to let go of more than that. My inhibitions, my barriers. I've never been with anyone who put me first like this. Never wanted so badly to meet someone in the middle. I want to have him, too.

Have him. Not forever, but for tonight. Because I can't really have him. Because this can't be more than what it is right now, in this moment. We're in my hotel room, not at my home, and I'm only here for the month. Dammit, and I shouldn't think about it, shouldn't dare to wish that it's any different than this. I can't. I shove the thought out of my brain so it won't bring me down off my high.

I reach down, rub my hand along the length of him and die a little. Oh... So unfair that he's still wearing his pants. I pull on his jeans, pop open his fly. He makes a very sexy groan as I slip my hand under his waistband, breaks the kiss off as he grabs my wrist.

I stare up at him, almost drowning in the blue of his eyes as he moves my hand away. "I want to make you feel good, too," I whisper.

He shakes his head. Slowly brings my arm over my head and holds it there. "No. Just you this time."

He's totally in control, and for this one moment, I let him be. Grip the sheets again like I'm holding on for dear life as he shifts down the length of my body. He moves so slowly, planting a trail of hot kisses as he descends, the skin he leaves behind burning for his touch again. He keeps sliding down, down so he's lying between my legs, one of his hands squeezing my waist, the other caressing me. Teasing me. Tormenting me. A shock jars through me as his tongue touches me, flicks against me over and over. Learns me. Memorizes everything about me. Finally, finally pushes into me, wet and hot and making me spiral up off that hard edge.

"Oh, God. Connor…"

I dissolve beneath him, sharp waves of ecstasy obliterating everything in my world except for him.

19

CONNOR

Alex cries out my name, and I close my eyes and focus on letting myself feel her and everything she's willing to give me. Hold onto her, revel in how her smooth legs tense against my shoulders, how a shudder courses through her. How she lets everything go in release as she comes undone. I love the way she tastes, and I don't let up on her, not even when she pants and grabs at my hair. Not even when she begs.

"Please..."

I push my tongue into her one more time, lick her long and slow before directing all of my attention to her sweetest spot. Feel her shudder again, hear her moan, slide my fingers inside her to enjoy the aftershocks of her orgasm before pulling out.

I kiss her legs, shift my body up so I kiss her belly, drag my tongue around her hot navel piercing. Wait for her to come down so I can do it to her all over again.

"Connor." She's breathless, her voice jagged. "I want you."

I want her, too. So badly, but I don't want this to be about me. I hesitate at her words, shut my eyes, work to get myself under tighter control.

I don't ever do this. Yeah, I generally try to make sure that whoever I'm with gets something out of it, too. But that's a bonus. Icing on the cake. Something to make me feel better about using whoever I'm with, to ease the guilt about it solely being about the sex and then walking away afterward. This is different. This is just about Alex, and I don't want to walk away from her tonight.

I raise up, move to lie next to her. I graze my hand against her cheek, and she turns her head to face me.

"No, sweetheart." I trail my fingers through her hair, cup the base of her neck, shift us so she's resting her head on my shoulder. "Not this time."

She searches my face for what feels like forever, her chest rising and falling as she sighs. Her eyes are beautiful and full of wanting, and my body is all messed up because I've fooled it into thinking that it's going to be with her. Though if she asks me again, I might not be able to say no.

"Okay," she finally whispers.

Her whole body relaxes, her cheek lying against my arm and her hand splaying out on my chest like she's trying to feel in my heart the effects of what we just did. I don't ever do this either. Don't stay with a woman in her bed if I can help it. Don't do the pillow talk thing. But she feels too good lying against me to make me want to get out of bed, let alone move.

Eventually, I do move. But only to undo my jeans the rest of the way so I'm more comfortable. I reach over and grab the down comforter to cover us, the only sound in the room being the movement of our bodies over the crisp sheets as we rearrange ourselves. Her breathing becomes more regular, slower. My instincts tell me that I should go if she falls asleep, that to stay the whole night with her would make things awkward between us in the morning. But that's habit speaking for me, and I decide that unless she asks me to go, I'll stay.

I hear a door open and click shut as one of her parents enters the main part of the suite, footsteps and another door close. Alex starts in my arms.

"Hey, Connor?" she whispers. "Could you lock the door that goes to the suite?"

I shift away, stare at her. Her eyes are still closed, her face relaxed and serene. "The door was unlocked that whole time?" I hiss. "You're kidding me."

She opens her eyes and gives me a lazy smile. "Don't worry. They don't come in here without knocking first. But just in case, you know?"

"Yeah." I get out of bed and flip the dead bolt.

I walk back to the bed, Alex watching my every move, and even though I'm standing in only my undone jeans, I'm comfortable being here with her. Like hanging out together in her room is something we've done before.

She rolls over and crawls to the edge of the bed, and I stare at her legs and try not to think about the fact that she's not wearing underwear under that little skirt. She grabs her t-shirt from the bed and pulls it on, and I cock my head at her.

"That's a damned shame, you know. You getting dressed."

She stands and faces me with a mischievous gleam in her eye. "I have an idea."

I smile back. "What's that?"

"You still have your pool card? The one that can get us in after hours?"

I nod. "I do. You want to go for a swim?"

She walks up to me, places her hands on my chest, tilting her head up and smiling at me. "Yeah. If you're game."

Her hands start to move down my body, and I catch them in mine, lift both of them to my lips before she can do any more damage.

Damn, I might fucking well explode by the end of this night.

"Let's go."

I bring all of my stuff down to the pool with me, not wanting to overstep whatever the boundaries are by going back to her room when we're done. There's a half moon out that lights part of our way, and I manage to sneak myself and Alex into the pool area undetected. Even if someone were to catch us, I hooked up one of the night security guards with his job last year, and I know he'll look the other way if need be.

Cruz is right that I do have connections here, though probably not nearly as many and to the extent that he thinks. My connections are out here trying to make it, just like me, and yeah, they help me out sometimes and I help them out. Not because I'm keeping track of things, not because I'm planning on cashing in on what I think is owed to me later. Not like my brother.

I'm still angry over the idea that Cruz thinks I owe him for running to the gang for protection. That he blames me for the lot in life that *he chose*.

I understand the fear, the desperation that he felt back when we were kids because I was right there with him and felt it, too. There were plenty of times when our father had his tweaker friends over after Cruz and I went to bed. When we could, we'd sneak out of the house and go over to Elle's because we didn't feel safe. When we couldn't, we'd take turns keeping watch for each other. Cruz slept with his baseball bat in arm's reach more often than not.

But to take matters into his own hands like that. To run to people even more dangerous and unpredictable than our father was. To turn to them for help... I can't even begin to understand why he did it. I guess that's one of the differences between us. When we were a lot younger, we talked about packing up, running away and trying to find our mother, but neither of us could disappear on Elle. She's an only child, and we were like her brothers.

Hell, Cruz might as well blame Elle for everything because her being there in the same city kept us from running away. He probably does, the fucker.

"You're thinking about your brother, aren't you?"

Alex is floating on her back in front of me, but she swims over to me right before she asks, her gaze questioning. The dividers are reeled in for the night, and we have wide-open water all to ourselves.

"Yeah," I admit. "How can you tell?"

She shakes her head. "Because you're here with me and you look positively pissed off."

I laugh, but there's hardly any humor in it. "Sorry. You're right. I shouldn't be thinking about him right now."

"Can't help what you think about. Or at least I don't know anyone who can."

I smile a little. "You always call it like you see it, don't you?"

She swims up to me and rests her hands on my shoulders as I catch her by her hips.

"Maybe a little too much. My mouth gets me in a lot of trouble a lot back home," she admits.

I stare at her lips, that beautiful mouth. "I don't doubt that."

"You know what I mean. Not like that." She rolls her eyes but laughs softly, and I bring her closer. Her arms wind around my back as she wraps her long legs around my waist.

My God, she's incredible. I press my forehead to hers and close my eyes.

"Dammit. What are you doing to me?"

Her fingernails scratch through my hair and send a shiver down my back. "Giving you something better to think about."

She says it in this throaty voice that's sexier than hell, and my hand cups her face. I feel her melt against me as I stroke her cheek with my thumb.

"Yes, you do that. Definitely."

Her lush lips curve into a smile. "Good."

I lean forward and kiss her. Try to let go of everything but her, and she makes it so easy. Her arms wind around my neck, and I rub my hands over her thighs. Hell, I want her so much I might lose it. But I also want to keep holding her in my arms like this. She's so warm and soft, and I love how close she feels to me right now. I just want to keep kissing her under the half moon.

The water is cool, but there's enough heat between us to compensate. It's burning slower than before, our kiss almost lazy but with a rhythm that taunts me with what I know could be, if I only ask for it.

But I don't want to ask for it. There are dozens of women in this city that I could use to get myself off whenever I want to. I don't want any of them, though.

Right now, I only want this.

I take the kiss deeper, my hands sliding over her body, and Alex makes a sound of pure desire. She pushes herself back from me, just enough so she can get her hand under the waistband of my boxer briefs. My eyes roll back in my head as her fingers close around me.

"Let me use you," she whispers.

I must be fucking insane. I *am* insane. I take Alex's hand and move her away from me, even though every instinct in my body wants to push her against the wall, wants to take her here in the pool and say to hell with the consequences. But I tighten my grip around her waist. Get a grip on my resolve at the same time.

Her eyes cloud with confusion, and I push her hair back from her ear and lean in, brush my lips against her earlobe as I clarify my actions.

"I want you. You don't even know how much I want you. But not like this, not tonight."

Not tonight. It's basically the same thing I said to her upstairs. I know it holds a promise, and I'm willing to make it. I don't wait for her answer before I kiss that beautifully long line of her neck. She closes her eyes and shivers, and I take her right hand in mine like we're dancing, wind my other arm around her back and spin her around. Her eyes fly open as a laugh escapes her, and I grin at her. I dip her nice and low before bringing her back up to me again.

She smiles, and it's just for me. "Connor Vincent, you're crazy."

"Your fault," I retort.

She leans away, lifts an eyebrow. "How is this my fault?"

"Because Alexis Lin, you're so amazing that you make me fucking crazy."

She laughs again and shakes her head. "So what's your plan for tomorrow? You have to work?"

"Actually, no." I kiss her forehead, closing my eyes and breathing her in before I answer. "I sort of put myself on administrative leave for a couple of days until I'm sure Cruz won't pop up on me when I'm with any of my clients."

I hadn't meant to bring him up, and I immediately regret spoiling the moment. Her forehead creases in a frown, and I wish I could kiss it away.

Less than a day of idle time and I'm feeling out of my element. If it wasn't for Alex, I'd be alone right now. My life is normally all about work, and I can see that now that I actually have time off. Aside from Elle and maybe Neil, I don't actually know anyone here, not really. And it might be because I'm feeling the high from being with Alex right now, but I wish I had room in my life for more. Room for her.

No. She's here on vacation, and her answer about what she's doing with me makes sense. She's the perfect distraction for me, and I know I can't be anything more than that to her. Still, everything we've done together (except for the night we first met) beats anything else I've ever had since moving to Vegas.

"I'm sorry you guys hate each other. Did you ever get along?"

I shrug. "Yeah, sure. We were close growing up. But then we drifted apart as we got older and focused on different things. Had a falling out right before I left for the military."

"What happened? He didn't like you leaving?"

"No. That wasn't it." I stiffen without meaning to, but Alex remains relaxed in my arms. She waits while I deliberate.

"There was a girl…" I briefly shut my eyes. "Her name was Laura, and she was the only girl I ever loved." The words feel uneasy on my tongue as I say it, especially while I'm holding Alex. "We were together for two years." I stop, not sure I can say the rest. Besides Elle, I've never told anyone any of this.

"When was this?" she asks softly.

"We started dating when I was sixteen." Sixteen. Nine years ago. I can't even totally swallow it as I hear myself say it. It had felt real back then, but really, what the hell does a sixteen year old know about love? It probably sounds stupid to Alex, but if it does, she doesn't say anything.

"I'd already started training for the SEALs." I look at her, wondering how much detail to give. She's listening, so I go on. "You don't have to be enlisted in the Navy to become one, but if you're a civilian, you have to work toward what's called a challenge contract. You have to prove yourself physically, psychologically, mentally. Elle's dad knew a guy who's a former SEAL. He was willing to train me, and I worked my ass off to get to where I needed to be."

I take a breath and release it. "Laura acted like she was supportive of it. But we were young, and in retrospect I think maybe she wasn't that cool with it. And I took her support for granted. Even before we graduated high school, I threw myself into training big time. Hardly saw her. I was living with Cruz in an apartment he was paying for with gang money, but I didn't know it at the time." I grit my teeth, shaking my head at my own stupidity. "Believed him when he came home beat up so bad he couldn't see straight and told me it was a school fight. Didn't see what was going on with him because I was so stuck on myself."

"You were trying to do something with your life. You shouldn't be ashamed of that," Alex says quietly.

I don't respond. I can't defend myself for what I'm about to say, and now that I've said as much as I have, I have to keep going. "The three of us would go to parties sometimes, and whenever I bailed, Cruz and Laura would go without me."

"Oh…" Alex breathes it out like she gets it, and I know what she's thinking. But she doesn't, and now I feel like I really need to get to the punchline.

"I came home one night, was something ridiculous like three hours late for a date with Laura." I swallow hard, suddenly feeling like there's a fucking fire in my chest burning me from the inside out. "Found her passed out cold in his bedroom. Cruz dropped some shit in her drink, and he took full advantage of her."

A little strangled sound comes from Alex's throat, and I plead at her with my eyes and pray she'll understand.

"Roofied?" she whispers.

"Yeah. She got really messed up from it, never spoke to either of us again. Not that I can blame her." I run my hand over Alex's shoulder, down her arm to take her hand. "That's why I suspected what was going on with you at the club that night."

She grips my hand, her eyes brimming with empathy. "Oh, God. Connor. I don't even know what to say —"

I can't make myself stop talking. It's like some valve opened in me that was shut tight for seven years and needs to let everything out.

"You don't have to say anything." I raise our hands out of the water, stare at our interlaced fingers as the realization strikes. "Believe it or not, I think helping you out at the bar, even being with you now, is letting me make up for it. Like I can finally move past all of that."

She releases her breath in a rush as she takes her hand out of mine, the other one slowly sliding off from my shoulder. I stare at her in surprise as she untangles herself from me, as her expression shuts down.

She floats away from me in the water, and I reach for her. "Alex…"

She kicks over to the wall and climbs out. Turns to face me with a smile that belongs to someone else. "Good night, Connor. I'm tired and going up to my room now. Thanks for the swim."

I frown at the switch in her. It's like she totally shut me out. "Can I see you tomorrow?"

"If you want to," she throws over her shoulder without looking back. "You know how to find me."

I don't know exactly why what I said made her upset, what made invisible walls come up. I thought I'd shown her a good time tonight.

Fuck. I was just thinking about this. She's only here through the month, and we were just having fun. She seemed cool with me talking to her about things, even that stuff about Laura. But it looks like I might have misjudged that. I don't know.

All I know right now is I hate watching her walk away from me.

20

Alex

Winning means knowing when to walk away. Those had been Dad's words as applied to gambling at the tables. But it doesn't just apply to the tables. What I've been doing with Connor is gambling too, and it may come with bigger stakes than playing with that stack of cash that's in my vault.

I avoid the pool for the rest of the week. Even though I hate every second of the gambling, I suck it up and spend more time with my dad on the floor. I convince my mom to hit the spa and go shopping with me instead of going to the pool. A few times, I catch her looking at me like she wants to ask what happened with Connor and me, but she doesn't. Elle comes over once to catch a movie with me and another time to do lunch, but she also needs to work and put in some hours for her social work internship this week.

Besides that, I spend time moping in my room and thinking about *why* I'm moping. It had shaken me to hear Connor tell me that he was basically using me to get over his ex-girlfriend. And after he said he didn't want to use me.

Yeah, it doesn't feel good, knowing that stuff about Laura. That was too heavy for me. I don't want to be held responsible for that, for wiping Connor's conscience clean.

I wake up for the day, not even knowing what day it is, and press my face into my pillow to stifle my groan. This is why I don't do this. This is why I don't let people get too close to me. When I do, something like this happens.

I'm already way too close to Connor. What happened between us – in my room, at the pool – stirred up too many emotions in me. Way more than any other time I've messed around with a guy. And there's no way I can let myself get attached to him like that. June will be over before I know it. I'll go back to my normal life where I'm focused on school, work, and the few friends I have back home. And he'll move on to someone else. For the short term, I told Connor I'd help think of a way to deal with Cruz (and I'm doing a crappy job of that by avoiding him), but even if I do, then what? And what happens when he goes back to work?

I think I know the answer to that. Bottom line is that I already lost too much of myself to Connor without meaning to. I don't like feeling this way. It makes me too vulnerable, sets me up to get hurt, and I need to distance myself before I lose anything more.

But the problem is, I already like him. I *like* Connor.

Mom hasn't been bugging me to get up at any particularly time for the past few days, but she knocks on my door pretty early, and I moan as I drag my ass out of bed. I only got about five hours of actual sleep earlier this morning after lying awake and… Okay, so I might be a huge hypocrite because I made that statement before about it being pointless trying not to think about things, but I watched random crap on TV for hours while doing just that – trying to not think about things. Finally gave in and thought about all of this until I passed out from sheer exhaustion at six in the morning.

The knock comes again, and I frown as I shuffle across the room. Must purge all of these thoughts before I see Mom.

I give her a big smile when I open my door, grimacing inwardly when I see she's dressed for the pool.

"Hi, Mom. You feel up for some shopping? Spa? Early lunch?"

"Pool?" she says hopefully. "I really need to get back into my exercise routine. I've been so dreadfully lazy." She lingers in the doorway to my room as I half-heartedly comb through my top drawers for a clean swimsuit. "Unless Connor's coming and you'd rather not have your mum around?"

"Oh, Mom." I pluck out a navy blue halter-top bikini, kind of wishing I had something that would cover me a little better. "First of all, you're not lazy. You're on vacation and have the right to relax a bit. And second, if Connor's coming, so what?" We're about an hour later than we usually go down to the pool, anyway.

I don't mean to sound snappish about it, but that's how it comes out. Mom gives me a shrewd look and glides into my room, perching on the one of my chairs. I look away, try to forget about how Connor looked sitting in that same chair the other night.

"All right. I haven't said anything for several days now because I wanted to see if you'd snap out of it, but you haven't. What happened between you two? And don't tell me 'nothing,' because I can tell when my baby girl's upset."

I'm running a pick through my hair, but I put it down with a sigh. "Honestly, nothing really. I'm not upset, Mom. I just don't want this summer to be all about him. I want to keep my options open, you know?"

"Alexis." Her voice is uncharacteristically sharp. "You don't let yourself have options. You make it impossible for anyone to get close to you."

I whirl around, my jaw almost to the floor. She looks back at me, her expression totally solemn. Mom never says stuff like this to me. If she does give me a hard time about guys, it's to the extent that she has so far with Connor – encouragement but nothing heavy.

She lifts her hands, palms out in an attempt to placate me. Maybe because I look like I feel right now. Defensive.

"I'm not saying it has to be Connor," she adds quickly. "You're young, and I know how intent you are on your studies right now. But I worry about you sometimes, baby girl. That you never see a boy more than a couple of times before you decide he's not worth it. That you won't know what love is when it comes your way."

"Mom…"

I look away, my face burning, but it's too late because she's already seen it. Seen more than I've been willing to admit to myself. When Connor told me about that girl Laura, he said he'd loved her, but he didn't even have to tell me. I could see the agony in his eyes that spoke for him. I was just thinking about this, and it's true – I've never felt that strongly about anyone before, and I can't deny anything my mom's saying about me now.

"Remember when I told you I used to sing in a club?" Her voice is raw with some of her own pain.

"Yes." I nod, my face still averted.

"It was more of a pub, and it was when I lived in England. What I didn't tell you is that I did it because of the first boy that I ever loved."

I stare down at my hands, my fingers knotting in the straps of my bikini. I don't look at her, but I listen.

"Your Gran sent me to a boarding school in England. You know that." She draws in a shaky breath. "We used to have arranged social functions, chaperoned dances, that sort of thing. I met him at one of those when I was fifteen. His name was Ian, and we saved all of our dances for each other."

I look over at her, and she's smiling gently at some distant memory. "Mum and Dad had already moved over here by then, but I stayed in England. Ian and I went to university together. His family owned a pub, and I would sing there every night while he played piano." She rests her gaze on me, and it's mostly happy but there's sorrow in it, too. "When I was up there on stage, I thought I could have done that for my entire life, Alexis. Be with him."

"Why didn't you stay with him?" I whisper.

"Because your grandad died, and my mum was all alone over here. She needed me." Mom lifts her shoulders delicately before dropping them.

"Okay, then why didn't he come with you?"

"Oh, Alexis. It wasn't that simple. His family needed him, too. We wrote letters to each other for a while, but he eventually met someone else, and I met your father."

Mom rises from the chair, so elegant and refined and wise. Everything that I'm not. She glides over to me and places her hand on my arm. "Don't misunderstand me. I have no regrets. I love your father dearly, and I wouldn't trade having you for the entire world, baby girl."

I stand there like I'm paralyzed, unable to move, unable to speak. Trying to understand why I'm so sad that she didn't wind up with Ian instead of my dad.

She gives my arm a gentle squeeze and floats away, her voice drifting over her shoulder. "I'll leave you to get dressed and then we can go down to the pool together. See if your boy is waiting for you."

Connor's not there, and I get mad at myself because I'm disappointed.

I know it's not because we're later than usual in getting down to the pool. Or because I've skipped a few days. It's because I brushed him off the other night. Took off running after he opened himself up to me in ways that I never imagined possible. He made me feel so damned good, he made me feel so special and desired, and he wouldn't take anything in return. And what did I do? Blew him off because he was honest with me about his past.

I sink down on one of the chairs on the pool deck and grab my phone from my bag. I still have his number on it from when he'd called me the other day, and I pull it up and stare at it. Think about that look he'd given me when we were in my room, in my bed. Like he was revealing to me the real him and yearning for me to do the same.

I pause with my finger hovering over his number, my hand shaking slightly. Do I really want to call him? Or am I only feeling mushy, sentimental, and *not like me* because of the story about lost love that my mom told me?

My phone rings in my hand, and I jump. I recognize Elle's cell number, and I blow out a breath and hit answer. Mom is doing her stretches next to me, and she shoots me a curious look that I ignore.

"Hey, Elle."

"Hey." She sounds on edge, and I sit up straighter, wondering if something happened. She clears her throat before rattling off, "What are you up to today? You want to meet for lunch or whatever? We need to talk plans."

Plans. I feel an irrational lightening in my chest, as I realize that – of course – this is where Connor is right now. He's with Elle, and they've been talking about how to deal with Cruz. That this is why he isn't at the pool.

"Sounds good," I say. "Do you guys want to come over here?"

Elle hesitates. "I'll come and meet you, sure. I don't know where Connor is, though. Haven't been able to get a hold of him all morning."

That shred of hope that was starting to bloom in my chest flits away in an instant, and I give myself a mental slap.

"*You* haven't heard from him recently, have you?" Elle's voice shakes me from my thoughts. Her tone is almost too casual, and I wonder if Connor talked to her at all, if he told her anything about what happened between us.

"Nope." No, I haven't seen Connor. Not since I spent a glorious night with him at the movies, in my bed, and ended it by being a bitch to him at the pool.

She and I talk for a minute more. I invite her to meet me and my mom at the pool, and then we'll decide where to go eat from there.

"Everything all right?" Mom gives me a concerned look before pulling her coverup over her head. She's limping a little, and I frown, my turn to be concerned.

"Yeah, that was Elle. She's coming over for lunch. But what's going on with you, Mom? Are you limping?"

"Oh." She makes a dismissive gesture with her hand. "I walked into something in the middle of the night. I'm dreadfully clumsy, I know."

She moves away toward the pool, and I shake my head. Mom couldn't be dreadful or clumsy if she tried.

I decide to skip the stretches and run in to the pool desk to leave Elle's name as my guest. Mom's waiting for me at the end of the pool when I get back, and we splash in together. I try not to think about the fact that I snuck into this water with Connor the last time I was here. I start to swim, waiting for my bubble to envelop me and quiet the unrest in my heart, but it never comes. Who am I kidding? I wish Connor was here, going all Navy SEAL and doing laps around us like he owns the pool.

Okay, this is not a big deal. I'll apologize the next time I'll see him. Play it by ear and see where things stand. And no matter what, I'm committed to helping with the Cruz situation. I'll meet with Elle, pass along any ideas I have to him through her if need be. I had a preliminary thought yesterday or the day before – that Cruz might have bluffed about not knowing anyone in the city.

Connor told me he thought Cruz found him because he paid off the guards. But Connor has been working with these people for longer, right? So that part doesn't make sense to me, that the guards would betray Connor like that. Unless of course, Cruz dropped tons of money on them, but even then, I'd like to think that *someone* would have been loyal enough to Connor to tip him off about Cruz.

I'll run it past Elle later to see what she says, but I think it's more likely that Cruz already has connections here. That he had his poker face on when he approached Connor, so to speak.

I think about this long and hard, and when I realize I haven't come up for air for more than a quick breath for ten full laps, I finally surface at the wall. My muscles burn as I hang onto the edge and focus on my breathing, and I look around the deck in tempered hopes that Connor will be here. But I don't see him, and it's like something deflates in my chest and leaves a big empty spot.

I like Connor, and *that's* why I want to help him. He's complex, and he's not always easy to be with. Yes, I'm a little ticked off at him, but I got through some of those layers of his, and I think he's worth it to me.

Connor's worth it. The realization of it fills me with a sudden panic. Because I don't have the slightest idea of what I'm doing. Because the idea scares me out of my damned mind. I'm pretty sure that Mom saw it almost right away, saw through those layers of his, but she's always been perceptive like that.

And Mom is…where exactly?

The lane on the other side of me is calm and still. I scan for her in the water, but she's not there. I turn and sweep the pool deck, see her bag and neatly folded coverup on the chair, her sandals sitting beneath. Maybe she got out to use the bathroom, but no, that couldn't be. I swear I passed her in the lane not too long ago.

The seconds tick by as I spin around in the water and look for her, and I try to put a lid on my increasing concern. There are three other swimmers going strong in the lanes to my left, and the lifeguard is sitting up in the lifeguard's chair. Wearing her earbuds, though, looking off into space…

Something's not right. I can feel it, like a pulse from the universe. My heart starts going a million beats a minute as I slip under the divider to my right to the empty lane. The sun is high, and the water ripples reflections back at me, blinding me. I shield my eyes, but then the sun suddenly slips behind a cloud.

I see something near the end of the lane. Something sticking out from under the lane dividers. *Someone.*

Mom. *Mom.*

"Hey!" I yell and wave my arms at the lifeguard, but the bitch can't hear me. "*Hey!*"

I don't wait for a response. I dive under the water and I'm off, kicking and pulling through the water as hard as I can to get to her. But my lungs feel like they're going to explode as soon as I get going, and I erupt through the surface again, only a few feet away. Not close enough. I scramble forward, aware of the lifeguard standing up in her chair and finally preparing to dive in.

I reach, stumble, my breaths coming in gulps, try to move through the water that suddenly feels like molasses. Try not to totally lose it. My fingers close around Mom's ankle right as the lifeguard splashes down into the pool next to me.

Someone runs over, shouts down at us. I scream at the top of my lungs without looking up, "*Call 911!*"

Fucking do it. Please. Please, God. Please don't let her die.

Mommy.

She's heavy, so heavy, and I tug at her to get her out from beneath the divider and throw my arms around her. She's like deadweight, and my stomach ties into a sharp knot when I feel how lifeless she is. I strain to pull her up, to get her head above the surface, but the lifeguard is stronger than me, and she finally manages to get Mom free.

Her lips are purple. Face bluish. Not breathing.

We pull her over to the wall, and the lifeguard hoists her out with the help of some guy who runs over to the side. I throw myself out of the pool after them, slipping, stumbling, wiping away my tears and trying to remember to breathe.

Mom.

My tears really start pouring down my cheeks as I stare helplessly at Mom lying there. As I watch her body jarring in a sickening rhythm with every chest compression.

A small crowd of people have gathered around by now, and they make way for me as I crawl to get closer, stagger to my feet and come to a skid on my knees. The lifeguard is still working, counting compressions, and my eyes zigzag wildly over Mom's body. Fingers and toes are purple. Face, chest, arms are blue. Leg is swollen. The blue. The puffy leg. Something jars in my memory. From one of my classes. Anatomy and Physiology last semester. But I can't remember…

"Mom," I wail.

Mommy. Wake up. Please be okay.

She's so limp, not moving except for when the lifeguard pushes down on her chest.

I can't move either. Not even when the paramedics get there and order us to please step back. Someone lifts me up to a standing position, but my eyes are glued on Mom's face.

Blue. Her chest. Not moving. Not breathing despite their attempts to revive her.

An arm is pulling me back from the scene now, and I thrash, try to wrangle myself out of the person's grasp and get back toward where they're lifting her onto the stretcher. Why aren't they giving her oxygen? Shouldn't they be giving her oxygen? The grip on me gets tighter, keeps me from getting to my mom.

I hear someone screaming.

I realize it's me.

The person holding me spins me around and crushes me to his chest, and I struggle and get away. Connor. I think it must be Connor, but I look up and it's not. Just some random guy who's trying to calm me down so I don't totally lose it.

"Alex! Omigod, Alex!"

I step back from the stranger and see Elle standing in the crowd, face pale, mouth open as she takes in the scene. She starts running toward me, and we charge into each other.

Her arms wind around me as my screams turn into sobs. *Mom.*

21

CONNOR

My pride won't let me go and see her.

I could have gone to meet Alex at the pool all week. But I can't bring myself to do it, not after she walked away from me the other night. Not when I let her in and she shut me out. Not when I know that seeing her will only make me want her. Not when she made it clear that I can't have her.

Fuck. It's like being with her messed up my wiring, and I can't make sense of my thoughts anymore.

I wake up with a void inside my gut again, knowing nothing I do to preoccupy myself will fill it. I think I might go out of my mind without anything on my docket for the day.

I grab one of the books off my stack on the night table, but my mind wanders and I stare at the pages without knowing what I'm reading. Staring at stupid shit on the internet only gives me a headache. My house feels sterile, empty, even though it's filled with plenty of distractions. State-of-the-art gaming system (hardly ever use it), entertainment system (don't feel like using it), tons of books to read (too distracted right now). I don't really do much here except eat and sleep. It's my home base, but now that I've been holing up here for the past few days, it strikes me how little it feels like home.

I've been down to the Strip for an hour or so everyday, but as Neil is still working with Maya, there's nothing for me to do there except to make my rounds. I've checked in with some the people that I interact with on a regular basis, but no one's mentioned seeing my twin. Good news in one sense, but I still don't know what the hell Cruz is up to.

I wander into the garage, stare at the space that's taken up by my bikes. The old beater Honda sport bike that I bought dirt-cheap off my uncle when I lived in Albuquerque, a remnant from my old life that I haven't ridden in almost two years. And the classic Harley that I bought off of a guy I know. It's about half-restored, but I can't even remember the last time I worked on it. Months. Maybe since winter. I tell myself it's because I'm busy, but deep down I know that's just an excuse. I could make time to work on it if I really wanted to. Aside from building up the clientele for the business and the list of women I fuck around with, what the hell do I really do with my time? Elle has music that she's passionate about, and I have what?

The garage is insulated, but it's still gets to be feeling like a furnace in here during the summer. I'd be crazy to work on it now, but I look over at the Harley again anyway, debating.

My phone rings, and I frown. Elle's been sending calls to my phone most of the fucking morning today, but I've been ignoring every single one of them. I have a pretty good feeling she's calling me about Alex, and I'm not in the mood to get chewed out for something I didn't do. I glance at the clock. I know Alex probably already went to the pool and is gone by now, and I feel something twist hard inside me.

My phone is still ringing. I go to silence it but see it's Neil. I pick up immediately.

"We need to talk," he says swiftly.

I immediately snap out of my funk, my senses going on high alert. "Maya. Is she all right?"

"Yes. But I need to meet with you before I have to pick her up this afternoon." His tone is curt, but it always is.

Maya's okay, but I know something happened. My forehead breaks out into a cold sweat, and I run into the kitchen, grab my keys, and am out the door as I'm still talking on the phone.

"Where?" I ask. Another call comes in as I get into the Audi, but I ignore it.

"The coffee shop in Maya's hotel. Hey, Connor…" He pauses. "I promise she's fine. A bit pissy because I'm not you, but I wanted to clear something with you regarding her protection."

"Okay. I'll be there in twenty."

My brain switches over into work mode as I back out of the garage. I'm obviously relieved that Maya's okay, though I'm of half a mind to tell Neil I'll take her back today. Neil wanting to see me in person doesn't surprise me. But it means he wants to gauge my reaction to something. I try not to guess what that something is going to be, but my instincts scream out the answer anyway.

Cruz. Neil must have seen my brother. But in what capacity, I have no idea. If Cruz is following Maya around after telling me he would leave her alone, I'll find him before the end of the month and kick him out of my city for good. The question is how. Even if Neil wants to meet me for some completely different reason, I still need to figure out how to get rid of Cruz.

Traffic isn't as shitty as it could be, and within ten minutes I'm taking the turn onto Las Vegas Boulevard. Alex's hotel is right across the street from Maya's, and I give it a quick glance before pulling into the far right lane, the one that'll take me to the valet parking at Maya's hotel.

I look again when I hear the siren. Traffic comes to a literal standstill as everyone ahead of me brakes and rubbernecks to see what's going on. I'm no exception, and I stare as the ambulance barrels up the drive from Alex's hotel with lights on and horn blaring to get through. It's too far away from me to see who's sitting in the cab with the driver, but an uneasiness creeps over my skin as the ambulance gives one more loud blare before taking the turn onto Las Vegas Boulevard. Probably someone thinking they're having a heart attack after losing all of their money. Or someone getting heatstroke at the pool.

The pool... I'm white-knuckled as I grip the steering wheel. The cars ahead of me start to creep forward again, and I follow, my eyes fixed on the ambulance as it speeds to the nearest light. I finally tear my eyes away, shaking my head. I'm just on edge because I'm thinking about Cruz.

It's lunchtime, but Neil is sitting at a table with a coffeepot and cups for both of us when I finally get to the restaurant. He gives me his customary handshake that's more like a bone-crushing punch.

"Good to see you, man." I'm jittery, too much for my own good, but I pour myself a cup anyway while Neil sits back and calmly assesses me. He and I have our temperaments in common, which is why we do well in this business in general and as partners. But I know he can tell that I'm off today.

He starts as I raise my cup. "She's something else, that Maya Coplin."

"Yeah. Can't argue with that."

"Didn't speak more than two words to me until last night. But then she had all sorts of things to say once we got in the elevator."

I'm not surprised to hear it. Maya regularly gives me the down-low on things when we're riding back up to her room. She's usually too eager to gamble to ever want to talk very much on the way down to the gaming floor.

The waitress comes over and takes our orders, and Neil makes a show of stirring his coffee while I wait for the details. If Maya spilling her guts in the elevator is typical, Neil's silence isn't. He doesn't waste seconds – Neil's *modus operandi* is one of efficiency.

"I'm assuming she told you about my brother?"

"Not in so many words." His expression is dark. "But it's interesting that you'd think so. She told me she's worried about your safety, Connor. So you tell me. What's the connection between your brother and the fact that she's worried?"

Neil and I went through a hell of a lot of shit together back when we were active SEALs. We don't keep things from each other, not when it has any sort of bearing on our business. I trust him more than probably anyone I know.

I drum my fingers on the table. Thinking of the bullet points.

"He showed up when I was with Maya, made some shit statement that might have sounded like he was threatening her." My hand clenches into a fist before relaxing, but I can't release the sick feeling in my chest. "In actuality he was threatening me, coercing me into getting rid of her so he could get me alone, but I completely understand if she felt like her safety was compromised."

Neil's face clouds over like a storm. "No, man. You didn't hear me correctly. She's not worried about herself. She told me she's worried about *you*. Since when does a client like this little lady worry about my buddy's safety? What the fuck have you gotten yourself into?" He leans forward, his gaze piercing and direct.

It's a valid question, and it's one I need to answer. My phone vibrates for what must be the tenth time today, and I hit silent without looking. After a second, I turn it off completely and look up to find Neil watching me with narrowed eyes.

"You sticking your dick where it doesn't belong, brother?"

Brother. It's what Cruz had called me when he was trying to appeal to me – unsuccessfully. Neil's use of it is different because it's actually meaningful.

"Maya? Fuck no." I shudder. "I don't sleep with clients. You know this."

"Right, right. No clients, no one with attachments. Just everyone else." He grins at me, but I don't smile back. I can't deny the truth. Or at least it's how it's been for the past two years.

"Cruz is affiliated with a street gang from back home," I mutter. "When I was there, they were solely a protection racket. Petty crimes and turf war stuff but nothing too big, though that definitely could have changed."

Neil nods, almost seeming to relax now that he has some concrete information he can process. "Not drugs? Gun-running? They involved with any cartels that you know of?"

"Don't know, but he…" I hesitate, trying to recall Cruz's words. "Honestly, I don't think things are going too well for him, is why he's here. Says he wants a piece of my action in Vegas." I fill him in on everything else Cruz told me, watching as Neil's expression transforms to incredulous, then murderous. It's not anything I'd ever want to have directed at me. I amend, "Yeah, I mean a piece of *our* action."

"Want me to have one of my guys take care of him for you? You wouldn't be implicated."

I know exactly what he means, and I'd be lying if I said I'm not tempted.

But Elle. I know she'd suspect my involvement, no matter how indirect, if anything happens to Cruz while he's in Vegas. I doubt I'd be able to live with myself either. No matter how much I despise Cruz for the past, I can't completely forget everything we endured together as kids, either.

"No. I'll figure out another way. But thanks."

"What do you propose to do?"

"I need to find out what else Cruz is doing here," I say. I hadn't vocalized this to Elle or Alex, but it's something that's been sitting in the back of my mind ever since I talked to Cruz. "He tried to make it sound like he's only here because of me, but then why stay here until the end of the month? He's gotta be involved in something else, maybe going ahead and messing around without me."

Neil nods curtly, sets down his cup with finality. "Agreed. I'll feed this through the system, have my people notify me when they spot him and who he's with."

Neil's specialty in the platoon was intelligence. He got out of the SEALs a year or so before me, and I know he's made different sorts of contacts in the city than I have. I suspect some of it's mob, but Neil made it clear a long time ago he's not directly involved in anything illegal, and that he's very careful to keep everything separate from our business. I made it equally clear that I don't want to know details.

"They need to be discreet. And not act, just report," I say firmly. "It's Cruz Marino. You need me to dig up a picture?"

He laughs, the sound completely humorless. "Discretion is a given. And no, if he's your twin, they already know what he looks like."

Meaning Neil's connections know about me. "I'm gonna pretend that doesn't make me nervous. No offense."

He shrugs. "None taken. I'll also see what I can dig up about his people in Albuquerque. We need to distance ourselves if he's in any way, shape, or form mixed up with a drug cartel. If it's just local, a protection racket like you say, we have more options."

Makes sense, as much as any of this does. I nod in agreement but also pick up on Neil's switch to using "we." We put a hold on our discussion as the waitress comes back with our orders, and I stare down at my sandwich in ambivalence. I don't even remember what I ordered.

"Timeframe," I inform him. "I'm supposed to meet with him at the end of the month."

"Good. We have time then. I'll get back to you as soon as I know something."

"Hey, man. Thanks." I hesitate, not knowing how to put the rest into words. That I'm afraid I'm putting him and his people at risk. But this is how he and I work. I got his back, he's got mine.

We talk about regular business until we're done with our lunches, and then we split up, Neil heading upstairs to take Maya out and me leaving the casino with nothing on my agenda. I wait for the valet to get my car, admittedly relieved that Neil confronted me about this and glad to have him in my corner. I wouldn't want to have someone like Neil as an enemy.

I wait at the stoplight to get back on the Boulevard, my eyes focused on the casino across the street. I'm automatically heading back to my house only because I have nothing else to do.

Screw it. Alex might not be at the pool anymore, but I have my entire day ahead of me. And like she said, I know how to find her. Pride can be damned right now. Having Neil offer his help to me and accepting it was humbling to say the least.

I glance behind me, abruptly edge over into the next lane, and get an angry honk of the horn from some jackass in a hurry to get into standstill traffic. I drive across the street but don't bother with valet this time and grab a spot in self-parking instead. The arcade of shops leading to the main casino is crowded with couples picking their way through overpriced restaurants, and I avert my eyes from their smiles and ignore their sounds of laughter as I pick up my pace to get through.

As soon as I get to the pool area, my instincts tell me something's wrong. There's an almost tangible buzz in the air, and I glance outside and see a few casino employees talking to groups of people. Like they're putting in extra time doing public relations. Or maybe crowd control after an incident.

The back of my neck prickles as I walk up to the front desk, and I wait impatiently to get the attention of the two employees, a guy and a girl. I know the girl – thankfully not anyone I've ever slept with – but they're whispering like crazy and on their smartphones instead of doing their jobs.

"Excuse me," I interrupt, irritation lacing my tone. "Did something happen out there?"

They look up at me, the girl's face initially startled but then relaxing when she recognizes me. She exchanges a furtive glance with the guy. Shit, I wish I could remember her name.

"There was an accident earlier," she says carefully.

"Yeah, some lady almost drowned," the guy says, a lot less carefully. "Her daughter and lifeguard saved her, but the mom was in bad shape. They had to take her to the hospital."

"Ryan," she hisses. "We're not supposed to talk about it."

Some lady and her daughter. I fight to get my breath as I think about the calls from Elle that I ignored not so long ago.

I take out my phone, trying to keep my hand steady as I turn it back on.

Six missed calls from Elle. One text.

CALL ME. URGENT. IT'S ABOUT ALEX

Holy shit. This can't be…

I hit send, but it goes to Elle's voicemail. Goddammit. I brace my arm against the counter as I try Alex's number. It also goes straight to voicemail.

I look up, my glance connecting wildly with the girl behind the desk. Lizabeth. I remember now that her name is Lizabeth.

Someone approaches the guy and asks about a guest pass, and I lean over the counter and beckon to Lizabeth. She comes closer, her eyes bright but expression still guarded as I try to force down the sick sensation in my stomach.

"Lizabeth, I understand the whole confidentiality thing. You're doing what you need to do." I lower my voice and turn my full force of my gaze at her, and she nods at me like she's mesmerized. "But I was supposed to meet a good friend here this morning. And she's sometimes here with her mother." I say the rest in a rush, before I lose it. "Were you here when it happened? Can you at least tell me what pool? Please…"

At this point, I'm not beyond begging, and I plead with her with my eyes. Sympathy floods her expression, and she throws a glance at Ryan, even though he hadn't seemed to care about releasing the information.

"Okay…" She sighs while I simultaneously hold my breath. "It was at the lap pool. The mother had a heart attack or something."

"What did she look like? And the daughter?"

"The mom was blonde. Maybe kind of strawberry-blondish hair? Her daughter was about my age? Tall with long red hair…"

216

The words strike me like a punch to my gut, rend me apart. I back away from the counter, my chest feeling like it's collapsing.

"Which hospital?" I demand.

Her eyes become as big as saucers. "Desert Springs. Connor, is this your friend?"

I shove away from the counter and run like hell. Don't remember going through the casino or parking garage. Operate on pure adrenaline. Hands shaking. Thoughts a mess.

The only thing I can think about is her.

Should have been there for her. Shouldn't have been so stubborn. Should have answered Elle's calls. God, I hope Alex wasn't alone when her mom had the heart attack. Hope someone had been there with her, hope Elle or someone else is with her right now.

I pull into the hospital entrance, snag a spot in the parking lot by the E.R., and stumble out of the car, noticing Elle's Honda Civic in the lot. I run into the waiting area, and I spot Alex right away. I'm out of my fucking head by then.

She's wrapped up in a blanket, legs drawn up to her chest, chin on her knees but with tangled hair falling over her face like a curtain. Elle's sitting in the chair next to her, a cup of something in her hand and her phone pressed up to her ear.

"Well, his wife is in the *emergency* room right now, so yes, I'd say this constitutes an emergency, wouldn't you?" she says with acid. "Now please. *Find. Him.*"

Alex is trembling so hard I can see it from here. Fucking hell. I could have been with her this entire time. Should have been. Or if I'd only answered my phone, I could have found her father and brought him here.

Maybe I still can. I take a step back, but before I can turn away, Alex slowly lifts her head and looks straight at me. She's crying, her face pale and her expression twisted with pain, but a deeper sort of agony flashes in her eyes when she sees me. Pain that's mirrored by what I'm feeling in my own heart.

I take a cautious step forward. Hold out my hand to her. "Alex…"

Her body wracks with a giant sob. I don't wait for permission. I make it over to her in three quick strides, take the chair on the other side of her. Put my arms around her and hold on tight, even when she stiffens. Keep holding on as she continues to cry.

I still don't know what's going on with her mother, but now's not the time to ask. Now's not the time for me to feel guilty or to berate myself for not being there for her earlier. Alex is falling apart in my arms, and fuck my pride. I need to be here for her *now*.

22

Alex

I don't know anything anymore. Don't know where they took Mom. Don't know if she's okay, though I *cannot* think about the possibility that she might not be. Every time the doors to the emergency room open, I jump out of my skin.

But there's nothing so far, no news, and having to wait is slowly killing me.

Don't know how long I've been sitting here. Or how long Elle and Connor have been with me. I'm sandwiched between them, Elle clinging to me on one side, Connor with his arm around me on the other. I rode in the front of the ambulance, and Elle followed in her car, got here sometime after me. Elle walked me to the bathroom so I could change out of my bathing suit and into my clothes – I vaguely remember someone at the pool handing me my bag along with Mom's stuff before I got into the ambulance with the paramedics, otherwise I'd still be in my bikini and towel. Elle got me the tea and blanket from somewhere. She talked me down from the ledge, calmed me down enough so I could talk to my dad and tell him what happened.

I don't know anything else. Except that I'm scared. Scared out of my goddamned mind.

The mechanical hum of the E.R. doors sounds as they open for the millionth time, and I stare at the woman in scrubs who's standing there holding a clipboard. A flicker of hope spreads through my chest, but it crashes down on me all over again when she calls out someone else's name. Connor tightens his arm around me, gives me a squeeze, and I close my eyes. How he knew I needed that right then, I have no idea. I also don't know how he even found out that we were here, but I'm guessing Elle called him.

I told her not to. Not to call him, because I knew seeing him would make me angry. And when I first saw him in the waiting area, looking so panicked, it drove up my pain to almost excruciating levels. I cycled through part of it when I was riding in the ambulance, worked through my anger over the fact that Connor hadn't been there at the pool to help me when all of that craziness happened. Not that anyone could have predicted this happening. Not that it's his fault he wasn't there in the first place – I know that it's mine for ending the other night so badly.

I'm mostly furious with myself for being so self-absorbed when I was at the pool. For thinking about Connor and nothing else when I should have been watching out for my mom. I can't get the image of her out of my head, of how blue she was. If I'd only noticed her sooner...

Connor's fingers trail through my hair. It might be the fact that I'm shell-shocked, but I don't feel anything besides anger in response to him being here. I stopped crying a while ago because I ran out of tears.

Eventually, I just feel cold.

We wait, and I alternate between watching the door going into the E.R. and looking out for my dad. It had taken forever to get a hold of him. Dad initially hadn't answered his phone or responded to my texts. It was Elle who thought of calling the casino, and she shouted at some poor person at the front desk until they sent someone to find him. Dad had been down the street at a different casino when he finally called me back.

"Dad, Mom's in the hospital. You need to come now."

That's all I'd been able to say before my voice had given out. Elle had taken my phone straight out of my hands, told him which hospital. I heard her tell him that I was fine and that my mother was in good hands. That hadn't been too long ago.

Elle's totally my hero right now.

She wordlessly passes me the cup of tea, and I wrap my hands around it for the warmth that never comes.

"Alex…What can I do to help you?"

It might be the first thing Connor's said to me since he got here. My neck feels stiff as I turn my head and look up at him. I'm already not doing so well in terms of getting air into my lungs, but my breath catches when I see how he's looking at me. I can tell that he's hurting for me and for my mom, and he searches my eyes like he's trying to get a sense of me, too. But I'm feeling too shattered inside to let him.

I don't even want to think about this right now, but I can't expect anything from this. Connor's here now, but that doesn't mean I should raise my expectations from ground level. I don't want to be all broken-hearted like Mom must have been when she said goodbye to Ian… I cut off my own thoughts before they become crippling.

"Nothing. Thank you." My tone is icy, and he looks confused, maybe even a little hurt.

I close my eyes to all of that, retreat inwardly even further. It hits me for the first time exactly how exhausted I am, but I can't rest. Not until I know how Mom is.

The longer I sit, the more I wind up sinking into my own head. I desperately try to call up the bubble that Mom always talks about. Try to use it to make myself strong but maybe also to keep myself numb. I think about Mom and all of her headaches, how she'd been complaining about being sore lately. Whether the painkillers were helping her, or whether they might have contributed. I'd handed the bottle of ibuprofen over to one of the E.R. nurses when I first got here because she wanted to know if Mom was taking any medication.

I also think about how I've been worried about her ever since Dad told me they were cutting the trip short. And how I've been running around doing my own thing or moping in my room instead of keeping an eye on her.

I lied to Connor before. I am a spoiled brat.

No clue how much time passes before Dad runs into the waiting area. He stops when he sees me, and there's so much anguish and terror in his expression that I can almost feel a fissure crack through my heart. The seconds slowly tick by as we stare at each other, and it's not until Elle or Connor peels the blanket off my shoulders that I get up. My legs are weak, and I wobble on my feet as I move to him. I'm vaguely aware of Connor lunging forward to steady me, but I ignore him and plod forward.

I swallow down the lump in my throat, focus on taking those steps forward as Dad does the same. My arms feel heavy, but I raise them, reach out to him. "Dad," I whisper.

"Alexis."

He grabs me in a hug that crushes all of the air out of my lungs. The room blurs out of sight through my tears as I hug him back. His hands close around my arms, gently but firmly as he pushes me back so he can see my face. He looks like he aged ten years since I saw him last night.

"How is she? Did they tell you anything yet?"

"No." I swipe at my tears. "Not yet."

I know Connor wants to do more for me. I know he and Elle both do. But that has nothing on how much I wish I could erase Dad's pain in this moment. More of those precious seconds tick by as we hold onto each other, and he starts to shake. My Dad, the one person in the world who I can always count on to make things better, is as scared as I am. I squeeze my eyes shut, my tears freely flowing as that realization pitches me into complete desperation.

What if we lose her? I can't be all that Dad has left in the world. I'm not enough.

The E.R. doors swing open, and I jump. A man wearing scrubs and a face mask hanging below his chin steps out into the waiting area.

"Ms. Lin?"

I clutch at Dad's arm for balance, the floor feeling like it just dropped from under my feet.

"Yes?" I squeak.

The doctor seems to notice Dad for the first time. "Are you immediate family of Grace Lin?"

He nods. "I'm Grace's husband. How is she?"

The doctor rubs his forehead and gives us both a stiff smile. Dad puts his hand on mine, and we stand together and listen. I went to the bathroom not too long ago, but I suddenly feel like I have to pee.

"Your wife is in relatively stable condition at the moment, but she's not out of the woods yet."

Stable condition. Not out of the woods yet. I start breathing again, the words repeating themselves in my head. Careful phrasing that doctors use in an attempt to reassure but at the same time try to prepare people for the worst. Only there are no words that can prepare anyone for the worst.

He's still talking, and I try to concentrate on what he's saying, recognizing some terminology from my anatomy and physiology classes. Deep vein thrombosis. Pulmonary embolism. Two broken ribs from when CPR was administered. Oh, Mom... I grip Dad's hand a little tighter as he goes on to explain, and my own heart aches as he tells us that Mom hadn't had a true heart attack. Her heart had undergone arrest in the pool but they were able to confirm with a scan that it was because of a blood clot from her leg that traveled to her lungs. Had we noticed her being short of breath? Had she complained of chest pain prior to this?

My dad looks as shell-shocked as I feel. Mom had complained about being sore, begged off from swimming, was limping but dismissed it. She must have felt what the doctor is describing but downplayed it because she hadn't wanted us to worry. I saw some of the signs, but I hadn't put any of it together.

My legs feel weak, and I glance over at the chairs where Elle's now sitting next to Connor. I wish for all the world that I didn't have to stand here and listen to this. The doctor is still talking, throwing out specialized terms left and right. Terminology that not even I understand and I'm sure my dad doesn't, either, and I'm starting to become angry on top of everything else. The doctor looks young, can't be more than a few more years older than me. He seems competent, but his bedside manner leaves a hell of a lot to be desired.

"She'll be on bed rest with anticoagulant treatment until we can be sure that there's no danger of clots reforming. And of course, we'll need to do an echocardiogram to check for damage to her heart."

"Please. May we see her?" Dad manages to keep his voice steady, but I can pick up how anxious he is.

"Yes. She's sedated now but you can see her." He hesitates. "Your daughter said your wife didn't have any underlying medical conditions. Is this correct? Is there any family history of clotting issues?"

Dad's posture grows rigid, and I look at his face. White as a sheet.

"Grace hasn't ever had an…embolism. But her father had one. That's actually how he died." His tone takes on a different kind of agony as he averts his eyes from me.

What? I blink, the rest of me feeling paralyzed at the news, over the fact that I'm hearing this for the first time. I had never known my grandfather because he died before my mother had met my dad, but I was always under the impression that he had passed away because of a simple heart attack. But they must not have thought the details were important to tell me. Maybe not, but it still comes as a shock.

"Good to know," the doctor says. "I'd advise running some extra tests, with your consent of course, to see if she tests positive for one of several possible genetic clotting disorders. And of course there's always diseases like diabetes and lupus which come with the increased risk of deep vein thrombosis…"

He goes on and on about possible tests while I go into a mild trance. Some of those diseases he's mentioning are heritable, and if my grandad had the same thing, it's possible that Mom has it, too. But I'm jumping ahead of myself now, and I don't want to take the next leap and think about what it might mean for me...

"...No matter what, Mr. Lin, I promise we'll get down to the cause of this. Hematology is my specialty," the doctor says a little smugly. "Your wife is in good hands."

"Thank you," Dad says. "I'll sign the consent forms for the testing, of course. It's best if we know."

I need to know, too.

23

CONNOR

"God, I'm such a mess inside, for all of them." Elle sits next to me, her head leaning against my shoulder. We've been here all afternoon, and she's been trying to entertain me for the past hour by reading me random stuff from her phone. I've been tolerating it.

"Yeah, I know," I say.

"Like I don't see my parents very often, but I think I'd be wrecked if my mom had a heart attack or embolism or whatever."

I don't respond to that. If Cruz hadn't told me our father was still alive, I wouldn't have necessarily assumed he was. And to hear that our father was dying did nothing to me emotionally. He's been dead to me for years.

"It kinda makes you think about your own mom, you know?"

Okay, Elle. You can shut the fuck up now.

She jerks away from me, her hand over her mouth as what she said finally hits her. "Oh, shit. Connor, I'm such an asshole. My head's not on straight right now. I didn't mean to…"

"I know," I interrupt.

I sound like I'm on repeat today, but I don't know what else to say. I'm not gonna tell Elle that it's okay, because it's not. She hits herself on the forehead with her fist and invites me to do the same. But the damage is done. Her words make me think about my mom.

I haven't allowed myself to remember her for years, because my most vivid memory of her was from that day that Cruz and I came home from school and she was gone. We tore through the house to find a lot of her stuff missing, and then we waited all afternoon for her to come home. I finally gave in by evening and called my dad at work – something we were never supposed to do. Cruz yelled at me the entire time to not call him. He was right. We both got our first bad beating from our father when he got home that night.

All of my hope slowly died as the days and weeks passed. It was about six months before I could finally admit to myself that she'd never be back. By then, I stopped talking about running away and finding her. Cruz would get angry whenever I mentioned her, anyway. He knew from almost the day she left that she didn't want us anymore.

If I make myself try, I can remember – the way she snuck a special note into our lunches for school every day. How she always smelled like the flowers she arranged at the shop where she worked. The sound of her sweet, lilting voice when she told me and Cruz stories before bedtime. We didn't have many books, and the stories were usually ones she'd heard from her own mother or had made up herself.

Elle's my family now, and the only thing I know for sure is that we're here together, united. And that I want to be here for Alex, if she'll let me. She's been back out to the waiting area periodically throughout the afternoon to give us brief updates – or to give Elle the updates, since she hasn't once made direct eye contact with me – but she's been gone for almost an hour and a half this time.

I don't want to think about the things I loved about my mother. I don't want to remember. But as I sit here with Elle and with my thoughts full of Alex, those good memories release from where they've been locked up in my head for so long. Maybe because I'm pretty sure that's all that Alex is doing right now. Thinking about her mom and all the things she loves about her.

Right as I have the thought, Alex steps out into the waiting area, and she's like a shadow of herself. If I could erase her pain, I would. In a heartbeat.

Elle and I both jump up at the same time, and Alex looks a little surprised that we're still here, but it hasn't even been a question for either me and Elle. We both decided independently that we're not leaving until Alex does.

"She's sleeping." Her face is expressionless, her eyes dull. "They'll run some more tests later. My dad told me that I should get some rest. And he wants me to go get dinner, but whatever."

Her words almost slur at the end, and Elle exchanges concerned glances with me. I'd run down to the cafeteria and grabbed something for both of us while we were waiting. I think about doing the same thing now, but Alex might want something that doesn't taste like cardboard. And she might want to get out of here considering she's been here all afternoon and part of the evening.

"Did you eat anything today, hun?" Elle asks.

She shakes her head. "Dad had something to eat a while ago, but I'm not that hungry."

"But a girl's gotta eat." I call up the same words she'd used when we went out for burgers, when she was helping me cope with my own shit. When things were better for her.

She still doesn't look at me. "This girl's fine," she says, but there's no fire in it.

The two of them walk arm in arm to the exit, and I follow with Alex's bag, glad to be out of here.

"So, my dad's going to spend the night here with her, but they won't let both of us stay," I hear Alex tell Elle. She lowers her voice. "Can I stay at your place tonight? I told my dad I'd be fine in the room, but…" She trails off, like she's ashamed to say the rest.

I finish the thought for her in my head. She shouldn't stay in that empty suite all by herself, and she doesn't need to be ashamed of that. God, I want to take her in my arms so badly that I fucking hurt.

We step outside, and I pick up the pace to catch up to them. Elle hasn't given Alex an answer yet, and she throws me a panicked glance before commencing to chew on her bottom lip. I know she's stressing out because she has to go to work in forty minutes.

"Of course, hun," she says anyway. "Whatever you need."

I already knew this ten times over, but my cousin is a pretty incredible person. She anticipated this, and she's been trying to find people to cover her for the last hour, but no go. I know she'll risk getting in trouble at work by calling in sick at the last minute, that she'll do it for Alex. Like I know she'd do the same for me if I ever needed it.

"Elle has to work tonight," I interject, "but you can stay at my place if you want. There's plenty of room there, and I'll sleep on the couch."

Alex averts her eyes. "I'll go to Elle's and wait for her to get back from work. I don't need you to babysit me."

Her tone is cold, but I know she has to be hurting bad right now. Elle and I both heard most of what the doctor said, pieced the rest of it together while Alex was out of the waiting area, and all of that is heavy shit for anyone to have to deal with. Exactly why she shouldn't have to deal with it alone.

I know she has to be feeling pretty messed up inside right now, but I wish she'd let me in, just a little.

"I'll call in sick," Elle says quickly, but she looks worried. "It's not a big deal."

We get to the cars, and Alex lets loose with a drawn-out sigh. "No. I don't want you to have to do that. You've done too much for me already. I'll be fine until you get back."

Elle shoots me a wide-eyed look. I know her shift is seven hours long, and we don't even have to say anything out loud for both of us to know we're in agreement. Alex shouldn't be alone right now. This is a situation I can actually do something about, and I give Elle a slight nod. She blinks and takes Alex by the arm, steering her to the Civic.

"Okay, hun. I'll take you to my apartment. You can use my bathroom stuff, and I have an extra toothbrush you can use." She pauses before unlocking the door, looking dubious. "Unless you want to swing by your hotel room first to grab some clothes and other stuff?" I know what she's thinking, that Alex is a good six inches taller than she is and curvier all around.

"No. I'll be fine in this." She gets into the passenger side of the car, still dressed for the pool, in t-shirt, shorts, and flip flops.

"Okay." Elle shuts the door and runs over to me to grab Alex's bag. Her eyes are wild as she looks up at me, and she speaks quietly and quickly. "Connor, I haven't gone grocery shopping yet this week. I have jack shit in my fridge."

"Don't worry, Elle." I hand over the bag, my eyes fixed on the passenger side of the Civic. "I'll take care of it."

Elle is practically vibrating with nervous energy when she throws open the door to her apartment twenty-five minutes later. She's dressed in tattered black with extra spiky hair for work, her makeup excessive and dark.

She slips out into the hall and shuts the door behind her. "Fair warning. Alex doesn't want you here," she hisses. "She said as much as soon as we got here."

Ouch. But given how chilly Alex has been to me all day, I'm not that surprised. I'm not about to lie down and roll over, either.

"I know what I'm doing. Go to work, Elle."

"Okay, but I'm only agreeing to this because I can't get any of the other girls to cover me," she warns in a whisper.

"And because you know I care about Alex," I add very seriously. I feel the truth of my own words as soon as I hear myself say them.

"Yeah, that too." Her expression softens a little, and she critically eyes the bags in my hands. "Come in at your own risk." She rolls her eyes and pushes open the door.

Elle's apartment is essentially a studio with a kitchen and bathroom tacked on. It's small, but she's done well making every inch of it reflect her personality. Dark tapestries hanging on the walls next to provocative pieces of art. No TV, just tons of books spilling out of a tall black bookshelf and an overstuffed dark purple velvet couch to read them on. A bed with a black duvet and a sea of black and purple pillows.

Alex is sitting cross-legged in the middle of the bed, and she gives Elle an accusatory stare as soon as I step inside.

"I need to run in to work, hopefully not for the whole shift, but at least to open," Elle says firmly. "And I'm not leaving you alone."

Alex doesn't say anything to either of us, just turns away and lies face-down on the pillows. Elle hesitates, but I grab her around the neck in a hug, nodding toward the door as I release her.

"Get outta here," I say. "See ya soon."

"Bye, Connor. Bye, Alex," she says loudly.

Alex doesn't move, but I do. I take the t-shirt and sweats out of one of the bags and lay them on the bed a safe distance from her. They're mine, and they'll be way too big on her, but I'm betting it'll be more comfortable than what she was wearing at the pool.

I walk over to the kitchen area and take out the remaining contents of the bags, putting away most of what needs to be refrigerated but spreading the rest of it out on the counter. I start cutting up vegetables, half an eye on Alex.

"Is there anything you don't like?" I ask.

My question is met with silence, and I let it go. I resume dinner prep until she lifts her head from the pillow and glares at me.

"Right now? You."

I set the knife down on the counter, wipe my hands on my jeans, and walk over to the bed. She stiffens, and I sit down on the edge of the bed and look at her, keeping my expression carefully neutral.

"Alexis…"

She closes her eyes. "Don't call me that."

"Why not? It's your name," I point out. "Look, I gotta say this. I'm sorry for whatever it was that made you so mad at me at the pool the other night. I'm sorry I wasn't there with you today when everything went down – it kills me that I wasn't. I understand that your mother's not in the clear yet and that you're probably terrified right now. But I'm here for you."

Her eyes are still closed, and she's lying perfectly still. I take a chance and reach out, lay my hand on her leg. Feel her tense up but keep it there.

"I care about you," I say firmly. "And there's no way in hell I'm letting you stay here by yourself right now. So be angry with me if you want to, but I'm not leaving."

She sits up, her leg almost kicking at me in her haste to move out of my reach, her eyes glazed with unshed tears.

"You want to know why I'm angry?" she spits out. "Do you really want to fucking know?"

She's lashing out, and I'm the closest target. And I'll take the hit because I meant what I said. Because I care about her, a whole hell of a lot. Maybe more than I've admitted to myself until now.

I meet her anger with as much calm as I can. "Tell me."

"Because," she snaps. "I was thinking about you at the pool this morning. I was thinking about how I could help you, about that whole Cruz thing, about how I really wanted you to be there swimming with me."

I stare at her, frozen in place as she gets up on her knees so she's eye to eye with me. Her tears are streaming down her cheeks now, her voice strangled. "I was thinking about you the whole time that my mom was stuck under a lane divider. I was thinking about *you* when I should have been paying attention to my mom. *She almost died because of me!*"

She yells the last bit and comes at me with fists flying, hits me squarely in the chest, struggles when I wrap my arms around her and pin her to me. I hold on as she fights to get free, as she shouts obscenities.

I close my eyes and hang on. Wait out the storm.

She eventually stops shouting, stops fighting and starts crying hard. I press my lips to the top of her head as she soaks the front of my shirt with tears, wishing more than anything that I could shoulder it all for her – the pain, the guilt, the anger, the grief. But I can't because she has to work through this herself. I don't know how long it takes before the storm recedes, but eventually the only sound in the apartment is her breathing as she tries to gain control.

The cool girl, always in control of her emotions. I want to tell her that it's okay. That it's okay to let go, especially now.

"Alexis," I say. "What happened to your mom isn't your fault. It would have happened anyway, even if you hadn't been thinking about me."

I reach up and take her hands, hold them and push her away from me so I can look at her. Her cheeks are slick with tears, her lower lip trembling, and it doesn't matter. She's so beautiful.

"You can't protect the people you love all of the time," I say. "That's life."

Her breath hitches, and her eyes search my face with something like desperation. Like she desperately wants to believe my words but doesn't know how. And in that moment, I realize how much I need to believe it myself. I've always blamed myself for Laura because I hadn't been there to protect her from Cruz. Thought that if I hadn't been late coming home that night, that Cruz wouldn't have drugged her. That he wouldn't have ruined her life. And while that might be true on some level, what happened to her wasn't my fault – it was Cruz's.

I look into Alex's eyes, seeing her struggle with the truth of what I said as I try to do the same. For years, I've let my guilt over that incident prevent me from getting close to anyone. I've let my guilt shape all of my relationships with women.

All except for this one.

"Sweetheart, your mother didn't almost die because of you." I place my hands on either side of her face, gently wiping the tears from her cheeks. "You didn't give her the embolism."

Her face crumples as she sags against me, and I hold her. But this time, it's not to restrain her. This time it's to show her that I'm here for her, in no uncertain terms.

She whispers something that's too quiet for me to hear, and I stay very still and wait for her to say it again. She draws back from me, reaches up to touch my face.

"I care about you, too," she murmurs.

I lean down and kiss her cheek, and she turns her head and very gently presses her lips against mine before releasing me. It's sweet, and I lay her down on the bed and lie down next to her.

"You're so beautiful," I say.

"Whatever," she rasps. "I'm pretty sure I look like hell."

"Nope. Beautiful." I stroke her hair. "And I'll keep telling you until you believe it."

She closes her eyes, and I do the same. My body immediately reacts to her as she rolls over so she faces me, her breasts, hips, and long legs pressing up against me. She feels so fucking good, but I work to keep myself in check. Now is not the time.

She makes a small sound, and I open my eyes to see her looking at me. I watch as pain floods her expression again.

"See?" Her eyebrows draw together in a frown. "I'm doing it again, thinking about you when I should be thinking about my mom."

I give her a small smile, reach up and smooth her frown away with my fingers. "Your mom knows you're thinking about her. I don't know her that well, but I'll bet you anything she wouldn't want you worrying yourself sick about her."

She stares at me and sighs. "You're right. She wouldn't. I can't stop worrying, though."

"Well," I say, tracing my index finger down her jawline. "That's where I come in. I'm here to distract you."

Her lips part, and damn if I don't want to kiss her.

"Connor…"

I pull away from her, get out of bed and concentrate on stamping down my desire. I want her, yes. No question. But it wouldn't be right if I did anything about it, not now. I don't want to take advantage of the situation, don't want to take advantage of Alex.

Although maybe the old Connor from only a few weeks ago would have.

"Come on." I hold out my hand to her. "Distraction time. Help me make dinner."

24

Alex

I can't breathe. I'm drowning. Disoriented. Can't tell which way is up. It's so dark that I can't find the surface. I fight for it, swim as hard as I can, but my limbs suddenly feel like they're encased in the earth.

My eyes fly open to a dimly lit room, and I gulp for air. Strong arms immediately tighten around me as I thrash around.

"I got you, sweetheart," I hear him say.

Connor. I grip onto his shirt and press my face against his shoulder, finally able to breathe.

He's got me. He totally does.

I open half an eye and remember that we're in Elle's apartment. I remember making these huge frittatas with him and both of us being so hungry that we ate an entire one apiece. I remember taking a really long shower and brushing my teeth with the toothbrush Elle gave me, changing into Connor's t-shirt – so yummy-smelling – and cinching his sweats around my waist as tightly as I could so they wouldn't fall down.

Don't remember falling asleep in his arms, but I think I must have needed it. I remember lying down on Elle's bed with him before that. Listening to him talk about everything like he was reading me bedtime stories. He told me a little bit about what it was like to be in the SEALs, about his friend Neil and how they work together now. He went back further than that and told me about the crazy workouts he did to prepare for all of that when he was a teenager. Back even further…

I run my fingers over his arm, and he tenses but then relaxes. He told me about the day he got that scar, about his father and Cruz.

Connor doesn't move as I trace over the shiny skin of his scar with my hand. I lift my chin, stare at his face, breathe in. His scent surrounds me. From his clothes. From him.

I missed him this week. Now that he's here, I could get used to this.

"Hey," I say. My voice sounds hoarse.

"Hey." He pins me with that vivid blue gaze, and little explosions go off in my chest and make it harder to breathe again.

"What time is it?" I manage.

I'm lying on his arm, and he lifts his wrist from behind me, his gaze flicking briefly to his watch before resting on my face.

"Ten-thirty."

At night? Really? It feels like it's two in the morning. I must have crashed not too long ago, but I suddenly feel hyper, like getting all of that anger out of my system somehow gave me my second wind.

He goes on. "Elle texted me a while ago, and I told her you were asleep. She doesn't have to work her entire shift and will be back within the hour."

At the mention of a text, I scoot away from him and reach down to my bag for my phone. Dad had left me a voicemail, and I hit the button to listen, my hand shaking. Connor's eyes are on me the whole time, but I focus on the message.

I start breathing normally again and send Dad a quick text, my fingers still trembling as I type.

Got your message. See you in the morning. Love to you and Mom

"Well." I sit up and hug my knees to my chest. "She's sore and exhausted, but whatever they gave her to break up the clots is working. They need to monitor her to make sure they dissolve completely and that she doesn't develop any new ones."

"Good. That's good." He sits up next to me and puts his arm around me. "I'll take you to the hospital in the morning if you want."

"I'd like that." I reach out to him and hesitate. Drum up the nerve and run my hand through his hair, like he always does and as though I have a right to. He closes his eyes, like he's enjoying it.

"Hey, Connor?"

He opens his eyes and smiles at me, and it's full of sweetness. Maybe there's some relief in it, too. "What?"

"I'm really sorry I took off on you that night at the pool. I was mad at you for saying that you were using me to get over Laura, but I should have told you that instead of just taking off like that."

His smile vanishes, genuine surprise taking its place. "Oh. Wow." He raises his hand like he's going to push it through his hair again, but it falls to his side. "Alex, I got over Laura a long time ago."

I stare down at my toenails, at a chip in the blue polish on my big toe that needs to be fixed. This whole thing still stings when I think about it, but I want to give him the chance to explain this time. I hear him exhale, but I don't look at him.

"I'm over *her*, but I still feel bad about what happened to her. And okay, honestly, I admit it did cross my mind – when you were sitting on that bench outside QE2 and we first figured out you got roofied. Elle even said to me something like that, that I needed to make up for the past…" He stops and makes a quick gesture of his hand, like he's waving that notion away. "But that's it. I guess I really meant that the more time I spend with you, the more I realize how much of a better place I'm in now."

Look at him.

I raise my head and see that same emotion in Connor's eyes from before, from when we were together in my bed. The color rises to my cheeks, my own feelings muddled as my brain tries to fit that look into what he's saying to me. I try to ignore the fluttering in my chest and make myself chew on this for a minute.

I don't think he's trying to bullshit me. I know more about him now, about where he came from, and if I can help Connor realize that he's in a better place now, I'm totally okay with that.

"So I guess I could have found that out if I'd only asked, huh? Instead of blowing you off?" Ugh. "I seriously don't know who that crazy person was."

He shakes his head. "I do. It was this really cool girl. And I happen to like her, so watch what you say." He gives me a stern look. "And stop trying to find new ways to blame her for everything."

My grin appears out of nowhere, and I lean over and give him a quick kiss. It feels good, almost more intimate in a way than when we go at it full bore. Familiar. Comfortable.

His eyes shine at me, and I know I surprised him again, but in a good way. "Elle's gotta be on her way by now. You'll be okay here tonight if I leave?"

I don't want him to leave. I almost tell him that I changed my mind, that I'll come and stay with him at his place, but I stop myself just in time. Maybe he's right about it not being my fault, but I still think the universe slapped me in the face today and that I shouldn't ignore that.

"I'll be all right. Thank you. For being there for me today."

I hope he can hear the sincerity in my voice, feel the gratitude that's filling me up right now. His lips part as though he's going to say something, but then we both hear it and look over at the door at the same time. The sound of Elle's key in the lock reminds me. "Oh. We still have to talk about Cruz…"

"You have a lot on your plate right now. Don't worry about Cruz." He touches my chin. "There are much better things to think about, anyhow."

I reach out and rub my hand over his jaw, loving the roughness of his stubble. Happy that he was stubborn and followed me here. Glad that he opened up to me. I bet he doesn't usually tell people the things about himself that he told me tonight. I'm glad that he felt like he could.

I watch him get out of bed and greet Elle as she walks into the apartment, and I smile as he gives her a big hug and strict instructions to take good care of me. Mom is still in the forefront of my mind, but I think it might be okay for me to also be thinking about Connor. Going to his house wouldn't have been a good move. Given how desperate I am for comfort right now, I have a pretty good idea that we wouldn't have just slept. I don't want to have sex with him only because I happen to need someone right now. That would cheapen what we have.

I'm not even sure what it is that we have. I just know that it's good.

Connor shows up at Elle's to pick me up bright and early. It's only seven, but I'm ready to go. He looks like he just got out of the shower, and he smells fresh and manly like the shirt I'd slept in last night. I changed back in my clothes from the pool again, leaving Elle where she's still crashed out in bed. She'd been wiped out when she got home from work last night and tried to stay up with me, but we both wound up falling asleep almost right away. So much for my second wind.

"How's your mom doing today?"

"Dad said she's tired but doing well, considering." That was all he said when I called him this morning, even after I pressed him for more details. I could hear from his voice that he hadn't slept very much, and I'm anxious to get to the hospital.

I notice that Connor's holding a cardboard tray with four steaming cups from Starbucks, and I smile.

"Do you need a pick-me-up this morning?"

He shrugs, looking a little embarrassed. "Not exactly. I didn't know what you liked, so I brought you some options."

That's almost enough to melt me into a pile of goo. I don't clutch my heart or anything, but really, that was so thoughtful of him. I pick out a frappuccino, he takes a plain coffee, and we leave Elle her choice of the other two and a note that says we went to the hospital. Hotel first, though, so I can look more like a human being. And Dad had asked if I could please bring him a few things from the hotel room.

Connor takes my hand as we walk to his car, and I pretend to be totally absorbed by drinking my coffee but I'm secretly looking at him. He's frowning as he unlocks the car and holds open the passenger side door for me, and I have to wonder how much doing all of this for me is getting in the way of his own life – work, Cruz, everything. I'll let him know when we get to the hospital that he's not obligated to stay.

We're both silent as we go to the hotel via some side streets that he knows, and he waits for me in the living room of the suite while I get ready. I'm already showered, but I change my clothes, do my makeup, and throw my dad's stuff together. I wind up packing a second bag for myself in case I decide to spend another night at Elle's. She'd offered last night before she fell asleep and had even given me a spare key, and I may take her up on the offer. I scan through the suite, and it takes me only a fraction of the time to know that I prefer the cramped, messy studio apartment over the empty, pristine suite.

Connor's standing by the window talking on his phone when I'm done with everything I need to do. There's something about the way guys talk on the phone to each other, like they have to make their voices more manly-sounding or something. Connor's maybe doing some of that posturing but not a lot. His tone is brisk and business-like, and I'm guessing he's talking to Neil. I don't want to eavesdrop, so I go back into my room with my two bags to wait.

I remember Connor telling me that he essentially took administrative leave, which I assume means he turned over his work to his partner, until he could get a handle on this Cruz thing. Man, if I ever run into his twin, I might need physical restraints to keep my claws in. He sounds like a douche.

I wonder if they're identical or fraternal. If I ever do get the chance to meet him, it would probably be weird either way. Not that outward appearances are everything. When I first met Connor, I thought he was gorgeous but also a total dick.

I'm grinning to myself right as Connor walks into my room. He looks almost relaxed now, and I direct my momentary glow at him, but my smile fades as he stops short and stares at me.

"What's wrong?" I instinctively look down, wondering if my shirt is inside-out or something.

"What's so funny?" he asks at the same time. "Nothing's wrong. You look great, is all."

"Thank you." I smirk at him. "And I was thinking about what a jerk you were when I first met you."

He laughs, and I surprise myself by laughing with him. Just for a second, but it feels good despite my sides hurting a little from crying so much yesterday. Connor walks over to me and takes my bags.

He winks. "You need to work on your sweet-talking skills."

I poke him in the ribs. "That's more or less what you said at the bar."

"Yeah, I remember. Unfortunately." He shifts both bags into one hand and takes my hand with his other. "I don't know why you're even with me."

With him. I think about that the entire elevator ride downstairs and most of the way to the parking garage. Not sure if Connor said that deliberately, if he wanted to let me know that he considers us to be together. I mean, obviously we're together in the literal sense right now, but I wonder if he thinks of himself as something more.

I'm *not* going to ask him what he meant. I don't think that all things necessarily have to be defined like that. And I've had guys get all needy on me after a couple of dates and demand to know how I feel about them or ask what we "are." My gut reaction has always been to run screaming in the other direction.

I ask instead, "Everything going okay with work?"

"Yes." He puts my bags in the back seat of the car as I get into the passenger side. "My client was being…stubborn for a day or so and not playing as much as she needed to. Things are much better now."

"Oh." I think about this as he gets behind the wheel. I know he's probably being deliberately vague because of confidentiality, but I'm curious about what he means by things being better. "Do you get paid depending on how much time they play?"

"No, we charge a fee based on number of days and evenings we block out for that client, regardless of how much they play. But it's always in a high roller's best interest to get out on the floor." He shoots me a sideways glance. "You know, to work off all of the comps."

I frown. I know Dad must need to work off all of the things that the casino has comped him, too. But with Mom being in the hospital... I think about the changes of clothes and toiletries Dad is having me bring to the hospital right now. I hope he doesn't completely get in a bind because of this.

I feel bad even thinking it, and I know I have no place to ask my Dad if he's even thought of that. Not now. Not when Mom's "not out of the woods yet." The casino will have to understand given the situation, right? I sip my coffee and stare outside at the Strip. It's relatively dead right now compared to peak hours, but this city is always awake, always working.

Connor turns in the visitor lot of the hospital like he's going to park, and I touch his arm.

"Hey, you don't have to come in with me if you don't want. You put a lot of time in yesterday."

His jaw tightens, and he's silent as he pulls into the first open spot. I stare off into the distance at the hospital. Maybe I'm feeling wimpy and tired, but geez. Could he possibly have parked any farther?

I'm about to make a quip to that effect, but when I face him, he looks annoyed.

"So we're clear, I'm not putting in time with you. I do things because I want to do them, and I'm here because I want to be." He tone is definitely irritated, but then his expression softens. "Unless you're telling me that because you'd rather me not come, then say the word. I promise I won't be offended."

I like that he said that, that he called me out and spoke his mind. He once asked me how I did the same thing, but he's not so bad at it, either. I'm glad that he finally figured it out. And I'm glad that he wants to be here with me, because he's been pretty great – comforting me, distracting me, keeping me from stressing out too much.

"Oh, by the way..." He reaches behind my seat and produces a bouquet of flowers. "I picked these up for you. For your mom."

My jaw drops as he sets the arrangement in my lap. It's an assortment of pink and purple blooms including some pink orchids like in the high roller room. Absolutely gorgeous. No idea when he would have had time to do this, considering he was at the hospital all afternoon and then with me until late last night.

"Connor. They're beautiful. Thank you so much. How..." I stop, swallowing the lump in my throat. First the choice of coffee and now this. I'm officially a melty mess.

"I know someone who works at a floral shop." He shrugs. "I called in a small favor."

I beam at him, my eyes feeling teary. My God, what is the matter with me? I'm not used to riding this kind of emotional roller coaster, but that's what this whole week has felt like.

He cocks an eyebrow. "You laughing at me again? Or crying? I can't tell."

"Not crying. And laugh at you? Nope..." I sigh as I get a bona fide case of the warm fuzzies. I know I'd be a nervous wreck if I had to be here by myself right now. "You really *are*

Prince Charming. That gruff thing you do is all an act, isn't it?"

He shakes his head at me. "I don't know what you're talking about. You're crazy, you know that?"

I smooth my hair back and smile. "Yes. Yes, I am." I put my hand on the door handle. "You coming with me, or did you park all the way out here so I could get my exercise?"

"Crazy," he mutters as he gets out of the car, but I can see his dimples.

Dad is waiting for me outside Mom's room, and I'm worried all over again as soon as I see him. He had sounded dead tired on the phone, and I can tell by the dark circles under his eyes that he probably didn't get any sleep. And this is for a guy who normally stays up late playing.

I immediately feel bad, wondering if I should have insisted on hanging out at the hospital last night. The nurses had said only one of us could stay in Mom's room, but I could have crashed in the waiting area, where Connor's stationed right now.

"How's Mom?" I ask, peering at him. "And how are you?"

"Neither of us got too much sleep. They were in throughout the night taking blood and adjusting her IV drip. She says she's feeling okay, but you know your mother. She has a hard time admitting it if she isn't." He frowns. "The nurses have already given her a couple of reminders about how she needs to communicate everything she's feeling."

Sounds like Mom. I stare down at the bag I'd packed for him. "I take it you'll be staying the night again?"

He nods. "I may go back and forth during the day, but I'll be staying nights here until she's discharged, if they'll let me. Your mother wants me here." His forehead is still creased as he directs his concern to me. "What about you? Are you all right?"

"Yes, I slept over at Elle's last night," I admit. "And my friend drove me here this morning. Did they give you an idea of when she might be discharged?"

"Not sure. She'll be on bed rest for a while so they can monitor her. Depending on how things go, they could decide to release her and treat her as an outpatient, but either way, she's going to need time to heal."

I can almost feel the stress flowing off of him in waves. I wish so badly that there was something more I could do.

"Dad, you need to take care of yourself, too. What can I do for you?"

He puts his arm around me, rubs my back. "Me? Nothing. But go and say good morning to your mother. Make her happy."

I walk into her room after giving him the hug of a lifetime.

Mom's eyes are closed, and I fight back my tears when I see how pale she is. Her hair is lank, and the dark shadows under her eyes combined with the horrible fluorescent lighting make her cheeks look sallow and sunken in.

I set down Dad's bag inside the door and Connor's bouquet on the counter, when she opens her eyes.

"Morning, baby girl." She gives me a wan smile.

"Hi, Mom." I think about what Dad and I both know, that she's good at hiding her pain. She's so incredibly strong, and I have to be the same for her right now. No matter how scared I am.

I perch on the edge of the armchair that's already pulled up beside the bed and reach over and take her hand. She squeezes it. "I'm being taken care of by all of these lovely nurses, and I keep thinking about how wonderful you're going to be once you get your certification."

"Aw, Mom..." The tears finally start to flow, and I wipe them away with my free hand. "I have to get through nursing school first. But I'm glad they're being good to you." I can totally see how my mom would have charmed the staff in no time flat.

"They are, despite having to poke and prod me with those terrible needles all of the time. And the extra tests on top of that. Why your father agreed to those, I'll never understand."

"Dad told the doctor about grandad," I say softly.

Her breath catches before she briefly closes her eyes. When she opens them again, they shine with unshed tears. "Yes, well... I suppose that's what they're doing, seeing if it's something that's in the family." She takes her hand from mine and places it on my shoulder, only a small shake belying her nerves. "I don't want you to worry about any of this, Alexis. I knew I wasn't feeling quite like myself right after we got here. I was worried, but I thought it was the change in humidity, elevation, something that would go away. But I was daft to keep it from you and your father. My leg was hurting for a while, and..." She sighs. "...quite frankly, I made up what I said about running into something so you wouldn't worry. I promise to keep both of you in the loop from now on."

I can tell she's beating herself up over it, like I had been all day yesterday. We are so much alike, my mom and I.

"I wish I could make everything all better for you, Mom."

"I wish I hadn't ruined everybody's holiday." She sighs, and her whole body seems to sink a bit more into the hospital bed.

"Stop. You didn't ruin anything," I say. "If it was going to happen, I'm glad it happened when you weren't alone." I shudder, thinking about how things might have gone down if she'd been home, with Dad at work and me living in my own place.

"Yes, I suppose so," Mom says thoughtfully. She closes her eyes again, and this time she keeps them shut. She says so quietly that I have to strain to hear, "This may be horrible of me to think, but I'm glad that your father has had to take a break from all of the gambling." Her lips twitch, her eyes still closed. "Though I do wish it had been because of a different reason."

"That's not a horrible thing to think." I ask her the same thing that I asked my dad. "What can I do for you, Mom?"

"Oh, I honestly can't think of anything. Come for another visit later today?"

"That's a given. But seriously, there's nothing I can do?"

"You can tell me about Connor," she murmurs. "Have you seen him lately?"

"Yes..." I think about how Connor told me stories last night as we were lying together and how it had eased my worries. Mom opens her eyes, watching me with a look of anticipation. If this will help her take her mind off of things, I can do that for her.

I don't go into too much detail, but I tell her how he showed up at the hospital, how he came to Elle's and brought me his t-shirt and sweats to sleep in. How he stayed with me until Elle got home so I wouldn't be alone. About the coffee this morning. And the flowers.

My cheeks feel rosy by the end of it, my belly warm.

Mom looks tired but is smiling at the end of my narrative. Her eyes sweep through the room and land on the flowers. "I had an inkling when I first met him that he was a keeper."

I feel myself grow even redder. "I'm having fun with him, Mom. But I don't know how this can possibly go anywhere after this summer. He lives here, I live in New York."

"Then don't decide now. Wait until the end of the summer." She closes her eyes. "New York isn't the only place in the world that has a nursing school."

"Uh huh," I say skeptically. "I can't believe we're even talking about this. I've known the guy for not even two weeks."

"Pssh," she whispers. "A week, a month, a year. What does it matter? If something is meant to be, it's meant to be. You have one more semester of your nursing pre-requisites?"

"Maybe even less if I can do a few courses on-line," I say, thinking about the summer classes I didn't take. I glance over at the door, but it's still firmly closed. "Mom, seriously. What are you saying? Does this have to do with the Ian story and how the two of you were meant to be?"

She opens her eyes, and I read genuine surprise in them. "I shared that story from that part of my life so you knew that your old mum has a heart," she says softly. "And Ian? He was my first love, yes, but I don't think I ever truly believed he and I were meant to be. If that were the case, I wouldn't have let him get away so easily."

I blink. "But I thought you said you could have stayed with him forever."

"Well, maybe I did at the time," she admits. "But you know... no one will ever love me as much as your father does."

Her eyes settle on the door to the hallway, and I watch as her face brightens despite her pain.

"Oh." I smile at her, though she's not looking at me. "Mom? Of course you have a heart. A pretty amazing one."

She sits up and reaches for me like she's going to give me a hug, but then winces and falls back again. I gasp and lunge over to her to help, but she waves me away with an audible sigh.

"Are you all right?"

"I will be." Her eyes settle on my face again. "You have an amazing heart too, baby girl. Don't forget that."

25

CONNOR

The second Alex's father walks over to me in the waiting area, I'm in uncharted territory. Laura's parents were divorced, and she snuck out of the house to meet me more often than not so I wouldn't have to deal with her mother. And there's been no one else except for the occasional one or two-night stand.

Fuck. Twenty-five years old, and I've never had to make small talk with the father of a girl I liked before. Seriously, how did I dodge that bullet this long?

I rise to a standing position from my chair as he approaches. I can see bits of Alex in him, especially in the way he carries himself. There's a sort of confidence in both of them, something that speaks to how they like to stand on their own and not rely on others for much of anything.

He strides up to me, looking at me directly as he holds out his hand. "James Lin. You're a friend of my daughter's?"

I shake it. "Yes, sir. Connor Vincent."

He gestures to the chair I just vacated. "Have a seat? I wanted to speak with you for a minute."

Oh, shit. I don't know why my immediate response is to feel defensive. Maybe that's normal. Either way, I brace myself for the inevitable questions that he's going to ask me about my intentions regarding his one and only daughter.

"I've seen you around quite a bit," he starts. "In the high roller rooms. What's your line of work, Connor?"

Interesting. Didn't see that coming, though maybe I should have. "I provide asset security for players. For high rollers," I pause before adding, "such as yourself."

"I see." He looks thoughtful, and I make the quick decision before he goes on to say anything. If he's considering hiring me, I'll have no choice but to decline because of conflicts of interest.

I can't work for you and like your daughter as much as I do.

The thought sends my head spiraling in a completely different direction. Because I would actually turn down this job if given an opportunity. Because I haven't looked at or even thought about another woman since that night at the concert when I danced with Alex.

"Not a bodyguard then?" he asks.

My work brain clicks the rest of the way into place as I consider why he'd ask me this. For clients like Maya who put themselves and assets like jewelry on display, personal security is part of the package. After all, the entire reason I'm in this gig is because some shithead tried to knock her down and steal her purse. But this can't be why Alex's father is asking. Alex told me about his background, that he's a hard-working guy who likes to treat his family to the high roller lifestyle on summer vacations. I have a few other clients like him, and I can see for myself that he doesn't flaunt what he has. So why ask about personal protection?

"Not specifically, though personal safety is a natural extension of protecting someone's assets," I explain. I look at him shrewdly as I add, "Why?"

He stares back at me, and I see it. Fear. There's something he's afraid of. Maybe even someone specifically. The look is gone in a literal blink of an eye though, and he gives me a wry smile.

"No particular reason. I know you and Alexis have been spending time together." He hesitates. "Forgive me for not being direct with you from the beginning, but I did ask around about you. You have a solid background and an excellent reputation with your clients. This city is full of individuals with unsavory backgrounds, and quite honestly, as Alexis' father, I feel better knowing she's around people who are safe."

This conversation keeps revealing more and more surprises. He had me checked out. Sounds like it was strictly in the business sense – not in regards to my personal life, thank God. I vaguely wonder if one of the people he talked to was Maya, but I'm not going to ask. Whether it was Maya or someone else, I can say with pride that I know that I have a good reputation and that my clients can all vouch for the fact that I'm good at what I do.

Alex walks into the waiting area right then, and she stops in her tracks when she sees me talking to her dad. Her face flushes, and I can't help but smile at her.

"Alexis." Her father stands up as she walks over to us, relief written on his expression and uncertainty on hers. "Did you have a nice visit with your mother?"

"Yes, but I'm afraid I tired her out, because she was dozing off at the end." She glances at me. "I see you met Connor?"

"I did."

"It was a pleasure, sir," I say, rising to my feet.

"James," he says with a nod, and I catch Alex's look of shock out of the corner of my eye. "Please call me James."

"I'll be back this afternoon, Dad," Alex calls out, but her father is already walking away.

Neither of us have eaten yet, and we decide to go back to Elle's place. As I drive there, we agree to drag Elle's ass out of bed and make breakfast. Alex seems more relaxed now, and I'm glad. Not that she was acting anxious when I picked her up an hour ago, but I imagine that seeing her mother had to have made her feel better.

"I love being out here for the summer, but that's one thing I do get sick of," Alex admits. "Constantly eating out or doing room service. And then I have to work in a restaurant when I get home. Yuck."

I glance at her before I make the turn onto Elle's street. Alex doesn't seem like the type to stick with something she doesn't like.

"If you don't like the restaurant, why not do something about it? Why not get another job?"

She shrugs. "I've thought about it, but it's good money, for one thing. And only temporary until I finish school. It's really not too bad." She shoots me a sideways look. "And if you must know, I've kind of had a crush on one of the cooks for forever."

I pull over in front of Elle's building and turn off the ignition. "Yeah? What's he like? Tell me about him. Or her."

Alex laughs. "It's a guy. No way. Why would you even want to know that?"

"Because. I'm interested in what you find worthy of a crush."

I rest my arm on the back of her seat, and her smile slowly disappears as I focus all of my attention on her. It was a simple question, one I asked out of pure curiosity, but her eyes search mine like she's waiting for more. I don't even know how I'd answer my own question. I suppose I used to think I had a specific "type" of woman I went for, but being with Alex kind of destroyed that stereotype. She's vibrant, headstrong, sensitive. Resilient as hell. She's nothing like any of those other women I've been with. Or maybe I just never gave anyone else the chance except for in a physical sense.

No, there's definitely some of that, but the women I've been with have been focused mostly on sex, too. On using me exactly like I used them, and then losing me.

Fact is, Alex is someone I can actually see myself with. For real, not only for one or two nights like all the others.

She clears her throat, and I'm glad she can't read my mind right now. "I don't even know if that cook is 'worthy of a crush,' as you say. He's just eye candy, you know? Something nice to look at during an eight-hour shift." She drops her gaze down into her lap almost shyly. "Not anything like you."

This warmth explodes out from somewhere deep inside. I'm not even sure I can put into words how I feel, not exactly. Just that I crave these moments with her. That when she lets me in like this, it makes me want a lot more of her. And that I want her, more than I think I've ever wanted anyone before. But not just physically. I also want to know more of what makes Alex her, and that realization throws me.

"Not anything like me? What, I'm not nice to look at?" I joke.

She looks up at me again, and her shyness gives way to a smirk. "C'mon. You know you are. Total eye candy. But eye candy I can actually talk to."

I grin at her. "Ah, that's the secret to my charm? My shitty conversational skills?"

She shakes her head and pushes open the passenger-side door. "Yeah, that's it."

We climb the stairs to Elle's apartment – her studio is one of two situated upstairs from a tattoo shop that's run by one of her friends. It's a totally fitting place for Elle to live.

Alex digs out her key from her bag as we get up to the landing. "If she's still sleeping, I guess we'll surprise her with breakfast in bed."

I'm about to say something not so funny again, but my guard goes up as Alex freezes outside the apartment, key raised to the door but stopping short. I hear it, too. The unmistakable sound of a bed rhythmically thumping against the wall, and it's definitely coming from Elle's apartment and not from across the hall. I might have thought it was funny if it was anyone else, but this is Elle. Overreaction or not, my first instinct is to beat the shit out of the guy who's banging my cousin right now.

"I don't think she's sleeping," I grumble.

Alex stares up at me, her eyes widening when she sees my jaw twitching. She takes hold of my hand and tugs on it, not letting go until we're back on the sidewalk in front of the building.

"Hey," she says cautiously. "You know Elle's a consenting adult, right? And that she does have a boyfriend?"

"Sorry," I mutter. "I know. That doesn't mean I like to think about her getting laid, let alone hear her doing it. She's like my little sister."

"I get it. The protective big brother vibe." She pats me on the arm. "You big softie."

"Ha." I roll my eyes, but I know what she's doing, that she's trying to make me lighten up about it. "Right. I get that a lot."

Alex gives me her sunny smile, but some of her happiness is tempered by the worry that I know has to be there. I like the way we can still banter back and forth like this, even now with her being stressed out about her mother and with me having Cruz as an intrusive pain in the ass in my life.

It strikes me that I haven't really been thinking about Cruz that much lately, maybe not as much as I should be. Part of that is because I know Neil has his people out there scouting him out for me and there's not much I can do until he gets back to me. But it's also because I've been with Alex, and she has this way of distracting me. I haven't talked to Neil yet this morning, and I remind myself to do it at the earliest opportunity.

We're still standing out in front of the tattoo parlor with the sun beating down on us, and Alex starts tying her hair back into a knot at the base of her neck. My eyes drink up that sexy line of her neck, my body instantly remembering how it felt to kiss her. I let my gaze slowly travel down her body, and I torture myself by also remembering how I kissed her everywhere, how she'd laid beneath me in her bed.

She stops, like she can feel the heat of my gaze, her hands stilling and eyes fixed on mine when I look back up at her face. Not taking my eyes off of her, I reach out and tuck a loose strand of hair behind her ear.

The gesture seems to shift something in her mood, too, and she lifts her hand, running her fingers across my cheek. Her touch mesmerizes me, the look in her eyes only inflaming my desire for her.

She drops her hand, linking it with mine. "So should we make breakfast at your place then?"

It takes me a second to find my voice. "You want to go to my house?"

"Yes." She shoots me a sideways look that's definitely feisty. "I'm sick of restaurants, remember?"

Today must be a day for firsts, because I've never taken a woman to my house before. Elle's maybe come over three or four times in the past two years, but that doesn't count. It's true that I did invite Alex over last night, to stay the night even. But that was different. That was because she needed to be with someone, and it could have been me or Elle or anyone else she knows.

We get back into the car, and I drive her over to my house. Not because she needs to come over but because she wants to. I shouldn't read into it, or I'll drive myself fucking crazy.

Too late.

I live about fifteen minutes west of the Strip, and Alex stares out of the window on the drive over, still holding my hand but completely silent. Like she's either processing everything that's happened or trying not to think about things too much. I try to focus on the road, but I'm already reacting to her being next to me, to her absently running her thumb over my palm, to the warmth of her skin. Damn if I can't think straight because my blood flow is not going anywhere near my brain at the moment.

She watches with an almost detached interest as I go through the security gates. It's one of dozens of the same sort of communities in the outskirts of Vegas, and I'd chosen it because it was pretty much a straight shot to the Strip off West Flamingo. The house had been a foreclosure, and I jumped on it when I first moved here because it was a good investment. It came with some extras that I don't need, but with other perks like a swimming pool and gym down the street.

The house itself is decent, three bedrooms over two stories and not nearly as excessive as some of the others in the area, but Alex gawks at it as I turn into the driveway. "You live here by yourself?"

"Yeah."

I know it's more space than I need. I did actually offer to rent Elle a room once I moved in, and she thought about it for two seconds before we both laughed it off. We would have driven each other crazy. Or if my feelings twenty minutes ago had been any indication, I would have lost it if I had to deal with her bringing home a string of guys.

Alex immediately hones her sights in on my bikes as I pull into the garage.

"You're a bike guy. I think I knew that when I first met you. Why don't you ever ride?" She gets out of the car and steps over to check things out.

I move to stand near her. "Because it's not the greatest thing in the world for transporting clients. I don't even think I have the Honda registered anymore." I shrug. "And the Harley obviously still needs a lot of work."

"Huh." She turns and faces me with a glint in her eye. "I don't know – if I were ever your client, I think I'd probably like that mode of transport."

"If you were ever my client?" I take one slow step toward her. "I'm afraid I wouldn't be able to take you on as my client, Ms. Lin."

Alex takes another step closer, tilting her head up to look me squarely in the face. It's already way too hot in the garage considering the time of day, but her move makes it escalate another degree. Or ten. "And why is that, Mr. Vincent?"

"Because I'd want to kill anyone who looked at you the wrong way."

Surprise registers in her eyes, but it's gone in an instant. She says coolly, "Yeah, that wouldn't be very good for business, would it? Well, maybe you could get the Honda registered and take me for a ride sometime."

I regard her seriously. There's no real reason I've let the Honda collect dust for so long. It's been sitting here mainly because I haven't bothered with it, but I honestly do miss riding it. My God, she's actually making me consider this. It's like she sees these things in me and somehow knows how to draw them out.

"Come on." She's already walking to the door that leads to the mudroom. "Give me a tour."

The grand tour should take less than five minutes, but Alex extends it by taking in everything in each room, even though there's not a whole lot. She runs her fingers over the marble countertop in the kitchen, snagging two apples from the bowl I keep on the counter and tossing me one before we walk into the living room. She sits down for a few seconds to test out the couch – a microfiber sectional and the most comfortable thing in the house – before getting up again. Her hands run over the gaming system as she asks me what games I have, and she nods as I tell her the titles that mostly involve shooting things, blowing shit up, or strategizing to shoot or blow shit up. She goes outside and circles the small backyard – I pay someone a nominal fee to maintain what little landscaping I have, but hardly ever go out there myself. She wanders through the two bedrooms upstairs, one of which I use as a study, and the other pretty much empty except for some stuff I still have stored in boxes. I suppose I should set it up to be my guest room someday, but I never have guests.

"I haven't done much with the upstairs," I say.

She doesn't respond, but she walks through the bathroom adjoining both bedrooms and then turns to face me, curiosity in her expression. "Don't tell me you sleep on the floor. Where's your room?"

I hesitate. "Master bedroom and bath are downstairs."

I hadn't meant to save my room for the end of the tour. Maybe I wanted to skip it, subconsciously or whatever, because it's my personal space while the rest of the rooms are just rooms. But Alex is already bounding down the stairs, and I shake my head and follow her. My bedroom is off a short corridor that runs back from the kitchen, and I catch up to her in the kitchen as she pauses to throw away her apple core.

"It's kind of a mess," I warn as I lead the way.

She stops inside the doorway of my room. "Um… Hardly."

Okay, so it's probably obsessively neat by most people's standards, but it's messy for me because the covers are still thrown back on my bed from when I got up this morning and last night's clothes are lying over the back of my leather recliner. Alex walks through the room, and I stand back and watch as she pauses to look at the stack of books on my nightstand.

I can guess why she wanted to come here. I see what she's doing because I do it too whenever I step into clients' hotel rooms – check out the way they use their space, pay attention to their personal effects. I can tell a lot about their personalities that way.

That's exactly why I haven't ever had anyone over here, why I don't ever invite women over. Because I'm not comfortable letting anyone in. But I smile a little as Alex tests out the recliner, kicking her feet up and giving it the equivalent of a thumbs-up with a relaxed sigh.

Yeah, I don't mind letting her in. Not at all.

I still don't make a move. Not until she drops her purse on the chair and kicks off her sandals, gets up and walks over to my bed, and leans against it. Not until she trails her fingers over my sheets and looks at me in a way that's shy and inviting at the same time. I've been holding myself back since the pool accident because I haven't wanted to take advantage of her. But that look, direct and wanting and from beneath her lashes. It's enough to drive me insane. She knows exactly what she's doing, knows what she wants, and so do I.

This need fills me, this crazily intense need to be next to her, to feel her skin, to kiss her. To taste her again. It takes me mere seconds to walk over to her, but the time seems to stretch out. I focus on the way she's looking back at me with hunger in her eyes. How her beautifully lush lips part as I advance on her. The way her breath quickens when I come to a stop in front of her.

I kiss her, and I'm not soft like I've been with her before. I'm greedy this time, want more as soon as my mouth takes hers. She rises to meet that desire, steps into me and presses her body close as I push my tongue into her mouth. I run my hands up and down her back, over her ass and down to her thighs, lifting her up so she's sitting on the bed and I'm standing between her legs. She makes a small sound in the back of her throat as I shift her forward so she's nestled against me.

It hasn't even been an entire week since we kissed like this, but God, I think I was starving for her. And I don't want to stop until we're both satiated.

I find the hem of her shirt and grab it, force myself to break off the kiss so I can pull it over her head and chuck it to the floor. She presses her hands against my stomach before sliding her hands up and doing the same with my shirt, and we face each other, both breathing hard.

I know I can please her, but it's so much more than that. I know all too well what it's like to feel alone, to turn to someone solely for the physical gratification. I'm not going to let it be like that between me and Alex. No fucking way.

It wouldn't be like that. There's already more than that between us, and I know it.

"I want you. All of you." My voice is raw, my feelings stripped down to be just as raw as I wait for her response.

"Then take me," she whispers.

Fuck yes.

I run my hands over the sensitive hollow of her throat, down the perfect line of her collarbone, over the gorgeous curves of her breasts. She reaches behind her back and unsnaps her bra, getting rid of it completely, and I squeeze her as I lower my lips to her neck and follow the same path. Move lower until my mouth covers her nipple, teasing her with my tongue before taking it between my teeth. She moans, pain and pleasure shooting through me as she digs her nails into my shoulders.

Her hand grips and releases my hair as I give her another gentle bite then suck. I lift her leg, run a hand under her thigh, marvel at her smooth skin. She hitches up her skirt so she can get even closer to me, and fuck, I want her so badly right now, want to feel all of her against me.

But I want her mouth again first, and I rise and take it, rubbing her nipple between my thumb and forefinger and making her moan against my lips. I take the kiss deeper, slower, loving the way she matches my rhythm, meets me stroke for stroke. It only heightens my need for her because I know that's exactly how it's gonna be when I finally lose myself in her.

I grab her legs, reach under her skirt and work her panties off her as she pushes herself up to help me. She reaches down, jerks open the button on my pants, and unzips me in one swift move. I love how she doesn't hold herself back, how she knows what she wants and goes for it.

I groan as she slips her hand between us and frees me from my boxer briefs. Her fingers close around and squeeze me, stroke me long and hard, and holy God, I'm going to lose it if she keeps that up. I move her hand away, taking over and rubbing myself against her sweetest spot, feeling her wetness and getting off on the little noises she makes as I tease her.

"Please," she whispers.

I want her to lose control. I want to get back down on my knees and taste her, make her be on the verge but be with her when she goes over the edge, but then she grabs my shoulders and pulls herself forward. She tilts her hips up to meet me, and we get too close. I shut my eyes and use all of the control that I have to pull myself back. God, I want it, but not yet.

She whimpers. "If you say you don't have condoms, I'm going to die."

"No dying. I have them," I growl.

I run my hands through her hair, descend on her mouth and kiss her until our breaths come out as hard pants. Push her so she falls back on my bed, grab her skirt, and pull it off. Stare down at her gloriously naked body as I get out of my jeans and kick out of my boxer briefs. Watch her as her eyes travel down the length of my body and then up again like she's drinking in the sight of me.

She's in *my bed*, and she's so fucking beautiful. The way she's looking at me right now stirs up feelings in me that I thought were dead. This isn't about running through any scripted moves that I know I can use to drive her wild. This is about me and her, about just us in this moment and whatever we want to make it.

I want her to be mine.

I have to separate from her to get a condom from my wallet, and I throw an extra one on the bed before I sheath myself. I kneel down, kissing her thighs and squeezing them as I dip my head and lick her, taste her, flick my tongue against her and into her. She arches her back, grabs the sheets, and I hold on and love her until I can feel that she's nearing the cusp.

"Connor…"

I love hearing her say my name.

I pull away, move back over her body, rasping my tongue over her skin, over her other nipple before drawing it into my mouth. Her fingers knot in my hair, grab at me as her body tenses beneath mine, but I don't move. I take my time, suck hard as I slip my finger into her wetness and feel her tighten around me.

I move up, cup her cheek and run my thumb down her jaw. I'm nearing the limits of my control, but this already feels better, deeper, more satisfying than anything I've ever done with anyone. I lower myself so I'm positioned perfectly to take her.

Her lips part, her eyes closed.

"Alexis," I whisper.

She opens her eyes, and I drown in the depths of her desire.

"Tell me you want me."

"Oh my God," she whispers. "I want you, Connor. So much."

I kiss her deeply as I rock into her, and she cries out against my mouth as she takes all of me.

Holy shit, nothing can feel this good.

I linger, give her the chance to really feel me, let myself feel all of her, and she's so fucking perfect. Perfect because we fit together so well. Perfect because she's reaching inside me in a way that I've never felt before. She grabs my arms and digs her nails into my skin as I start moving again, and I take it slow, make it last. Drive that delicious burn deeper and deeper until it's everything that I know.

I know she's getting close when she starts quickening her movements, her sounds building in urgency. I move faster, harder until I feel her body start to tremble, and she stiffens beneath me and cries out. I close my eyes as I feel her come, let myself go right after because I can't hold back any longer.

I bury my face in her neck and hold her tightly, shuddering as she takes everything. As I give her everything I have.

Damn. I think I'm done for.

I'm already falling for her, hard.

26

Alex

Oh dear sweet God.

I run my hands over Connor's sweat-slicked body, feeling him completely as he takes his own bliss. The shocks continue to roll through me, my breaths synched with his as he collapses on top of me. I don't want him to move, but he pulls out and rolls over to lie next to me. My eyes close as the heat between us makes me languid, and I smile to myself as he reaches down and squeezes my hand.

He shifts away from me, and I open one eye, mourning the fact that he's leaving the bed but simultaneously enjoying the view as he walks to the bathroom.

I don't always get there when I'm with a guy, but that's because they're usually mostly intent on themselves, on running to the finish without me. Not like this. I feel like I connected with Connor in a way that I never thought would happen for me. He didn't just have sex with me. He actually made *love* to me, and I can still feel all of him. It makes me want more of that connection, more of him, period.

I'm maybe a quarter-asleep when he comes back. I feel him move again so he's lying on his side, facing me, and the warmth of him sends sharp tingles down my spine.

"You okay?" he murmurs in my ear.

"So much more than okay," I murmur back.

I open my eyes and look at him. He's staring at me, and the look in his eyes makes my heart stutter. Desire, passion, his whole soul bared for me to see.

I reach up and put my hand on the side of his face, and he braces himself up on an elbow and leans in to kiss me. Slow and deep and so very sexy. Sending little sparks through me that keep me from coming down all the way.

"Mmmmm." My eyes flutter shut again as I make the sound of pure contentment, and I feel him smile against my lips.

He pulls away again before I'm ready for him to, traces lines on my shoulder and down my arm. "What do you want to do today, love?"

Love. He's called me sweetheart before, like that time at the bar when he was being sarcastic, and I know that's kind of his thing. I'm not that girl who goes all soft when a guy calls her all of those ooey gooey names, but there's something I like about Connor calling me that. Love.

I drag my eyes open again and blatantly enjoy the sight of him. Run my fingers over those strong shoulders and across his chest. Place my palm so I can feel his heartbeat.

"I want to do this today," I say, but my stomach growls loudly in protest right after.

He grins at me. "You need breakfast."

My stomach may be grumbly, but I object. Maybe I'm still working myself down off that glorious high, but I feel so close to him, and I want to get even closer.

I'm not going to lie to myself and say that it's not totally scary feeling this way, wanting more of an emotional connection to Connor. But I'm going to take a chance this time and let myself feel this. Because I like the fact that he stood back and let me into his personal space this morning. I like the fact that he lets me see past that gruff exterior when I'm with him. I like the way he makes me feel so special and how he breaks down my walls like they're not even there.

And scary or not, I like him way too much to run away.

"I just need you right now," I murmur.

My hand is still pressed against his chest, and I can feel his heart start to race. Those blue eyes of his blazing at me the entire time, he takes my hand and kisses my fingers, one by one.

My eyes close of their own volition as he draws my index finger into his mouth and sucks on it.

"Kiss me," I whisper.

He kisses my palm, but then his lips cover mine as we meld together. Our arms winding around each other. Our bodies aligning with a quick shift of movement so we can feel more of each other. He keeps kissing me, and I lose myself to the rhythm. Slow. Sexy. Like he's relishing me and making me melt a little more with each caress of his tongue.

I run my hands over his hard-cut body as he grabs another condom. He's ready for me, already hard again and pressing into my thigh, and I never came down all of the way, never stopped being ready. I take the condom from him and give him one long, slow stroke before rolling it on, loving how his eyes close and the sound of his groan. Loving how I can do that to him.

He gets to his knees and lifts me up, pulls me so I'm straddling him and holds me close. Oh, God. There's something really hot about him wanting me to be on top, about him relinquishing that control he likes so much. His hands run down my sides, his thumbs stroking my skin, his grip tightening on my hips.

"You have no idea what you do to me," he says in a husky voice.

I smile at him. "It's the same thing you do to me," I whisper.

I look into his eyes as I raise myself up, and a jolt of nerves slashes through me. It's only for a second though, and it dissolves, leaving me with nothing but desire for him. I've never felt this way about anyone before, and it's so, so good. Better than good.

He's breathing raggedly or maybe it's me. I'm in total control, and I don't move.

"Alexis..." he says roughly.

I take his mouth again, so softly, as I make us one, and oh God, it's like he's made to fill me up. He keeps his hands on my hips as I move with him, but he lets me set the pace. And he keeps looking at me, and there's so much emotion in his expression that I almost can't take it. But I keep looking at him too, and it intensifies everything between us. Physically. Emotionally.

I love this.

I love being with you.

I don't want to let you go.

I close my eyes. Let myself concentrate on how he feels and how he makes me feel, on the electric shocks radiating through me as I lower myself so I can take all of him. Let the friction and heat build as his hard body grinds against mine.

He leans forward and kisses my neck, sucks on me as one of his arms wraps around my back and draws me even closer. I run my hands through his hair, dig my nails into his shoulders as I move faster, as those currents of electricity keep building. My breath escapes as a gasp as I feel him grow even harder, and I know he's close when he grabs my hips with both of his hands. I start moving fast and furious until those shocks explode to fill me, and I wind my arms around his neck, moaning as my body is overcome with pleasure.

He shudders in release at the same time, and we cling to each other, his mouth finding mine and kissing me until we can't breathe. He lifts me off him, lays me back on the bed as I turn into a pile of jelly. Lies next to me and kisses me again, long and lazy. I kiss him back, just as lazily, drape an arm around his neck and curl up against him, but he moves away and lays the covers over me.

"Stay here. I'm bringing you breakfast in bed," he says into my ear.

I snuggle down into Connor's pillow, sighing and letting the drowsiness win.

I don't hear him move away for a long time. I'm on the verge of sleep when I feel him smooth back my hair and kiss my forehead.

I wake with a start to the smell of breakfast, and I clutch at my pillow until I remember where I am. Not my pillow. Connor's.

I sit up and see the tray on the side of the bed. He owns an actual tray for serving breakfast in bed, but it looks brand new (or just really clean). I wrap the bedsheet around myself and crawl over, smiling when I see that Connor made me the works. Coffee, juice, French toast, bacon, eggs, and a decent selection of fruit. Seriously. He can be so unreal sometimes.

The shower's going from the master bathroom adjoining the bedroom, and I nibble on a piece of bacon and let myself bask in happiness for a moment.

My phone buzzes from my bag on the chair, and I grab a bunch of grapes and scoot over to the edge of the bed. It's a text from Dad, telling me that Mom is sleeping soundly and he's going to head back to the casino for a short while. I know that Mom is glad that Dad has a break from gambling, but I think about what Connor had said and can't help feel relieved that Dad is taking care of his obligations to the casino to cover all of the comps.

My phone is almost dead, and I can't remember if I packed the charger. Actually, I'm pretty sure that I didn't, which means I'll have to stop by my hotel room to get it because Connor and Elle both have different phones than me. Just as I have the thought and am shuffling back over to the bed in my sheet, a call comes in, and this time it's Elle.

"Hey, Elle," I say cheerily. "Have a little fun this morning?" Hello pot, please meet kettle.

"What?" She sounds confused, and then she lets out an embarrassed laugh. "Oh, hell. Did you come by the apartment a while ago? Because Wes stopped by for a minute."

"I hope for your sake it lasted a lot longer than a minute," I laugh. Damn but I'm giddy right now. "What's up?"

"Okay, so two things. First, I'm singing next Friday night at this small but really cool venue on West Charleston. I mentioned to Trey after the Alysa's Empyre concert that I might want to start again, and he arranged the whole thing, even got me a backup band on short notice. It's some buddies of his, and they do covers so I'll have to figure out what songs of theirs I can do."

I can hear the excitement in her voice even though I can tell she's trying to hold herself back and downplay it. "Elle! That's awesome. What time?"

"Nine o'clock. Oh, and I obviously wanted to tell Connor this too, but he's not answering his phone right now. Is he with you?"

I glance at the bathroom. "Yes. He's busy right now, but I'll tell him."

"Okay." She doesn't question it, plowing onto the second thing like she's anxious. "The other thing, and this is for Connor too, but Cruz just stopped by, right as Wes was leaving. He told me he needs to get back to Albuquerque on Wednesday now."

"What?" Wednesday is two days away. Panic settles hard in my chest, and I throw the sheet off me and start grabbing my clothes from the bed and floor. I hop on one foot and stumble into my underwear, the phone pressed against my ear. "What does this mean?"

"He said he wanted to see Connor tomorrow night, and at first he tried to make it sound all social and shit, but I called him on it." She sounds worried, and I wonder what all else Cruz said when he talked to her. She probably feels like I do, like I totally failed Connor by not even talking with him about what he was going to do. I didn't even see him for all of those days, and with that stuff with my mom… Crap. I wrangle my shirt over my head, my face burning with anger and some shame. But tomorrow night isn't right now, which means we still have time.

"You told Cruz you knew what he was really up to?"

"I did," she admits. "Honestly, he didn't seem that surprised."

"Okay, so Connor needs to tell him that he'll give him an answer at a later date. He said the end of the month, so he can wait until the end of the month."

Elle sighs loudly. "That's the gist of what I told Cruz, but he didn't like that. He got mad at me."

Mad? I bristle at the thought. "He didn't hurt you, did he?"

"No, no," she says quickly. "But he wasn't happy that I thought I had the right to say anything about it. I think Connor might be better off telling him no right now. Or I've actually been thinking…" She hesitates. "I know some people and probably so does Connor – acquaintances, no one that we're really tight with – that we could send Cruz to. You know, to appease him so he'll back off."

"No, Elle," I say firmly. "That kind of guy doesn't just stop at a little bit. If you or Connor give him anything, then he'll keep coming back for more." The water stops running, and I hurry up and say, "Hey, Connor's getting out of the shower now. Let me talk to him and then I'll call you back, 'kay?"

"The shower? Where are you?"

I bite my lip and the bullet at the same time. "At Connor's house."

"For real?" she practically screams into my ear. "He never takes anyone to his house. Alex, what is going on between you two? Are you..."

"Not now. Hey, we'll figure this out, okay?" I say it loudly, to counteract her screechiness, but I have to stop her from going there. "Gotta go, but I'll call you back."

I end the call and hear the bathroom door open at the same time. Still wearing nothing but my underwear and shirt, I turn around, hoping I don't look as rattled as I feel.

Connor is standing in the doorway, a towel wrapped around his waist, his body still wet because he probably heard me yelling and came out right away to investigate. His hair is darkly plastered to his forehead, a concerned expression on his face as I drop the phone.

He looks so, so beautiful that I want to cry.

The next fifteen minutes go by in a blur. I manage to keep my emotions and angry commentary in check, reporting to him first what Elle told me and then my own harebrained ideas on the subject. He listens to me until I'm done, the tight muscles in his jaw the only sign that he's upset.

Turns out that Connor's also considered that Cruz might already have connections here and that Neil has "people" (I'm afraid to ask exactly what that means) tailing Cruz to see who they are.

"So you haven't heard from Neil yet?"

"No, but I'm going to call him now." He steps up to me and plants a quick kiss on my lips, his gaze holding mine with an intensity that makes me reel. "I'll take care of this. Thank you, love."

I nod, and he grabs his phone and walks out of the room, already speaking with Neil before he's out of earshot. He's all business-like and efficient, and I'm glad that he's so level-headed because it helps me be the same. I decide to take my turn in the bathroom and run out to his garage, grab my bag from the trunk of his car, and sneak back into his room. The sneaking turns out to be unnecessary because I can hear Connor's voice coming from upstairs on my way through the house.

I take the quickest shower in history, brush my teeth, and run a pick through my hair so it won't dry all tangled. Stuff my clothes from yesterday into my bag and throw on a new shirt and skirt. Keep my makeup simple and light.

It takes me a total of ten minutes, and Connor is dressed and waiting for me in his room when I get out. He's walking around restlessly, not exactly pacing but pretty close.

"Neil has some preliminary information for me, and I'm going to the Strip to meet him right now," he says without preface. "Do you want me to drop you off at the hospital to see your mom? Or you're also welcome to stay here."

Obviously me coming along isn't an option, not that I thought it would be. I remember my dad's text. "I'll stay here," I say.

He nods distractedly. "I should only be an hour or so, but in case you get bored, there's a clubhouse with a pool about a block east of here. I'll give you the code for it and also the one for my front door if you want to go."

I keep my face intentionally blank as he quickly writes down both codes down on a piece of paper in bold blocky handwriting. It's maybe silly of me to think anything of it, but it is sort of like he's giving me a key to his house.

I can tell he's itching to go, but I dig through my brain for something to say.

Be careful.

I don't want anything to happen to you.

He's already halfway to the door. "See ya soon," I say.

Connor stops in his tracks and turns around, reaching me in four long strides. He slides his hand around to the small of my back, holding me there as he kisses me. It's sweet and soft and hot all at once, his tongue purposefully slow as he kisses me. I clutch at his arms in an attempt to keep centered. He ends it way before I'm ready for it to end, touches my cheek, and gives me his old cocky grin before he sets off. I watch him walk out the door with that swagger of his. Damn.

I pick at the rest of the breakfast for a few minutes but decide to take him up on his offer to use the pool. I'd thrown in one of my swimsuits when I packed, more out of habit than anything, and I grab it and put it on under my clothes. I dig out my flip flops and kick them onto my feet, wrapping up my hair into a loose knot at the base of my neck. Don't know if there are towels there or if Connor has special ones he uses for the pool, but I snag the towel I used for my shower, and also grab my phone, sunglasses, and piece of paper with the codes before taking the breakfast tray out to the kitchen.

I root around in the lower cupboards until I find a mess of tupperware containers and dig through until I can find matching lids. I save what will keep and scrape the rest into the garbage before stacking the dishes into the dishwasher. I guess I could have left the tray, but it's maybe habit from working in the food business or from my Gran and her aversion to wasting food.

I dig around some more and find another mess of recyclable shopping bags in a drawer. Don't know why, but I'm glad that not everything in this house is perfectly neat and stacked. I untangle one of the bags and stick my stuff for the pool into it, fill my water bottle, throw on my sunglasses, and I'm out the door. It beeps behind me to let me know it's locked.

It's late morning, and the sun immediately fries me as soon as I step onto the walk. Connor had told me that the clubhouse was a block or so east of here, and I take a second to get my bearings before heading left.

His neighborhood is super quiet, the houses all stucco-walled ghosts with empty windows for dead eyes. In actuality, I know that I'm not seeing anyone outside because it's over a hundred degrees out as opposed to whatever everyone has their air conditioning set to. That, and probably most people here have jobs that they need to go to. Still, it feels a little creepy.

"Alexis."

My heart leaps in my chest as I hear Connor call out my name. But his voice is scratchy, like he's been yelling for hours when he's only been gone for less than thirty minutes.

I whip around, and a gaping hole forms in my gut when I see the man walking toward me from across the street. I knew they were identical twins, but I'm still not prepared to see someone who looks so much like Connor.

Cruz.

He's even dressed like Connor does most of the time in a simple dark t-shirt and jeans, though he's wearing cowboy boots, which I can't see Connor ever doing. And there's a severe quality to his face that is so *not* Connor, like his features have been hollowed out by some darkness from his past. His frame is skinnier, lankier. His hair is longer and greasier, darker (probably because of the grease). His eyes glimmer as he closes in on me, and maybe I've watched too many movies in the past week because the thought automatically pops into my head. He's like one of those supervillains from an alternate universe. Like the anti-Connor.

"Hey, baby." Even though his lips look so much like Connor's – dammit, I must stop thinking like this – they turn up in a distinct leer.

I back away from him, noticing the gun that he's openly carrying in his belt. I force myself to breathe evenly, try to keep my cool, but I'm actually freaking out inside.

"What do you want?" I take another step back. And another. I'm only four houses away from Connor's, but I'm wearing flip flops. Even if I did manage to outrun him, I'd have to dig out the code and punch it in before I could get inside.

I wouldn't make it. I'd never be able to get there before Cruz, let alone get inside safely. Not even if I'd had a key instead of a code.

My heart sinks at the realization, but I somehow dig out some new resolve at the same time. I need to take a stand, talk to him and bide some time until someone drives by that I can flag down. Someone has to drive by soon, right? Cruz isn't answering me – he's just eating me up with his eyes in a way that's making my skin crawl.

"How did you get past the security guards?" I demand.

I notice a For Sale sign in front of the house where he came from. We're on the other side of the street from Connor's, and I'm guessing that Cruz has probably been lying in wait inside this empty house for a while. I can totally picture him breaking in and waiting until he had the opportunity to get to Connor. Or get to me.

And now that he has me, now what?

He coughs out a brittle laugh. "Those underpaid cop wannabees? They didn't need very much convincing."

I swallow hard as he takes another step toward me, and I take a step back like we're doing some terrible dance routine.

"What do you want?" I repeat, hating the fact that my voice breaks at the end.

His eyes narrow into slits. "I need to convince my little brother of something, and I thought I could pass the message through you."

Pass a message through me? What the hell is that supposed to mean, that he's going to leave me for dead or something for Connor to find? The panic explodes to fill me, and I whirl around and run. The clubhouse. There will be other people there. I might not even need the code. I can draw attention to Cruz once I get there.

I sprint down the street, but I don't get very far before Cruz grabs me from behind. I open my mouth to yell, but he clamps a hand over it, pinning my arms to my sides with his other arm. I grit my teeth and buck against him as hard as I can, try to stomp on his foot with my heel, but all that happens is that I lose my flip flop and sear the bottom of my foot on the sun-baked asphalt.

He may be lankier than Connor, but he's incredibly strong, his arms like iron restraints thwarting my attempts to break free, and my kicks and jabs don't deter him. His breath fills my nostrils, and it's smoky and rancid, like burning plastic.

"Shhh. Don't fight me, baby," he whispers in my ear. "I'm not gonna hurt you. I just gotta tell you something, and then I'll leave. *Comprendes?*"

I blink back the moisture forming in my eyes as I try to nod my head to let him know I understand. He doesn't seem to realize how hard he's holding me though. Not that he would care.

"You tell Connor that if he doesn't agree to help me, my associates won't help out your father as agreed."

My dad? Oh my God. I squeeze my eyes shut, choking against the stench that's rolling off of him.

"See, it turns out that I have friends here, and they've been watching you and your family. Your daddy's been making some bad decisions this summer, but it only got worse when your momma landed herself in the hospital. Lucky for him that my friends cut him a sweet monetary deal. An all-expense vacation, if you know what I mean, and he gets the whole year to pay them back."

I tear away from him enough to violently shake my head back and forth. I don't understand everything he's saying to me, but I understand enough. No. He's full of shit. There's no way Dad would have involved himself with the criminals that Cruz must be talking about.

"If Connor doesn't give me what I asked for, then I go to my friends and tell them to renege on the deal. And trust me." He presses his cheek against mine, and this time, I do retch. "You don't want them to do that."

He lets go of me, and I'm in such a hurry to get the hell away from him that I pitch forward. I catch myself on the asphalt with my hands but not before I skid on my knees. He walks around to stand in front of me, and I lift my head and glare at him.

"Go fuck yourself, Cruz."

"I'd rather you do it, baby."

He laughs, and the sound is so much like Connor when he's happy and lets himself go that my tears finally spill over and run down my cheeks.

Cruz drops down into a crouch, and I make myself meet his gaze and hold the eye contact. I'm pretty sure that what I can smell on his breath is the smoke from hard drugs of some kind, that he's high, and that's why he's so strong. That this is why the look in his eyes isn't totally sane.

"Tell my brother, bitch."

My throat is closed up, my lips dry and my heart in pieces as I fight to say the words.

"I'll tell him," I whisper.

27

CONNOR

I meet Neil at a different restaurant this time, giving major pause when I see that he's not alone. He's in a booth with Maya, and they're sitting across the table from one another and leaning in close like they're partners in crime. Looks like she got over her reservations of working with Neil, which is good. What's not good is having Maya involved in this any more than she already is.

Neil's dressed up like a biker today in a black leather riding jacket and black jeans, a total contrast to Maya in her light blue off-the-shoulder evening dress. He spots me first, gives me a curt nod, and Maya follows with a tight smile. She slides over in the booth for me, and I sit after a brief hesitation.

"How are you, gorgeous?" I say, but there's too much heaviness in the air around us for it to be like it usually is. She looks as great as always, but her face has a hardness to it that I haven't seen in her before.

"Your brother is either going to get himself killed or arrested," she says with venom. "And even if neither of those things happen, we need to take him out before he smears your good name all over this city."

Maya can be cool and controlled, especially when she's out on the floor, but I've never seen her like this. Not so direct. Not so harsh. Or maybe I did get a glimpse of it that time she asked me to get her cigarettes, when she asked me about what I was doing with Alex.

I look at Neil, who stares back at me with his standard expression of complete neutrality. He shrugs. "Mrs. Coplin is a smart lady. I'd listen to what she has to say."

Interesting. He's having Maya break the news. Or maybe she's the one who came across whatever information they're about to tell me. I almost call him on that but stop myself at the last second. He's right. Maya is a smart lady, and I've always known it. I focus all of my attention on her and listen.

"Your *brother*," she says, almost spitting out the word, "has been making a nuisance of himself with all of the wrong individuals."

She looks around, casting a quick glance over her shoulder, even though we're in the corner booth in the back of the restaurant. Neil has a vantage point to see the rest of the restaurant, and I follow his line of sight to a guy dressed like a tourist in a Vegas t-shirt, shorts, and ball cap. He's facing away from us and looking out into the gaming area, and I wouldn't have picked him out of the crowd if I hadn't been looking for him. I'm guessing this is one of Neil's people that he has looking out for Cruz. And apparently watching out for us, too.

Maya leans in close to me. "There are people that you don't cross in this city. You know this. You're one of the good ones, Connor, or maybe you've just been lucky in being able to keep your nose clean and stay away from all of that.

But if Cruz keeps doing what he's doing…" She trails off, her palms up in the air before they fold neatly in her nap.

I get it. Vegas is a mix of people with varying and extreme levels of power. I'm at one extreme, haven't wanted any of that, have only wanted to do my own thing while figuring out my next move in life, but Cruz is a totally different story.

"So you've identified who he's gotten mixed up with then?" I ask. I don't want to know specific names, and I doubt Maya would ever tell me. But if he's getting involved with the organized crime sector, I'm going to have to put an end to that right now. And if this is the case, I might have an idea of how to get Cruz the fuck out of my city.

She nods. "There's a consortium. All of them have legit connections to the gambling industry, but Neil and I know that at least some of them are involved in racketeering, setting up illegal gambling via other channels, that sort of thing."

Neil speaks up from across the table. "And I know a guy who knows a guy." He gives me a humorless smile. "This person is in the collection business for the consortium, and he tells my guy that Cruz has been poking his nose into that area." He leans forward. "These guys who collect are some really bad motherfuckers. But maybe that's why your brother feels like he'd be right at home with them."

Maya presses her lips together, stares down at her hands. "You understand that it's better if you don't know any more than that, Connor."

Not going to argue that point. And I'm not totally blindsided by this, either. I already knew Maya has been building her own connections in the city for the past few years, but I wasn't totally sure of the nature of them. And I do understand. I understand that my brother's trying to edge in on a racketeering scheme that undoubtedly has links to organized crime. And that he's way over his fucking head. I'm grateful for about the millionth time that I chose to change my name so there isn't an overly obvious connection between me and Cruz for people who've never met me face-to-face.

"I don't need to know more than that." I glance between them. "Will you two be all right working together for a couple of more days?"

Maya laughs, and it has a hard edge to it. "Of course we'll be all right. Turns out Neil and I have more in common than I thought."

She digs out a cigarette from her purse, but the restaurant is one of the places in the casino where she can't smoke, and she drops her hand and frowns.

"Let's go for a walk," I suggest.

Maya nods and signs off on the check, and we slide out of the booth, Neil waiting until she and I are standing before pushing the table back and squeezing through. Maya slips her hand through my arm like she always does, putting the cigarette between her lips. Neil appears on the other side of her, a lighter in hand.

"Thank you, darling," she mutters as he lights it. She draws and exhales, her gaze connecting with mine with some unease in it for the first time since I got here. "Before you fill us in on your plan, I need to tell you something else. I'm out after this trip, Connor. I'm done. My business back home is a giant mess because of some poor decisions." She blows out smoke as she simultaneously sighs. "Not all on my part, but I had a very bad business manager and didn't realize what was going on for several years. It's been a really good ride, honey. I couldn't have done it without you."

I suspected something was going on, with her mood shifts, bagging out on the games, and the phone calls, but I don't know what to say to this. She does seem uncomfortable about it, but she's also calm, like she's updating me on the regular news of her day. She squeezes my arm and glances over at my business partner. "I've already told Neil this, and he's kindly offered to go after my old manager, who's conveniently fled the country, by the way. But that still wouldn't get me out of this mess."

"Maya…" I discard the formalities again because in this moment, she's just Maya and I'm just me. But she has it all wrong. I couldn't have done any of this without her, wouldn't have even considered doing what I do if Maya hadn't given me the opportunity. "You've been incredible," I say, and it's an understatement. "If there's anything I can do…"

She waves a hand dismissively. "No. If I'm struck with inspiration, I'll let you know, but you have your own problems to deal with at the moment. So, what do you propose to do about Cruz?"

The three of us stop outside the hotel's ticket office, like we're conferring upon shows we want to see, and I lay out the details of my plan. Neil and Maya take turn asking questions until I'm pretty sure we get it all the way right. It's a gamble, but we all agree that aside from getting someone to put a bullet in Cruz's head – not an option – it's the best plan that I have.

Neil's gaze bores into mine, his mouth set in a hard line. "You want to take one of my guys with you for backup?"

"No. I have to do this alone. But there is one more thing before I go." I huff out a breath, raking my hand through my hair. "I'm going to give my girlfriend your phone number. Cruz made a point of telling me that he knows about her. If something happens while I'm gone, I want her to be able to call you."

I'm in a hurry, and the words come out without me thinking. My girlfriend. It doesn't feel strange to say it, though.

There's Elle I have to worry about, too, but she's almost always around people. But more importantly, no matter how resentful Cruz is toward Elle for leaving him in New Mexico,

I know he loves her. And I can't kill Cruz outright or have him killed because he's my twin brother.

Maya interrupts my thoughts with a sharp look. "Is this the girl from the high roller room?"

I nod. "Yeah. Her name is Alexis Lin. She'll probably be spending most of her time with my cousin, but I need to be sure she has someone else she can turn to if she needs to, you know?"

Neil gives me a chin-up nod. "You got it, man. I'll personally make sure she's covered."

Maya says abruptly, "You can count on me, too."

You can't protect the people you love all of the time. It's what I told Alex when her mom went into the hospital, and it seemed so clear-cut at the time. Everything is easier when you distance yourself from it. I knew I could count on Neil, but I'm surprised by Maya's gesture. But I'm appreciative. She slides her hand free of my arm and surprises me a second time by getting on her toes and planting a kiss on my cheek.

"Good luck, honey. We'll be thinking of you."

I give her a quick squeeze before letting go, and Neil gives me a bone-crushing handshake. I need to get on the road right now if I'm going to make it there by dark, and I don't have the option of even stopping by my house. I also can't risk Cruz finding out where I'm going and ideally, don't want him to even know that I'm leaving town.

I take out my car keys and hold them out to Neil. "How do you feel about trading cars with me for a few days?"

He grins at me and digs his keys out of his pocket. "The Audi? You got it. But I didn't take the car today. If you don't mind riding the Ducati for eight hours, she's yours."

I bark a laugh. "I don't mind one bit. Don't scratch up the car."

He shrugs out of the jacket and hands it to me – it winds up fitting me all right. "Don't scratch up the bike. It's all gassed up. Helmet is locked on it."

Perfect.

I walk away, feeling a sharp pang in my chest as I think about Alex all by herself at my house. Waiting for me to get back. I need to give her Neil's cell number so she has it. But I'll call her when I'm on the road, tell her just enough so she knows I won't be around for a couple of days, and make sure Elle picks her up.

I'll explain everything to both of them when I get back. When all is said and done.

It's time for me to go back home.

28

Alex

Cruz is either an apparition or a waking nightmare, I can't decide. One minute he's there, and the next thing I know I'm standing by myself in the middle of the street staring at the place where he used to be.

I try to breathe, but the air feels too thin to properly move into my lungs. I'm not going crazy. Cruz was actually here. He was in my face, and I can't move because I'm shaking so hard.

There's no way I can tell Connor exactly what Cruz said to me. No freaking way. Because if I do, Connor will give him what he wants, and it terrifies me partly because of what that would mean for Connor and partly because I know he would be doing it for me. But if I don't tell him, my dad is in danger, and that scares me even more.

I squeeze my eyes shut, my brain almost throbbing from the effort of trying to work this all out in my head. What the hell am I thinking? My dad is *already* in danger because he made a deal with some pretty terrible people. That is, if Cruz was even telling the truth.

My eyes snap open, and I finally force that badly needed breath into my chest. I'll find out for sure by talking to my dad, by asking him what's going on. I need to be direct but also approach this carefully, to talk to him about this in a way where he'll tell me the truth. Including the truth about where he got the cash that he gave me on my first day out here.

A car door slams shut from right next to me, and I have to swallow back the scream that's in the back of my throat. I hear a voice say hello and look up to see a woman standing in front of the house with the For Sale sign. She's wearing a suit and stockings in one hundred plus degree weather, her makeup and hair all very professional. Obviously a realtor.

"Hello?" she repeats brightly. Her glance skates down my sweat-soaked t-shirt, short skirt, and single flip flop before landing on my face again with confusion. "Are you here to see the house?"

The house? Laughter bubbles out of my throat, and I clap my hand over my mouth to stifle it. Holy crap, I'm totally losing it. Scratch that. I may have already lost it, but I can't stop and choke out a laugh that sounds like more of a sob. Hearing it jars me, makes me almost panic with the thought of how I'm in danger of losing so much right now. But I have to hold it together and fight so Dad, Connor, and I all come out ahead of this little game Cruz is playing. Somehow.

"No. God, no," I reply to the stunned realtor. "I'm not here to see the house."

I limp a few steps away until I can kick my poor naked foot back into my flip flop, stoop down to where the bag with my stuff is lying – I don't remember dropping it – and make a beeline to Connor's house. My hand is trembling when I dig out the slip of paper with the code on it, but I manage to punch in the numbers and get the green light to come on. I huff a sigh of relief when I hear the click, and I push my way into the house.

My back sags against the door as I dig out my phone from my bag. My battery's almost dead, but I need to call my dad and then Connor.

I punch Dad's name in my contacts list.

C'mon. Please answer.

I bite on my thumbnail as it rings, immediately hanging up when it goes to voicemail. I call the hospital, get redirected twice until I finally get to the wing where my mom's room is, and ask the nurse if my dad is there with Grace Lin. His text from earlier this morning said he was going to the casino for a while, but maybe he's back.

"This is his daughter. I don't want to wake up my mom in case she's sleeping, but could you tell me if he's there?"

"Grace Lin... Oh, yes, your father. No, I'm sorry. He left a while ago, but your mother's awake. I'll transfer you now."

"Wait…" I protest, but it's already ringing.

"Hello?" My mom's sweet, clear voice comes over the line just as another call comes through. My heart jumps when I see it's Connor. But I'll have to call him back.

"Hi, Mom. I hope I didn't wake you."

"Not at all," she assures me. She sounds tired but also happy. "Did your father call and tell you the news?"

"No, I haven't talked to him." My chest feels tight as I say it. But at the same time, Mom sounds positive, and I'm glad for that. I can't hear the same tinge of pain that was in her voice earlier.

"Well, maybe he wanted me to tell you," she says, and I can almost hear her smile over the phone. "The echocardiogram showed that my heart suffered no permanent damage. According to my physician, I'm very lucky."

We're all very lucky in that sense. "That's great news, Mom. Told you that you have an amazing heart." I put my hand over my own heart, the relief I feel almost incapacitating. "I'm coming over to visit you soon, so I can celebrate the news with you in person."

"Oh, dear. I would love that, but my lovely attending nurse is coming in a bit to give me a horrid sponge bath. I hope she'll wash my hair, because I look like the zombie child of the Bride of Frankenstein."

I smile at the image. "I'm sure you don't."

"I'm sure I do," she says firmly. "I sent your father to the hotel this morning and told him not to come back until after lunch when I look more presentable. Give me a few hours?"

Another call comes in, this time from Elle, and I ignore it, too. "Count on it. And Mom? I love you."

"Love you too, baby girl. See you in a while."

I end the call, my relief at hearing the news muted by everything else that's going on. But at least now I know that Dad is at the casino, which means plan B. I'll call a cab to take me to the hotel, and then I'll go find him. And then visit Mom.

But first, I go to my missed calls list to return Connor's call. I stare at my phone in dismay as the display goes black. Crap. Totally dead.

Okay, no problem. I just need to find a land line. I wander through the house in search of a phone. It's strange being here without Connor, like I can still feel his presence. He told me he hadn't done much with this place, but even so, there are touches of him everywhere.

I go through every room in the house. Twice, and even check the garage. Yes, there are touches of Connor everywhere, but no land line.

Shit. I'm stuck here without a car and without a way to call anyone. I could go to the clubhouse and ask to use their phone, but Cruz might still be lurking out there. Plus, I'm not sure if I remember Connor's phone number from memory. I sink down on his couch and stare at the coffee table, the numbers I'd seen on my display scrambling in my head. I might be able to remember Elle's if I think hard enough. Or I could just chill and wait here for Connor to come back…

I drop my head in my hands, annoyed with myself for not remembering to pack my charger. The fact that both Connor and Elle had tried to call me within minutes of each other is unsettling, to say the least.

My head jerks up when I hear it. In the distance, the whining and almost anxious sound of an engine accelerating up the street. It's coming closer, and I stand up as I hear it approach the house. Connor?

The sound dies as the car screeches to a halt, and I tense up as I hear a car door slam shut. From right outside the house. Connor would have pulled into the garage.

I freeze, goosebumps popping up along my arms and legs as I hear the footsteps coming up the walk. Not walking. Running.

I jump when a fist pounds against the door.

"Alex?" the voice yells. "Alex!"

Elle.

I run to the front door and throw it open. Elle gapes at me, her expression frantic and pissed off at the same time as she waves her phone at me.

"Holy shit. I've been trying to call you on your cell."

"My phone died." I stare at her, my heart sinking. "What's wrong? Is Connor okay?"

"Your phone died," she mutters. "Okay, so he just called me, hun. I think he split town."

I'm only vaguely aware of how maniacally Elle drives us to the Strip. I crumple up the piece of paper she gave me into a ball, my pulse hammering in my ears.

Connor left town. He tried to call me but when I hadn't answered, called Elle instead and told her to pick me up. Made her write down this phone number before giving her some line about having to take care of business and that he'll be out of touch for a couple of days. Elle had protested (rightly so), but he hung up before she could get any more out of him and now all of her calls are automatically going to voicemail.

"So you're pretty sure he was on the road?" My throat feels raw, like I just breathed in fire, but I force myself to swallow.

"Um, yeah. There was so much traffic noise in the background, it was hard to hear him. Pretty sure I heard a semi's airbrake, so it wasn't city noise either. Like he was standing on the side of the interstate or something."

Seriously, I may be at my limit of what I can take right now. Still totally freaking about my dad. Not having any idea if I should be worried about Connor or furious that he left for some mystery destination. I settle on both. He would have tried to feed me the same line if he'd gotten a hold of me, and I'm worried about Cruz being responsible.

I shake my head. It doesn't make sense. Even if Connor did call from the road, why wouldn't he have been inside his car? My anger slowly morphs into dread.

"Elle, you don't think he was like… oh, I don't know. Taken against his will or something? Or is it possible he just bailed?" As soon as the words are out of my mouth, I know how wrong they feel. He wouldn't do that.

She snorts. "Connor? No fucking way." Her eyes briefly flick over to me. "I know you two have gotten pretty close physically and what-not. But he's the kind of guy who follows through with things. And he knows how to take care of himself, believe me."

I guess I know all of these things. I also think about what he said about killing anyone who'd look at me the wrong way. At the time, I thought he'd been mostly joking. Mostly.

"That's part of the reason he's been by himself so long, cuz he's all about self-preservation," Elle adds as she takes a sharp turn onto Las Vegas Boulevard. "But you know, I think he did really like being part of something when he was with the SEALs. And I also think he really likes you. Like, *really* likes you. If he left, it was for a good reason."

I *really* like him too. I'm already heartsick over the news about my dad, but a different sort of agony layers on over that to think about the possibility of Connor being in trouble.

"This isn't helping," I sigh. "I'm worried about him."

"Yeah, well, me too." Elle chimes in with her own heavy sigh, braking to narrowly miss a car that cuts in front of us. She lays on the horn and flips the other driver the bird, adding, "He'll be okay, though. He always is."

I want to believe Elle, but I still have a really bad feeling about all of this. Cruz approaches Elle, accosts me, and then Connor takes off? But there's no way Connor would have known about Cruz getting up all nice and close with me before he took off.

Either way, I think Cruz somehow knew Elle would call up Connor in a panic and spur him into action – which essentially is what happened. And then he sprung on me and hit me with the info about my dad like I'd walked into a trap. The more I think about it, the more I think that this was Cruz's full intention. What a manipulative bastard.

And maybe everything's simply coming to a head now, but I'm going more than slightly crazy not knowing what Connor's up to.

We run upstairs to my room, where I stick my phone on my rapid charger to power it up again. Dad's not in the room, but I head straight for his desk. According to his schedule, he has a break right now, but that could have changed given the fact that he's been at the hospital. I read across to see what was on his schedule for the past two days. The high roller room downstairs, the one across the street, and a place called Maxwell's Room. I've been to the first two, which will hopefully make it easier to get in and check for him, but I don't know where the third place is.

"What's up, hun?" Elle flits over to my side.

"You ever hear of somewhere called Maxwell's Room?"

"Lemme see." She whips out her phone and does a search. "Okay, so it's across the street, but hold on..."

I wait impatiently while she pores over the screen, the seconds dragging out to a full minute.

"C'mon," I protest. "What is it?"

"It's a pretty exclusive place, and it looks like you need a ten thousand dollar buy-in to play there." She looks at me skeptically. "I'm not sure how these places work, but I don't know if they would even let you in."

"I don't need to get in," I point out. "I just need to see if my dad's in there."

I know I'm not being totally rational. I could wait in the hotel room for Dad to come back, but there's no guarantee he's planning on coming to the room anytime soon. And Elle's comment makes me wonder. People in these places protect their privacy as much as they protect their money, and my dad is no exception. That's exactly why trying to find him when Mom was hospitalized took forever. No one had wanted to locate him, let alone interrupt his play, and it was only because of Elle reducing some lower-pay scale employee down to tears that we were able to get word to my dad.

"I have an idea, just in case," I say. It's a crappy and impromptu idea, but it's better than nothing.

Elle tails me as I storm back over my room, watching as I tear through my closet to find the nicest dress I own. It's an evening dress in steel-gray satin, backless, and makes me look like I'm at least five years older. I'd only brought it with me on this trip because my mom picked it out for me and insisted I wear it out sometime for dinner. I sweated most of my makeup off before, so I fix myself up and borrow one of my mother's necklaces and a bracelet.

But the most important accessory is in my vault, and Elle's eyes become as round as dinner plates when I pull out the stack of cash. The size of it fluctuated a lot with each day I spent on the floor with my dad, but I have just over fourteen grand now.

Elle gapes at me. "First of all, you look gorgeous. But the money. Dude, what's that for?"

"Just in case," I repeat grimly. I check my phone and see that it's almost halfway charged. Good enough.

"Come on. We gotta go."

Elle and I are outside on the pedestrian bridge when he calls.

Dad hadn't been in any of the gambling rooms in my hotel, so we're going down the list. It must be a million degrees outside, and I'd been rethinking the brilliant idea of wearing this satin dress.

"It's Connor," I hiss down to Elle.

Seeing his name on my phone's display makes me break out in more of a sweat. I hurry in my heels over to the side of the bridge, Elle hanging back but with her entire expression clearly reading, *Omigod.*

"Hello?" My voice cracks.

"Alex…" He sounds relieved but funny too, like he's far away somehow. "I've been trying to reach you. Did Elle come and get you? Did she give you Neil's number?"

My jumbled thoughts fall away at hearing his voice, my mind suddenly sharp. He doesn't sound like himself. There's distance between us, but not only in terms of location. It's a little loud on the pedestrian bridge, but if I try hard enough, I can hear some of what sounds like interstate noise, like Elle described.

"I'm with her right now, and yeah, I got the number. Thanks for the babysitting service," I say in what's maybe too angry of a tone. I don't bother to clarify that I left the number balled up on the floorboard of Elle's Civic. "Where are you? Did you leave town?"

"Yes, but I can't tell you anything more than that, love."

Oh no, he doesn't. Connor doesn't get to shut me out like this, not after his brother lay in wait for me and grabbed me like that in the middle of the street. Not when my father might be tangled up with people that Cruz knows.

I close my eyes and make myself breathe, remind myself that he has no idea what happened earlier today.

"No one forced you to leave, did they? Are you alone?"

"No one forced me. And yes, I'm alone."

"You're coming back?" My eyes are still closed, but I can feel Elle's pointed stare.

"Of course." He sounds genuinely surprised.

"When?"

"A couple of days maybe? Alex…" He hesitates. "I left because I need to take care of something very important, and I'll tell you everything when I get back. But I can't right now, and I need you to trust me."

I do. I do trust you.

I'm not going to ask him how dangerous his situation is. I won't call him on the fact that he *could* tell me right now, if he really wanted to. I know exactly what he's doing. He's trying to protect me by telling me as little as possible. While my immediate instinct is to tell him what he can do with that security guard act, the way he asks me to trust him gets to me, gets through the rest of my walls.

I lower my voice. "Does this have anything to do with Cruz?"

A pause, and then, "Yes."

It feels like we're playing twenty questions, but something almost like despair fills me at the idea that the time I get to speak with him might be that limited.

"Connor… Promise me you'll be careful."

"Always am."

"Yes, okay. I know." I fight the temptation to roll my eyes. "But promise me you'll be careful *this time.*"

Because I don't know what I'd do if I lost you.

"I promise." He hesitates. "We probably shouldn't call each other from this point on, not until I'm out of danger. Stay with Elle if you can tonight, but if you'd rather stay at my house or your hotel room, let Neil know. And don't tell anyone I'm out of town, not even Elle."

He just said "out of danger." I bite back my comments, that I strongly object to him being *in* danger in the first place. That Elle's not an idiot and was already able to figure it out for herself. And that there's no way I'm going to check in with this business partner of his that I don't even know. What, is this guy going to stand outside Connor's house or outside my room all night with his gun drawn? No thanks.

"I'll stay with Elle," I say simply.

"Good." I hear him blow out a breath, or maybe it's the wind. "I need to get going, but I just wanted to…"

Hear my voice right before you go do something extremely dangerous?

"…make sure you were okay."

"I'm fine, Connor." I'm not going to tell him what happened with Cruz today. There's nothing Connor can do about it now, it would make him mad, and I can wait until he gets back to share that story. Or hopefully I won't even need to. I swallow hard, thinking about this morning. How can everything go from paradise to hell in such a short time? "Come back to me soon, okay?"

"I will." His voice changes, sounds pained. "There's nothing I want more, love."

Say something else before he ends the call.

Tell him how you feel about him, how important he is to you.

"Me too," I say softly. "I'll see you soon."

He ends the call, and I look down on Las Vegas Boulevard into the crowd of tourists. Hundreds of terrible secrets hidden down there, ill intentions, greed, malice. There could be dozens of people like Cruz walking around, looking for a way to take advantage of someone else, a way to destroy someone else's life.

But I'm sure there are also a fair number of people down there who are carrying all of those dreams that they still believe in, like Elle. Or who have scars and harsh pasts like Connor but are still willing to take a chance on people and love them. Like the person that took a chance on me.

I took a chance on Connor, too. And I care about him so much. More than I've cared about anyone.

Why didn't I tell him that? Because it would have been on the phone, and there's something too impersonal about that. But at least then I could have been sure that he knew.

"Shit, Alex. Are you ever going to tell me what he said?" Elle takes hold of my arm and gently shakes me out of my daze.

"He's taking care of some things, like you said." My voice is monotone, and it sounds dead to me. "He's alone, he's going to be careful, and he'll call when he's finished."

"That's it?" she demands, but then she looks at my face, and her mouth turns down in a frown. "Girl, you okay?"

"Yes," I say truthfully. "I'm okay." Because I have to be.

Turns out Elle was right. Trying to get into Maxwell's Room is like trying to get into a popular club when your name's not on the guest list. The guard posted outside the doors is like a tank, and I've already asked if he could relay a message to my father (assuming he's inside). That request only got me stony silence. I doubt the family emergency card and the I'll-talk-to-your-manager route will get me anywhere with this rock.

I smile to hide my frustration and continue hacking away at him. I've done everything save batting my eyelashes and waving my fourteen grand under his nose. "You can't turn me away if I have the money to cover the buy-in," I protest.

"You didn't come here to play." He speaks over my head, a testament to how little worth he's attributing to me. Damn him.

"I wouldn't be carrying around this kind of cash if I didn't want to play," I bluff, reaching into my purse. Man, if this works, I may actually try my hand at poker.

"Oh, honey, no. What are you doing?"

I recognize the soft Texan drawl and whip around to face the gorgeous blonde who's Connor's client. She's accompanied by a muscular black dude who is looking at me with undisguised interest. This has to be Neil, and my face has to be beet red.

They're standing behind me like they've been waiting for me to get my ass out of the way so they can get into Maxwell's Room. Probably listening to the whole thing. Despite my embarrassment over this entire situation (I'll get over it), the practical side of me brightens at the prospect of being able to find out if my dad is inside.

"Honestly, I'm just trying to find out if my father's in there," I admit in a low voice so Stony Face won't hear. "If you're going in, would you mind –"

"Hold on," she interrupts.

She steps away from me before I can describe my dad to her, and I watch as she simultaneously flashes a card and a stern look at the guard. He steps back and opens the door for her like she's royalty, and she sweeps through the doorway, leaving me and Elle alone with her security.

I stare at him. "Are you Neil?"

He smiles, and there's warmth in his expression I didn't expect. "I am. And you must be Alexis."

I don't know how to respond to that, to the fact that he knows who I am. Obviously Connor told Neil about me if he gave me his phone number, but I can't help be curious as to what else Connor told him about me. I'm rescued from having to say anything either way when his client emerges from the room.

"We'll come back a bit later, Neil," she says in a quiet voice, and he nods like any of this makes sense.

She takes my arm in a firm grasp and leads me away from the doors. Neil is hot on our tail, and Elle walks next to him. I catch her looking at him like she wants to eat him up for dessert, and I almost snicker. Almost.

"Your father's not in there," she says in a low voice.

I raise my eyebrows, surprised. "You know him?"

"Yes. We've never met, but I know who he is." Her blue eyes appraise me coolly. "My name is Maya Coplin, a friend and client of Connor's. And I of course know who you are, Alexis. You're Connor's girlfriend."

I'm already feeling emotionally wracked from the ups and downs of this day in general, but yikes. I don't even know if I believe in defining relationships like that, but the fact that Maya did means that Connor thinks of me as his girlfriend. But it's okay…it's okay that he does.

Connor…I want him to call me and tell me that everything's all right and that Cruz is gone. I want it so badly that it hurts.

Maya gives me an astute look as though she can tell what I'm thinking and asks, "Have you had the pleasure of meeting Cruz yet?"

I check her out like she's doing to me, noticing how her eyes narrow and her lips turn down in distaste at the mention of Connor's brother.

"Oh boy, have I ever," I say bitterly. "Just met the guy today, actually."

She suddenly steers me toward the entrance of a theater. The doors are closed, and she squeezes around a set of poles holding velvet rope and walks to the entryway, which serves as a sort of alcove with privacy. I follow, seeing Neil out of the corner of my eye move to block the alcove with his muscly form, with tiny little Elle to keep him company.

Maya holds me with her gaze. "Tell me exactly what happened."

I still need to find my dad, and I don't know why I bother telling her what happened with Cruz. Maybe because she just helped me by scoping out the oh-so-exclusive Maxwell's room. Maybe because of the look she gave the stony-faced guard that wouldn't let me through. Or because she introduced herself as Connor's friend in addition to being a client.

She leans forward, seeming to hang on every word I say, smiling at me when I'm all done. It's not exactly a happy or friendly smile.

"I have a proposition for you," she says. "Your father has basically involved himself with some very ruthless people. But I think I may be able to help, if he's willing to help me."

Ruthless people. Maya stares at me with this gleam in her eye, and I see that this is a woman with power. She might be a client of Connor's, and while she might have a lot of money that needs protection, there's nothing about her that speaks to weakness.

I know I have to make a choice right now, need to figure out how much I'm willing to gamble.

Winning only comes from knowing how much you can stand to lose. That's what Dad told me that day he first took me out on the floor, and I finally think I get it. My dad jumped from what was probably minor financial trouble to even bigger problems with these ruthless criminals. Connor's out there putting himself into some dangerous situation to get rid of his brother, and I have a feeling that he's doing it as much for me as it as he's doing for him.

I should have acted on the signs that my dad wasn't acting like himself and pressed the issue more. I shouldn't have wasted precious time assuming the worst and ignoring Connor for a good part of a week when I could have been spending that time with him. We could have come up with a plan together instead of him having to do this alone.

But maybe that's also too many "could haves" and "should haves." The people I care about have already lost enough. Too much time wasted. Too much pain endured. I'm not willing to let them lose anything more.

I look Maya in the eye. "I'm listening."

29

CONNOR

It was one in the afternoon by the time I left Vegas, right at the end of the fucking lunchtime rush. I stop twice to call Alex – the first time only managing to get through to Elle but succeeding the second time. I let myself have that brief moment to hang onto Alex's voice, to let myself realize the gravity of what I'm doing right now. To let myself wish I didn't have to leave her.

After that, I shut everything down and go into survival mode, like I do when I'm on the job, only even more so. More like I did back when I was going through SEAL boot camp and trying to emerge on the top. Back when I realized pretty quickly that it didn't matter how on top of the group I was. I just had to survive.

Same thing here. I need to get through this, and then I can go back home, to my real home in Vegas where Alex is waiting for me. And see where things go from there.

I get to the outskirts of Albuquerque in less than eight hours, silently thanking Neil and his Ducati and the fact that I don't hit any major traffic along the way. I stop at the city limits to gas up and make a second stop at a cheap motel to pay forty bucks for a small but reasonably clean room. The place is far enough away from the city that I'm fairly sure it's in neutral territory. Neil's people had recommended a safe radius around the city, and the last thing I want to do is to sleep on some gang's turf.

Hopefully I won't even have to stay the night. I'd given myself two days in case I needed it, but if luck is on my side, I can blow town late tonight, stay somewhere way the hell away from here, and be back to Vegas tomorrow.

I don't have anything with me except for the clothes on my back, wallet, phone, and Sig. I go into the room anyway to take a piss. Maybe also to regroup and to try to shrug off some the tension that's in my back and shoulders from riding for so long. I haven't eaten since I briefly stopped in Arizona to grab some shitty fast food, but I'm pumped full of adrenaline right now and not hungry.

My phone's been off since I last used it to call Alex, and I keep it off and leave it in the room so I don't run the risk of it being confiscated. The closest connections I have in the world are eight hours away, and everyone I plan on seeing while I'm here is mostly a stranger to me. But I have to use those old relationships to my favor to get Cruz out of Vegas and back here where he belongs. For good.

First things first. Before I do anything about Cruz, I have to take care of some personal business. Neil did some basic research for me after I left Vegas, texted me the info while I was in transit. Just an address. I didn't tell him the significance of it, and he hadn't asked.

I'd looked up the address on my phone as soon as Neil sent it to me, and now I follow the route to the southeastern part of the city. It's a nice neighborhood, on the outskirts of the city near the air force base, and the houses look on the newer side and like part of an actual community. They probably pass ordinances here about things like noise control and what kind of landscaping they require.

It's almost nine-thirty by the time I pull up to the two-story house. I hesitate with the motor idling, taking note of the newish BMW SUV parked outside the two-car garage. Compared to the one I grew up in, this house is practically a mansion. The upstairs is dark, but the first-floor windows are lit. My gut twists in a knot as I catch a glimpse of movement behind the sheer curtains covering one of the windows.

Laura's house.

It's in a neighborhood a class or two above the area Laura grew up in, too. Back then, I always thought of her as being privileged, but in retrospect, I know that's not really true. I only thought that because of *her* – how perfect she looked all of the time. But we went to the same school, and she grew up in a neighborhood that wasn't all that different than mine.

Neil hadn't mentioned if she lived with anyone or had a family, but then again, I hadn't asked. But this place is too big for her to live in alone.

I kill the engine. Fuck it. This is the last time I'll be here. Now or never.

I get off the bike and walk up to the front door, knocking before I lose my nerve. The footsteps approach quickly, the tread light enough to make me think it's a woman. I glance down at myself and think about how I must look in the black biker jacket at this time of night, but the door opens with a chain in place before I can do anything about it.

Laura's suddenly looking through the crack in the door. She still looks good, same platinum blonde hair, same creamy skin, but I wasn't lying to Alex when I said I was over her. I check her out, but it's an objective assessment. I feel surprisingly detached about it. Almost like when I run into any other woman I've slept with. Except for Alex.

"Cruz…" She has glasses on, a book clutched to her chest, and she frowns heavily as she speaks my brother's name. She slowly lowers her glasses. "Connor?" she whispers.

"Hi, Laura."

She blinks at me like an owl while I search for something else to say. I didn't think it would be totally easy to do this, and it's not. The sight of Laura dredges up my old feelings of guilt, ties my tongue into knots. I'd had a lot of time to think about things on the ride here. Thought long and hard about what I would say to Laura when I saw her, but that doesn't mean I came up with anything good.

Before I can work out something to say, she shuts the door. I cringe inwardly, my guilt immediately mixing with disappointment, but honestly, what was I expecting? I mostly wanted to come here to see for myself if she was doing well. If the house and vehicle are any indication, she's at least financially secure.

I turn away to leave, but I'm surprised when I hear the chain slide back. Laura slips outside to stand on the stoop and quickly shuts the door behind her.

"My husband is upstairs putting our daughter to bed," she hisses. "I haven't seen you in forever. What are you doing here?"

She's still beautiful, her hair short now, her features obviously matured since we were teenagers. I notice that she's a little round in the middle, but I'm not about to travel down that slippery slope and ask if she's pregnant – in case she's not.

"I'm passing through and wanted to stop by." It's not a lie. "And I know it's been a long time, but I've always wondered how you were doing, if you were happy."

"Oh…" She blinks again, and her brow furrows even deeper like she's wrestling with her own thoughts. Her expression finally clears as she looks me up and down. "You look really good. And yes, I'm pretty happy," she says with a small smile.

"I'm glad." I mean it because she deserves it.

"Yeah." Her hands land on the bump on her belly. "We're expecting number two. Our daughter's already five."

"Congratulations," I say. "That's great."

"What about you? Are you still in the Navy? Are you married or…" She trails off, her gaze dropping again. Probably looking for a wedding band.

"I'm good," I say. "Not actively in the Navy anymore. I'm in Vegas now. Not married, but I'm seeing someone." It feels good to say it. Although it makes me think about how Alex is too far away from me right now.

"Lucky girl… You look really amazing, Connor."

It's not at all what I'd expected her to say. The closing the door in my face thing, that's more of what I thought would happen. Laura continues to look at me like she's struggling with something she wants to say, and I watch as she inhales.

"I'm so sorry for before," she whispers. "I know it's too much to ever ask for your forgiveness, but I need to apologize for what happened between us."

I stare at her, the apology sending me spiraling into a stupor. She has no reason to say she's sorry. I'm the one…

"This is crazy, but I was just thinking about this the other day, and here you are," she says quickly, like she's afraid that I'll bolt. "I've always felt so bad for cheating on you with Cruz —"

"What?"

"You were just so into all of that training stuff for the Navy…" She squeezes her eyes shut for a second. "No, no, none of it was your fault. You were good to me, Connor. But I was selfish and stupid, and…well, already drunk and wanting to party that night, and Cruz was right there."

Holy fucking shit. She's serious. She's saying this like she made a decision to take those drugs and have sex with my brother. Even if I believe her, I've held onto it for so long. Too long. The guilt over what happened to her. My anger at Cruz. But it suddenly all becomes muddled as I try to understand what she's trying to say.

My head hurts as I fight to process this, and I swallow my pride and ask, "You wanted to take those drugs…and sleep with him?"

Her cheeks become a mottled pink. "I…Yes. I didn't really know what I was getting into with the drugs, but I wanted to have some fun. I'm so sorry. I knew how you felt about that stuff, but Cruz offered, and I did it anyway. I was so ashamed about it afterward, especially when I found out that you're the one who called the ambulance for me. And Cruz and I…Yeah." She hangs her head. Actually fucking hangs her head while I wade through my shock.

"I hope you'll find it in your heart to forgive me someday," she whispers. Her hand holding her glasses reaches out for me, but she reconsiders at the last second and drops it.

I feel this heaviness lift from my heart like Laura said or wherever I've kept it for so long. I wasn't a good boyfriend like she says, but we believe what we want to, right? And all these years, I had it in my head it was Cruz's fault – and mine. Never once did I think that Laura wanted it. I believed he took advantage of her because that was what I needed to believe.

My feelings toward Cruz aren't much different. His actions had been deliberate. Laura's admission doesn't mean that Cruz is without fault or that I wasn't a bad boyfriend. But I think I might be able to finally walk away from this now.

"Thank you, Laura. For telling me the truth, and I'm sorry that I was so self-absorbed back then." I smile at her, my face feeling stiff. But it's because of the ride and the stress, not because I don't feel what I'm saying. "Take really good care of yourself. And that husband and those babies."

She lifts her gaze and meets mine, relief flooding her expression. "I will. Have a good life, Connor."

That's the plan. To have a good life.

Laura slips back into her house, and I shake my head as I walk back to the bike. Holy hell.

I take off to head back to the city. It's getting late, and I have to keep moving.

It's been a long time since I've been back, but as I pull into the city, the streets feel as familiar to me as they ever have. I distinctly remember the long bus rides I took out of my neighborhood to get to the YMCA, working on my school assignments along the way. I'd take the bus out there after school almost every day for nearly a year until I bought the Honda off my uncle. Did lots of homework on that bus line.

I drive that same bus route right now but in reverse to get to my second stop of the night. Before I head to the place that's my ultimate destination, I need to do one more thing.

I get to my old neighborhood, and it's as run down as I remember. Old beater cars and bikes with engine parts littering some of the dirt yards, teenagers glaring at me with way too much suspicion as I drive by. It's past ten at night, but grandparents are yelling at little kids from some of the porches of the houses that sit in bad repair. I'd never known my grandparents because they'd died before I was born, but I remember that being common here, to have multiple generations and sometimes other extended family crammed in the same crowded living space. The corner store has the same types of kids that it always did, loitering against a wall framed in graffiti claiming whatever gang's turf it belongs to this month.

All this time I thought Cruz was solely about control, but he really lost his control when he succumbed to the power of this place. We were both surrounded by it, but I refused to let any of it drag me down.

Having to live with my father's abuse was ultimately what made Cruz turn to the street gang and what made me hell-bent on getting the fuck out of this place. It's what tore Cruz and me apart when we really should have turned to each other. When it really comes down to it, that's why I can never forgive my father for his decisions, because he scared away my mother, because he drove an irreparable wedge between me and my own brother when we could have stood together as a family.

He cheated us of everything we deserved, and I don't want him to ever forget that.

The one thing I hadn't checked on prior to coming here was whether or not the old man still lives in the same place. But the second I turn onto my street, I see the same old beat-up blue Ford pickup truck parked in front, and I know he's home.

I pull up in front of the small two-bedroom house and kill the engine. It's a lot like it was when I'd left, but now the brown stucco is chipped and even more badly stained. The porch looks like it's falling apart, the roof missing tiles, the front lawn nothing but dirt and rock. I don't know how often Cruz comes here, but I get my answer as soon as I take off my helmet. A kid in the street points to me, shouts Cruz's name. I hear either his father or older brother correct him and say my old name.

Connor Marino. Connor's come home.

Except that's not who I am anymore, and this will never be home to me. I ignore the buzz, the steadily increasing volume of murmurs and sounds of doors slamming shut as more people come out to witness the show.

I have no idea what state my father will be in when I see him. He was already pretty much gone ten years ago, and I don't even know if he realized what a fucked-up childhood he gave me and Cruz. The lung cancer Cruz claims he's dying from may be karma in action, but if it releases him from his misery, that's a lot more than he deserves.

I'm still sitting on the bike, waiting for it, waiting for the hatred to fill my heart and give me the impetus to do this.

But the hatred doesn't come. I stare up at the single lit window coming from the front room of my father's house, and while there's a pit in my stomach, I can't feel anything but the dull edge of resentment.

The porch light turns on and the front door cracks open as I'm looking at it. He steps out onto the porch a few seconds later.

My father. Every instinct in my body urges me to run, but it's like muscle memory acting up from being trained to do a task over and over again. The fear is old, a ghost from my past, and it has no place in me anymore. I feel nothing for him as he shuffles forward, as he holds his hand up to his forehead and squints down at me.

He's not the same man I remember. He must be in his late fifties by now, but he looks like he could be twenty years older than that. His dark hair is graying and thin, his skin sallow with cheeks sunken in, his frame that I'd always remembered as being solid now emaciated. His shoulders hunch over as a cough wracks out of him, and he goes for a good minute before he can stop.

"That you, Cruz?" he calls out, but it sounds weak compared to the angry, bitter voice that he always used with us.

I get off the bike and set the helmet down on the seat, the screams from the kids on the streets dying down as I walk up to the house, as everyone watches. I don't care about these people. There might be one or two faces I recognize from here, but I wouldn't exactly call this place a community.

"No," I say in a flat tone. "Not Cruz."

He stops squinting, his eyes widening to almost comical proportions.

"Connor," he rasps. He stumbles off the porch and down the steps, almost falling in his haste. "Son. You came home."

I think of all the things that have been running through my head during the last leg of the drive. That this isn't my home. How this man was never my father because of the abuse he doled out, and how he has no right to call me his son. How I wouldn't care if I came here and found him dead.

He starts to cough again, and I stiffen and watch as his body shakes uncontrollably, as he wipes spit and blood from his lips when he's done. I don't move, just stand on the walk in front of the house that acted as both my home and prison for sixteen years of my life.

I might not like it, and God knows that I fought for the majority of my life to escape it, but this is where I came from. From this man, this place, this house. These are my roots, and while none of that defines who I am, there's some value in remembering it because of how far I've come.

"Son," he repeats, like he's trying to convince himself that's who I am. "I'm dying. Did Cruz tell you? They claim there's nothing more they can do for me, but those fucking doctors…" He shakes his head.

I could have guessed it even if he hadn't told me. He looks like he's already gone but obviously not at the point where he's accepted it. If I do feel the slightest bit of sadness for him, it's because I'm sorry he pushed us all away. He spent his entire life making sure he lost everyone who could have helped him through this.

Even now, the expression in his eyes isn't totally lucid, like the only comfort left in his life comes from painkillers and whatever other drugs he's on. Or maybe he finally pushed himself past the edge of sanity.

"Then I came to say goodbye." I keep my voice steady. "I won't be back after this, not even for your funeral."

There's a gleam in his eye that might be tears or maybe a flash of anger, but he was always so messed up in the head that his emotions remain a mystery to me, and I can't tell which.

I could go on and say a lot more, but I leave it at that. My father made it so no one will mourn for him when it's all over for him. And yes, I can't change the fact that I'm his son, but I won't think about him after he's gone. There's nothing even remotely good about him that I want to remember.

His hand has a tremor in it as he reaches for me, but I turn around and walk away.

30

Alex

Things are going to be okay. They have to be. Good things are already in motion, and I have to believe that the universe will continue working in positive ways.

Except I haven't heard from Connor since that one short phone call. I go over my conversation with him again and again, thinking about everything he said to me. All I succeed in doing is driving myself crazy. Connor said he would be gone for a couple of days, and at the time I hadn't argued the point or asked him what he meant by that. A couple of days could mean two if he meant it literally, or it could mean longer.

Dammit. Even two feels like too long, especially if he's not going to call and check in. But Neil had echoed the need for no communication until we hear from Connor first. Figures.

We're all sitting in Maya's suite right now – Maya, Dad, Neil, and I. Elle had to leave a couple of hours ago for rehearsal with her cover band, and I'm feeling restless and starting to wish I went with her. Neil and I are on one side of the room watching a movie on low volume so we don't disturb Dad and Maya.

That's one good thing that I could focus on if only I had the mind to do it – the deal that my dad and Maya made. Vegas winds up being a smaller place than I thought, and it turns out that while they hadn't known each other before, Maya had known "of" my dad and the fact that he's a CPA. I didn't hear the details, but the gist of it is that Maya has a business back home that's really messed up and that my dad is going to help her sort out her books. In exchange, Maya agreed to bail Dad out of his own mess by paying off his gambling debts with the people he'd gotten himself tangled up with. Apparently what he owes is a mere drop in the bucket for her compared to the fines, legal fees, and potential jail time Maya will face if she doesn't get her business in order.

I heard her say that she wants him to go with her to Texas for a week or two at the end of the summer but that they should be able to do most of the work electronically. And instead of coming back here next summer, he'll spend it working for her – Mom is welcome to come and stay with him in Maya's guesthouse. I heard Maya tell Dad that she's done with gambling, and it looks like Dad will be for a while, too. At least for the rest of this summer and the next one.

That's pretty much all I know, and for now it's enough. As long as my dad isn't in trouble with these people anymore, I'm happy. And I'm also secretly glad that Dad will be on a mandated break from gambling – I think he and Mom could both use that break. I can always come out here next summer by myself to visit Elle.

And Connor. I know I'll be out here a lot more than just the summer to visit Connor. Assuming everything works out okay.

I need to call or text him. Or at least try. I glance at Neil out of the corner of my eye, but he's been watching me like a hawk every time I make a move to even look at my phone. He keeps insisting on no texts either, despite my protests.

The movie is the latest installment of the Avengers movies, which is normally my kind of movie. But all I can think about is the double feature that I took Connor to on our first sort-of-date and how much I wish he was here.

Neil sort of resembles Heimdall, sentry of Asgard, having stoically watched over me ever since I ran into him. He even stood watch in the waiting area earlier while I visited my mom (she loved the satin dress, which I unfortunately am still wearing) and grudgingly admitted to me that he knows one of the aides on hospital staff who'll keep an eye on her room. It's all because one of Neil's guys that was supposed to be following Cruz reported losing him. I confessed all about Cruz accosting me outside Connor's house when Neil asked, and he insisted that these extra security measures are what Connor would want him to do.

Seriously, I feel like I'm being treated like a princess locked in an ivory tower. I'm going to go out of my mind.

"Hey, you know what?" I say brightly. "I think I'll go and watch Elle rehearse."

Neil looks at me sharply. "Not a chance, sister."

I cast a look of desperation over to my dad, but he's focusing on something on the laptop screen. He doesn't seem to be aware that Neil has me under house arrest, but he also doesn't know what happened with me and Cruz, either.

I make a big show of sighing. "I have to pee, too. Do you want to come and stand outside the door while I do that?" All I get is a steely glare in response, and I change my tone to be more serious. "C'mon, Neil. Elle's boyfriend is friends with the drummer or something and will be there, too. And I'd just go over to Elle's apartment to sleep right afterward."

Maya overhears me from her side of the room and calls over, "Why don't you go with her, Neil? Then you can go home and get some rest when she goes to Elle's."

Maya has been pretty cool all day. She insisted on ordering all of us room service – from two different restaurants – and even offered to order me a cot if I want to stay here when my dad goes back to the hospital to be with my mom. She occasionally banters with Neil in an almost flirtatious but completely harmless way. And with my dad, she's been one hundred percent professional. I've heard her ask him a few times if he wanted to call it a day until tomorrow as it's getting late. I can see why Connor likes working with her.

Neil hesitates, and I know he's considering it. I make myself withhold further commentary until he finally nods.

"Fine," he says. "I'll drive you over."

"Okay, thanks," I say. "Give me a minute?"

I make that trip to the bathroom and then go over to my dad. He's in work mode, his brow creased in concentration as he clicks and scrolls through something on Maya's laptop. I lean down to give him a kiss on the cheek.

"Night, Dad."

He looks up at me, startled, and leans back and stretches. "Oh, good night, Alexis. I'm heading over to the hospital in a while, so I'll talk to you in the morning."

"Okay. Give Mom my love."

He smiles and nods but doesn't turn back to his work right away. "Be careful," he says solemnly. He looks at me very seriously, and I can read concern in his eyes and also regret. I know he feels terrible about the bad decisions he made, and I wish I could do something to alleviate that. I hope working to help Maya will help him, too. I think it will.

I need to go back across the street to my hotel room to get my stuff, and Neil tells me his vehicle is in the parking garage downstairs and that we'll head there first. He grabs a black duffle bag from behind the bar before we leave Maya's suite. He doesn't say what it is, and I don't ask as we head for the elevators. I've spent the better part of the day with him, and he's about as talkative as Connor was when I first met him, meaning not very much at all. I wonder if the two of them ever get together on a social basis and if they hang out and not talk a lot.

From what I can see, Neil seems like a good guy, and it's obvious that Connor trusts him implicitly. I don't think that Connor trusts very many people.

I raise my eyebrows in surprise when we get down to the parking garage and he walks up to the Audi. It has to be Connor's, unless Neil owns the exact same make, model, and color, in which case that would be creepy.

"Your man and I traded vehicles for the time being," Neil says off-handedly. That answers that question. I watch as he sets the black bag in the trunk before opening the passenger side door, not just unlocking it but holding it out for me like Connor does for me. Like a gentleman.

I ignore the "your man" part of that, pressing him for more information. "Why did you have to trade vehicles?"

Neil doesn't say anything until he gets behind the wheel, and I think he must be ignoring the question. He gives me a pointed look until I put my seatbelt on. "I imagine he wanted to slip under Cruz's radar." He smiles to himself as he starts the car, like he's enjoying a private joke. "Plus, I think mine gets better gas mileage."

I shoot him a look. I was already guessing that Connor went somewhere kind of far if he needed a couple of days, but this seems to clinch it. "Where did he go, Neil?"

He presses his lips together as he backs the car out of its spot, and I know I'm not going to get an answer.

"Well, at least tell me what he traded you for," I say lightly.

"My Ducati, and may the good Lord help him if he doesn't get it back to me in one piece." He glances at me. "Racing motorcycle."

"I know what a Ducati is," I say simply, and we both fall silent after that.

Neil pulls around to the service entrance in the back of my hotel – I'm pretty sure the same one where Connor parked when he made sure I got to my room that fateful night I got roofied. Funny to think back on that night. It feels like a long time ago. Like Connor is the same person that he was that night but also a little bit not. And the same with me.

"Why don't you give me your key, and I'll run up and grab your bag," Neil says, holding out his hand. "Unless you need something else."

I think quickly and shake my head. "No, the bag is fine." I'd packed for a few days, in case, and I drop my key card into Neil's hand and tell him which tower and room. But he's already out of the car because Connor must have told him my room number. He keeps the car keys with him and pushes the button to lock me inside as he walks to the service entrance.

I watch Neil open the door and disappear, and it takes me about that long to decide.

I'm not supposed to call Connor, but I want to leave him a voicemail.

My phone only shows me one out of five bars for service – maybe because I'm in a concrete tunnel, but the Strip is notorious for that and unpredictable. I unlock the car and get out, hurrying past the service entrance to the end. There's cigarette smoke hanging in the air like someone was just standing against the wall with one, and I think about the guy (Jordi? Jordan? I can't remember and it doesn't really matter) from that night after the QE2, how he'd pretended to be all nice and walk me inside at Connor's request but then proceeded to run his hand over my ass at the first opportunity. Asshole. He's not out here on a smoke break though. No one is.

As soon as I get a second bar on my phone, I hit Connor's number. It goes straight to voicemail, which simultaneously worries me but maybe is a tiny bit of a relief. It means his phone is off, which also means I'm not disturbing him by calling. I just hope his phone is off because he decided to keep it off, not because someone took it from him.

Connor can take care of himself. You know this.

I take a breath as I hear the beep.

"Hey, Connor. I know you said not to call. But we're all okay and Neil has been great. Maya too." I hesitate. "I had an incredible time with you this morning, and I wanted to tell you that I...can't wait to see you. Hurry back to me."

I end the call, my hand shaking for some stupid reason. Okay, I don't know why that made me feel better, but it did. I start to walk back to the car when I hear a slow clap coming from behind me.

My heart is in my throat as I spin around. Cruz is standing at the end of the tunnel, and his greasy-ass hair is even greasier than when I saw him out in front of Connor's house. He has a glass of liquor of some sort in his hand, and his eyes are rimmed with red.

He raises his glass in a toast and sneers. "Congratu-fucking-lations to the happy couple."

I gape at him, my anger overriding my fear. "Seriously, do you have nothing better to do than to follow me around?"

"I wasn't," he snaps. "I've been having a guy keep an eye on Connor, which means he winds up following you half the time. But my guy lost him sometime yesterday, and here you are in his fucking car. Any idea where he is?"

He moves toward me, and it's almost a stagger because he's stinking drunk. God, he's so...nasty. I wrinkle my nose against the smell of smoke and sweaty body odor. But I stay where I am, don't move away from him this time. I know I should run like hell, but I'm also so sick of Cruz's intimidation bullshit.

I lift my chin and meet his glare with one of my own. "I don't know where he is," I say truthfully.

"Well, I do. Want me to tell you?"

I hesitate, just enough, and he pounces on the opportunity.

"Your boy Connor ran back home to his ex-girlfriend."

He flips back his hair from his face while I force down the bile that rises in my throat, trying desperately to keep my game face on. No way. He's deliberately trying to mess with my head, and I'm not going to fall for his little mind tricks.

But Cruz looks agitated, almost like there's panic underlying his pissy drunkenness. Something is going down, and I find it hard to believe that it has to do with a fight over an ex-girlfriend.

I keep my voice steady. "I don't believe you."

"No?" He advances and shoves his hand at me, and I take a step back and wince, but then I see that he's just holding out his phone to me.

It's an e-mail from a Laura Rivera. Laura. *The* Laura? I can smell the whiskey on Cruz's breath, and I swallow down the nausea and make myself read it. It's dated today. From an hour ago.

Dear Cruz,

I know I haven't been the best about staying in touch with you, and I'm so very sorry for that. I can blame life and how busy I've been, and that's been part of it. But honestly, I need to confess to you that I've always felt so guilty and terrible for how you and I snuck around on Connor all of those years ago. I think that I thought by avoiding you after he left for the military that I would be able to deal with it, but now I know that the only way to move on is to face it head on.

This probably isn't making sense to you, is it, me writing to you out of the blue? I have no idea if this is even still your e-mail address or if you are reading this, but the reason I'm writing after all of these years is because Connor found me. He tracked me down after seven years and came to my house tonight to see if I was happy...

Game face, officially dead. I feel the blood drain from my face, and my lungs don't seem to be working anymore. Cruz yanks his phone back from me before I can finish, and I'm torn between demanding to see the rest of it and wanting to scrub my eyeballs clean of all that. But that wouldn't erase it from my memory.

"So you know what this says to me, bitch? That you didn't give him my message."

"I didn't have a chance to before he left," I snap. "Connor evidently had other plans in the works."

I don't intend for there to be resentment in my tone, but that's how Cruz can take it if he wants. Yes, let him think he won this round. I'm admittedly confused by what I'd read in that flowery e-mail of Laura's. I don't like it, not one bit. Don't like the fact that Connor tracked her down and visited her, and a brief flare of jealousy rips through me as I imagine what that reunion must have been like. I want to tell Cruz exactly what he can do with his e-mail and phone in general, but I clamp down on my emotions in time.

I catch myself before I blurt out that his threat is meaningless now, that my dad is no longer tied up to Cruz's "associates" – if they are truly his or not. But I don't know whether or not Maya actually took care of all of that yet or if it's still something that needs to happen. Either way, I know that it wouldn't be a good idea for me to say anything, especially not with that crazy look in Cruz's eye. The ice in his drink clinks together as he brings the glass to his lips with a shaky hand and downs the entire thing. He tosses the glass into the road, shattering it into a million pieces. Classy.

"Yeah, well maybe you can hang with me until we know what those plans are, huh, baby?"

Cruz lunges for and grabs my arm, and I have a sick feeling in my stomach that's part déjà vu and part panic because there's no one around to help me. I'm wearing my high-heeled sandals, and I stomp down on one of his damned cowboy boots as hard as I can but teeter as my heel breaks off of my shoe. I doubt he even felt that, but it distracts him enough for him to let me go. I scramble away from him, yelling at the top of my lungs as I race toward the end of the tunnel. I'd have to pass him to get to the service entrance, and I'm pretty sure this street curves around in a second to the shopping arcade entrance.

"Come back here, bitch!"

I throw a glance behind me and see Cruz groping for his gun. Holy crap, *he's going for his gun.* My thoughts crash together all at once as I run without looking back. If Cruz wants to use me as a hostage or as collateral or whatever he's thinking, he needs to keep me alive. But the look in his eyes was so murderous. I can't count on that. I hope Connor gets my message.

I hope you're safe please be safe please be okay…

A gunshot explodes in the tunnel, and I scream and drop to the ground. My arms fly over my head. Eyes squeeze shut. Pulse pounds in my ears.

I'm okay I'm okay I'm okay

"Drop it, you piece of shit!" a voice booms.

I dare to open my eyes and see. Cruz is standing still, his hands slowly lifting in the air, gun still in one hand. I can't see behind him, but I know that booming voice belongs to Neil.

"I said, drop it. Slowly and in front of you. Or your brains are going all over the place, cuz that's what I have in my sights right now."

Cruz nods and very slowly crouches down. He places the gun down on the asphalt in front of him, his eyes burning with hate at me the entire time. I can finally see around him to a sight even scarier than Cruz – Neil in all of his controlled fury, stalking toward us from the open trunk of the car with a scowl on his face and a semiautomatic rifle in his hands. Cruz straightens, and the barrel of the gun follows his ascent. I scramble to my feet and step back.

"Smart job, cowboy. That was a warning shot. Now kick your Smith and Wesson to the side."

Neil had fired off the shot, not Cruz. Not that it makes what happened any less freakier. Cruz does as he says, and I stare dumbly at Neil as he tips his chin up at me like he wants me to pick up Cruz's gun. I have no desire to take it, but I can see an angry tic in Neil's jaw, and I rush over, scoop it up, and make a mad dash to stand next to him. Neil's standing in close-range to Cruz now, the barrel of his gun still pointed at Cruz.

"Tell this lovely woman right here that you're sorry for the trouble," Neil commands.

"I'm fucking sorry, bitch," Cruz spits at me.

Neil's posture becomes even more rigid, and I hear him mutter a curse under his breath. I brace myself for it, convinced that Cruz is going to die right here and now for all of the crap that he pulled today.

"I'm gonna let you go, Cruz," Neil growls. "But only because I'm following orders, otherwise you would have been a stain on the sidewalk by now. Show your face anywhere near my man Connor and his woman again, and I will hunt you down. And don't think I'll be generous and shoot you. I'll feed you piece by piece to the sharks at the aquarium while you watch."

Neil hasn't moved or lowered his weapon since he came outside, but Cruz takes a step forward and spits again, this time on the concrete a few feet in front of Neil's feet. He turns and walks away without so much as another glance, disappearing around the corner and leaving Neil and me all alone in the tunnel.

Neil lowers the rifle by his side, his big hand closing over mine to take Cruz's gun.

"That won't keep him away, you know," he mutters as he walks to the car. "He'll try to seek retribution, but he has no idea what kind of trouble he'll be in if he does."

This whole thing is happening because Cruz is dangerous. That's what Connor warned me about in the first place, but I didn't really believe how dangerous until now. I kick off my shoes and follow him, my brain closing off because I can't process any of this right now.

"Speaking of trouble… I'm in trouble, aren't I?" I say in a shaky voice.

He hits me with a dark look that gives me a chill. "Why did you get out of the car? Were you trying to call Connor?"

I nod, and he puts the guns in the trunk and slams it shut. "Jesus, Alex. Don't call Connor right now, okay? He's meeting with Cruz's people, and they're not as nice about shit as I am. What if they took his phone off of him during discussions when you called? Might as well have Connor hand them your phone number on a piece of paper."

I wobble on my feet, which may be the effect of his words or because my heel broke off. More likely because of the gunshot.

I hold out my phone to him, and he shakes his head at me, his lips drawn in a thin line.

"That's yours. Despite what you think, I'm not here to police you. Just to protect you." He peers at me. "You okay?"

"Yes," I say, and I'm surprised to realize that I am. I'm rattled, but okay.

"Good," he says curtly. "Now let's go get Elle."

I get into the car, already resigning myself to being under house arrest for the rest of the night.

31

CONNOR

Last stop, gangster central. Now that I've made an official appearance in my old neighborhood, I know that I have no choice but to go and do this. I may not have been back there for seven years, but that place still felt like Cruz's stomping grounds. I'm banking on his people already knowing I'm here, on them waiting for me at my next stop. If they aren't there, this will have to wait for tomorrow. But I'm hoping for the opposite.

I ride to 4th Street, pass the small side street where Cruz and I used to live. According to Neil's sources, Cruz still lives there. Not alone but with a new member of the group, a kid no older than fifteen or sixteen whose face still shows evidence of the beating he took for his "jumping in" initiation. I don't bother going past our old place, heading straight for the greasy 24-hour diner around the corner instead.

I've been here before with Cruz, after I moved in with him when I was seventeen. Once when he specifically

introduced me to Martin, and that was when I finally figured
out what was going on with my brother. But by then, it was
too late. I never knew his last name – still don't – but I do
know that once you commit to a guy like Martin, you don't
ever get to back out.

Martin is sitting in a booth today, the same one that's
against the back wall that he was sitting in when I first met
him. He sees me as soon as I step through the door, stares at
me as he casually sips a cup of coffee. His hair is jet black
and pulled back in a ponytail, his eyes an unusual shade of
amber. His nose is crooked from being broken, his mouth set
in a hard slash of a line in a pock-marked face. He's as ugly as
hell, but there's some intangible quality about him that
somehow commands loyalty and respect from his people.
When I left, he'd been in his late thirties. When you're the
head of a local gang and haven't gotten your throat slit or
shot in the head by then, forty-some-odd years old is
practically geriatric. Martin is sharp, has a good sense for
business, and he's careful. I wouldn't have come here if he
was as much of a wild card as my brother.

Last time I saw him, he'd been with a girl who looked
twenty years younger than him. A beautiful girl from the
neighborhood who he probably handpicked to be his bitch
for the next few months, like a stray cat that was starving for
attention. Same thing this time, same type of girl, but now
she's about thirty years younger. Standing on the end of the
booth is his personal bodyguard. I think I recognize him
from when I lived here, or maybe not. They're a dime a
dozen, these guys from the neighborhood.

I don't know if he gives them a signal or what, but two
guys get out of a booth near the front. I quickly size them up
– one is about my age, wiry and with a long scar slicing across
his cheek, the other is taller and bulkier than me, obviously
the muscle of the two but looks like he might be in his late

teens. Muscle looks to Scar almost in deference, and I focus my attention on the smaller guy as they both approach me.

They don't look surprised to see me.

"Arms out, *gringo*," Scar commands. I'm the same as Cruz, half-Latino, my mother's side of the family mostly Irish, but I know they're using the term to label me as the outsider.

I do as he says because I want to talk to Martin. Muscle moves as if he's going to pat me down but shoves me hard in the shoulder instead. "Jacket off. You know the drill."

I glower at him, but I shrug off the jacket and subject myself to the inspection. Scar is definitely the more dominant one of the two, and he keeps his face blank as he watches Muscle pat me down roughly but efficiently. The Sig comes out of my holster right away, and I put up with the rest of it because I have to.

"You don't have a phone on you?" Muscle demands.

"No." I refrain from pointing out that he was the one who searched me, and no, I obviously don't have a fucking phone on me.

"Well, we'll keep your piece nice and safe until Martin is done with you," Scar says coolly.

I nod curtly, not liking it but knowing I don't have a fucking choice. It's their territory, their rules. My nerves are tightly wound – can't exactly help that – but I have a lid on my emotions. I have to stay in my head and show no fear. I'm here on a mission, and I'm not leaving until I see it through and can walk away with the results that I need.

Martin's been watching the show the entire time, and there's a gleam in his eyes when I meet his gaze. Curiosity? Interest? Approval? I don't care. I don't care what he sees in me because I'm not going to waste more breath on him than absolutely necessary. But first, I have to wait for the invitation.

Martin sets his cup down and leans back, beckoning to me with a deceptively lazy wave of his hand.

"Sit, sit," he says. He whispers something into the ear of the woman next to him, and she slides out of the booth after giving me a shy but interested glance. The thug standing to the side of him stays.

Martin smiles at me, and something about it reminds me of Cruz. Wolfish, like he's feeling things out before the kill.

"I would say 'welcome home,' but judging from your activities tonight, I have a feeling you're not here to stay," he says.

I incline my head. "You've always had a good handle on your territory, Martin."

He waves away the platitude. "You came here alone, Connor. I must admit that this surprises me. I would have heard if Cruz was dead, which is one of the possible explanations of why you have returned here without him." He leans forward. "So where is he?"

I don't know if he's insinuating or asking if I killed Cruz. I don't suppose it matters. Martin is shrewd and a strategist at heart, and I know he's choosing his words carefully so he can feel me out. I thought about this potential meeting for much of the drive, had talked this part through with Neil and Maya before leaving home. We decided that it would be best to keep my answers as simple and truthful as possible. Martin's bullshit meter has been honed with years of experience, and the way his amber eyes are probing me right now, I know he could pluck out a lie in no time flat.

"He's in Vegas, and he's alive," I say just as carefully. "But he won't be for very long if he doesn't stop what he's doing. He's messing around in big dog territory, and they'll piss on him. Or kill him."

A flash of impatience crosses Martin's expression. "That's interesting you would say this, because this is all news to me, Connor." His lip curls in disgust, and it's obvious he doesn't like it, not being in the know. "Care to fill me in? Because all he told me he was going to do was to convince you to come home."

My eyebrows lift in genuine surprise, and Martin sees it. I know he sees it, and his face darkens in response. Never once did Cruz tell me that his mission was to bring me back here. Thinking back, yeah, he started off by telling me our father was dying. Maybe that was his half-assed attempt to get me to say I'd come back, but if it was, that plan royally backfired. Either way, he didn't make that particular intention clear at all.

I want to ask when Cruz's deadline was to bring me home, but Martin's not the type of guy who answers questions without getting his own questions answered first. Maybe not even then. I have to try to appease him, and disclosing the information I'd gotten from Neil and Maya is part of my eventual plan anyhow.

"Cruz has been trying to edge in on a suspected racketeering scheme. So far all he's managed to do is make contact with some of the low-level grunts of the operation. But if he starts edging his way in any deeper, he's going to piss off the big players, and they'll retaliate."

Martin doesn't respond, those eyes of his feeling me out more effectively than any lie detector. But I'm not pulling any fast ones here – this is the truth. There's real danger for my brother and for Martin's gang if they don't call Cruz back home, and that's what I'm going for.

"And how do you know this?" he finally says. "Do you have connections with this group?"

"No," I say honestly. "I would never get involved with these people. But when Cruz showed up and told me he was going to stay until the end of the month, I had him tailed to see what he was up to." I shrug. "Apparently while he was having me tailed at the same time. Must be a twin thing."

Martin throws his head back and laughs, and it's not a happy sound. It's almost maniacal, makes me uncomfortable to listen to, and I can almost feel an increase in tension in his thug and in the guys guarding the front of the diner. I don't imagine he's a guy who laughs often, and it's like he's unleashing a little bit of that madness when he finally does.

He shakes his index finger at me, still smiling widely. "No, you had him followed because you are no fool, Connor. Cruz isn't either, though perhaps in this case his ambition got in the way of his judgment." His brow furrows. "Cruz has been like a son to me, or a younger brother. But if he's acting rashly and without my consent, there's little I can do about it."

He'd wash his hands of Cruz to save the gang at large. Not surprised to hear it. But in some fucked-up sense, I can *almost* understand why sheer desperation would make someone flock to a guy like Martin. Why someone who had nothing would be willing to fight for and maybe even die for the lifestyle. Cruz did it not only because he wanted to protect us, but because he didn't have a father figure or family in general that Martin and the gang eventually became. I know he wanted me to jump in with him, that in his mind it would have been the best scenario, a happily-ever-after ending for both of us.

I wonder how Cruz would feel now, to hear Martin say that Cruz dug his own grave and needs to lie on it. But that still doesn't solve my problem of needing my brother to leave the city, and my need to protect my name and the people I care about.

"These people in Vegas," I say, "they won't stop with him. If they take Cruz out, they'll get retribution by coming after your group. Cruz is your agent, and he's out there representing you whether you gave your consent or not."

I look Martin hard in the eye, watch as comprehension settles in his eyes and sets hard in his jaw. Now's the time to make my plea.

"You need to call Cruz back home," I say. "And keep him here for good."

Martin breaks eye contact with me for the first time since I entered the diner, snapping his fingers loudly and calling the waitress over.

"*Más café!*" He practically slams his coffee cup down on the table as he orders more, his eyes narrowing as he turns back to me. "*¿Quieres un poco?*" he asks, as though remembering his manners.

I lift my hand off the table and gesture that no, I wouldn't like any, before dropping it again. Need to stay focused, even though this conversation is testing my stamina beyond any physical test I've ever put myself through. I have so much at stake, so much to lose, so much to look forward to if I come out on top of this. And I just have to make it a little bit longer because I feel like I'm in the homestretch – I laid out my concerns, expressed the danger to Martin and his gang in what I'm pretty sure was a non-threatening manner, and now I have to wait and see what he says.

Worst case scenario is that he tells me to fuck off and take care of my own problems. I have a feeling he won't do this. But he could ask for something else from me in exchange for him pulling Cruz out. I sit patiently as the waitress refills his coffee, feeling the exhaustion creep over me like the grease coating the table. I almost reconsider the offer of coffee, but I don't want to take anything from Martin.

"Why did you come all this way to tell me this in person?" he demands as he mixes a shitload of sugar into his coffee. "What's in it for you?"

"Cruz is still my brother," I say simply. "We have our differences, but I also don't want him to get killed."

It's not a lie. I'm still working through what Laura revealed to me earlier tonight. What she confessed to me changed things but it didn't. It changed things because Cruz didn't drug and have sex with my girlfriend without her consent. But the fact that he got her so drunk and high that she had to have her stomach pumped, the fact that he went ahead and fucked her – I still can't forgive those things. But that doesn't mean I want him dead.

Martin leans back in the booth, his fingers tapping against the table and his eyes like amber stones. "You want him out of your neck of the woods, is that right?"

"Yes."

He sips at his coffee, addressing me over the rim of the mug. "You're intelligent. Smart enough that I don't think you'd try to lie to me, to make up a story and risk meeting with me simply because you want your brother out of your hair. Am I right?"

"Yes, that's right."

He stays silent for longer than necessary, makes me sweat it out as he decides on his answer.

Finally, he nods.

"I have a cousin who lives in Henderson. I'll give you his number, and you call him tomorrow, make arrangements with him to send Cruz home. Either go with him to collect Cruz, or you can deliver him to my cousin, whatever you prefer." His eyes gleam at me. "But no guarantees that this is forever. If there does turn out to be an opportunity for us in Vegas as Cruz seems to think, we will be back."

I keep my opinion to myself, the opinion that Maya and Neil shared that their small operation doesn't stand a chance in Vegas. And I work hard to hide my relief even though all of my nerves are buzzing with tension. I want to ride full throttle out of this god-forsaken place, but I simply nod back.

"Thank you." I hesitate, then decide to press my luck. "To be clear, you and I are even. I owe you nothing, and you owe me nothing."

He chuckles, and I brace myself against the sound escalating to a laugh, but it never comes.

"*Sí, sí.* Consider us even, Connor." His eyes glimmer, and his mouth twists into what might be a smile. "Unless you'd consider joining us."

"No, thank you," I manage to say without choking. "But I say that with all due respect, sir."

I can't wait to get the fuck out of here, but I force myself to go through the formalities. Shake hands with Martin, wait for Scar to give me back my piece and resist the urge to punch him in the face when he takes his sweet old time examining it before finally handing it over. Doing it deliberately, of course, to test my patience or to throw his weight around and be a dick about it. Probably the latter.

"That's a nice jacket, Marino," Scar says. "My brother has a bike. He'd look good in that."

Whatever the fucking hell. I just want to get out of here, and I take my wallet and keys out of the pockets before shoving it back to him. I make sure I clip him hard on the shoulder in the process.

"You can have it," I say. "But that's all your entire operation is ever getting from me."

I walk out of the diner, and they let me.

Cruz chose his lot in life, forged his own bonds, and there's no way I can talk or barter his way out of that. I imagine that he'll be punished when he gets back, but I got the sense from Martin that he values Cruz, does see him as a member of the family and hopefully an asset. It's the best I can do for him right now.

I stop by the motel on my way out to grab my phone and throw my key on the front counter before taking off. It's the dead of night, but there's no way I'm going to stay in this city one second more. I hit Route 40 and ride hard and fast, chilled to the bone in only my t-shirt and jeans, but I keep riding even when I feel the exhaustion settle hard into my body. It's a good two hours until I hit the next major city right before Arizona, and I don't slow down until I get there.

I ride around until I find a hotel that displays a sign for underground parking, and I hide Neil's bike to the side of some guest's big SUV in one of the dark corners far in the back. I'm shivering when I stumble into the lobby – not having the riding jacket sucked, and I make a mental note to buy Neil another one or two to make up for it. The late-night clerk at the front desk gives me a curious look as I ask for a room, but I ignore it and shell out cash, not even caring at this point how much it is.

I walk into the room, throw the helmet on the chair, kick out of my shoes and jeans, peel off my shirt, and collapse on the bed. Alex swims through my thoughts as I close my eyes. I desperately want to call her, to hear her voice, but I can't fucking move to get my phone. First thing tomorrow.

It's late, and I'm dead-tired and need to sleep so I can hit the road before daybreak. But I lie awake for a while, listening to the sounds around me. Laughter in the hallway as people come back from the bar. Some jackass' car alarm that goes off outside the window for a full five minutes before someone bothers to go outside and deactivate it. I toss and turn to lie on my back and eventually rest my arm over my eyes.

I'm used to sleeping alone, but God, I wish Alex was here with me right now.

32

Alex

I wake from a nightmare and bolt up to a sitting position, a knot in my stomach as I look around the room. I can't remember if I'm at Elle's or at Connor's or if I'd gone with the cot in Maya's living room, and I blink and look at a room I don't recognize.

I hug my knees to my chest, everything that happened from last night flooding my head with unwelcome clarity. Cruz had pulled a gun on me last night, and Neil had driven straight to Elle's rehearsal afterward. He brought both of us to stay at his house, saying he'd sleep on the couch for the night. Saying it was the safest place for us until things calm down.

I need this madness to be over.

My phone is sitting on the floor, where I'd left it to charge last night, and I climb out of bed and dive for it. Nothing. No messages or missed calls from Connor. I close my eyes as the disappointment mixes with worry and a hell of a lot of fear.

I huff out a breath and open my eyes again, picking up my phone and calling Dad.

He picks up right away. "*Baobèi!* Great news!"

It takes me a second to equilibrate between the freak-out level of stress I'm feeling in comparison to the giddiness of his tone. But I'm relieved that he's okay and didn't get a visit from a certain evil twin at the hospital last night.

"What's the amazing news?" In contrast to him, I just try my best to sound normal.

"Your mother tested negative for the genetic clotting disorders. The physician also said he doesn't think it's lupus, though he'll recommend our regular doctor monitor that when she get home."

I close my eyes, relief washing through me. "Oh my God, Dad. That's so great! Do they know yet when they're going to discharge her?"

"Not yet. Though she's anxious to go home."

I listen as he tells me that home will mean back to the hotel because apparently, flying increases the risk of blood clots and might have actually been a contributing factor to the one in her leg. She and Dad are following the physician's recommendation to not fly back to New York until July, and he tells me that he'll soon be moving both of us to a different suite in the hotel. He seems apologetic as he explains to me that it won't be a VIP suite and will be a lot smaller, and I tell him that sort of thing doesn't matter to me.

"I'll come by a little later if that's okay?" I say, trying not to sound as dead as I feel. "I still need to have breakfast and stuff."

And find out if Neil's heard from Connor. I need to do that most of all. I realize I have no idea what time it is, and I quickly peek at my phone's display and see that it's already ten-thirty in the morning. I'm surprised I slept for so long.

"No hurry. Your mom is trying to kick me out of the room to make herself pretty, even though she always is."

"I know," I say, a small smile finally making its way onto my face.

"I'm meeting with Ms. Coplin at two. Maybe you can be at the hospital by then to keep your mother company?"

"Not a problem. Tell her I'll see her soon."

Neil's house is actually a condo that's attached to three other units, and the bedroom I'm in looks like it doubles as an office. I walk out of the guest room, half-expecting to find Neil standing guard somewhere with his semiautomatic. Instead, I find Elle in the kitchen, her hair standing on end and eyes red from crying and probably no sleep.

I rush over to her and grab her in a hug, trying to stop the panic from welling up in my chest. "Hey, you okay? Did something new happen?"

"Oh, aside from my cousin losing his fucking mind and trying to take you hostage last night at gunpoint, and not knowing if my other one is alive? No."

I freeze. "Connor's alive. He has to be."

"Oh God, I'm sorry." She sniffs and squeezes me back before pulling away. "I should be asking you if you're okay. Are you freaking out?"

"I'm fine." I force a smile, strictly for her benefit. "I'm more worried about Connor than myself right now."

We both turn around as we hear the sound of the garage opening, and Neil enters a minute later with drinks from Starbucks in one hand and what looks like a shake from In-N-Out in the other.

I stare at him suspiciously, but he averts his eyes out of either discomfort or respect. I'm wearing the only pajamas I'd had in my bag – a silky tank top and shorts pajama set – and it doesn't leave a whole lot to the imagination. But this is no time to be overly modest, and I storm over to him.

"A frappuccino and a chocolate shake? Did you talk to Connor this morning? Is he okay?" I demand as I take the former from him.

"I talked to him," he admits, and my heart skips one or two beats. "He's on his way back."

"He's okay," I repeat. My knees feel weak, and I glance over at Elle and exchange looks of relief. I scoot around the counter to the kitchen table and sink down into the nearest chair, feeling sick as I think about what Neil had said about Connor meeting with Cruz's people. Equally nauseous when I remember the e-mail Cruz had shoved into my face. If it's even possible, I hate Cruz even more for planting any seeds of doubt about Connor in my head, but that was his whole intention, wasn't it? But the e-mail said Connor had stopped by to see if she was happy, not anything else. Given what he told me about what happened between them, I can't fault him for that.

Neil nods, but he's still not smiling, and my hope mixes with anxiety. "I'll let Connor fill you in on all of the details later. There's one loose end we have to tie up, and I'm leaving you girls here until we take care of it."

Whoa. I glance over at Elle and see her face crumple. Weak-kneed or not, I can't let Neil leave us with such vague and shitty information, not when it has to do with all of us. I rise and fold my arms across my chest.

"Uh uh. You and Connor don't get to do that. Keep Elle and me in the dark while you guys run around and play hero. Whether you like it or not, we're involved in this. Cruz is Elle's cousin, too. And he followed and threatened me — *twice*."

"Yeah." Elle stalks up to Neil in all of her five-foot-two glory and jabs a finger at his chest. "You need to tell us what you're doing." She sniffs hard again. "Are you gonna kill him?"

"No." He stares down at Elle in surprise and takes a few seconds to collect himself. "We're not going to kill him. We're going to send Cruz outta here. Connor went to Albuquerque to arrange for Cruz to get a permanent one-way ticket out of Vegas."

Elle's jaw drops, and I quickly process this new information. Okay, so this means that Connor "arranged" this with the people in Albuquerque – Cruz's people, his gang? That explains the secrecy and why he didn't want Elle to know he even left town. If she'd leaked it or if Cruz had been able to force the information out of me, he would have retaliated. But he does know Connor was in Albuquerque, thanks to Laura's e-mail, which means he might have put it together.

"But Cruz isn't just going to lie down and take it if Connor tells him, right?" A chill courses through my body and makes me shudder, and Neil looks across the room like he's trying to find me a blanket.

"Cruz will have no choice once we deliver him to his people." Neil's expression closes up as he realizes he's said too much, and I know I'm done getting any more answers from him.

This is all going to be over soon. I don't know exactly what I'm doing, but I stride out of the kitchen and over to the guest room with renewed purpose.

"Alex?" There's a warning in Neil's voice. "What do you think you're doing?"

I spin around. "If Connor's on his way back, let's go find Cruz now so he can 'deliver' him. The sooner the better, right?"

It's Neil's turn to look incredulous. I continue into the guest room, and he follows me as I grab clothes out of my bag.

"Hold the phone, sister. My orders are simple. You and Elle are going to stay here until it's all done."

I whirl around with a t-shirt and bra in hand, and Neil looks down at his feet.

"Your orders? What, is Connor your commanding officer, and are Elle and I really and actually under house arrest?" I snap. "You can't keep us here all day."

"It's what Connor –"

"– would want." Maybe it's an overreaction on my part, but I'm standing by my guns this time. If the guys get to do it, then so do I. "I'm not going to run off by myself. I'll go with you to find him, and Elle can come too if she wants. Or maybe she wouldn't want to, but she should be given the choice."

Once I get going, I can't stop myself. "What are you really afraid of, Neil? You made it sound easy, or was that a lie? Are you expecting a big shoot-out? Or are you more afraid of what Connor will do if he comes back and finds out you didn't have me locked up 24-7?"

I turn around again so I'm facing away, not caring if he sees my back as I change out of my pajama shirt and put on my bra and shirt. Neil doesn't say anything in response, and I pause as I hear murmurs from the living room and a door open and close. Huh. Okay, so I probably pissed him off by calling the shots or embarrassed him with my forwardness, but he'll be back and then we can go from there. Not that I haven't appreciated his concern, but –

"No, love. Neil was afraid of what it would have done to me if something ever happened to you," a low voice says.

I spin around, my hand flying to my mouth as a strangled sob comes out of my throat.

Connor.

Connor is standing in the doorway, and he's looking at me like I'm the last person left in the world.

I run up to him, and he steps into the room and catches me around my waist. His skin feels hot, like he's been out in the sun forever, and I press up against his heat and throw my arms around his neck. He stares at me with depths of blue layered with need and concern, and oh my God, he'd better kiss me right now.

Please.

Please tell me you're here right now because you're mine.

His beautiful lips smile at me before they take me, and I melt into him. His kiss is hard and desperate this time, like he's dying to have me as much as I'm dying to have him. His hands slide down and run over my silk pajama shorts before lifting me up into his arms, and I know it with a staggering amount of certainty. I know it in my heart.

This is where I belong. With you.

I almost wither when he breaks away from me.

I reach up to touch his face, run my fingers through his hair. Across his shoulders and down his chest. He catches my hands in his and raises them to his lips. His eyes search mine, simultaneously reveal everything about himself and delve into the depths of me.

I whisper. "You're really here."

He smiles. "I am."

I breathe, really breathe for the first time since he left. "Don't leave me like that again."

His grip on me tightens. "I won't."

I feel more for this man than I ever have for anyone. I lean into him, hugging him to me like I'll never let him go.

I can't remember what doubt ever felt like.

"Thanks for your message," he murmurs into my neck.

I draw back and place my hands on his shoulders, run them down his back. I need to touch him, and I can't stop.

"You're kind of a jerk for not calling me back," I say.

"I'm sorry. I wanted to surprise you. Thanks for ruining it." He smirks and traces my lips with a fingertip.

I put my hand over his to still it, not believing his words. "You wanted to *surprise* me?"

His eyes fill with so much emotion for me that it renders me powerless. "I woke up this morning and heard your message. I called Neil instead of you, and yes, told him not to tell you I was coming back because I wanted to surprise you."

"Well, it backfired because Neil told me," I inform him. "And of course I knew you would come back. He also told me what you need to do, and I'm coming with you."

"I heard. I was in the garage, and I heard everything." His eyes twinkle, and he shakes his head. "Obviously I went about this all wrong. I should have consulted with you ahead of time to make sure it would work out."

"Obviously. You need to keep me part of things." I shoot him a look of disapproval. "What were you even thinking?"

He grins at me and shoots back, "What did I ever do with my fucking life before I met you?"

I don't answer him, just take his hand in mine and press it against my heart. I've never felt so strongly for anyone before, and now that I have it, I'm asking myself the same question. And now that he's back, I think that I know I can't stay away from him. We'll figure out how to make it work. I believe it because I want it more than anything.

"I don't know. But that doesn't matter anymore, I don't think." I still need to finish getting dressed, and I tear myself away from him. I slip out of my pajama shorts and get into my skirt, loving how he watches me.

"Well? Are we gonna go finish this, or what?"

Connor has to have driven way too much in the past twenty-four hours, but we pile into the car without even a question of who's going to be behind the wheel. Maybe Connor was the one in command when he and Neil served together after all.

I call shotgun out of habit more than anything else, almost reneging because it means Neil has to squeeze together with Elle in the back seat. No one objects, though, and I listen to the two of them banter back and forth and decide that it's okay.

I glance over at Connor as he takes us to an address just east of Vegas, in Henderson. He looked it up on his GPS as soon as we got into the car but his eyes are completely focused on the road now. I watch out of the corner of my eye as the dot on the screen moves closer to the starred destination, like a lit fuse that's steadily shortening. Like time slipping away.

"I can always transfer, you know," I say.

He looks over at me. "What?"

"I can transfer schools. There's nothing special about pre-nursing requirements that I can't do them anywhere." He's looking at the road again, and I'm hoping it's because traffic is bad. "I'm not saying I'm necessarily deciding now, just mentioning it as an option."

He brakes a little too hard behind a stopped line of cars, and Neil and Elle's conversation dies down as we all pitch forward.

Connor turns to face me, his gaze blazing into mine. "You'd do that? What about your parents? Your life back in New York?"

"People move away from their parents all the time," I say quietly. I'm pretty sure Elle and maybe even Neil are eavesdropping hard, but I don't care. I pause to catch my breath, my next words coming out in a rush. "Of course I need to see how my mom's recovery is going to look. But besides them, my life in New York doesn't have anyone in it worth staying for. Maybe I'll wait until the end of the month to decide."

The entire car is silent until a horn sounds from behind us, and Connor has to look ahead as traffic starts moving again. There's more color in his cheeks, and he might be breathing slightly harder than normal.

"You can decide sooner than that if you want," he finally says. "End-of-month deadlines never seem to work out for me."

He actually said that. He's indirectly telling me he wants me, and the hope inside my chest threatens to explode. "What about your life? Would me being here mess things up?"

He reaches over and takes my hand, his fingers closing around mine. Shitty traffic or no shitty traffic, he turns to look at me again, and the amount of emotion in his eyes is heart-stopping. "I thought we agreed. I need to keep you part of my life."

"Okay. I'll look into what's involved when we get back."

"*What?*" Elle screeches from the back seat. "Are you for real thinking about moving out here? Omigod, you guys!"

I catch her look of utter shock from the back seat, but I'm flying too high to say anything. Connor shoots me a lopsided grin that's thoroughly contagious, and it's crazy that I'm smiling so hard considering what we're driving out to do right now. But I'd wanted to tell him, wanted to bring it up while I thought of it. If I learned anything over the past few weeks, it's that you need to listen to your heart. But you have to act on it, too. Because sometimes you lose the opportunity, and you're damned lucky if you can get it back.

We didn't say anything about living arrangements and of course if I wind up doing this, I'd need a job to pay for my expenses. But those are just details. Details I can handle. Details are easy.

I check the GPS again and see that we're almost there. My heart stops for a second again but for completely different reasons.

"All right." Connor clears his throat, and his tone is all business. "I'll drop myself off at the house, you follow. Neil, I need confirmation that your guy still has Cruz's location."

At first I think he's talking to me, and I totally panic. We're dropping Connor off? I don't like the sound of this, but I'm also not in control of this situation. Connor is, and I hope it stays that way even when he's with whatever gang connection this house belongs to in Henderson.

Neil speaks up from the back seat. "Just did. Cruz is at the bar at his hotel, having lunch with some lowlife collector. We should be good, but my guy will contact me the second he makes a move."

Connor nods and gives my hand a quick squeeze before releasing it. "Are you ready for this?"

I start. I'd wanted to come, but that's not really a question I can answer. How can anyone be ready for something like this? "For what? What do you have to do?"

"Don't worry about what I need to do, love." His tone isn't quite as brisk as when he'd spoken to Neil but it's close. "Can you follow us? Hell, I didn't even think to ask – do you even know how to drive? I know not everyone from New York does, but Elle can drive if you –"

"Hold up. Yes, I know how to drive, and you're probably thinking about people from New York City. But *me*, drive?" I stare at him, trying to comprehend but failing, half an eye on the GPS that says that we're right around the corner from this gangster's house.

He nods. "Neil was originally going to drive, but now he can come with me as my backup. It's easy, love. Everything's arranged. They have no reason to try to lose you. You're just following with my car."

"In case you do lose us, I'll text Elle here with the address," Neil says helpfully.

Okay. Okay, I can handle this. I nod mutely as Connor pulls in front of a small stucco house. He leans over and kisses me, his hand cupping my cheek, his tongue caressing mine way too briefly before he pulls away.

"See you in a few minutes." He touches my chin and gets out of the car.

I nod again even though he's already walking up to the house, and my voice might be in the giant vortex in my stomach. I don't know.

"Omigod," Elle whispers as Neil gets out and shuts the door with a boom that shakes the whole car. "This is totally crazy. You okay to drive, Alex? Want me to?"

"No, I got this." My throat is suddenly dry, my voice scratchy, but my eyes are fixed on Connor and Neil as I slide over to sit behind the wheel. "How are you? I know you were kind of close to Cruz growing up…" I trail off, not wanting to let my feelings about Cruz slip out. I have nothing but terrible things to say about the guy, and that would be me being nice.

"Yeah, well. He used me to get to Connor. He held you at gunpoint and was connected to the people that messed with your poor dad. And he lied to me about being off the drugs, and about a lot of things, actually. I used to think he could come around, but it's obvious he can't." Her voice is bitter, and she ends with a sigh. "I know this is terrible, but he was always happiest when he was with that gang. Maybe he belongs with them."

She stops, and I know she's thinking the same thing I am. Cruz doesn't belong here with any of us.

Connor and Neil are coming out of the house now with a guy who doesn't look much like I'd expect for having gang ties – although what do I really know? He looks around my dad's age, has a full head of dark hair that's going gray, with half his face hidden behind big brown sunglasses. His attitude exudes a seasoned sort of confidence as he leads Connor and Neil to a grey sedan. If he does notice me sitting behind the wheel of the Audi, he doesn't give any indication.

"Don't look right at him," Elle hisses. "If you don't know what he looks like, he can't kill you."

"Holy crap." I roll my eyes. "Seriously, Elle. What movie is that from?"

"Just sayin', hun." She slumps back in her seat and is thankfully quiet for the rest of the drive.

We follow the sedan for what feels like forever because of traffic and honestly, because every second Connor sits in that car with that guy pushes my limits of sanity. But we finally pull up to what I assume is Cruz's hotel. It's one of the older casinos on the outskirts of the old Vegas on Fremont Street. They pull into the open parking lot off to the side, and I follow. Follow. I just need to follow.

"Now what?" I ask.

"Now we wait, I guess," Elle says quite reasonably.

I pull into a spot in a row behind them, and we wait. Elle sings softly to herself the entire time, and I stare straight ahead and try to remember to blink now and then. Connor said that this would be easy, that this was all arranged, and I assume he meant from when he went to Albuquerque. I have to believe that he was telling me the truth. And if he's not, I'm going to kill him. Figuratively and not literally, of course.

Being with Connor definitely keeps things interesting, that's for damned sure.

They come out exactly sixteen minutes later, the sunglasses guy with his hand on Cruz's shoulder. Connor is walking right behind them, with Neil lagging maybe a half step behind that. I stare hard at Cruz, try to see whether he looks pissed off about all of this or broken, but he looks stiff, his face a total blank. He stumbles forward as he steps into the parking lot, and sunglasses guy's hand falls off his shoulder.

Cruz straightens and spins around, and I gasp as he takes a swing at the older guy. But Connor moves with lightning-fast speed to intervene, pushing sunglasses guy out of the way before throwing a hard punch to Cruz's face. He falls back, lands flat on his ass in the parking lot, his hands over his face. I can see all the way from here the blood spurting through his fingers from where Connor undoubtedly broke his nose. Yeah, Cruz is going to have a hell of a ride back to Albuquerque.

"Damn," Elle says from behind me.

My thoughts exactly. I feel like cheering. I wish I could get an instant replay of that.

Connor stares down at him for a good minute, and maybe says something to him or maybe not while Cruz glowers back up at him from the pavement. They may be identical twins, but they don't even look related to each other at this moment. Connor can be the guy in control a lot of the time, but he's real. He has real emotions and real heart. A pretty amazing heart, like my mom once said about me.

I watch as the evil twin staggers to his feet and turns away from his brother. He doesn't look at Connor again as sunglasses guy shoves him toward the sedan.

Connor did it. We all did. Dad and Maya are going to help each other out. Mom is going to recover. Elle is singing with a band next week, for the first time in a long time. Connor raises his head and locks gazes with me through the windshield, and I finally let myself smile at him and dare to believe what I've hoped. That we're going to be okay now. That Cruz won't be back.

Connor gives me a slow smile, showing me his cocky grin that I love so much, and I feel the rest of my defenses crumble to dust as my heart completely fills with the possibility of us. Mom gave up her Ian and found my dad, but everyone's story is different. I can't give up the chance to be with Connor.

I didn't know before meeting him that my heart needed to grow up so much. I never thought that my walls would come down for someone like him. I want him with his flaws and all, and he wants me even given mine, and I think that's how it's supposed to be when it finally happens. People lose enough as it is in this world, but sometimes the universe is kind to us, gives us someone who won't walk away from us no matter how hard things get. Someone who we can be honest with and trust.

Sometimes the universe throws someone unexpected in our paths so that we can finally see who we really are.

Connor and I are going to be fantastic together. We already are.

EPILOGUE

CONNOR

Maybe I could have done things differently. In dealing with Cruz. In not forgiving my father before he died. But both of them are gone now – Cruz back to Albuquerque to sort out his own shit and my father to his grave. So yeah, maybe everything this summer could have gone down another way, but I can't think like that. I'm done letting guilt follow me around like it's my shadow.

And all I have to do is wake up in the morning and see Alex by my side to know that I did all right.

It's already the end of July, and she'll be flying back to New York with her parents tomorrow, but then she'll be packing up her stuff to move out here. To live with me. It blows my mind, but she's been staying over at my house a few nights a week this past month, and I can't wait for her to officially move in. I shuffled my schedule around so I can take time off to help her move. Doubt we'll need an entire two weeks, but it's what she asked me for, and I suspect she wants to make a vacation of the road trip.

I dismount the Honda when I see her come out of UNLV's Student Services building. I've been working on the Harley restoration in my spare time, but it's not ready to ride.

Alex walks toward me, her hair blazing like the sunset. Her face lights up like I'm the best thing she's seen all day, and I know that I did a hell of a lot more than all right.

I reach for her, and she slips her hand into mine. "How'd it go?"

"Great. I'm all set. Looks like I can get everything done in the fall if I take two on-line courses. It's going to be a busy semester."

I give her hand a quick squeeze. I already have secret plans to give her one of the rooms upstairs for her workspace. Neil's in on the surprise and is going to get most of it set up while we're gone.

"Don't worry. I'll leave you alone so you can study."

We get to the bike, and she pivots around and faces me with a frown. "Hey. I'm moving across the country to be with you. You'd better not leave me alone."

I slide my arm around her and pull her close, and her frown gives way to a smile as I lean down to kiss her. I wouldn't be able to leave her alone if I tried. But she pulls away, placing her hand on my cheek and sighing.

"C'mon." She detaches herself from me, walking over to the bike before we both burn to a crisp on the sidewalk. "We're going to be late."

I get back on the Honda and kick-start it, the rumble of the engine becoming a low growl. Wait for her to get on behind me, loving the feel of her arms sliding around my waist and her thighs pressing up against my legs. Neither of us are perfect, but we fit together perfectly in a lot of ways.

"Ouch," she says into my ear. "You could have at least parked in the shade."

"You're welcome to sit on my lap if the seat's too hot for you," I tease, and I can't see her face but know she's rolling her eyes.

"Your sweet-talking skills still suck," she says. "Good thing I love you."

I laugh as I hit the throttle, and we're off. It's the best damned thing in the world. That she loves me.

We arrive early to the club, and there's already a line to get in. But we walk right through, Alex dressed to the nines and on one of my arms, and Grace looking beautiful and elegant on the other. Walking both of them in makes me feel like a fucking rock star, but it's not me on stage tonight. It's Elle who put our names on the guest list at the door, and I couldn't be more proud of her.

When we get inside, there's a fair number of people crowding the space, and we grab a spot at a high table in the back of the bar. Grace sits down in one of the chairs right away, shooing Alex away when she expresses concern. She's been slowly but surely recovering from her embolism, assuring everyone that she feels stronger every week. And she insisted on coming tonight, said she wouldn't miss Elle singing for the world. Alex stands next to her mom, and as I go to the bar to get us drinks, I hear them talking about the classes Alex will be taking in the fall. I know living on different sides of the country will be hard for them, but I promised Alex we'd visit as often as we can.

It's not like we have to be stuck in Vegas forever, anyway. I still haven't decided on what I want to do in the long term, but Neil keeps trying to convince me to get my engineering degree. Talks it up almost every time I see him and says we could go in business together, again. I'm thinking about it, but I also want to keep my options open. And for now, I'm not in a huge rush to change careers. The security thing isn't something that Maya just handed to me on a platter like I used to think. I have a good name for myself, and it's a name I built myself.

Not just any name. Vincent isn't only Elle's middle name and her mom's maiden name. It's my mother's maiden name, too. I can think about my mother a little more these days without it hurting so fucking bad, and I think a big part of that is because Grace has treated me like her own son ever since she got out of the hospital. Even before that.

I get back with our drinks right as Elle comes out on stage. She spots us standing in the back and waves like a maniac. We wave back, but Elle's eyes close and she starts into her first song right away. Her voice is smooth and sultry, and she sounds damned good. This is her debut with her new band. She worked her ass off for a month to pull everything together, and I know she's had to use a lot of her connections to get this initial gig.

Alex nestles up to me, and I run my fingers through her hair, lean down and breathe in her scent as Elle's voice and the notes of the song play over us.

"I can't believe I got the cool girl to fall in love with me," I say into her ear.

"Who, me?" Alex turns to face me and gives me a smile that makes my temperature skyrocket.

I cup her face in my hand and kiss her, forgetting for the moment about all of the other people in the room. It's just her and me, and her arms wind around my neck as her body presses into mine. My grip tightens on her waist and brings her even closer as she dances, as she moves against me in time to the slow rhythm of the song.

God, I love her. I can't get enough of her, and I doubt I ever will.

We finally break apart, and Grace smiles at us and speaks over the song. "Go out there and dance, you two. Alexis, if you don't take him out there, I will."

Alex buries her face in my neck, and I laugh and tighten my arms around her before taking her out on the floor to dance. She's so fucking incredible, she's mine, and we have real plans to be together.

Life is unpredictable, and it never works out the way you think it's supposed to. I wasn't looking for Alex this summer but she found me and I found her, and whatever happens next, I know we'll figure it out. Because what she and I are building together – it's worth the risk.

I've lost people I once loved, but that doesn't mean I have to make it through all by myself.

I've lost enough. It's time for me to finally live.

The End

Second Chances ∙~ Book One